Gears of the Sun

By

Nicoline Evans

Author: Nicoline Evans – www.nicolineevans.com
Editor: Christie Stratos – www.proofpositivepro.com
Cover Design: Nicoline Evans

To my beta readers and everyone else who has offered support (in all ways, shapes, and sizes) during this entire process—thank you!

The Solarpunks of Quintessence

Thermapunks

Element: HEAT
Location: Fyree
Hearts contain the Source Flame
Gears made of Gold
Veins filled with Magma
Lead Family: The Dawes

Thermapunk Sub-faction(s):

• Pyropounks; fire faction within the Pyro-Argo Militia. They combat the moon monsters.

• Steampunks; work at the Steamery and collect water for Fyree.

• Welders; specialize in repairing metal structures with fire.

• Thermadocs; medical mechanics who specialize in healing/repairing Thermapunks with ailments.

Terrapunks

Element: MINERALS
Location: Terra
Hearts contain Uranium
Gears made of Chrome Silver
Veins filled with Petroleum
Lead Family: The Horrigans

Terrapunk Sub-faction(s):

• Tinkiepunks; gadgeteers who maintain the geared world of Quintessence.

• Revopunks; they skate in continuous loops atop the giant terra gears, keeping them turning.

• Digipunks; miners of Terra.

• Terrapunk Guards; patrol the basic workings of Terra.

• Stone Patrol (Stoneheads); serve and protect the Horrigan family.

• Terradocs; medical mechanics who specialize in healing/repairing Terrapunks with ailments.

Aeropunks

Element: GAS
Location: Gaslion
Hearts contain Helium
Gears made of Copper
Veins filled with Liquid Nitrogen
Lead Family: The Holloways

Aeropunk Sub-faction(s):

• Pilopunks; aviators of the sky.

• Argopunks; gas faction within the Pyro-Argo Militia. They combat the moon monsters.

• Gas Spinners; conservationists of the solar shield.

• Aerodocs; medical mechanics who specialize in healing/repairing Aeropunks with ailments.

Hydropunks

Element: WATER
Location: Hydra
Hearts contain Ocean Water
Gears made of Zinc
Veins filled with Octopus Ink
Lead Family: None

Hydropunk Sub-faction(s):

• Nautipunks; pirates of Hydra.

• Watermen; specialize in channeling their water hearts and dousing fires with ocean water.

• Hydrodocs; medical mechanics who specialize in healing/repairing Hydropunks with ailments.

The Gods (as seen in this series)

Solédon – god of all suns
Lunéss – goddess of all moons
Incarna – goddess of mortal & demi-god souls
Matrigaia – goddess of mortal & demi-god lives
Marlodon – god of the seas

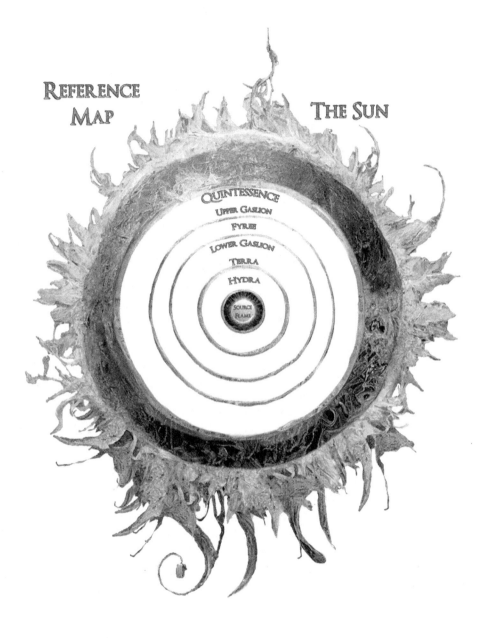

REFERENCE MAP   THE SUN

QUINTESSENCE
UPPER GASLION
FYREE
LOWER GASLION
TERRA
HYDRA
SOURCE FLAME

May all of your curses turn into blessings

Chapter 1

The sky exploded.

Glittering moondust showered the sun-kissed land of golden gears, catapulting debris off the fallen airship in every direction. A large chunk of space rock ricocheted into Emmeline's window, shattering the glass and startling her awake.

Emmeline raced to her balcony to find a lingering plume of black smoke and flames hovering in the sky. Fire and gas—a lethal combination.

Fire.

Emmeline looked down at her hands—her geared joints showed no signs of fire, but inside her heart, the source flame raged.

She was a Thermapunk—rulers of heat and keepers of the flame. Every Thermapunk was born with fire in their hearts, and through the power of heat, they reigned supreme.

Another detonation rained ash over the land. Moondust fluttered all around Emmeline as she scanned the sky for her brothers.

Cyrus, Helix, and Solís led the Pyropunk Militia—a warrior faction of the Thermapunks—into battle daily. They fought moon invaders regularly, all while protecting the thin solar shield of flares that encased this world. They fought alongside the Argopunks, who were the fighting faction of the Aeropunks. The Argos used their element of gas to take flight and create lethal chemical combinations for the Pyropunks to detonate.

Argopunks circled their most recent spot of detonation, assessing the damage and rescinding their deadly cocktail back into their gaseous hearts.

A hollering cheer echoed through the morning sky.

Moments later, three whooshing whirlwinds tore past Emmeline, tangling her long golden hair into knots.

"Hey!" she shouted.

The third golden blur circled back, slowing as it reached Emmeline.

Solís came into view.

"Sorry, sis. That victory is too great not to celebrate."

Bare-chested beneath his harness and secured safely in the sky by the power of gas and aerophysics, he caught his breath. His shoulder gears churned, giving motion to the titanium wings strapped to his back, and the helium tank situated between them kept him afloat.

"Who'd you get this time?" she asked.

"Monsters from the Moon of Rage. They came with their leaders." A devious smirk stretched across his handsome face. "We eliminated them all."

"That's great!' Emmeline cheered. "The war has really shifted in our favor ever since you, Helix, and Cyrus formed the Pyropunk Militia."

"Just happy to help. Makes Dad's job easier, too."

"And mine, eventually," Emmeline added, her excitement growing.

"You're going to do great at the detention center."

"That's the plan," she agreed confidently, though lines of doubt in her expression revealed her reservations.

"Dad is lucky to have you," he added, sensing her worry.

Emmeline changed the subject. "How long did it take you to get used to flying?"

"A few months. We had been training to dive, so switching our focus to the sky was a little jarring. But it didn't take too long to adjust. I just wish I was allowed to refill my helium tank during off-hours, too."

"Why can't you?

"The Aeropunks strictly monitor our consumption of their helium." Solís sighed. "I dream about flying free."

"That would be nice," Emmeline agreed. "Freedom."

"There's no such thing," Solís reminded her. Though his tone was playful, he spoke the truth. Every Solarpunk was bound to specific duties that kept the sun healthy.

He added, "Quintessence is a tinkering prison of gold. Beautiful and impressive, sure, but a prison all the same."

"You carved your own path," Emmeline reminded him.

"Out of necessity. If the world didn't need warriors in the sky, I'd be working alongside Dad." He grinned. "I'd be your boss right now."

"Thankfully, you're not."

He flew a little closer and playfully tousled the hair atop Emmeline's head.

"Stop!" she yelled, swatting him away.

Solís laughed, then turned his attention to the sweet aroma wafting through the air. The marbles in his gut rolled faster as he investigated the scent.

"Mom's making a victory feast." His entire focus shifted to his rumbling stomach. "See you there."

Solís took off, disappearing again as a golden blur.

Though she was excited to begin her journey as a monster wrangler at the detention center, her anxiety toward the responsibilities that awaited her was all-consuming. Today marked her first day of training with her father. She would travel to Hydra—the sea that existed within the center of the sun—where the family business resided: Dawes Detention Center for Demons. Though Emmeline was the youngest in the family, her brothers were too important to the war effort to help, so the obligation to take over the business landed on her. Emmeline was expected to take on a leadership role when she turned sixteen. She glanced at the clock on her wristband.

Two months until she celebrated her sixteenth soul day.

"Come get your marbles!" her mother shouted from the kitchen.

Melora Dawes, her mother, was the epitome of punk perfection. Though her high-ranking status among society was untouchable, it hardly matched the air of pretention with which she carried herself.

Her voice startled Emmeline from her thoughts.

Emmeline got dressed, tossing on a white blouse with short, trumpet-laced sleeves, and latching the straps of her canvas corset around her waist. She grabbed a pair of ruffled taupe bloomers, clipped a brown bustle skirt to the back, and then fastened her leg harness and pistol to her thigh. Thigh-high boots covered the rest of her legs and she raced downstairs for breakfast.

"My window shattered," Emmeline announced.

"I'll hire someone to fix it," Melora replied as she assessed her daughter, visibly annoyed by her outfit choice. "What is that?" she spat, waving her thin hand at Emmeline's clothes. Her wrist gears were perfectly greased, making no noise as she criticized her daughter.

"You told me last night to dress nice today," Emmeline countered, hip gears creaking as she sat down at the table.

"Then why do you look like a harlot?"

"Excuse me?"

"Your legs are always showing!"

"I don't like pants," Emmeline replied simply.

4

"You ought to be wearing a dress! You have an important meeting today."

"My outfit is fine."

"Even your hair is all wrong."

Emmeline clutched the long golden braids she had knotted into her hair, unsure what was wrong with them, then scowled.

"Where is my food?" she asked.

Melora sighed as she placed a bowl of golden marbles and a cup of liquid grease in front of her.

"You will continue to attend etiquette classes," her mother insisted. "I don't want the crude nature of the Nautipunks to rub off on you."

"I won't have time," Emmeline argued.

"You will make time. Now, eat."

Emmeline rolled her eyes and shoved five marbles into her mouth. They hit the back of her throat with a clang, then ricocheted down her throat chute and into the holding pan. She tossed another five marbles into her mouth, gearing up to have enough energy for a long day in Hydra. Though she ate her hearty meal, she was unable to hide the frown on her face. Anxiety replaced her excitement, and she stared at what remained of her breakfast.

"What's wrong, Emmeline?" Cyrus asked as he charged through the back door. Helix somersaulted through the front door and Solís entered through the open window. A burst of life during an otherwise dismal breakfast.

Emmeline glanced up at Cyrus. "Nothing. I just lost my appetite."

Solís scoffed, "You're *always* hungry."

5

"I've seen you eat more than the three of us combined," Helix added, then smirked. "It's impressive."

Emmeline stared at her bowl. They were right, her appetite was normally insatiable, but right now, all she could think about was her first day in Hydra.

Melora clicked her tongue, interjecting into their conversation. "It's not about hunger, or even taste—it's about keeping your gears healthy and moving. The marbles keep your insides turning, without them, you'd stutter to a stop."

"I know," Emmeline grumbled. She threw another marble into her mouth and felt the clinking clang of it pinballing down her throat into the holding pan, which methodically released each marble into the elaborate mechanism within her gut. Her gears turned a little quicker now, reinvigorating her spirit.

Feeling better, she gobbled up the rest of the bowl, filling her body with thirty golden marbles. Clinking and clanging, creating a quirky melodic rhythm, they found their place within her intricate system of inner gears. Marbles were the kinetic fuel that kept every Solarpunk going.

Her brothers stomped around the kitchen, filling their bowls and loudly recalling their morning victory.

"Did you see how they combusted?" Helix said through a mouth full of marbles.

"I've never seen anything like it," Cyrus noted. "They weren't solid at all. They were made of dust and dirt."

"Easiest defeat yet," Solís chimed in. "And we took out their leaders, too."

"Today's triumph was well-earned," Melora said. "Eat up and rest. There's no telling when a new group of invaders will arrive."

Emmeline finished her last sip of grease and burped quietly.

"Victory," she said, pleased with her empty bowl.

Helix responded with a louder burp of his own, speaking through the belch, "Victory!"

Cyrus and Solís joined in, saying random, congratulatory words through loud burps.

"Champion!"

"Triumph!"

"Enough!" Melora chastised. "Time to go."

Emmeline wore a silly grin on her face as she placed her bowl into the sink. She reached into the jar of marbles and grabbed a handful—snacks for later. As she walked past her brothers at the table, she waited until her mother had left the room to deliver one final farewell belch.

It was louder than she anticipated, which signaled Melora to peek around the corner. When she realized the burp came from her daughter and not one of her sons, her expression shifted to horror.

"Was that you?" she asked, sending Emmeline's brothers into a fit of laughter. Melora clicked her tongue, shook her head, and remarked, "I thought I had a daughter, not a fourth son."

Emmeline grinned sheepishly before darting out of the room to join her mother.

Atop her piled and flowing golden hair, Melora placed her top hat, which was decorated in tulle and feathers. A strip of lace masked her pretty golden eyes, and the thin feathers attached to her high-necked blouse danced as she moved swiftly toward the door.

Emmeline grabbed her own top hat, which was shorter in height and decorated with metal buttons. Her brass-rimmed goggles clung tight to the brim, ready for wear.

It was time to meet her fate.

Quintessence was the sun of this galaxy—one of many in the expansive universe, but the primary source of heat in the galaxy they called home. The Solarpunks lived inside a pocket of oxygen within the sun. Here, they controlled the warmth delivered to the surrounding planets and moons. While Thermapunks controlled the flame, they could not exist without gas, water, and minerals—Aeropunks, Hydropunks, and Terrapunks. These four groups of Solarpunks kept this orb of divine ether functioning; they ensured a healthy sun for the mortals living on the surrounding planets.

Despite their equal contribution, the Thermapunks reigned supreme. They had final say in all matters, as all matters often began or ended with fire.

Emmeline glanced up at the swirling solar shield, wondering how often Solédon, the god of all suns, checked on them. As decreed in His holy doctrine, the Solarpunks were given two tasks: provide heat to the mortals living on the planets that rotated around Quintessence, and protect the source flame from those who wished to steal its fire.

Moon monsters invaded often with the intention to steal fire, which is why her father, Montgomery Dawes, created their family business—Dawes Detention Center for Demons. Within this complex world of gears and wheels was a prison where the captured moon monsters were kept.

The Dawes family airship, a steel-plated aircraft, hovered next to their floating mansion in the sky. Emmeline stood beside her mother as Regis Morrell, their personal Pilopunk, chauffeured their trip to Hydra. The Pilopunks were another subgroup of the Aeropunks, and they acted as stewards to the nobles of Quintessence, using their gaseous hearts to fly the Thermapunks around. Regis was trained in pyroaeronautics and utilized Melora's source flame to fuel their flight. With fire, they flew faster than the standard helium-ships.

Regis did not speak as they drifted through the sky. He wore an aviation cap rimmed with gold cords, and his black suit was tailored with precision. Proper in appearance, just as Melora demanded. Like all Aeropunks, his copper gaze held a pinkish-orange gleam. Unlike the others, though, his eyes repressed unspoken discontent.

"Good morning, Regis," Emmeline greeted, hoping to coax a smile out of their silent pilot.

He nodded in reply, expression stoic.

She did not push any further. One day, she'd get him to smile, but today, the pressure of what awaited her in Hydra was her primary focus.

Anxiety shifting to excitement, Emmeline's spirits lifted. She reached into her pocket, snatched a golden marble, and tossed it down her throat. Eating provided great comfort. The marble clambered down the chute, landing at the back of the holding pan. One by one, with timely exactitude, the marbles from breakfast launched into the intricate workings of her gut. Melodic and precise, they kept all her vitals functioning with healthy accuracy.

She tossed another golden marble into her mouth, letting it roll around on her tongue before swallowing.

High above Quintessence, Emmeline looked over the side of their fast-moving ship to observe the intricate workings of the world below. There were two groups of Terrapunks: the Revopunks and the Tinkerpunks. The Tinkerpunks were not bound to the terrain, instead, they hustled around the golden geared orb, tinkering with the springs and greasing the joints as the wheels rotated.

Emmeline could not see the Tinkerpunks from the sky, but the Revopunks were impossible to miss. They were massive as they tore across the landscape. Their feet locked into the moving terrestrial gears, they skated in monotonous order, keeping the chains of Quintessence in motion. They moved in specific migrations, never breaking pattern or veering off their designed course.

"Do you think they're sad?" Emmeline asked her mother.

Melora shook her head. "They are angry; they always have been. If we showed them the smallest bit of mercy, all would be lost."

"Why?"

"For one, they are walking bombs. Even the hint of a flame would detonate their uranium hearts, and the petroleum coursing through their veins would fuel the blast. Secondly, though I hate to admit it, they are smarter than us. Their tinkering skills are more advanced, and without the restrictions we've placed on them, they could overrun us—like they have in the past."

Though Emmeline felt sympathy for the Terrapunks, she understood the reasoning behind this enslavement. In past wars, their nuclear capabilities combined with fire almost caused the annihilation of Quintessence.

"Don't you agree?" Melora asked Regis, whose stoic expression twisted with forced compliancy.

"I do," he answered.

Melora laughed, then spoke to Emmeline. "It's one of the few things our groups can agree on."

Regis steered the airship, crossing over the sprawling city of golden gears—roadways, bridges, and buildings all made of turning wheels. They spun and churned, which rotated the orb. This consistent revolution kept the sun alive.

As they crossed the horizon, the elaborate gates to Hydra came into view. Titanium rods elongated and crisscrossed, the barrier was unbreachable without permission; access was granted from below.

Emmeline held her breath as they approached.

It was time to meet her destiny.

Chapter 2

"My loves," Emmeline's father greeted from his floating airship beneath the gates of Hydra. "You will be delighted by the news today."

"Good news?" Melora asked, surprised. "Last I heard, there were still monsters roaming free."

"There will always be new monsters to catch," Montgomery said, optimism undeterred as he inserted his master key — the only key of its kind — into the gates of Hydra. Five counter-clockwise twists within the lock and the stretched springs began to recoil. The gears turned and slowly, the gates opened.

"We caught another," he announced with delight as Regis lowered a rope ladder over the side of the airship. Melora and Emmeline climbed down. Four rungs from the bottom, Emmeline leapt off and landed on the steel planks of her father's ship.

"What kind of monster was it this time?" she asked, prepared to embrace her destiny as a warden in this watery prison.

"A ferocious beast from the Moon of Discord."

"Where did you find it?"

"Where they always are — deep beneath the sea. We dragged it up and caged it. Now we are looking for any potential offspring."

"Can I see?" Emmeline asked as her mother finished her hesitant climb down the rope ladder.

"Of course, that's why you are here!"

As soon as Melora's feet touched the ground, Montgomery instructed his Pilopunk to set course. Avery Morrell, daughter to Regis, zipped across the world of

Hydra like a true sea-savvy pirate. The Morrell family had loyally served the Dawes family for decades.

Avery did not make eye contact with Emmeline; in fact, she showed no interest in her arrival at all. Emmeline brushed aside any feeling of offense—she had enough to worry about.

Montgomery's ship had billowing mauve sails, which helped direct their course, and the metal vessel was held in the sky by four thermal balloons draped in gold-chained nets. A pair of golden dragon wings adorned to each side of the stern helped steer the vessel and served as a reminder to the Hydropunks of Hydra that he was not one of them—he was from above.

"I've heard the Hydropunks are awful," Emmeline confessed.

"As a whole, they're not so bad. Most of them live on the many Roves scattered across the ocean and mind their own business," Montgomery explained.

"What's a Rove?"

Montgomery pointed into the distance at an anchored island comprised of stacked homes, markets, and pipes to the world above.

"That's Smuggler's Rove—there are tons of Roves scattered all over Hydra. It's an island of junk, really. But the Hydropunks seem content living in disorganized filth."

"I thought they were pirates? Don't they live at sea?"

"Ah, yes. The sub faction of Hydropunks that we work with are indeed pirates. They call themselves Nautipunks, and they truly are a thorn in my side. But they do good work. I couldn't have wrangled all these moon monsters without their help."

"Are they dangerous?" Emmeline asked.

"Very. I'd argue that they are their own breed of monster."

Emmeline gulped.

"The fire sets us apart," Montgomery noted, seemingly reading his daughter's mind.

"How? They don't need fire to thrive," she argued.

"No, they get plenty of power from the strength of the sea," he agreed, then smirked. "But they can never leave." He pointed toward the faraway gate in the sky, the only exit from this shadowy, cavernous place. He then patted the side wall of his giant, fire-fueled ship. "With this vessel, we can fly or sail, unlike the Nautipunks, whose steel tanker ships are bound to the water. They can sail, they can submerge beneath the sea, but they cannot fly. Not without fire and gas. They have some sneaky ways of getting around, but as a rule, none of the Hydropunks are supposed leave Hydra."

Emmeline returned her gaze to the ocean.

The source flame existed deep beneath the sea, rotating slowly at the center of the Quintessence. Obsidian rock surrounded it, containing the molten lava radius that extended for a nautical mile in all directions. Light peeked through in various spots—naturally formed cracks, damage inflicted by the moon monsters, and small fissures where golden tethers extended fire into the world above.

Only the Thermapunks could get close to the source flame—Hydropunks were burned alive on the rare occasions that they had tried. Their hearts were made of water, a necessary component in this orb of ether, but extraordinarily limited in capability. One might argue that they were just as imprisoned as the monsters here.

Fiery rays filtered through the ocean, reaching the surface and casting light from below. Many of the

Nautipunks' ships were decorated in mirrors, which helped blind their enemies and deflected more light into the world above the sea.

The light came and went, moving with the tides, and Emmeline's eyes struggled to adjust between each wave.

A blinding beam aimed toward them indicated the arrival of a Nautipunk man-o-war.

Montgomery turned to Emmeline.

"Show no fear," he advised.

Before Emmeline could reply, a raspy voice shouted up at them.

"Ahoy, Montgomery," the scallywag greeted. "Are ye here to see the kraken?"

His ship was made of metal and bones, and the skull at the bow had mirrors for eyes. Emmeline was still blinded by the light.

"Indeed," Montgomery replied, pulling Emmeline forward. "Meet my daughter, Emmeline. It's time she learned the ropes down here."

"A pretty lassie she is." His tone dripped with covetous desire. "Though, would be prettier if she smiled."

Emmeline lifted her six-barrel pistol out of her leg holster, cocked the hammer, and aimed it at the pirate.

"Are ye gonna shoot me?" the Nautipunk captain asked with a laugh.

"Tell me to smile again." She pulled the trigger and shot the stuffed raven off his feathered tricorn hat.

"Blimey! That was me favorite pet!" He pulled the sword from his belt, and his crew of pirates did the same. "She coulda killed me," he growled at Montgomery.

Gun still aimed at the pirate, Emmeline growled, "If I wanted to kill you, I would've shot you between the eyes."

15

"Her aim is perfect," Montgomery explained with pride. "She learned to shoot from me."

"Beautiful and dangerous," the Nautipunk stated, his desire more potent than before. "I mean ye no harm, but me crew don't particularly love the landlubbers."

"I live in the sky, not on land," she informed him without lowering her gun.

"But ye have never been to sea before."

"What of it?"

He chuckled, placing his sword back into his scabbard, then addressed her father. "She'll do just fine in Hydra. Lemme take ye to the kraken."

Adrenaline racing, Emmeline couldn't lower her gun. Her father gently placed his hand on top of the pistol and lowered her aim.

"You did good. Now relax."

Though she showed no fear, her hands trembled. "Why'd you let him talk to me that way?"

"It's part of the process. You have to earn their respect. You did well."

"Did he do the same to Cyrus, Helix, and Solís?"

"Yes."

Agitated, but relieved, she recollected her wits and asked, "Who is he?"

"That's Red Fang Ralph—the most amicable Nautipunk captain of the lot."

"Why do they call him Red Fang?"

"Because he adds the blood of monsters to his grog."

Her eyes widened; this pirate drank the blood of his prisoners. "And he's the easiest to deal with?"

"By far."

They followed Red Fang's pirate ship, flying high while Ralph's boat hovered atop the surface of the sea, filtering in and spitting out the powerful tides to stay aloft. The boat was impressive; full skeletons of deceased monsters and Nautipunks were secured to both sides of the ship. Fastened with metal strips and bolts, the zinc bones of the Nautipunks retained their gears and moved as the wind spun their wheels. Emmeline watched in amazement—five thousand ghosts waved at her from their eternal prison.

A grumbling roar echoed so loud, Emmeline fell to one knee. She braced herself and squinted, hoping to adjust her vision to the ever-changing light. As the sight before her came into focus, she saw them: five colossal monsters imprisoned in titanium cages.

Beneath them was a sprawling assortment of connected cages containing monsters less visible, but the five stood apart from the rest.

"These are the first five monsters we ever caught," Montgomery explained. "After them, we built more condensed and sustainable cages, but easy access to the original five helps with our research."

"What are the monsters in the cages below?"

"Offspring of the five you see above. If we ever come across a new species of monster, we'll build a sixth large cage. But let's hope that never happens."

Each of the five original prisons were suspended above the water by steel beams. The bars crisscrossed in disorderly patterns, creating triangles and diamond cut-outs that the monsters peered through.

Red Fang Ralph anchored his ship directly below the cages, then used his spear gun to hook a long rope to the nearest cage. As the rope retracted, he flew into the air and latched onto the side of the cage. His arrival angered the monster inside. Red Fang Ralph swiftly avoided the creature's claws, which viciously tried to impale the pirate through the gaps.

"What is he doing?" Emmeline asked her father.

Montgomery shook his head. "Trying to collect some blood for his cocktails, I'm sure."

"That creature is filled with rage."

"That is an Ogre of Irritability from the Moon of Rage. He was our first catch, but his offspring are everywhere. Not nearly as big as he is, but one day they'll grow to his size."

"And we have to capture them all?"

My father nodded. "Our work is never-ending."

She felt the burden in his voice, a burden she soon would help him carry.

Melora sat in a cushioned chair at the back of the airship, sheltered by an ornate canopy of metal coils. Unbothered by the screeching roars of the monsters, she sat there, blissfully disinterested, stitching buttons onto a pair of gloves.

Emmeline looked back to her father and asked, "Can we fly closer?"

A mischievous grin crossed his face. "Of course!"

Avery cranked the wheel, which turned the gears and added friction to the engines that propelled the ship forward. Misty vapor whistled from the bells attached to the bow.

Upon reaching the closest cage, Avery slowed so Emmeline could take a good look at the creature inside. Massive, but sluggish, this monster moved in slow motion. It sensed their proximity as it turned its head. Beneath clay-covered eyelids, black caverns of emptiness stared through Emmeline. An ice-cold shiver slithered down the gears of her spine.

A growling grumble resonated from the monster's gut, causing its bared fangs to chatter.

"Don't let the slow nature of this Behemoth of Fatigue fool you," her father whispered. "This monster consumes the brightest stars, smothering their glow. If it touches you, you're lost to its darkness."

Emmeline clenched her fingers into fists, suddenly aware that she was ill-prepared for her fate.

Her father instructed Avery to fly onward.

The second cage held a smaller creature, but its wild energy made up for its lack in size. A giant pair of iridescent wings extended from its back, ripping through the air at dizzying speeds. It ricocheted from wall to wall, traveling in a blur of color as it screeched one word repetitively: Mine.

"That's a Hellion of Obsession," her father explained.

"Its wings are so colorful," she said, captivated by the beauty.

"They are dragonfly wings. Be wary of their glamour. This monster uses illusions to lure its victims."

"What does it do to them?"

"This monster makes their victim sick in the mind. It gives life to their darkest, most repressed desires. Sometimes, it even births new derangements. If it seizes you, it will twist you until you are consumed by your own darkness. It will swallow the light until your obsession becomes all that you can see."

"Why?" Emmeline asked, horrified.

"We aren't sure what they get out of it, only that it is a vicious weapon used against us. I lost my first Pilopunk, Charles, to this Hellion of Obsession. The beast spat into Charles's eyes and the poisonous saliva embedded into his brain. It wasn't until Charles jumped off the side of our airship a few weeks later and drowned at sea that I realized the extent of the damage. Charles wanted to be free—he had expressed that to me many times in subtle ways—and the hellion gave that desire life; Charles viewed death as a logical path to liberation."

"These are wretched creatures," Emmeline commented, her confidence wavering.

"Without us, these monsters would steal the sun's flame and our galaxy would crumble."

Emmeline nodded, mustering any courage that remained. She understood the importance of this job.

The third cage held the Demon of Destruction from the Moon of Demolition. The bars confining the massive beast were bent and dented.

"Will it get out?" Emmeline asked.

"No, but it fears no injury in its attempts."

The demon slammed its rock-hard head against the bars, howling pure rage. Crimson blood flowed from the fresh wounds on its forehead, streaking down its face like war paint. The whole cage shook atop its golden pedestal, and the welded metal holding it from falling into the sea had formed countless fissures.

Emmeline pointed. "Are you sure it won't get out?"

Montgomery lowered his magnifying spectacles, and after closer inspection, snapped his fingers.

"Welders, line up!"

Five Thermapunk welders with infrared goggles and waist harnesses emerged from the crew.

"Repairs are needed on cage three. May Solédon watch over you."

"Ascent," they replied in unison, before tossing hooked ropes at cage three and launching themselves off the side of the ship. As their hooks snagged the demon's cage, its fury amplified. It reached its bloody arms through the cracks, attempting to seize the welders as they worked. They soldered through heated palms, turning their fire onto the monster any time it got too close.

The monster's anger surpassed the pain, and it continued its fight, creating a volatile workspace for the welders.

Montgomery waved Avery onward and they reached cage four where Red Fang Ralph still fought the Ogre of Irritability.

This monster was quick, but its massive lumps of boiling anger often prevented it from reaching its full range of mobility. It couldn't lift its arms due to puss-filled sores on its shoulders, and its legs could only move so fast, as the chafing cysts on its inner thighs rubbed together painfully. This creature was wretched to observe. Still, despite the clear agony it lived within, the ogre fought back. No regard for its own well-being and blinded by rage, it slammed its body against the cage, hoping to knock Red Fang Ralph loose.

Montgomery glanced at Emmeline, ready to explain, but saw the look of horror on her face and reconsidered. "I think you get the idea."

She nodded. "Red Fang Ralph has lost his mind."

"He lost it years ago," her father revealed.

The last cage held the newest prisoner: a Beast of Panic. This monster had wings, and it flew in monotonous circles.

Montgomery explained, "If you break its routine, it loses its ability to breathe, so it'll steal the breath from the nearest bystander in order to survive. This obviously kills the bystander, but the beast resumes its routine till it's disturbed again."

The weight of this responsibility hung heavy on Emmeline's back.

"And all of these monsters came from the moons in our galaxy?"

"They did. Long before your brothers formed the Pyropunk Militia, we weren't so good at keeping them out of Quintessence. Often times, we did not even know they were here. They infiltrated silently, always reaching the source flame. For a long time, the strength of the fire killed them, leaving us with little to worry about, but as they grew smarter and arrived with better strategies and tools to steal fire for themselves, we had to smarten up, too. At the time, our air defenses were weak and they always reached Hydra, so it landed on the Hydropunks and Thermapunks to stop them from leaving with fire. That's how our family business came to be."

"Why are there still more to catch within the sea? Doesn't the Pyropunk Militia stop any new ones from entering Hydra?" she asked, her voice tinged with dismay.

"They do, but the damage the monsters caused down here is immense. Before we became aware of the moon monsters infiltrating our world, and before we found ways to stop them in the sky, they burrowed here in our sea and reproduced. Those that breached our borders long ago left an everlasting mark."

"Can't we just kill them?"

"We've tried, but it's not as easy as it may seem. Like us, they were born from the primordial gods. Killing a demi-god takes time and specific instruction. Very few methods of elimination work."

"I will pray to Solédon," Emmeline said. "He has to help us."

22

"He can only do so much. Remember—Lunéss, the goddess of all moons, is His sister. Solédon created us to protect this sun. He created us in retaliation to Lunéss's refusal to wrangle Her moon monsters."

"Perhaps that will be my first goal—learn the secret to killing these horrifying creatures. I will make Solédon proud."

"It's a lofty, but noble goal. If you succeed, you would make our job easier. For now, focus on the tasks within our control: hunting and wrangling the monsters, while keeping the Nautipunks in line."

Red Fang Ralph reappeared. Swinging carelessly from the mainmast, he lifted his flask and hollered, "Ye ho! A bloody great success."

"Indeed. But our work is never done," Montgomery reminded him.

"Aye, ye scurvy dog! Live a little!"

"Enjoy your bloody rum. We hunt again at dawn."

"Give me yer flame and I can hunt by meself."

"Ah, and so you can share the flame with your whole lot of Nautis?"

Red Fang Ralph spat in reply, then took a hearty swig from his flask. "Ye got me pegged wrong. I want that flame all to meself."

"You can't fool me; you want to see the Thermapunks fall from grace."

"It would be a pretty show," he sneered with a roguish laugh.

Montgomery raised his brow, but chose to ignore the threat. "Until dawn."

"Until dawn!" Red Fang repeated, twirling around the mast as his crew sailed their ship away.

"Are you ready for the hunt?"

Eyes wide, Emmeline nodded. She suppressed her rampant fear.

"I'm ready," she said, clutching her nerve-wrecked stomach. The marbles fell one by one, keeping her gears turning. The intricate workings of her body were delicate, as they were for every Solarpunk in Quintessence. Tinkering gears, propelled into motion by a daily consumption of marbles, kept them alive. It was one of the few things that the Solarpunks shared; it was one of their limited, but profound similarities.

Emmeline observed the Nautipunks as Avery flew her father's airship toward the gates of Hydra. As different as they were, they were just as bound as her.

The monsters were far away now, yet they remained vivid in her mind. They terrorized her thoughts, replacing the excitement she once felt with dread.

Her gaze lifted toward the sky and the sensation of flying soothed her nerves. A foreign consolation—she had never felt drawn to the sky before—but comforting all the same. The farther they soared, the farther away the monsters became.

Emmeline was determined to remain optimistic.

Unrelenting bravery would see her through.

Chapter 3

"Are you ready for your first hunt?"

Solís's voice woke Emmeline from a deep slumber.

"Get out of my room," she mumbled, rolling over and covering her head with a pillow.

"It's time to face the day," Solís declared, jumping onto the end of her bed and bouncing up and down, forcing Emmeline to get up.

"Why are you so annoying?" she groaned.

"I'm your brother. That's what I do."

"Go bother someone else."

"I'm excited for you!"

"You shouldn't be."

"Why?"

"It's terrible down there."

Solís chuckled. "Not a fan of the monsters?"

"No!"

"At least they're in cages," he offered. "I have to fight them in the sky."

"They roam free in the sea, too. I'll have to fight them underwater."

"Try to focus on the good parts. You get to go diving, you get to go on a chase." His golden eyes lit up from the imagined thrill. "It's going to be a rush."

Emmeline wanted to be brave.

"You're right. I'll be fine." She sat up in bed and realized that her left hand had gone numb while she slept. She twisted her elbow gears to return the feeling to her fingers.

"You need to drink more oil," Solís suggested.

"I didn't ask for your advice."

"Don't do a dive with ungreased gears. You'll rust."

Emmeline groaned. "Get out of my room!"

Solís picked up a pillow from a chair near the door and tossed it at her as he left. Too disoriented to catch it, the pillow smacked her in the face.

Emmeline fell back onto her bed in defeat.

The unpredictability of the forthcoming hunt haunted her.

"Time to go!" Melora shouted from downstairs.

Emmeline rolled over, smothering her face in her pillow. When the air thinned to nothing and breathing became a struggle, she sat up with a gasp. Soon, she'd be leagues below the sea with no access to air. Soon, she'd be breathing through a tank.

It was time to be brave.

Despite her newly formed trepidations, she was conditioned to embrace the sea—that was where she was trained to be. Determination focused, she dragged herself out of bed.

She had monsters to catch.

Emmeline retrieved her swimming corset. Top and bottom laced together with thick strips of stitched leather, she pulled the suit up her torso and tightened the straps till the fit was snug. She knotted her long golden hair into a singular braid that reached the middle of her back. Overtop of her swimming suit she wrapped a long ruffled skirt and put on her leather bomber jacket.

Emmeline examined herself in the mirror. She skipped smudging black eyeliner on, since the water would only wash it off. Her innocence and inexperience were enhanced by her fresh face. With a grumble, Emmeline grabbed her stick of black grease and smeared the darkness around her eyes. If she couldn't feel like a warrior, she had to at least look like one.

Combat boots on, but unlaced, she stomped downstairs.

"Why are you wearing makeup?" Melora asked. "You're going diving today."

"I don't want to look like a child in front of the Nautipunks."

Melora did not argue. In fact, she seemed to silently agree.

Emmeline added, "I'm starving."

"You slept in too late—you'll have to take your marbles and grease to go."

"I can eat quick," Emmeline insisted, taking a swig of grease before lifting the bowl of golden marbles to her mouth and swallowing them one by one in methodical rhythm. They rolled down the chute of her throat and into the holding pan where they'd eventually be shot into the rotating pattern of her inner gears.

One more swig of grease and Emmeline felt rejuvenated.

"I'm ready now."

Melora grabbed her top hat and led Emmeline out to the airship.

"You don't have to come," Emmeline offered. "It'll be rather boring on the ship while we're beneath the sea."

"I have crochet work to do. I'll be perfectly entertained."

Melora marched onto the airship. Emmeline dragged her feet as she followed.

The ride to Hydra was smooth. Emmeline watched Regis intently, wondering what the silent steward's story was. She lost track of time as she crafted a backstory and personality for Regis in her head.

"We're here," Melora announced.

Montgomery was waiting for them at the gates of Hydra.

As soon as their airship was close enough, he inserted the master key into the lock, turned it five times, and the tinkering gears of the elaborate gate unlocked in an intricate and orderly fashion. Latch by latch, the metal barrier shifted. Bars crossed under and above one another, creating room for the Dawes's airship to enter.

Regis lowered the vessel enough so the rope ladder could reach Montgomery's ship below. Emmeline and Melora climbed over and Regis waited for them in the world above Hydra.

After relocking the gates, Montgomery climbed down from the top deck and instructed Avery to set sail. Attention focused on the task at hand, Avery navigated the strong wind currents above the sea without ever glancing at Emmeline or Melora.

Montgomery's crew of Thermapunks bustled around the ship, working and cleaning while the boat made its way to their hunting location.

Melora took her usual seat beneath a canopy of coils, while Emmeline stayed close to her father.

"We'll be hunting for eggs today," he told her. "The moon monsters often lay them near the source flame for the heat."

"What do they look like?"

"Each species of moon monster lays different looking eggs. When we get down there, you'll follow me and I'll show you some examples. Today, you won't go off on your own. You'll stay by my side."

Emmeline nodded, relieved.

The source flame burned within the ocean. Though it was protected by a thick layer of obsidian rock, its heat and light still radiated for miles in every direction.

28

"If the source flame is protected by a thick shield, how does its light shine through?" Emmeline asked.

"Through cracks and fissures collected over the centuries."

"Why hasn't the ocean water seeped through the fissures and extinguished the flame?"

"The source flame functions exactly as the gods designed it; it has a force field around it that water cannot penetrate. Thermapunks can access the flame, and the monsters have created gadgets that can access the flame, but water cannot infiltrate," her father explained. "Not unless we fail in our duties as Solarpunks."

Emmeline thought of Solédon, the god of all suns. She then thought of Lunéss, the goddess of all moons and mother to the monsters.

"Do you think Solédon and Lunéss hate each other?" she asked her father.

"I have to assume that they foster a ripe rivalry, considering the war that rages between their celestial creations."

"I wonder if the suns in other galaxies have as much trouble with their moons as we do with ours."

"One can only speculate."

They had reached the spot of their dive. Montgomery anchored the floating ship with an anvil. Weight tossed overboard, he unreeled the attached chain until the magnetic pull of the flame held the anvil securely in place.

"Put this on." He handed Emmeline a metal helmet. Tubes extended from the base like octopus arms and connected to a tank that he helped strap to her back. She stepped into the airtight jumpsuit her father pointed to, and he helped secure the helmet to the suit.

"This will keep you alive underwater," he explained, then asked, "Do you remember the breathing techniques I showed you?"

Emmeline nodded.

Montgomery continued, then pointed to a lever with two buttons attached to a tube on her sleeve. "This is the BC. It stands for buoyancy control. Press up to fill your suit with air, press down to deflate. Acquiring buoyancy is key to diving."

"I might struggle at first."

"I will help you." He then handed her four finned cuffs. "These will help you move through the water. Secure them to your wrists and ankles and you'll be swimming in no time."

Emmeline locked one cuff to each of her extremities, and with ten solid twists of the tiny crank on each cuff, the fins began to flutter.

Clanging bells and creaking bones sounded through the misty horizon. Through the haze, Red Fang Ralph approached on his pirate ship of metallic death.

"Why are they here?" Emmeline asked, her manageable anxiety rapidly escaping her control.

"The more eyes, the better."

Red Fang Ralph dropped his anchor, situating his boat directly below Montgomery's.

"Ahoy, ye old seadog."

"Greetings, Ralph. Are you ready for the day's hunt?"

"Always!" he said with a growl. "I live fer the hunt."

"And your crew?"

Red Fang Ralph stuck his fingers in his mouth and whistled, summoning forth his top divers.

A beautiful young woman with wild red curls that hung to her waist stepped forward first. Her green suede tricorn cap cast a shadow over her devious blue gaze. A nasty neck wound left the interior zinc gears of her neck visible. They churned methodically as she assessed the Thermapunks.

"This here is Ruthanne the Heartless," Red Fang Ralph said. "She's the best diver of me lot."

Ruthanne spat overboard, unimpressed by the compliment paid by her captain.

This was the first female Nautipunk Emmeline had ever seen. The sight was jarring and wholly inspiring. An untouchable force of strength among the lowliest of men—Ruthanne showed no fear. She wore her many scars as a warning to those who meant her harm, and her name acted as a cautionary reminder—she was a heartless mercenary who held sympathy for no one.

A surge of fear-inspired determination surged through Emmeline. Ruthanne was an image of courage, and Emmeline intended to emulate that energy.

Behind her stood a boy … or a man—Emmeline struggled to determine his age. He didn't look much older than her, but his shoulders slouched as if he carried the weight of a hundred lifetimes.

Red Fang Ralph yanked him forward.

"Straight Leg Louie is new to me crew. He'll need ter prove himself today." He slapped the side of the boy's head, knocking his shaggy brown hair over his icy blue eyes. Louie took the beating without argument.

Emmeline felt his pain.

Red Fang Ralph barked, "I can't have a lubber aboard me ship."

The rest of his crew cheered and grumbled in agreement.

Though Ruthanne's stoic stance did not budge, her eyes shifted to Louie and she gave him a subtle wink. Emmeline observed, intrigued—they seemed to know each other well.

Unlike Emmeline and her father, the Nautipunks did not need helmets or suits to hunt beneath the sea. They were born to swim; designed to traverse deep water.

Straight Leg Louie and Ruthanne the Heartless stepped onto the banister of the middle deck. Ruthanne tossed her hat to a fellow crewmate and knotted her long hair into a braid. Beneath her decorated waistcoat she wore a two-piece corset that revealed even more of her battle scars. It also revealed how the Nautipunks were able to swim under water for long periods of time.

Large translucent claw-mark scars ran across her rib cage, and underneath the old wounds sat a tank of air where her gear-churning lungs should've been. Visible only because of her battle scars. Ruthanne twisted the notch at the base of her neck before diving into the sea. She disappeared into the water without making a splash.

Straight Leg Louie ripped off his billowing white poet's shirt, revealing the chest of a young man who had not yet seen war. Flesh intact over his intricate inner gears, not a single scar decorated his body.

Emmeline caught herself staring.

So did Louie.

His sapphire stare met hers.

Swirling pools of glimmering blue captivated Emmeline—his gaze was infectious.

A brief smirk crept across Louie's face before he dove into the water.

Teeth clenched, Emmeline cursed at herself internally. She needed to be invincible like Ruthanne, not develop fleeting feelings for a lowly Nautipunk like Louie.

"They can breathe underwater?" she asked her father.

"Their tank lungs fill with oxygen while they're above the water, and they use what they've stored when they're beneath the sea. They replenish each time they finish a dive."

"That's convenient," she replied, fidgeting within her bulky gear.

"Are you ready?" Montgomery asked as he closed the front vent of Emmeline's helmet and twisted the top of her tank, releasing breathable air into her suit.

"As ready as I can be." She thought again of Louie. "Won't their gears rust without protective gear?"

Montgomery shook his head. "Diving is part of their design. When submerged beneath the sea, their gears are continually greased by the octopus ink that runs through their veins. They'll never rust."

"Gold shouldn't rust either," Emmeline argued.

"The salt in this sea is particularly dangerous to precious metals. It corrodes gold, silver, and platinum faster than regular metals."

Emmeline fidgeted in her suit, uncomfortable from the itchy waterproof fabric and the weight of her heavy helmet.

Montgomery smiled. "All of that discomfort will vanish once we submerge. You remember the hand signals I taught you?" Emmeline nodded. "Good. Stay close to me down there."

He grabbed her hand and together they stepped onto a wooden platform extended off the side of their flying ship. Members of his Thermapunk crew turned a large wheel, which activated a pully system, and the platform began to lower. Inch by inch, the water grew nearer.

Emmeline's gut gears churned uncomfortably—she hated to admit it, but she was terrified of the unknown. Ocean spray splashed their covered ankles, and she could feel the frigidness of the water through her suit.

"It's freezing," she said, the gears of her spine chattering with a shiver.

"Your body heat will fill your suit and you'll adjust to the water temperature. And once we're deep enough and closer to the source flame, you'll see how the water temperature changes."

Emmeline groaned. Cold, scared, and unprepared—she did not wish to continue this hunt.

The platform came to a jolting halt a few inches above the volatile sea. Tumultuous waves crashed into the board repeatedly, knocking Emmeline and her father around.

"Time to hunt," he exclaimed with a devilish grin before extending one foot off the platform and stepping into the sea.

Without a splash, he disappeared.

Emmeline panicked.

She glanced up at the crew of Thermapunks above, who all frantically waved at her to follow her father's lead.

"Go now, or you'll lose sight of him!" a Thermapunk shouted down at her.

A giant wave slammed into the platform, knocking Emmeline off balance. She swayed ominously, back and forth, unable to regain her posture.

Another wave crashed into her and she fell.

Participating in this hunt was no longer a choice.

She was swallowed by the sea.

Chapter 4

Emmeline sank fast.

The weight of her golden gears sent her plummeting to the ocean floor. She flailed, frantically searching for her father while turning the keys of her finned wrist cuffs, hoping they might help her swim.

She cranked the key until the gears were wound enough that the fins began to move. They fluttered ferociously against the water, and while they did not magically teach her how to swim, they did slow her descent. The farther she fell, the warmer the water became. Her father was right—everything felt different at greater depths.

Away from the volatile space where water met air, the world beneath the sea was serene. Muffled silence stretched in every direction, beautiful tides of blues shimmered in the light emanating from the source flame situated at the center of the sea. Emmeline struggled to believe that monsters lived in this peaceful place.

Around the orb of fire that gave Quintessence life was a shield of obsidian rock. It had many surface blemishes where the light shined through. The conditions here kept the flame safe: unbreathable air, unbearable temperatures—no monster or punk, besides the Thermapunks, could reach this place without risking their lives to do so.

Just as Solédon had designed.

Emmeline looked above to see that Red Fang Ralph, Ruthanne the Heartless, and Straight Leg Louie swam many leagues above, a safe distance from the heat of the flame. They circled where she fell, unable to offer assistance or advice.

Her calmed heart resumed its panic. She thrashed her arms, hoping she might teach herself to swim, but it was no use. She couldn't figure it out.

As she fell closer to the obsidian ocean floor, the heat from the source flame grew stronger. Sweat beaded along her hairline and dripped down her forehead. Her hands instinctively raised to wipe it away, but the glass shield of her helmet was in the way. She rapidly blinked her golden lashes to keep the salty droplets at bay. It was no use. The sweat dripped into her eyes anyway, blurring her vision as she neared the black rock.

A strong grip snatched her bicep and turned her around. Dizzy from the vertigo, it took a moment for her father to come into focus. He floated in the water gracefully, no panic or urgency in his suspension. His cuffs fluttered, but he did not rely on them—he relied solely on his strategic breathing and the buoyancy created by his BC.

Emmeline recalled the lesson he gave her: Breathe in to rise, breathe out to descend. Combine the two in rhythm to float.

She refocused her frightened energy on her breathing.

Breath by breath, she found her buoyancy. As she settled into a steady cadence, her father demonstrated how to use the BC. He pressed up and a small amount of air filled Emmeline's suit, making floating easier.

Montgomery added a little more air into her suit, then gave her the "OK" signal—a circle formed by his thumb and pointer, with his other three fingers raised.

Emmeline nodded, mimicking the gesture.

He swam forward, never losing buoyancy, and Emmeline copied his movements exactly. Broad arm strokes and small legs kicks, assisted by the finned cuffs they both wore, guided them forward.

36

She was doing it—she was swimming. She was successfully hunting for monster eggs alongside her father. She thought of her older brothers, Solís in particular, and how proud they'd be of her. Jealous, too. Only she was being trained to perform such perilous quests for the family business.

Emmeline's excitement returned.

As they traversed the perimeter of the obsidian sphere, Montgomery pointed out strange objects and anomalies to Emmeline. She always looked to observe whatever he wanted her to pay attention to, but without the ability to speak, she did not yet understand their importance. A few strokes forward and a stark white rock covered in jagged knobs came into view.

Montgomery swam down to the object, carefully lifted it with his gloved hands, and turned to show Emmeline.

"Monster egg?" she asked, mouthing her question clearly so her father could lip-read.

He nodded and placed the egg into the satchel he wore across his shoulder.

They continued onward, scouring the dark land directly below. Emmeline found herself suffering from intense tunnel vision—the sea was so massive, to stay focused she could only concentrate on that which was directly in her sight.

From above, the muffled and distant sound of clanging metal forced Emmeline's attention upward. Ruthanne the Heartless was slamming her speargun against the large metal buckle of her belt. She pointed at a spot off Montgomery's trajected path.

He looked to where she indicated, then gave her the "OK" hand gesture.

Montgomery led Emmeline to the location. There, they found a red egg covered in black fuzz. Montgomery showed it to Emmeline before securing it into his satchel.

Aware now that she needed to widen her gaze, Emmeline fought off the luring tunnel vision and carefully scanned the ground in all directions, determined to find an egg.

The expansive ocean was endless, and it was inadvisable to wander too far from her father, but she also wanted to prove her worth. She wanted to contribute to this hunt.

She swam a little slower, vigilantly scanning every inch of the ground within view. Montgomery swam farther away while she lagged behind, futilely searching the barren oceanscape for anything that looked like an egg.

A blinding glimmer flashed across her peripheral vision. Attention turned, she located a shiny silver pearl the size of her palm.

It did not look like the eggs her father had found thus far, but it also wasn't obsidian rock, so Emmeline swam down to confiscate the foreign object.

Her father kept swimming, his image growing smaller as he got farther away. She knocked on the side of her helmet, hoping to make enough noise to turn his attention, but he did not hear her. She looked up and saw that Straight Leg Louie was keeping pace with her from above. He gave her the "OK" hand signal, indicating that he would wait. Nerves calmed—someone had eyes on her— she continued her dive.

When she reached the large silver pearl, she lifted it into her hands and was surprised by its lack of weight.

Her father had caught on to her detour and was now wading in place, waiting for her. Emmeline held up the pearl. Montgomery squinted from where he hovered, and then gave her the "OK" gesture before waving for her to return.

Giddy with excitement, Emmeline placed the pearly egg into her satchel and hurried to catch up to her father.

Back on his tail, her forward strokes were filled with accomplishment. She felt brave, she radiated confidence—maybe this calling suited her after all.

Focus lifted from the obsidian ground, Emmeline noticed Straight Leg Louie ahead, swimming fast and with intention toward an unknown darkness. She tapped her father's foot, grabbing his attention, and then pointed at Louie's charge.

As Montgomery's attention turned upward, Louie collided with a wiry creature made of tangled black cords and shimmering translucent flesh. It had giant dragonfly wings that pounded the water, propelling it forward at an unnatural speed. A piercing screech filled the serene ocean, forcing Emmeline to cringe. Horribly unpleasant, her insides shuddered at the sound. The monster was small but fierce, and swam in dizzying circles around Louie. The Nautipunk managed to pierce the monster with his speargun, slowing its manic pace, and as the creature fought its new constraints, its shrieking became decipherable.

"*Mine,*" it screeched repeatedly.

Emmeline now recognized this monster as a Hellion of Obsession.

Though Louie had him seized, the monster continued to fight, and Louie struggled to keep the wily creature captured. Red Fang Ralph and Ruthanne the Heartless swam to his aid, but they weren't fast enough. The monster snapped the rope and broke free. Spear still lodged in its gut, it tore toward Emmeline.

All the calmness she had found vanished. She had no weapons to protect herself, only a paring knife for skinning small fish. Emmeline retrieved the small knife from her boot strap as her father placed himself in front of her, unveiling a steel sword from the scabbard across his back.

The monster was not deterred. The hellion dove headfirst into Montgomery, taking the steel hilt to the neck. Buoyancy destroyed, the force of the collision sent Montgomery plummeting toward the ocean floor. His sword remained lodged in the monster's throat.

Emmeline was on her own.

In the distance, she saw Ruthanne and Ralph racing toward her, but the monster was already too close. They'd never reach her in time.

Both hands firmly gripping the handle of her paring knife, she held it outward, ready for impact. She closed her eyes, terrified, unwilling to witness her forthcoming death.

As the monster collided with her, its talons dug into her biceps and seized her. It dragged her at incredible speeds, pumping its translucent wings with great strength against the ocean current.

This was it.

This was the end.

Emmeline opened her eyes to see spears launching and missing the hellion's head. Her father was nowhere in sight, but the Nautipunks were tailing the monster, Louie in the lead. He swam faster than Ralph and Ruthanne, and was gaining distance on the hellion.

The hellion's grip tore through Emmeline's suit, allowing water to leak in. The trickle was slow, but significant. If she did not break free, she would drown.

The monster began to chant:

"*Ad lunam lu—*"

Emmeline seized her paring knife and stabbed the monster's ankle.

The hellion roared, but did not let her go.

Determination relentless, Emmeline thrust the knife into the creature over and over, undeterred by its stubbornness.

She would prevail.

The hellion *would* let her go; she would not stop until she was free.

Additional spears flew overhead, narrowly missing the hellion's skull. Louie was in reach now. His silver-blue gaze held murderous resolve.

Close enough to grab her, Louie seized Emmeline's boot and climbed up her body.

Latched tightly to her, his body covered hers. He pressed his forehead to her helmet and mouthed, *I've got you.*

Emmeline's heart gears turned violently, threatening to jam. Fear, hope, excitement—she trusted him. As he climbed onto the back of the hellion, Emmeline continued to do all she could to help. Paring knife in her grip, she kept digging at the fresh wounds in the monster's legs.

She could not see what was happening above, but the speed at which she was being carried away slowed and Ruthanne and Ralph were finally catching up. The hellion howled and released Emmeline. She tumbled out of its grip, somersaulting to face the fight above. As she fell through the water, dropping farther away from the battle between the monster and her savior, Louie impaled a giant spear through the top of the monster's skull. His stoic stance atop the creature's shoulder did not flinch as the head of the hellion imploded, scattering black cords and viscous membranes in all directions.

The monster fell, lifeless, to the obsidian boneyard, and Louie lifted his body, resuming his swim.

Water was seeping into Emmeline's suit at an alarming rate.

Dread at an all-time high, she flailed, unable to regain buoyancy without a functioning BC.

Montgomery was charging toward her from below, and the Nautipunks raced to her from above. Sea water slowly filled her helmet.

Louie reached her first. With the force of a tidal wave, he scooped her into his arms and catapulted toward the sky. The water in Emmeline's helmet now covered her mouth. She looked to Louie, who held her gaze as he propelled them to safety.

His confidence was calming.

She wanted to believe in him; she wanted to survive this, but she wasn't sure how long she could hold her breath.

The water rose above her nose.

A quick glance up filled Emmeline with dread—the sky was so far away.

"Look at me!" Louie shouted, his muffled words audible despite the water in her ears.

She did as he asked, but he was blurry through the tears that welled in her golden eyes.

As they fell from her bottom lashes, the oily droplets joined the sea water filling her helmet.

Louie moved quicker. Octopus ink greased his gears at an accelerated rate, helping him kick his legs faster.

The world flickered black—Emmeline was losing consciousness. Helmet brimming with water, she was completely submerged. Unable to hold her breath any longer, she began to cough, and water entered her mouth. She was choking, and with nowhere left to go, the water was now filling her body.

Her body went limp in Louie's arms as he rocketed toward the sky. Eight more solid kicks and they soared into the open air above the sea's surface. Louie ripped the helmet off of Emmeline's head, freeing her from the watery prison, and gently shook her head to force the water out of her mouth. The Nautipunk ship was anchored nearby, and he swam with her in his arms to the ladder his crewmates had lowered for them.

Emmeline's body slung over his shoulder, he climbed.

Red Fang Ralph and Ruthanne the Heartless emerged shortly after and followed him onto their ship.

Louie tossed Emmeline onto the deck, ripped off her diving suit, and straddled her where she lay. Concentration unbreakable, he massaged the gears of her lungs, coaxing them to turn and expel the water they held. Gear by gear, he worked his way from the middle of her sternum up to the middle of her throat. Water began leaking out of the sides of her mouth.

"It's working," Montgomery shouted as he crested the top of the ladder and raced to Louie's side. Out of breath, he begged, "Keep going."

Louie pressed his fingers into her sternum and with a gentle touch, cajoled her lung gears to turn.

More water expelled from her body.

"Why did the kraken target yer lass like that?" Ruthanne asked Montgomery.

"I don't know," he replied. "They usually run when they see us."

43

"Maybe she smells like grog," Ralph wondered aloud, clutching his throat, realizing his thirst. "Wish I had plundered meself some of its blood before we shot the beast down."

"We defeated the kraken, thanks to ol' Louie here." Ruthanne slapped the back of Louie's head as he continued to help Emmeline. "Seems the lubber earned his stripes."

Red Fang Ralph groaned, unwilling to agree with Ruthanne. Instead, he snatched a mug of grog from one of his crew and swigged the contents. After the final gulp, he shoved the empty mug into the belly of the crew member he took it from and burped.

"Ye know where ter find me," he said as he departed, stumbling toward his captain's quarters.

Emmeline was still unconscious.

Louie never lost focus. He worked her gears a fourth time, assisting in the release of the water.

The water pooled in her mouth, gurgling and spilling over her lips. Louie turned Emmeline onto her side and slammed his fist into her upper spine.

She awoke with a gasp, then began gagging on the water pouring out of her mouth. Three solid heaves, and Emmeline was saved. All the water that had entered her body was now expelled.

Louie slashed his palm with a blade and forced Emmeline to drink a quart of his octopus ink blood.

"We don't want you rusting on us," he said in response to her look of confused disgust.

When he finally let her go, she let out a violent cough. Out of breath, but recovering, her surroundings came into view. A raggedy crew of Nautipunks surrounded her, watching intently as if her survival was sheer

44

entertainment. Ruthanne stood within the circle, arms crossed and watching with a scrutinizing glare. Knelt to her right was Montgomery, who held her hand close to his face, rejoicing in her recovery.

Still straddling her was Louie. His silver-blue eyes held great concern.

"Are you okay?" he asked.

Emmeline recalled all that had transpired—the hunt, the retrieval of monster eggs, the arrival and demise of the hellion. Louie protected her through it all.

"Thank you," she said, voice hoarse.

"That monster took a liking to ya," he said, then smirked. "Can't blame it, really."

Emmeline blushed.

"Okay, that's enough," Montgomery interjected, lifting Louie by the arm and pulling him off his daughter. "We've had enough excitement for one day."

"Yer goin' to roughhouse the punk who saved yer daughter like that?" Ruthanne barked.

"It's okay," Louie insisted. "I was being cheeky."

"Still!" Ruthanne argued. The entire crew of Nautipunks grumbled with displeasure.

Montgomery turned to Louie, eager to dispel the sudden tension. "I am eternally grateful to you. Please don't mistake my haste to depart as disrespect. I just want to get my daughter home."

Louie raised his arms in surrender. "All good by me. Next time, give her a real weapon, though."

"I will," Montgomery conceded. He extended a hand to Emmeline and helped her to her feet.

"My bag," she said, remembering the pearly silver egg inside.

Montgomery picked up her tattered dive suit and satchel. She took them from him and followed him to the edge of the Nautipunk ship.

The Thermapunk crew on their airship above were already positioned and lowering a rope ladder.

"You first," Montgomery instructed Emmeline. Suit shoved into her satchel with the pearl egg, she tossed the bag over her shoulder and looked back at Louie.

He gave her a playful wink.

Embarrassed, she turned back around and swallowed her unwelcome delight. Climbing the rope ladder, she grinned, realizing she had found more than just monsters in Hydra.

Chapter 5

Safely on their airship and out of view from the Nautipunks, Montgomery grabbed Emmeline by the shoulders and gazed intently into her eyes.

"Are you okay?" he asked.

"I'm fine." Her stomach grumbled. "Just hungry."

He reached into his pocket, retrieved five golden marbles, and handed them to her. She consumed them feverishly as he waved over one of his Thermapunk crew members, who began lathering a stinky salve onto Emmeline's bicep wounds.

"What's that?" she asked, golden marbles chuting down her throat and joining the choral of churning gears in her gut.

"Healing ointment. It was created after we lost Charles to the Hellion of Obsession. The salve will extract the poison and save you from losing your mind."

"Louie touched it, too," Emmeline said.

"They have the salve. He will be okay."

Emmeline nodded, relieved, and winced as the crewmate wrapped golden gauze around her biceps.

Montgomery continued, "I've never seen a Hellion of Obsession—or any monster for that matter—target one of us like that before."

"It came right for me."

"We need to figure out why."

"Maybe the egg I found belonged to that monster."

Montgomery's intrigue piqued. "Show me."

Emmeline ripped her damaged diving suit out of her satchel, tossing it to the ground, then reached to the bottom of her bag and retrieved the large silver pearl.

It gleamed in her bare palm.

Flesh to stone, the magnetic pull she felt from this artifact was potent. A subtle darkness shadowed the overwhelming light and filled her with courage. Emmeline looked to her father to see if he felt it, too.

His expression did not shift. He felt nothing from the stone.

Still wearing his diving suit, Montgomery lifted the silver pearl into his gloved hands and then hurled it onto the ground.

Emmeline gasped as it hit the metal deck with a loud clang.

The egg remained intact.

"It isn't an egg," her father revealed, his smile knowing.

"Then what is it?"

"It is a silver sea stone. This type of rock is very common across the sea floor."

"It's the only one I saw down there."

"Once we cover more area, they'll become a common sight."

"It isn't made of obsidian, though," Emmeline argued, greatly wanting to have found an egg. "It doesn't look like it came from the source flame shield."

"Still, it's just a rock. Watch what happens when I do the same to the other eggs we found."

Montgomery reached into his satchel with his free hand, lifted the red egg with black fuzz, and hurled it at the ship deck. It cracked immediately, leaking gray goo, and the exterminators within the Thermapunk crew quickly eliminated the fetus within.

Emmeline flinched and looked away as they ripped the head from the tiny body.

Montgomery handed them the second egg he had found and they left to deal with it elsewhere.

"See," he said, still holding the stone. "These silver sea stones have been in our ocean for centuries, and never once has one hatched." Montgomery smiled. "I can see why you thought it was an egg though. It's the right size and very unique in appearance."

He picked up the silver stone and walked toward the edge of the ship.

"Wait!" Emmeline raced to him. "Don't toss it."

"Why not?"

"I'd like to keep it."

"What for?"

"As a souvenir of my first hunt."

Montgomery grinned. "The first of many."

He handed the stone back to her.

Emmeline held it to her chest, unsure why she found such comfort in the stone. Clutching it to her heart of fire, the shadows returned and the overwhelming trauma from the day's hunt felt far away.

"What happened?" Melora asked, charging toward her husband and daughter.

"A little mishap," Montgomery explained. "No need to worry. Everyone is alright."

Melora scoffed. "She looks worse than a fried Tinkerpunk."

"Gee, thanks," Emmeline grumbled.

"Where is your helmet?" she asked.

"Somewhere at the bottom of the sea," Emmeline replied before walking away.

Melora glared at Montgomery, who immediately began rambling a wordy and slightly left-of-center explanation.

On the opposite end of the ship, Emmeline took a seat next to Avery.

Avery was just as quiet as Regis, so being in her company was a lot like being alone. She flew Montgomery's airship toward the faraway gates in the sky, gaze never straying from her duty.

Still cradling the silver stone like a baby, Emmeline observed the Pilopunk in silence. Avery was only a few years older than her, and like Emmeline, she was thrust into a fate designated by her family history. Most Pilopunks wore tidy black suits decorated in gold buttons, corded stripes of honor, and winged star badges. Their shoulders were covered in ornamental epaulets and most wore wedged garrison caps or peaked service caps.

Avery did not fit the Pilopunk mold. Instead, she wore the standard attire of most Argopunks—a leather aviator cap lined with wool, large aviator goggles, and a bomber jacket with a fleece collar. Unlike the fighters who wore flesh-hugging spandex pants for mobility, Avery opted for ruffled shorts that showed much of her thighs, and her knee-high boots ended right below her churning knee gears. On her buckled waistband were the tools of her trade: a golden compass, an assortment of wrenches, a silver beaded abacus, and a single-shot pistol.

Though she was small in stature, her confidence crafted an enormous aura. Her quietness was not a result of timidness or insecurity, it was a choice. Emmeline sensed that Avery had no patience for meaningless exchanges.

Emmeline wondered if they had enough in common to break the invisible barrier between them.

"You're quiet, just like your father."

Avery exhaled audibly, clearly annoyed by the comment.

"He has lost much to the duties of this job," she replied.

"I didn't realize."

"Ask your father. He knows."

"I will."

Avery went silent again. Emmeline spun the stone in her grip, unable to let her curiosity go.

"And what about you? What's your story?"

Avery's orangey-pink gaze held no sympathy as she spoke. "I was born into a family that serves your family. I am here because I have no other choice."

Emmeline gulped. "Surely you could do something else if you wanted to."

"Could you?" she questioned.

This forced Emmeline to pause.

"I suppose not," she finally replied.

"We are all prisoners. Some of us just sport fancier titles."

Emmeline felt foolish. She hadn't meant to insult Avery.

"What would you like to do instead?"

"It doesn't matter."

"But it does," Emmeline insisted. "One day, I'll be in charge, and maybe I can help."

Avery's shoulders relaxed as she side-eyed Emmeline. Tension lessening, her expression softened.

"While I appreciate that, I'd rather not daydream about improbabilities."

Emmeline stood. "I get it. Just know that the offer will still stand whenever I take charge of this ship."

Avery nodded, her baffled intrigue displayed plainly across her face. As she returned her focus to the gates high above, Emmeline fell back into her coiled metal chair. The tension between them was gone and the bridge of friendship had its first plank.

Emmeline's thoughts returned to the traumatic afternoon she had endured. It was no wonder she found solace in silence. She tried to relocate the momentary sense of accomplishment she had felt beneath the sea. For a minute, she had seen herself excelling in her leadership role at Dawes Detention Center for Demons. For a fleeting second, she felt at peace with this fate.

Then the monster stripped her of her short-lived confidence, forcing her to rely on others for rescue. Louie—the handsome Nautipunk who tangled her clarity into terrible knots.

A smile crept across Emmeline's face as she recalled his protective grip and pretty eyes. The shadows clouding her vision cleared momentarily as she imagined the playful grin he wore every time he looked at her.

The stone sat heavy on her chest, pressing down on the gears of her ribcage.

Her blushing thoughts about Louie vanished as the shadows returned. Visions of flight pierced the darkness, lulling her into a dream about beautiful flying monsters luring her to join them. Standing on the railing of her balcony, she teetered on the edge with one foot off the railing. All she had to do was jump.

"Wake up, sleepyhead," Montgomery said, shaking Emmeline awake. "Time to leave Hydra. You can sleep on the family airship."

Montgomery's work ship was safely docked in the sky near the gates, and Avery was already soaring into the world above Hydra using a pair of copper wings.

"I wish I could do that," Emmeline said with a yawn.

"You'd need a helium heart to achieve flight," her father gently reminded her.

Emmeline grumbled while stumbling to her feet, holding the stone tightly and traversing toward the rope ladder dropped from above. She shook her head, forcing her senses to return, and dropped the stone into her satchel. Before making the climb, she recalled her conversation with Avery. She turned to her father.

"What happened to Regis?" she asked.

"What do you mean?"

"Why is he so sad, or mad, or whatever he is?"

Montgomery's smile vanished. "Remember the story I told you about Charles? The Pilopunk whose mind was consumed by a Hellion of Obsession?"

"Yes."

"He was Regis's brother."

"Oh," Emmeline said with a gasp, now fully understanding Regis's resentment.

Montgomery nodded. "Regis has not forgiven me. He believes that I should have protected Charles, but in my defense, we had never seen a monster like that before and I did not know how to protect *anyone* from it."

"He must not like that his daughter now serves as your Pilopunk."

"He hates it."

Emmeline grasped the complexity of this dynamic. All Solarpunks served the source flame, no one was free from duty, and many had to tolerate that which they despised for the greater good.

Aboard the family airship above Hydra, Emmeline raced to her private cabin and pulled a petticoat dress over her swimming corset. When she returned to the main deck, her father was locking the gates to Hydra and climbing aboard.

"You're coming home tonight?" Emmeline asked, confused because Montgomery spent most of his nights on his ship in Hydra.

"You had a tough first hunt. I want to be nearby in case you want to talk about it."

Emmeline smiled. "Thank you."

He kissed the side of her head, then made his way to where Regis steered the ship. They stood in silence, tolerating each other for the greater good.

Two giant balloons filled with helium were tethered to the masts with golden chains, and the Thermapunks on board fed fire into the intricate copper pipes that lined the deck. Using fire and gas, Regis controlled and manipulated the dangerous concoction. He was a skilled pyroaeronautic, and with fire, he was able to propel the airship forward without the need of wind.

They dropped the small Thermapunk crew off at each of their floating homes before reaching their own mansion hovering high above the land of golden gears in a strip of sky known as Fyree. One giant chain of braided gold tethered their home to the source flame burning deep within Hydra. The burning oxygen at the base of the home created a steady and stable heat flow that allowed the home to float.

These floating mansions made of gears, beams, and wires covered the sky, existing in Fyree, the second highest inhabited tier of Quintessence. Fyree was a strip of sky sandwiched between the lower and upper levels of Gaslion. All the Thermapunks lived here, high above the Terrapunks and Hydropunks below.

The Aeropunks lived in Gaslion—the airspace surrounding Fyree, both above and below. Some had homes situated within floating airships that floated above

54

the land and moved at the mercy of the solar winds. But most Aeropunks did not settle in one place. Driven by the desire to wander, it was a common sight to see Aeropunks using their gaseous hearts to travel above and below their tier. With fans propelled by gears, or wings made of metal rods and satin, they used their natural ability to travel freely.

The noble Aeropunks, led by the Holloway family, were the only ones who lived higher. They chose to exist out of reach in the upper levels of Gaslion. Like many other Solarpunks, Emmeline had never met the Holloways.

Regis parked the airship next to the lower-level platform protruding from the golden mansion Emmeline called home. Emmeline jumped off the floating airship and tore through the house. Montgomery called after her, but she wanted to be alone.

She grabbed a handful of golden marbles from the communal jar in the kitchen before retreating into her room.

Marbles tossed onto her bed, she raced to her third-floor balcony, which gave her a sprawling view of the world below. Emmeline knelt and rested her head on the gold railing, face pressed into the precious metal as she observed the daily workings of Quintessence.

Regis was already departing for the night. He turned the knob on the side of his neck which opened his helium heart, releasing gas and allowing him to float. With a large fan-pack attached to his back, he flew toward the lower region of Gaslion. Free, until a new day arose.

The sky was littered with Aeropunks, all of whom served the source flame. Most as Pilopunks, some as Argopunks, and an elite few as gas-spinning conservationists. These gas spinners monitored the thin layer of gas that formed the shield separating Quintessence from the thick layer of scorching hydrogen that radiated into the universe beyond. The fiery barrier was not impenetrable, but it made intruders think twice before infiltrating and slowed those who dared to attack.

Emmeline observed the floating Aeropunks, her curiosity heightened on this traumatic day.

A gentleman wearing a monocle sat in the large, curved pole of a propeller umbrella, reading the daily chronicles with one hand and turning a crank with the other. While his helium heart kept him afloat, the gears and wheels turning the blade above his head kept him moving. Without them, he'd have no control of his direction.

Emmeline's attention turned as a gang of young Aeropunks zoomed past, soaring in circles and chasing each other in a game of tag. Copper-rod wings strapped to their backs, they used their arm muscles to navigate the sky. The fastest of the group nearly collided with an elderly couple sitting on a bench with a fan attached. He shouted an apology before darting onward to catch up with his friends.

The elderly coupled was startled, but unharmed, and continued to rotate the gears of their contraption with foot pedals. Beside them, and outpacing them, was a trio of sisters riding airscrew unicycles. Also using pedals to turn the bladed wheel of their bikes, they effortlessly traversed the evening sky.

Their ingenuity was endless: rotor bowler caps, weathervane cloud skates, pinion bomber jackets.

Emmeline closed her eyes and imagined the sensation. Consumed by the sky, body suspended weightlessly—a serene peace she recognized. She had felt this way momentarily while underwater.

Her eyes opened.

Emmeline placed her hand over her fire heart—her purpose belonged to the sea.

A crashing blast against the solar shield shook Emmeline from her spiraling thoughts. Eyes to the sky, a giant black plume of smoke billowed above.

The upper level of Gaslion was engulfed in flames.

Nowhere was safe from the monsters.

The Aeropunks who were leisurely pedaling through the atmosphere now scattered to find safety. Dodging into nearby dirigibles and taking shelter in the homes of their brethren, they hid from the oncoming attack.

Pyropunks darted toward the solar shield, appearing from various nooks and crannies of the geared world. Emmeline's brothers rocketed out of the bottom level of their family home, whipping her with an unintentional gust of wind as they flew past.

Her long golden hair tangled in front of her face, blocking her view. As she swatted the mess out of her eyes, she watched her brothers soar toward a terrifying sight.

A massive mooncraft had breached the shield. Dripping in jagged crystals and beaming shadowlight over the golden sphere of gears, the invading ship inched through the solar shield, seemingly immune to the constant explosions detonating against their defenses.

The Pyropunks circled the bottom half of the mooncraft. Their metal wings made of indestructible titanium, they stood apart from the Aeropunk civilians who wore wings of copper. Tanks of helium strapped to their backs allowed them to fly like the Argopunks.

When the Argopunks joined the scene, they too wore titanium wings, but could fly without the tanks. Their helium hearts kept them levitated, and their geared wings thrust them forward.

Cyrus led the mission, pairing every Pyropunk with an Argopunk. Each duo held hands, spacing themselves strategically beneath the mooncraft. The Pryopunks fastened gas masks over their faces as Cyrus and his Argopunk partner took their place at the center of the formation, preparing to conduct the attack.

They counted down from three.

Emmeline could hear her oldest brother's booming voice from her balcony.

"Three ... two ... one!"

Her focus shifted between Solís and Helix, who began burning brightly at their centers. Fire hearts ablaze, they channeled the sweltering heat from the source flame deep within Hydra. As they and all the other Pyropunks shifted to blazing shades of red, their assigned Argopunks lifted their chins toward the sky, opened their mouths wide, and released chlorotrifluoride—the most flammable gas in existence—into the atmosphere.

Cyrus, who wore a gas mask, and his Argopunk partner measured the poisonous gas as it filled the space. They both checked their meter-gauges frequently, ensuring that they only released enough gas to destroy the ship. Too much, and the explosion could destroy the carefully assembled gears of Quintessence, too.

"Almost there," the lead Argopunk shouted to his soldiers. They kept their poisonous breath aimed at the mooncraft.

"Enough," Cyrus declared. "Foray!"

At his command, the Argopunks dropped out of the sky, falling at rapid speeds, while the Pyropunks lifted their hands and cast magmatic streams of fire at the enemy ship through fitted bracelets that connected to the veins in their wrists. Immune to the heat, they withstood the catastrophic blast as their fire combined with the chlorotrifluoride gas.

Watching from afar, Emmeline felt the explosion as a surge of heated wind.

The mooncraft imploded and shards of crystals rained over Quintessence. Emmeline raced inside and slammed her balcony door shut as the sharp rock shavings bulleted toward her. The catapulted shards hit the side of her golden home with ricocheting force.

Beyond her home, soft-shelled dirigibles and airships suspended by giant balloons were pierced and deflated, spiraling in dramatic freefalls as they crashed to the ground. She peered out the window to see that her family airship no longer hovered beside their home. It was lost to this battle.

Once the rattling assault of debris ceased, Emmeline cautiously stepped back onto her balcony and peered over the edge.

The land was littered with broken airships and injured Aeropunks. The giant Revopunks focused on lifting the wrecked airships off the damaged terra tracks. They could not let the gears of Quintessence stand still for too long; doing so risked the sun stuttering to a stop.

While they lifted the debris off the tracks, tearing apart and compacting the rubble into smaller pieces, the Tinkerpunks raced to repair the gears. With their skilled hands and tinkering minds, they quickly restored the tracks. One by one, the Revopunks resumed their monotonous loops.

Beyond the shield where the mooncraft had imploded, Emmeline witnessed the final demise of their intruders through the thin veil of fire. Moon monsters were burned alive beyond the solar shield, their screams violently echoing across the land.

Emmeline wanted to help those suffering below, but first, she needed to refuel. A quick dash to her bed, she grabbed a handful of marbles and popped them into her mouth all at once. Twenty in total, they clamored down her throat, fighting for their spot in line. Their clanking cacophony was matched by a deafening hum that reverberated through her golden skull. She fell to her knees, cradling her head.

Crippled by this debilitating migraine, Emmeline winced.

The force of the noise caused everything within eyeshot to shake—except the satchel where her silver sea stone sat.

She crawled to it, retrieving it from the bag and pressing the stone against her forehead.

The paralyzing noise stopped.

Emmeline breathed heavily, contemplating the cause of the migraine—it began after eating the marbles.

She lowered the stone from her forehead, perplexed. That had never happened before.

"Food is not the enemy," she said to herself, shaking the strange thought from her head. Ten golden marbles remained unconsumed on her bed. She shoved them into her pocket for later, then looked down at the stone through a shadowy vignette. The longer she held the stone, the quieter her mind became. It was soothing, it was serene, it gave her courage.

"Thank you," she whispered, before placing the stone onto her nightstand. Disconnected from it, light flooded the shadows and her fear returned.

She had to be bold, she had to help the fallen.

Confusion temporarily suppressed, she refocused her energy toward the devastating aftermath of battle and raced to the basement where her brothers would return to regroup.

If there was ever a moment to be brave, it was now.

Chapter 6

"The entire mooncraft almost got through," Helix said, pacing the room. He still wore his titanium wings, but they were bent and broken. "That has never happened before. Not since we formed the Pyropunk Militia, at least."

Streaks of char filled the lines of Cyrus' worried expression. "They must have developed new technology. Moving forward, we need to have guards stationed near the solar shield at all hours."

Emmeline barged into the basement.

"How can I help?" she asked.

All three of her older brothers gave her a quick look before ignoring her offer.

"They came with a full fleet, leaders and all. Different species of moon monsters than the last attack, but just as risky. Why are they suddenly sending their leaders on these suicide missions?"

"First, we need to determine how they got through the shield so easily," Solís said. He was wrapping his arm with golden gauze—it had been punctured by one of the crystal bullets. "Maybe we need to add more of the source flame to the shield. Perhaps it has weakened over time."

"Excellent idea."

"Can't do anything till we fix our wings," Helix noted, unstrapping his harness and letting the mangled metal poles tumble to the ground.

"I thought titanium wings were indestructible," Emmeline said, forcing herself into their conversation.

"They usually are," Helix answered, "but, as I am sure you noticed, we needed a much larger blast than usual."

"How'd you get back here with broken wings?"

"The Argopunks gave us a ride," Solís answered. His gaze narrowed on the gold bandages wrapped tightly around her biceps. "I heard you had a rough first hunt."

"There's no time to talk about that. Aeropunks are dying below. We need to help."

Cyrus raced to the window, assessing the aftermath of the battle for the first time.

"Emmeline is right. We need to offer aid."

"While we're down there, we can enlist a Tinkerpunk to fix our wings," Helix said.

Cyrus shot him a look. "Only if their hands are free."

"Our airship was destroyed," Emmeline informed them.

"There are other ways to get around," Solís replied, his expression mischievous.

"You've been keeping secrets from me?" Emmeline asked.

Solís laughed.

"You weren't old enough yet," Helix jumped in. "But you're almost sixteen now, and it's about time you learned how to sneak out of the house."

"Show me," Emmeline insisted.

"We belay and rappel," Solís answered while marching toward a floor door Emmeline had never opened before.

Five combination locks kept the exit secured. Solís leaned in close and turned the knob on each, carefully entering the codes. Three twists clockwise, one rotation counterclockwise, then half a spin back. He did this on each lock, using different combinations for each, before successfully unlocking the door. As he lifted the handle, a warm breeze entered from the outside.

"Where does it lead?" Emmeline asked.

"Nowhere," Solís replied.

"Then how will that help us?"

"Watch and learn."

Five carabiners attached to golden cords hung from a pulley system fastened to the basement ceiling. Solís chose one and latched it to the front of his waistband. He screwed the lever tight, locked it from opening, took two steps toward the lifted floorboard, and dove backwards through the opening.

Emmeline gasped.

He was gone.

She turned to Cyrus and Helix, who wore amused smiles.

"He's fine. Go look."

Emmeline tiptoed to the opening, cautiously peering over the ledge.

Solís bounced downward off the massive golden cord that tethered their home to the terrain, managing his speed through manipulation of the belay rope.

"He is insane," Emmeline commented.

"We all are," Helix replied. Hooked to one of the golden ropes, he launched his body through the door.

He howled with delight during his temporary freefall, then gracefully caught himself with two feet against the golden cord and a fierce tug of his belay rope.

"How am I supposed to learn how to do this if you all keep jumping without any explanation?"

"It's quite simple. First, you gear up. We wear belts designed for rappelling, so we don't need the harness, but you will." Cyrus grabbed a carabiner and a harness. He helped his sister step into the straps and secured them tightly to her waist. He hooked the carabiner to the metal loop and locked it. "Next, you need to know how to control your speed. This piece of metal here is a belay device. Tug the rope below it tight to brake. If you don't, you will freefall to a messy disassembly."

"Gee, great."

Cyrus yanked her rope and tugged her to the ceiling.

"Put your feet against the wall and practice."

Emmeline did as he instructed. She held the rope tight beneath her.

"Give it some slack," Cyrus said.

She did as he advised and fell to the ground.

"Ow!"

Cyrus laughed. "I didn't say to release it completely." He yanked her rope and pulled her back into the air. "Try again. This time, release the rope slowly, and tighten it to brake."

Emmeline took a deep breath, centered her focus, and gave it another try. Shifting the rope in smaller movements got her to the ground without injury.

"See, it's not so hard."

"I also don't have a deadly freefall beneath me."

"I'll stay right below you in case," Cyrus promised. "Let's go."

Cyrus hooked himself to a golden rope, then lowered himself over the edge, taking more caution than Solís and Helix. Emmeline got onto her hands and knees, letting her legs dangle over the edge while gripping the ledge desperately.

"What if I fall?"

"Trust the rope. The anchors put in place won't fail you."

She kept her gaze up as she pulled the rope tight with her right hand and released her grip of the door's ledge. With the rope in a braked position, she sat in the sky, swinging back and forth securely.

She smiled down at Cyrus.

"Good. Now, slowly lower yourself."

Heat from the fire blazing beneath their home hissed and blew hot wind into her face. She maneuvered the rope ever so slightly, lowering herself at a painfully slow rate.

"You can move a little faster," Cyrus encouraged. "Once you get below the fire, you can swing a little and bounce your feet against the tether. It's a good base board."

Emmeline kept moving at her own pace, refusing to feel rushed. When she lowered beneath the fire, she kicked her legs back and forth till her feet made contact with the tether. Its girth was so broad, she could plant both feet against it and use it to control her descent. Moving quicker now, she caught up with Cyrus.

"This isn't so bad," she shouted down to him.

"Soon you'll be launching yourself from the house like our knucklehead brothers."

"I don't know about *that*, but this isn't nearly as awful as I imagined. I feel like I'm flying."

"It's fun, but don't get too distracted. One slip of the rope and it's over."

"The fall would kill me?"

"Of course not, but it would mangle your gears bad enough that you'd never move the same again."

Emmeline heeded his warning and put her daydreams of flying aside.

"Hurry up," Solís shouted at them from where he stood. A giant magnetic platform sat below their home. The four beams holding it up were strategically placed between the orderly rows of terrain gears.

Two jumps before Emmeline reached the base, a fast-moving pack of Revopunks skated below the platform.

"It feels so different down here," she said as her toes touched the platform. She swayed back and forth, forgetting to release more slack. Solís grabbed her before she collided with the golden tether.

"You're a mess," he teased, releasing her rope. Her feet fell firmly on the ground.

"I did great for my first time," she argued.

"You're right ... you didn't fall. Good job."

Emmeline shoved him away from her.

"At least she didn't cry during her first rappel," Helix instigated.

Emmeline's eyes glowed with amusement.

"You cried?" she asked Solís.

"No! They like to say that I did, but I didn't."

"Okay, sure," Cyrus chimed in.

"It was nervous laughter," Solís insisted.

"Then why was your face covered in black oil when you reached the platform?"

"Sweat."

Helix cackled. "Sweat trails leaking from your eyes? Okay, if you say so."

Cyrus and Helix led the way to the platform ladder.

Emmeline pretended to cry as she walked past Solís, whose playful confidence had turned sour.

The ladder was fastened securely to the beam, and Emmeline climbed down after Helix.

Rows of tall terrain gears lined the land. Emmeline landed on the path beside her brothers. The ground between the gears was made of steel pipes painted in gold that filtered the heat from the source flame into the galaxy beyond.

Solís slid down the ladder last, latching his wrist gears to the railing and descending without using his feet.

"You're so cool," Helix teased.

"Cooler than you," Solís retorted with a smirk.

"At least he's not sulking anymore," Emmeline said, which instigated Solís to wrap his arm around her neck and press the side of her face into his chest.

"Get off me!" she demanded, punching his stomach and trying to break free.

He ignored her, chuckling as he walked forward, towing her along in his brotherly embrace.

"Let go! You smell," she exclaimed, pretending to gag.

"Like celestial flowers," Solís quipped.

Cyrus interrupted, "More like sweat and scorched moon monsters. We all reek of battle."

Solís let Emmeline go, grinning as she scowled and combed the knots out of her hair with her fingers.

As much as they bickered, Emmeline adored her brothers.

"Where are we going?" she asked, still feigning annoyance.

"The Tinker Market. There's one located three rows north of here," Cyrus answered.

Emmeline looked at both walls of fast-moving gears that trapped them on this path. The bottom halves of each wheel were lodged into a rut within the terrain, while the top halves stood at least five heads taller than Cyrus, who was the tallest among them.

"How exactly will we get out of this row?" Emmeline asked.

Cyrus pointed at the sky. "Aerial chainwheels. There's a loading platform up ahead."

Emmeline looked up for the first time since reaching Terra. An intricate grid of chainwheel cables netted the sky.

"I never noticed them from above."

"They blend in, just like the Tinkerpunks, who rely on them to traverse the land."

They reached the platform and an empty cable car awaited.

"Can we get a ride to the Tinker Market in Sector 3?" Cyrus asked the Terrapunk guard manning this station.

The Terrapunk grunted and waved them forward. Before Cyrus crossed the threshold of the cable car, the Terrapunk stepped in front of him. Silver gears covered in crud and grease, he held out his hand.

"We just saved the lot of you from annihilation," Cyrus argued. "You're really going to make me pay?"

"You made a terrible mess in the process," the Terrapunk grumbled. His voice was raspy and low. "Half the terrain was damaged by fallen airships. Loads of Aeropunks and Terrapunks were injured. Many killed."

"We are here to help fix the damage."

The Terrapunk held Cyrus's gaze, while the gears in his knuckles wiggled his fingers.

"Pay up."

Cyrus shoved his hand into his pocket and retrieved a firestone. The Terrapunk's eyes lit up with greed. Firestones were coveted by every punk without a fire heart, and due to their restricted lifespan, they were always in demand.

Cyrus placed the inactive stone against his bare chest. With his eyes closed, he channeled the source flame within Hydra. His heart began to glow, beaming light through his flesh and filling the firestone with heat. Once enough had transferred, he opened his eyes and disconnected from the source flame.

"Here you go." He tossed the scorching-hot stone to the Terrapunk, who had to bounce it between his hands till he was able to catch it in the thermapouch hanging from his waistband. For a limited lifespan the stone would emanate heat, and with it, many small contraptions could be powered.

Cyrus found a seat in the cable car. Helix hung from the overhead bars and Solís stood in a deep lunge between two poles. Emmeline sat beside Cyrus.

"How does this car work?"

"The Terrapunk guards assigned to this station lift us into the sky and lodge the roof gears of the cable car into the moving chainwheel above. Terrapunks are rhythmic beings—they can feel the precise tempo of the terrain gears—so their timing of the transition is often quite smooth. But don't be alarmed if there's a small jolt."

The cable car began to lift, and Emmeline gripped the side of her seat. The rise was slow and calculated. She closed her eyes and tried to locate the rhythm of the terrain gears—all she heard were the creaking gears of the cable car.

The small jolt Cyrus warned her about felt massive and their cable car awkwardly latched to the aerial chainwheel.

"Here comes the real fun," Solís announced, deepening his stance.

As the words left his mouth, the cable car went from zero to one hundred, zipping through the air at such great speeds, Emmeline instinctively tightened her grip on the sides of her seat.

Helix hung upside down from the overhead bars, swinging backwards from the force. Solís wobbled in his stance, attempting to stay balanced during the sudden acceleration.

Emmeline looked out the window. Revopunks raced in rhythmic rotations below, their skates interlinking with the terrain gears and propelling the chainwheels forward. They bladed on horizontal tracks running east to west that wrapped around the sphere of Quintessence, while the cable car the Dawes siblings rode traveled on a latitudinal path.

"How do we stop?" she asked Cyrus.

"There's a brake lever that we will collide with. It'll separate us from the main chainwheel."

"Won't that cause us to fall out of the sky?"

Cyrus shook his head. "We're almost there. You'll see."

Without warning, they jolted to a halt, sending Solís to the opposite side of the cable car and knocking Helix off of the bars he hung from. The aerial chainwheels kept spinning. A contraption overhead snagged the cable car by its roof bars and carried it to two columns attached to the station below. The cable car linked into the column gears and began its descent.

Emmeline marveled at the ingenuity. She was used to trinkets and gadgets motorized by spinning gears and spring-activated cranks, but she had never seen a system for traveling as complex as this. Powered by the skating Revopunks, who darted in a singular direction with their heads down, the intricate puzzle of chainwheels that crisscrossed the lower sky of Quintessence operated with precision.

Teamwork, even if it came out of necessity, kept the machine moving. Coordination such as this did not exist among the other punks. There was comradery, but little need for systems of nonstop productivity.

Emmeline understood the gravity of this perfect prison as the complexity of their essential duties surrounded her.

Without their obedience, without their willingness to participate and keep the gears turning, Quintessence would cease to exist.

"Get out!" a Terrapunk manning the station shouted.

Solís hobbled to the door, massaging his neck gears impacted upon his epic wipeout. Helix and Cyrus followed, and Emmeline exited last.

Standing atop the cable car platform, a nightmarish scene greeted them.

Unlike the orderly rows of towering gears near their home base, this section of the sphere was destroyed. Crashed airships and dirigibles had landed in the mechanism and jammed the gears. In some cases, the impact broke the terrain gears completely. Injured Aeropunks were everywhere—some alive and seeking refuge, others dead and scattered among the wreckage. Those who were able to walk used the liquid nitrogen in their veins to smother nearby flames.

"How do we help?" Emmeline asked.

"We have to fix our wings first," Cyrus explained as he selected a rod from the communal bin. The end he held had a lever and a loop to insert his arm, while the other end had an industrial-strength clamp. He continued, "Once they are repaired, we will be able to escort the surviving Aeropunks home. They'll get better care among their own."

"And what will I do?" she asked. "I don't have a pair of wings."

"Help the Terrapunks however you can, particularly the Tinkies. They'll need the most help rebuilding."

"Can't they lend me a pair of wings?" she asked.

"You wouldn't know how to use them, and there's no time to teach you. You'd only be putting yourself and whichever Aeropunk you were trying to help in danger."

He was right.

Her dismay was apparent.

Solís encouraged her, "You're a slayer of demons. You managed to eliminate a moon monster on your first hunt. You will do great."

Though it wasn't the whole truth, his encouragement lifted her spirits. There was much to be done in the wake of battle, and she intended to help however she could.

Cyrus lifted the clamp into the sky, snagged one of the metallic spheres that traveled on a slow-moving conveyer belt, and was carried away. Solís and Helix followed. Like all places on the ground level of Quintessence, the market sat on a platform that hovered over the terrain gears. When her brothers reached it, they released their clamps and fell a short distance onto the market platform. They placed the rods into the communal bin and disappeared into the bustling market.

Emmeline stood at the edge of the station platform and stared out at the sprawling wreckage.

An agonized scream echoed from below.

Pinned beneath a burning airship was a small Tinkerpunk. Mimicking Solís, Emmeline locked her elbow gears into one of the many ladders attached to the platform and slid down with speed. Landing with a thud, her knee gears buckled, but she did not fall.

"Help," the trapped Tinkerpunk shouted upon seeing Emmeline, while desperately trying to push herself out from under the metal aircraft. "The flames are nearing my uranium heart!"

Emmeline's fire heart swelled with fear—not only was the Tinkerpunk's life in danger, but all of Quintessence would perish if the fire reached her heart. Uranium became nuclear when exposed to the source flame.

There wasn't another soul around, only Emmeline.

The fate of the world resided with her.

Chapter 7

A tiny explosion burst in the center of the wreckage.

Emmeline shielded her face as metal shrapnel launched in all directions. The Tinkerpunk howled in pain.

"What was that?" Emmeline asked as the explosion settled.

"My foot!" the Tinkerpunk cried.

Emmeline raced to her side. She could not lift the crashed airship, which she realized now was her family's fallen ship, but she could absorb the fire.

Eyes closed with hands hovering near the flame, she channeled the power of her fire heart. In the lessons she had received as a child, she excelled at expelling fire, not rescinding it. Golden eyes shimmering with red flecks of determination, she mustered every distant memory of her teachings and focused on absorbing the flame. Bit by bit, the fiery entrapment left the debris and filtered through her palms. Slowly, and with great care, she defused the fire surrounding the bomb.

Emmeline's entire body blazed red as the fire filled her heart. Flesh temporarily translucent, her internal gears were illuminated where her outfit did not cover her flesh.

The Tinkerpunk stopped crying—the captivating sight of Emmeline's fiery glow distracted her from the pain.

"Only a few flares left," Emmeline said through clenched teeth. The transference shook her to the core. Though it drained every bit of energy she had, she refused to quit. Focus intense, hands shaking from the force, she growled and pushed through. Her resolve would save everyone.

"You're almost done," the Tinkerpunk encouraged.

Emmeline roared, matching the intensity of the fire that swelled in her heart.

One final flare remained.

Manic energy filled Emmeline's wide eyes. She reached out and snatched the flame with her hand, tilting her head back and dropping it into her mouth. It was an unconventional approach, but just as effective. With her eyes closed, she consumed the fire that had threatened to consume her world.

As it fell down her throat and entered her geared lungs, her fire heart seized the flare. It bounced like a magnet and joined the rest of the fire inside her heart. Crisis averted, her job complete, Emmeline fell to her knees, energy depleted.

"Wow," the Tinkerpunk said, still pinned beneath the smoking airship. "I thought for sure we were all done for."

"I'm glad I heard your cries, otherwise, we might have been," Emmeline replied through heavy breaths.

"Where will all that fire go? Will it stay inside of you forever?"

Emmeline shook her head. "I am directly connected to the source flame. Any excess fire my heart cannot hold will be transferred there."

"Thank you," the Tinkerpunk said.

Emmeline turned to look at the girl she just saved; her chromatic silver eyes glimmered with kindness. Today was her first time meeting any Terrapunks, and until this moment, she had assessed the lot as short-tempered and rude.

"You're not all the same," Emmeline noted.

"Of course, we aren't. Are all Thermapunks the same?"

"No," Emmeline answered, now realizing her judgments were nearsighted. "What's your name?"

"Gemma. And yours?"

"Emmeline."

"I appreciate your help. Any chance you can help me out from under this wreck of a ship?"

"I am not strong enough to lift it off of you."

"You don't have to be strong, you just have to be smart. I can help." Gemma's eyes darted to and from surrounding piles of rubble. "Find a long beam. Make sure it is solid."

Emmeline stood and scanned the area, searching high and low. A few glances at the sky revealed that her brothers had successfully repaired their wings and were now carrying Aeropunks home. Emmeline grinned, imagining their astonishment when she relayed the day's events to them.

"Any luck?" Gemma called out.

"Still looking!"

She turned the corner around the stern of her crashed family aircraft. A lengthy metal board from the airship lay detached on the ground. She dragged it back to where Gemma was pinned.

It was heavy, but she managed.

"What now?" she asked.

Gemma pointed at a coiled metal throne. "See that? Bring it here."

"This was my mother's chair," Emmeline noted as she dragged the heavy object to Gemma.

"This was your airship?

"It was. Not sure how it landed all the way over here, though."

"Just my luck to get pinned by one of the few airships fueled by fire," Gemma said with a deprecating laugh. "Place the chair next to me—it'll act as a fulcrum—then lodge the metal beam in this space here." She pointed to a small opening between the ground and the ship.

Emmeline did as instructed, breaking a sweat as she worked. Black beads of greasy oil streaked down her forehead.

Contraption configured, Emmeline was beginning to understand its design. She raced to the end of the beam opposite from where Gemma lay.

"You don't need to lift the whole thing, just enough so I can wiggle out," Gemma encouraged her.

With all her might, Emmeline pressed on the beam. The airship moved slightly, but not enough. She tried again, this time climbing on top of her end of the seesaw to use all of her body weight. She jumped up and down, shaking the airship and causing heavy pieces at the top to dislodge and fall off the backside. The weight of the ship was lightening and a few more jumps dismantled enough of the wreckage to render this task possible.

The airship lifted just enough for Gemma to frantically crawl out.

"Can you hold it one second longer?" she asked.

"Yes, but hurry!"

Emmeline used all her strength to keep the airship lifted while Gemma reached beneath it to retrieve her detached foot.

As soon as she was out from under the airship, Emmeline jumped off the beam. The large hunk of metal crashed with a loud thud.

"Thank you," Gemma said, attention focused on her detached foot. All the flesh was gone, only the silver geared skeleton remained.

Emmeline hobbled toward her, exhausted. "That looks painful."

"I've suffered worse," Gemma replied without looking up. Much of her tiny body was exposed through the thin white dress that hung loosely over her like an oversized sack.

Upon closer inspection, Emmeline noticed the many wounds her new friend wore. Both of her wrists were lined with thick scars, and her back had a gaping wound that revealed the gears of her ribcage and the geared organs inside. Worst of them all was the freshly stitched wound that ran across her neck.

"Why do you have so many scars?" Emmeline asked.

"Tinkering mishaps, gizmo contract disputes, battles for work among the Tinkies. This one," she pointed to her neck, "was given to me by a Revopunk. I was riding her back, greasing her skates, and when I was done, she kicked me off and I landed on the terrain gears. Almost decapitated me. I had to remove wired thread from the wound on my back to stitch my neck."

"Is that why it's wide open?"

She nodded. "It'll be like that forever now. The neck wound was lethal, my back wound was not."

"I'm sorry."

"It's just part of the life. Revopunks toss us around all the time. They're so angry. I should've been wearing my armor, but it was a busy day and I forgot."

"What will happen with your foot?" Emmeline asked.

"I'll reattach it. Watch."

Built into her hand were tinkering tools: screwdrivers, wrenches, pliers, needles, and precision blades, among many others. Able to retract only that which she needed, she extended a wrench. It protruded from her fist between two of her geared knuckles.

"Luckily, I still have the screws and bolts," she said as she lifted her leg and positioned the exposed gears of her foot with her ankle gears. Cogs interlaced, she pressed the metal joint to both connection points and reinserted the screws. With the wrench, she tightened a bolt to the end of each screw, securing the metal joint in place. Reconnected to her skeleton of gears, the marbles racing through her inner track could now motorize her foot again.

She stood and stumbled. Emmeline caught her before she fell.

"It's strange walking on a skeletal foot, but I'll get used to it," Gemma explained.

She took a few steps forward and found her balance.

"You make it look easy," Emmeline said.

"Wish that were so!" Gemma smiled. "Thank you for everything. How can I repay you?"

"No need."

"I'm a Tinkie! I work with artifacts from all corners of the world, even some trinkets from worlds beyond our own. I have access to the black market; I could swindle a deal for ya."

"I'll think about it," Emmeline conceded, reaching into her pocket to retrieve the golden marbles and refuel. "Want one?" she asked Gemma.

"No, thank you. I ate right before getting crushed."

Emmeline shrugged and tossed all ten marbles into her mouth. As the final marble fell, a dreadful noise echoed all around.

The deafening hum sent Emmeline to her knees. Hands cupped over her ears, she shook in pain.

"What's wrong?" Gemma asked, racing to her side.

"Don't you hear that?"

"Hear what?"

Emmeline's golden eyes widened as they lifted toward the sky.

"Not again," she groaned. "I have to go."

Emmeline stood and frantically paced with her hands still covering her ears. The healing wounds on her biceps began to throb.

"Where?" Gemma asked.

"Home."

"Why? What's happening?"

The noise grew so loud, Emmeline's sight began to blur. Patches of darkness strobed shadows across her vision. Dizzy from the flickering darkness, she did not notice her brother's arrival until she heard his shouts.

"What happened to her?" Solís barked at Gemma.

"It wasn't me!" She raised her hands in surrender and cowered against the fallen airship.

"She was fine when we left her."

"Stop," Emmeline managed to shout through the earsplitting hum. "She has been through enough."

"What's wrong?" he demanded, turning his confused anger back to his trembling sister. He grabbed her shoulders to hold her still, clutching the spots covered with golden gauze.

"Ow!" Emmeline shouted.

"Sorry," he offered, releasing her. His protective golden gaze was filled with worry. "Are you okay?"

"My head is filled with noise."

"Noise? Why?" he asked.

"A terrible migraine, I think," Emmeline said. "The joints in my head feel loose and they're rattling against my skull."

"That doesn't sound right. What caused the migraine?"

"I don't know."

Gemma stepped in. "She exerted a lot of energy while saving me. Perhaps that is to blame."

Solís took a closer look at Gemma, seeing all her fresh wounds for the first time.

"What happened to you?"

"Life."

"And I thought the punks in the Tinker Market looked beat up."

"I wish I could land a steady tinkering job there. I'm still stuck greasing the terra gears."

Solís's gaze shifted upward to the wreckage. "Is that my family's airship?"

"Yes," Gemma replied. "I was pinned beneath it. Emmeline saved me. Just in time too—the fire almost reached my heart."

Solís's chaotic wrath turned to awe. "That would have killed us all."

Gemma nodded.

Emmeline still shuddered from the horrible sound echoing through her head.

Gemma continued, "I owe her my life."

"We all do." Though his energy had softened, his guard remained intact. His wary gaze returned to his sister. "Will you be able to hang on if I fly you home?"

"Yes," Emmeline answered.

Solís moved the helium tank from his back to his chest. He bent to one knee and Emmeline wrapped her arms around his neck. Situated snuggly between his metal wings, she was ready to go home.

Solís loosened the valve of the tank.

"Don't forget my offer!" Gemma shouted as they rose into the sky.

Emmeline did not have the energy to reply.

They lifted higher toward Fyree, remaining subject to the whim of the evening winds. Using his shoulder gears, he motorized the titanium wings, while the helium lifted them upward.

Though she wanted to enjoy the sensation of flying, the unrelenting noise prevented any delight.

Solís flew through the open hangar bay at the base of their home. Cyrus and Helix awaited their arrival.

"What took you so long?" Helix asked as Solís landed gently. He knelt so Emmeline could slide off his back with ease.

"She saved all of Quintessence!" Solís declared, ignoring Emmeline's inability to look any of them in the eyes. It was too bright and too dark all at once. The noise had skewed everything—her senses were shot.

"What do you mean?" Cyrus asked, examining his ill-looking sister.

"Our airship landed on a Tinkerpunk. Emmeline saved the girl and everyone else before the fire within the ship detonated the Tinkie's uranium heart."

Cyrus and Helix stared at Emmeline, simultaneously shocked and amazed.

"I never knew you were such a badass," Helix said admiringly, a huge smile on his face.

"We have to celebrate," Cyrus cheered.

"I was just in the right place at the right time," Emmeline insisted, her expression twisted in agony. "I need to go."

"What's wrong with her?" Cyrus asked Solís as Emmeline raced toward the stairs.

"A migraine, apparently."

Emmeline heard mention of the family Thermadoc as she darted away.

Three flights of stairs, two long hallways, and she reached her bedroom.

Louder now, the noise pierced the backs of her eyes, forcing an anguished gasp. Shadows veiled the room. She fell to her knees and crawled, blindly feeling for her dresser—she needed a screwdriver to loosen the bolts of her skull and release some of the pressure. Oil drops leaked from her eyes as she searched for reprieve.

The desperation of her finger gear joints scratching against the golden tiles only added to the noise. She scrambled forward, slamming her head against the bar of her bed at full speed. The added injury sent her to the floor.

Collapsed on the golden tiles of her bedroom, she sobbed and recalled her brother's question: What had caused this migraine?

The golden marbles, she thought.

Every time she ate, she felt sick. Every time she swallowed marbles, a crippling migraine followed.

The sea stone, she remembered. It soothed her headache last time, perhaps it would work again.

Limbs heavy, body aching, Emmeline lifted herself off the floor, retrieved the cold stone from her nightstand, and pressed it against her face. Its cool touch soothed the heat sweltering inside her head and the world became quiet again. Oily tears of relief dripped down her face as she fell to the floor in exhaustion. The dramatic rise and fall of her chest matched the rhythmic sparks of her fiery heart. Lying motionless on the tiled floor with the stone held against her cheek, she surrendered to the luring pull of sleep.

The hammering wind coaxed Emmeline from her slumber a few hours later. Through squinted eyes she glanced at her wristwatch—it was the wee hours of morning when most of Quintessence was fast asleep. The air outside her window whipped violently, igniting her curiosity.

Stone still in hand, she went to her balcony to locate the cause of the raucous whirlwind. As the door opened, her long golden hair blew across her face, tangling into knots. She brushed it away, but the breeze kept gusting it in front of her eyes.

The pounding wind grew louder.

Determined, she twisted her hair into a braid, successfully keeping it bound.

Sights cleared, nerves paralyzed—to her horror, a Hellion of Obsession hovered outside her window.

Chapter 8

Nocturnal flares from the solar shield reflected off the iridescent film between the veins of the monster's wings, casting a colorful aura around its silhouette. Beauty and terror—Emmeline reminded herself not to fall victim to its enticing allure.

She crouched behind the golden bars of her balcony. Not hidden, but concealed, as she observed the monster.

The winged creature tore across the fiery sky, casting a shadow over the golden land of gears. The dark nocturnal glow of the solar shield lit the monster from behind, veiling its image in darkness. It left trails of silver light as it swooped in circles above her home.

What did it want? Why was it here?

Emmeline's gaze turned toward the Pyro-Argo air base. The Argopunks monitored the skies at all hours. They patrolled the cargo access ramp and the outer deck, their luminous pinkish-orange eyes always aimed upward.

Though their attention was lifted, none seemed to notice the monster in the sky. It flew undetected, dashing in frantic circles above her home.

Emmeline clutched the stone tighter, her amazement a mix of fear and wonder—was she the only one who could see the hellion?

If this were the case, the responsibility of shooting it out of the sky landed on her. Fists clenched, she allowed the fire in her heart to grow. Her golden eyes smoldered red. As she prepared to blast a stream of fire, the dark glow of the solar shield brightened, and the shadows veiling the monster lifted.

Emmeline gasped.

The arrival of morning light revealed an unexpected sight.

Divine in stature, elegant in nature, this was no monster—she was an ethereal creature from beyond. She soared with grace, her magnificent frailty an image of perfection. Her wide eyes and soft expression showed no signs of malevolence, no indication that she was a threat. As iridescent as her fluttering wings, her pale flesh glittered with color. Was she a manifestation of the primordial gods? Or was she just a lost traveler?

Emmeline's thoughts raced. Though she resembled a Hellion of Obsession, she also looked nothing like the wiry, frantic beasts in Hydra. What was she?

The woman flew with daring confidence and an air of invincibility, frantically looking for something unknown.

Emmeline stood from her hiding place, leaning against the rail with her arms spread wide.

"Who are you?" she called out.

Her voice caught the attention of the foreign beauty. As they made eye contact, the winged woman's confidence faltered and her determined expression shifted with shock.

Emmeline was not meant to see her.

As quickly as she had appeared, she was gone. She did not fly away, she simply vanished.

Impossible, Emmeline thought, but she was alone again, left with only the enticing memory of the beautiful monster.

The sight of this woman inspired both courage and fear; an itching sense of doubt now crept through Emmeline. The strict teachings engraved into her mind at a young age began to unravel—were the monsters truly evil? Or were they misunderstood creatures from other lands? If this visitor was malevolent, it would have killed Emmeline without a second thought. Instead, she left Emmeline unharmed. The question of this being's identity sent Emmeline's thoughts into a tailspin. A monster, a god, a creature from another sun, moon, or planet—the possibilities were endless.

"Emmeline!" her mother called from downstairs.

The summon snapped her back to reality. Emmeline was lying on the ground, cradling the silver sea stone.

Panic forced her to her feet.

Was it all a dream?

"Emmeline!" her mother repeated, her bellow echoing through the house.

Terrified to lose control again—be it the noises or the visions—she pocketed the stone and exited her room.

In the kitchen, her three older brothers sat around the table, devouring their marbles. Melora handed Emmeline a bowl as she sat next to Helix, who was still reveling in their recent victory.

"Despite the damage caused, it was our easiest defeat yet," he said, mouth filled with marbles. "And we took out their leaders, too."

"I still can't believe they risked so much," Cyrus replied.

Emmeline thought of the woman in the sky. She appeared as a monster until the light hit her face. Given a moment, her docile, non-combative nature was revealed.

"Maybe they just wanted to talk," she said aloud, unintentionally sharing her thoughts.

Her brothers looked at her in collective disbelief.

"They don't want to talk, they want to steal our fire," Helix countered.

"They are unintelligent monsters," Cyrus added. "You'll understand better once you've spent more time at the detention center."

"You can't possibly think that *we're* the bad guys," Helix accused.

Emmeline pursed her lips and scrunched her nose, regretting her outburst.

"Do you?" he asked.

"No, of course not," she insisted. "It was just a passing thought that I didn't mean to say out loud."

"Erase those thoughts," Helix demanded. "They will get you into trouble."

Though Helix was combative, Solís listened to their exchange with intrigue.

"What if she is right, though?" he said.

"About what?"

"About them wanting to talk. Their leaders were with them … same with the battle a few days ago. Two different sets of moon monsters arriving with their leaders onboard. They never used to do that. Maybe our strike was too rash."

"What could they have possibly wanted to talk about?" Cyrus argued. "Let's just say you're right—they're only interested in our flame. Even if they bartered with strategy or bribery or trade deals, we could never share the flame. It goes against every universal law. Fire cannot exist on the moons."

He was right—it was written in the holy doctrine.

Solís's expression tightened in thought. "I don't know what they could've wanted besides the flame either. But it's curious."

"Can't we just enjoy the victory without casting doubt upon it?" Helix asked with a groan.

"Helix is right," Melora said, stepping into their conversation. "Let's speak of happier matters. Emmeline, your soul day is rapidly approaching. I am planning a party."

"I don't want a party."

"Of course, you do," Melora countered. "Give me an invite list by the end of the week." She glanced at Emmeline's untouched breakfast. "And finish your bowl of marbles."

Emmeline grumbled and stared at the shimmering marbles. Afraid they might instigate another migraine, she had no desire to eat them. Her mother's oppressive stare bore into her, unceasing until she obliged.

She lifted a single marble and swallowed it. The moment it began to clamber down her throat, a slight chime rang through her head, filling her with regret.

"Melora," Montgomery called from the other room. "There's a tear in my knickers!"

Melora left the room to stitch her husband's pants. Cyrus and Helix finished their meals and departed shortly after, leaving only Solís and Emmeline.

The ringing in her head had stopped. This relief provided awareness—small, spaced out meals might be the way to cope.

She stared at the remaining marbles, zigzagging her spoon in the bowl.

"So, what do you want for your soul day?" Solís asked.

"Helium."

Solís raised his brow. "Why?"

"I want to fly."

"Since when?" he asked. "You've always been so excited to work with Dad."

"I still am. I've just been thinking that I need a hobby. Something to keep me busy when I'm home."

Solís stood from his seat at the table, knee gears creaking as he walked to the sink. After he dropped his bowl, he took a swig of oil and the black liquid coursed through his body, greasing his gears.

"You're a diver, not a flyer," he said after his final gulp.

"Imagine if I could fly above the sea. I could rule Hydra without a ship."

This forced Solís to pause.

"That's an interesting notion."

"So, you'll help?"

"Maybe, but after you've gotten more situated in Hydra. Focus on and perfect everything you've learned in school."

"Half of my schooling was Ms. Rickard trying to teach me how to be a lady."

Solís chuckled. "A terrible waste of her time."

Emmeline grinned. "Mother is trying to get me to return to etiquette classes."

"Being a lady will get you nowhere among the Nautipunks."

"Father keeps telling her that. So far, she's lost the battle, but she won't drop it."

"I'll talk to her, too," he promised.

"Thanks."

Solís went on, "And you will drop your quest to fly?"

"You said you'd help."

"Not anytime soon."

"Please," she begged.

"You do realize how hard it was to form the Pyropunk Militia, right? It took years to convince the Aeropunks to share their helium with us. We only get access during battles."

"Surely you can give me whatever is left in your tank after your next fight."

"First of all, they only leave us with enough to get to and from the base between battles. Secondly, I'm not helping you till I know you're settled down there."

Emmeline had stopped listening after his first point. "Maybe if I offer them something valuable in return."

"All they want is fire." His gaze was stern. "You cannot give them fire."

"I can give them firestones."

"They'll only accept real flames."

"Why can't we share fire with them? They aren't destructive like the Terrapunks."

"We don't share the fire because that is our only leverage. It is the only thing keeping the Thermapunks in power."

"Perhaps the power ought to be shared."

Solís laughed. "I doubt you'd maintain that stance once all your comfortable luxuries were stripped away."

"Like what?"

"Your personal Pilopunk to and from Hydra, the willingness with which the Tinkerpunks fix any trinket we bring them, the Nautipunks' non-combative compliance to a teenager's eventual rule over their ocean. Our stronghold of Quintessence serves you more than you realize."

"I just want some helium." She shoved her hand in her pocket and turned the sea stone between her fingers.

Solís examined his younger sister cautiously, trying to understand what she wasn't saying. After a moment, he concluded, "Flying won't solve your problems."

"I don't have any problems."

"That's debatable," Solís teased. He wrapped his elbow around her neck, pulled her in close, and pressed a hard kiss to the top of her head. He added, "I'm always here if you need someone to talk to."

Emmeline huffed.

"I'm fine," she said, pushing him off her.

"Of course, you are. You're a Dawes!" he declared as he left the room.

Emmeline swirled her spoon through the bowl of marbles.

She ignored her growling stomach begging for sustenance—she'd rather starve than be crippled by that sound again. Still, she was aware she needed some energy to survive the day.

This moment was a test—how many marbles were safe to eat? How many could she consume before the migraine began?

She ate a second marble.

The tiny chime at the base of her skull returned.

A third marble.

The ringing grew louder.

A fourth marble.

The sound began to fill her head.

A fifth marble.

She winced in pain.

That was it—that was all she could stomach.

Those five marbles would have to suffice. She carried her bowl to the kitchen counter, and after looking over both shoulders to make sure no one was watching, she dumped the remaining marbles back into the jar.

She reached into her pocket and gripped the sea stone. The noise in her head slowly dissolved.

Courage and confidence—the shadows carried her onward with deceptive comfort.

Chapter 9

Two giant balloons chained and tethered to golden baskets awaited her.

Regis and Montgomery were in one of the baskets, while Avery waited for Emmeline in the other.

"You're late," Avery barked.

Emmeline looked down at her wristwatch—the gears clicked as the seconds carried the minute hand past their designated departure time.

"I'm sorry. It's been a busy few days."

"Yeah, I heard you saved the world from certain doom." Though her tone was harsh, she wore an impressed grin.

Emmeline climbed into the basket and the balloon wobbled in the sky as her weight shifted its position.

Avery blew into a tube that ran into the base of the balloon, breathing helium into the aircraft. She then twisted a crank on the lantern, which heated the helium.

"Ready to go?" Montgomery shouted from the basket tethered to the other helium balloon. The goggles strapped to his forehead kept his shaggy golden-brown hair from blowing in his face.

"Yes," Emmeline replied. Though the shadows clouding her mind gave her confidence, they made it hard to focus.

Regis and Avery unknotted the ropes that docked them to the hangar bay, and both balloons began their guided float toward Hydra.

Emmeline peered over the side of the basket, in awe of their new ride. It floated peacefully through the air, hovering along at a much slower pace than their old airship. Emmeline enjoyed this speed—it paired nicely with the tranquil haze consuming her mind.

Avery broke the silence.

"First you survived a sea monster attack, then you saved Quintessence from a nuclear explosion. What other surprises should I expect to hear about you?"

Emmeline thought of the woman she saw in the sky. A monster, a god, a creature from beyond—or maybe just a nightmare that felt like a memory.

"Hopefully the excitement is nearing an end," she replied.

"I suspect that this is just the start of your heroic tales."

Avery was happier today, and Emmeline reveled in her welcomed levity.

"As long as these stories I collect are more of the 'saving-the-world' kind, rather than the 'I-almost-died' kind."

Avery laughed. "Fair enough. I enjoy the prospect of continued adventures working alongside you."

"Yeah," Emmeline said, focus foggy from the shadows. "We can turn our obligations into adventures."

Avery looked over her shoulder at Emmeline.

"You seem out of it today," she noted.

Emmeline let go of the sea stone hidden in her pocket.

"I'm fine, just a little tired."

They reached Hydra and Regis lowered their basket closer to the gates. Montgomery threw a rope ladder over the side of the basket and descended. Agile and fearless, he swung wildly in the open air as he made his way down. At the final rung, he entwined his feet with the rope, hung upside down, extended his arms, and inserted the key. He cranked the key until the lock disengaged. Hundreds of gears worked in unison, shifting and rotating, one by one. Each movement inched the gates open. Once the entrance was wide enough to drop through, Regis and Avery lowered their balloons into Hydra.

Operating on a spring, the gates were designed to only stay open in accordance with the turns of Montgomery's key. Moments after safely crossing the threshold into the watery center of Quintessence, the gears' rotation changed direction and the gates began to close.

Fueled by the lantern flames, the helium balloons lowered till they hovered directly above Red Fang Ralph's ship. He stumbled out of his cabin, eyes to the sky and a scowl on his face.

"Arr! No fairies allowed in these waters!"

"Very funny," Montgomery shouted in reply. "This is a quick visit—no need for my sea ship."

"I heard there was a bit of a calamity above."

"Yes. We had a significant air attack yesterday. The Aeros and Terras were hit the worst. We only lost the family airship."

"Ramshackled, eh? I suspect ye already have the Tinkies on the job."

"I do. A new airship should be built by the end of the week."

"Yer pistol proof! Ye lucky scoundrel. Me boat breaks and we drown." He spat. His envy radiated into the sky.

"You can't drown," Montgomery corrected him.

"Maybe so, but bein' adrift with no vessel and havin' ter swim back ter a Rove ain't no easy feat."

"More motivation *not* to sink your ship."

"Aye, but when battle beckons, ye answer the call."

Montgomery shook his head. "I still don't understand what the lot of you could possibly have to fight about."

"Respect! Honor! Grog!"

"Anyway, we will need to join you on your ship for today's work."

"Argh, if ye must. It'll cost ye five firestones."

"It will not cost me anything," Montgomery countered, his golden eyes blazing red.

Ralph lifted his arms in surrender. "Arright, arright! Come on down and join me crew."

Threats of fire maintained his dominance over the Nautipunks.

"Are you taking notes?" Montgomery asked Emmeline as he lowered his rope. The fire in his gaze still simmered.

"I am."

He nodded. "Good. Our fire is our greatest asset."

Emmeline better understood Solís's comment about fire being their primary leverage—if the Nautipunks had access to the flame too, they'd fight fire with fire and nothing would ever get accomplished.

Montgomery climbed down. Emmeline followed his lead.

Her combat boots hit the metal ship deck with a thud, and her gears creaked as she stood tall.

"Sounds like you need a little grease." The voice came from behind and was accompanied by a mug of oil.

Emmeline turned around to find Louie—smile wide and silver-blue eyes beaming. His white poet's shirt was tucked into a tight pair of britches, and his left earlobe had a gold hoop piercing. Though he was a Nautipunk, only his outfit matched the part—he did not speak like the other pirates, and he was much cleaner than his crewmates. His zinc gears were so polished, they churned without making a sound.

"Thanks," she said, accepting the offer and sipping the oil.

"Anything for you." He winked and tucked a lock of his shaggy brown hair behind his ear.

Emmeline blushed—annoyed that his presence filled her with giddy delight.

"You're a pest," she said. Though she meant to be harsh, the insult sounded playful.

"If pestering you wins me your favor, then I suppose that's what I'll do."

Emmeline pursed her lips together, agitated because she did not want to like him.

"You don't need to do anything," she replied. "You've already won my favor."

"I have?" His eyes glowed with spirited delight.

"I mean, you did save my life the other day."

He grinned, then teased, "This is true. Maybe you ought to be winning *my* favor then."

"Seems as though I've already done that." Emmeline smirked, then turned to join her father. Louie stood tall, grinning from ear to ear as she walked away.

"What's on the agenda today?" she asked her father.

"Look up," he said.

Emmeline did as he requested and gasped—a dead Hellion of Obsession was strung up with ropes between two of the masts. Head missing and arms stretched wide, its body hung limp. Still and lifeless. In this state, Emmeline was able to see the monster more clearly. Two arms, two legs, and smooth flesh. She remembered what its head looked like before Louie speared it: two eyes, two ears, one nose, a mouth, and a scalp covered with hair. Anatomically, it wasn't terribly different than the punks of Quintessence. Its insides were different, surely—Emmeline saw no gears at the monster's joints—and its specific features were uniquely foreign. Instead of feet with toes, it had talons, and they also had wings.

It very much resembled the woman in the sky.

Droplets of silver blood fell from the monster's talons onto the ship deck.

Emmeline looked closer—its wings were gone.

"Where are its wings?" she asked.

"They were chopped into pieces and divvied up among the Nautipunk crew—the material the wings are made of is valuable among the pirates. Great for trade."

"Why is it here?" she asked as the crew pulleyed a tarp to veil the carcass.

"The Nautipunks retrieved the body of the hellion who almost killed you. We will be using it as leverage while we interrogate the caged hellion at the detention center."

Emmeline instinctively reached her hand into her pocket for comfort. The stone did not fail her—it laced her vision with darkness and smothered the fear creeping up her spine.

She thought again of the woman in the sky.

"These monsters can communicate with us?"

"The Hellions of Obsession speak our language, luckily, but some of the others communicate in tongues we've yet to translate."

"I see."

She hadn't realized the extent of her trauma until being presented with the task of facing the monster who almost killed her again.

"You will observe and take notes," Montgomery said. "Interrogating our prisoners is usually only done upon capture, but in this scenario, we need to learn how a fully grown hellion wound up in our seas. I'd also like to figure out why it targeted you."

"I probably just looked like easy prey."

"Maybe," Montgomery replied, though he looked unconvinced.

Red Fang Ralph steered his ship toward the detention center, which sat a few nautical miles north of where they met beneath the gate.

The five large cages came into view. They appeared small at first, growing larger with each wave Red Fang's Ralph steered his ship through.

Louie leaned against the railing next to Emmeline, his shimmering gaze set on the horizon.

Emmeline turned her attention to him, but he never looked her way. The corners of his mouth ticked up ever so slightly, indicating his avoidance was intentional.

She took her hands out of her pockets and crossed them over her chest. Shadows lifted and senses vibrant, she turned her attention back to the sea, prepared to win this battle of stubbornness.

They stood there in silence until the tension became so awkward, Louie cracked a smile and laughed.

"This is a stupid game," Emmeline noted, still keeping her eyes averted from his.

"I win!" He gave her a gentle push.

"Excuse me?" Emmeline snapped to face him.

"You spoke first."

"You looked at me first."

"But you broke the silence," he said, his smile so charming, Emmeline struggled to feign anger.

She returned her attention to the sea. "I didn't know the rules."

"It's okay. Better luck next time." His playful banter fanned the embers in Emmeline's heart.

"I have a job to do, if you don't mind," Emmeline replied, desperately attempting to extinguish the fire swelling in her chest.

"Of course, you do," he agreed, wearing a forced frown and imitating her serious energy.

Emmeline cast him a stern side-eye, only to find that though he faked it well, he failed to eliminate the sparkle in his eye.

An involuntary smirk crept across her face.

"Go away," she demanded, though her attempt to be firm was soft.

Louie tightened his lips and shook his head. "I think I'll stay right here."

"Don't distract me when I have to work."

"I wouldn't dream of it."

Emmeline scrunched her nose, trying not to smile, when a deafening roar shook the boat. The Ogre of Irritability was in sight—every bit of delight left Emmeline's body.

They had reached Dawes Detention Center for Demons. At this proximity, the cages varied in size—some massive, some tiny, but all reinforced with titanium bars. Near the end of the row, a crew of Nautipunks were building a new featured cage. Equipped with blazing hot firestones, they were able to weld the metal rods together and assemble an impenetrable prison.

Emmeline buried her hands in her pockets, wishing to hide, but unable.

"Why are they building a new cage?" she asked Louie.

"For when we catch new monsters."

"So there isn't a new monster I need to be worried about today?"

Louie glanced down at her, his height more apparent than ever as his pretty gaze shifted from flirty to solemn.

"Not today, but maybe tomorrow, or the next," he said, no malice in his tone, just empathy. "Just this morning there was a report of a monster sighting a few clicks south of Smuggler's Rove. I suspect your father will send a crew to investigate after we deal with this hellion."

Emmeline gulped, almost choking on her oil-based saliva.

"Don't be afraid," Louie offered, his words sincere. "I'm here, and always will be."

Though she wanted to banter, his simple, genuine promise made her feel better.

"Thank you."

He nodded and offered his hand. She took it, removing her left hand from the stone in her pocket. The comforting warmth of Louie's hand in hers was all the support she needed.

Red Fang Ralph steered the ship to the smaller cage holding the Hellion of Obsession.

"Arghh, ye nasty kraken!" he shouted at the monster from the ship's wheel.

The creature was subdued and disinterested in its visitors. It kept its back turned to the pirate ship.

"Show yer face!" Ralph hollered. His crew launched hooked ropes at the cage, catching the titanium bars and anchoring the boat in place. The sound of clanking metal irritated the hellion, and it snarled in protest.

It stood on two legs, much like the punks of Quintessence, except each foot had four razor-sharp talons.

Emmeline recalled her diving suit being torn to shreds by the hellion's sharp grip. The wounds on her biceps were still healing.

She shuddered—Louie gently squeezed her hand.

As the monster turned to face its captors, it scanned the lot of them. Its wide, disc-shaped eyes were dark with fury. One by one, it assessed each punk on the boat. When its focus landed on Emmeline, the monster lingered, holding her gaze longer than the others.

"It's staring at me," Emmeline whispered.

"I see that," Louie replied, his worry apparent. Slowly and steadily, he pulled Emmeline back from the railing and began positioning his body in front of hers.

The moment it could no longer see her, the hellion's docile nature transformed. It catapulted its body against the titanium bars of its cage, slamming itself into its confines repeatedly and screeching inaudible words.

Emmeline peered from around Louie's shoulder.

In the midst of the monster's rampage, it locked eyes with Emmeline and jolted to a halt. Unmoving but frantic, it held her gaze and hissed, "Mine."

Chapter 10

"What does she have that you want?" Montgomery shouted, enraged that his daughter was being singled out again.

The hellion replied with a low growl. Its infuriated gaze remained locked on Emmeline.

She shuddered from where she hid behind Louie. Her hand returned to her pocket. The harder she squeezed the sea stone, the better she felt.

Her father bellowed, "Lower the tarp!"

At his command, the Nautipunks cut the ropes and the tarp fell. The slaughtered and mutilated hellion corpse was revealed.

Emmeline was no longer the monster's greatest concern—its wide eyes blinked and shifted upward, anger morphing into horror.

A bereaved howl echoed across the sea. The monster clutched the bars of its cage, face pressed between, and fell to the floor as its wings went limp.

"Tell us how this grown monster entered our sea," Montgomery demanded.

The monster did not reply.

"Tell me now!"

The monster ignored Montgomery's stern interrogation, keeping its sorrowful attention plastered on its slain comrade.

Aware that the monster had no intention of cooperating, Montgomery lifted his pistol and shot a tiny fireball into the monster's cage. Base bars wrapped in twine, the floor of the prison was set ablaze.

The Hellion of Obsession was forced to abandon its grief and fly. Wings reactivated, it hovered at the center of its cage, surrounded by flames.

"Answer my question or burn," Montgomery threatened.

The hellion hissed, and then spat.

"If you answer my questions, I will douse the flames. If you refuse, you will burn alive."

The hellion screeched in fury, wings pounding against the growing smoke.

"What do you want to know?" it asked, its voice deep and low.

Emmeline stepped out from behind Louie. Hearing the monster speak added a level of relatability—his words were clear, his tone was confident, and his diction revealed a level of education. This revelation added layers to the monster's allure—he had a personality, a past. He was a multi-layered being capable of intelligent thoughts and emotions.

The monster who once only hissed and snarled, now appeared as a man with depth.

Emmeline looked to her father, who showed no empathy.

"How did a full-grown Hellion of Obsession get past our solar shield and the Pyro-Argo Militia? How did it enter my sea?"

The hellion roared with displeasure.

"You will burn if you defy me," Montgomery warned.

"I cannot say," the hellion replied through clenched teeth. Fire sweltering, the growing flares lashed his wings.

"Then tell me why your kind holds such fascination with my daughter."

"Who?" the hellion barked.

Emmeline stepped forward. As the monster's attention refocused on her, his furious obstinance subsided. Suffering pushed aside, he reestablished his wits and his entire demeanor shifted. His black-disced eyes pierced through her with malicious desire.

"Come closer and I will tell you," he sneered.

"We will not—" Montgomery began, but Emmeline was already walking the plank extended from the ship's starboard. Her father shouted, "Come back!"

Emmeline ignored him, keeping her grip of the stone, desperate to feel brave as she faced her fears. This monster held the key to her questions: Why were the hellions so focused on her? And was the woman in the sky real, or just a dream?

The stone buzzed in her grip, electric with courageous energy.

The hellion closed its eyes, smiled, and bobbed his head to a melody only he could hear.

"Isn't it lovely?" he asked when she reached the end of the plank.

Over the crackling and whirring flames, Emmeline could hardly hear him.

"Excuse me?"

"The humming of home."

"There is no time for riddles. You will die if you don't cooperate."

"I will not die here," he responded, still swaying to the rhythm in his head.

Emmeline's expression tightened.

"What do you want from me?" she asked.

His disced-eyes opened. The darkness they previously held was replaced with glowing silver triumph.

"You know what you took."

"I took nothing from you."

"And yet here it is, delivered by you, beckoning me home." His grin was wicked. "Very unwise to covet it as you do. It will steal everything from you."

"What will?" she asked.

The hellion extended his arms, hands reaching for Emmeline, then began to chant.

"Ad lunam lu."

"What are you saying?" she asked, taking a step back.

"Accipe me!"

No warning, no fanfare—the hellion vanished.

Emmeline fell backward in shock, landing on the wobbling plank.

Gone.

She cursed beneath her breath.

A blaring, hand-cranked siren, accompanied by the outrage of the Nautipunk crew, made the roaring fire sound tame. Emmeline covered her ears and looked over her shoulder to find the furious pirates shouting at her. The only one not saying a word was Louie.

Montgomery walked the plank toward her.

The siren set to warn the world above of a monster breach subsided, and the loud crackling whir of the fire resumed as the soundtrack to this disaster.

"Where did it go?" she asked, as her father grabbed her hand and helped her to her feet.

"I was going to ask you the same question."

"How should I know," she objected, feeling guilty, but unsure what she had done. "I blinked and he was gone."

"Did it say anything to you?"

Her mind raced. "He kept mentioning home before he started speaking gibberish."

"Gibberish?"

"I was worried he was casting a spell on me or something."

"No, their only power against us exists in their touch. He did not touch you, so you will be fine. Do you remember what he said?"

"Ad lunam," she recalled. "Then something else. I can't remember."

"Ad lunam," Montgomery repeated, his thoughts consumed by this new information.

"Do you know what it means?" she asked.

"Not yet, but I will find out. In the meantime, we have to hunt the escaped monster."

"You think it's still here?"

"Where else would it have gone?"

The Nautipunks divvied up into search crews.

Louie led the divers. Stripped down to their swimming trunks, the assigned aquanauts lined the railing of the top deck, awaiting their signal to jump. Louie paced behind them, running his hand across each of their backs. Finger gears working overtime, he checked each of their hookups, making sure the seal of their tanked lungs was secured tightly to their inner tubes. As each member of the crew passed the safety check, Louie gave them a double tap on the nape of their neck, indicating they were good to go. One by one, they dove. Louie's rhythmic timing created a synchronized waterfall of bodies disappearing into the sea. He was the last to go.

He glanced at Emmeline, who watched him intently, afraid he might be mad at her like all the other Nautipunks. A flashing wink and smirk before he made his dive eased her worry.

Ruthanne the Heartless captained a fleet of smaller vessels.

Two large paddle wheels were attached to each side of her boat, and four members of the crew pedaled them forward. Ruthanne climbed to the top of the weather deck where she strapped a single-eyed ocular to her head and shifted between the various levers till she landed on her preferred lens. Placing an infrared telescope to her free eye, she scanned the sea.

Red Fang Ralph, with the assistance of ten other men, lifted an enormous grate from the floor of the main deck. With a heave ho, they maneuvered the massive piece of metal and revealed a fleet of submarines below.

Emmeline peered over the side of the opening.

"How will they get into the water?" she asked her father.

"You'll see."

Ralph jumped onto the top of the nearest submarine. After a quick swig from his flask, he cranked the top wheel, unlatching a hatch, then jumped inside. Two Nautipunks followed, while the rest climbed ladders into the lower deck. The top hatch was sealed shut and as the murmuring of turning gears grew louder, Emmeline and Montgomery took a step back.

With a lofty bounce, Red Fang Ralph's submarine launched out from the lower deck and landed on two long mechanical legs. Shaped like a fish with two giant stick legs, it swiveled in placed as Ralph got his bearings through a giant telescope that moved like an arm extended from the roof. Through the glass front of this walking contraption, Red Fang Ralph gave them a toothless salute as he launched his submarine into the sea with a hop.

A caravan of similarly shaped submarines followed suit, bounding with a spring over the ship's deck and landing with a splash.

While Louie, Ruthanne, and Ralph began their hunt across Hydra, Avery and Regis lowered the helium balloons. Of the Nautipunks, only the quartermaster, the coxswain, the lookout, and five able seamen remained.

"Who will be dousing the fire?" Montgomery asked of the lot.

"Reservoir Robert is a ripe chowderhead aboard this here ship, but he's our best waterman," the quartermaster replied. "He'll lead the charge."

"Robert and crew, please board the balloon with Regis," Montgomery instructed, to which the Nautipunks obeyed, shoving each other as they climbed aboard. They were stinky, rambunctious, and loud. Regis recoiled to the corner of the basket, holding his flying equipment with one hand and his nose with the other.

Montgomery and Emmeline climbed the rope ladder into Avery's basket. Safely aboard, they followed Regis to the flaming cage where the hellion had escaped. The monsters in the neighboring cages growled and recoiled from the fire, enraged by the residual punishment they were forced to endure.

As Regis steered his balloon to hover above the burning cage, Montgomery gave the order.

"Unload the power of the sea!"

The Nautipunks leaned over the edges of the basket, arms dangling overboard. As they channeled the power of the sea, their water hearts surged with the force of a thousand currents and gallons of seawater rained from their mouths and hands. Casting a vicious storm over the fire, the flames were extinguished in a matter of seconds. Spray from the shower misted into the neighboring cages. Some of the monsters enjoyed the splash, while others wailed in protest.

"Cease water!" Montgomery shouted.

Reservoir Robert sinched his faucets and stood tall. His comrades followed his lead.

"Thank you. Regis, you can return them to the boat."

A look of relief washed over Regis's expression as he lowered his balloon and delivered the Nautipunks to their ship.

Avery did not follow.

"Are we leaving Hydra?" Emmeline asked.

"Yes," her father answered. "The Pyropunks surely heard the warning siren, but we need to return to Fyree and give them details about the breach. Then you and I need to sit down and go over everything that transpired. Every detail needs to be analyzed if we hope to understand what happened today."

"Understood."

Montgomery gave Emmeline a curt nod.

As Regis lifted back into the air, Montgomery gave the order.

"Avery, take us home."

With her knees curled to her chest, Emmeline wedged herself into the corner of the basket, conflicted as she recalled the day's events.

Was she to blame for the monster's escape? If so, how? And why didn't she feel as bad as she suspected she should?

Hand shoved into her pocket, her fingers wrapped around the sea stone and she let the shadows soothe her discomfort. A vision of the winged woman tore across the darkness. The longer she recalled the mysterious creature, the more it felt like a dream—an impossible delusion cast forth by her sleepy imagination.

"You look tired," Montgomery said as he cupped the marble dispenser attached to his belt and pressed the bottom lever four times. Four marbles fell into his palm. Milky blue, reddish brown, pale purple, and pea green— he extended them to Emmeline.

"What are those?" she asked.

"Marbles to refuel."

Emmeline leaned forward, her expression a mix of wonder and disgust.

"Why do they look like that?"

"Oh, right. Melora only feeds you kids golden marbles. These are what the Terrapunks eat. They are made of clay."

Emmeline accepted the offering, holding the clay marbles in her palm. They weighed less than the golden marbles.

"Do they work the same?" she asked.

Montgomery nodded. "Some argue they work better."

"They aren't as heavy."

"Exactly—they move slower, so the energy they provide lasts longer."

She rolled the clay marbles through her fingers.

"They are perfectly round. How do they make them?"

"With firestones. They bake the clay and mold them."

"I never realized we didn't get our energy from the same source as the other punks."

"Aeros consume glass marbles, and the Hydros ingest black obsidian marbles from the ocean floor, or rounded sea glass."

"And those work just as well?"

"Yes. The main difference is the weight, and that golden marbles are a delicacy. Your mother buys them directly from the Tinkie who makes these clay marbles. She pays him with firestones." Emmeline examined the marbles.

"Eat up," Montgomery encouraged.

"I'm not hungry." She extended the pretty clay marbles back to her father.

He shook his head. "Keep them for when you are."

Montgomery sat on the floor beside his daughter.

"What's wrong?" he asked.

"I feel very confused."

"About what?"

Emmeline paused in consideration.

"Everything," she explained. "I was excited to join you in Hydra. I was ready and willing to accept my role. I took my training seriously and I was motivated to make you proud." She took a deep breath. "Then, I got here, and nothing was as I expected."

Guilt replaced Montgomery's concern. "You had a horrible introduction to Hydra. I'm not sure why things went so awry, but I promise I will always keep you safe. And one day, you won't need me because you'll have learned all that you need to know." He scanned her melancholic expression with empathy. "It's okay to be scared."

Emmeline pulled the sea stone out of her pocket.

"I keep this with me. It gives me courage. It reminds me that if I could survive everything that happened on my first hunt, I can survive anything."

"That's a great way to remind yourself how brave you are."

"Sometimes I think this stone holds magic."

"Magic isn't real."

"I know, but thinking that it is helps."

"Just be careful not to blur the line between reality and fantasy."

Emmeline nodded, then thought of the woman in the sky.

"Can I tell you something?" she asked.

"Anything."

"Ever since that day, I've seen strange things, and my thoughts are often clouded by shadows." She paused, afraid to say more. "I saw something that doesn't make sense."

"What?"

"A Hellion of Obsession—it appeared outside my bedroom window."

"Impossible."

"I know," Emmeline agreed. "It just felt so real."

"It's not surprising that you are having nightmares about those monsters after one of them nearly killed you."

"It wasn't a nightmare, though. If anything, it was a dream."

"You weren't afraid?"

"At first, yes, but then the morning sun illuminated her face and I saw that she did not arrive with malice. She was lost, and she meant me no harm."

"A lovely dream indeed, where monsters arrive in peace."

"What if it was a sign? Maybe there is more for us to learn about these creatures. Maybe there's more to them, maybe some of them are good."

"It was just a dream," Montgomery insisted.

"It felt real to me."

"Don't let the trauma you've endured soften your resolve. You want to believe these monsters are good because it makes them less scary. I get it, but you know what these monsters are capable of—you graduated from the academy with honors. Everything you were taught was true. Centuries of battles and conflict led us to where we are today. Remember your teachings."

Emmeline closed her eyes and rested her head against the basket, too tired to argue with her father.

Montgomery continued, "Perhaps you need a break to recharge."

"The sky has been calling me," Emmeline admitted. "I'd like to try flying."

"Flying?" Montgomery asked, his worry intensifying. He gently took Emmeline's arm and peered beneath the golden gauze.

"Are your wounds healing?" he asked.

"They don't hurt anymore."

He touched the edge of the wound—the salve had almost fully healed the large incisions.

"They're almost sealed," he confirmed. "I was beginning to worry you might be infected. Seems it's just a bit of lingering trauma. If flying will help, Avery can give you lessons. She can teach you how to fly helium balloons, or even the family airship once it is repaired."

"No—I meant on my own, with wings."

"Be realistic."

"My brothers do it every day."

"They are Pyropunks. They were only given wings and helium to help the Argopunks protect the sky."

"Imagine if I could fly within Hydra? I could rule the sea from above. No ship, no Pilopunk—I wouldn't have to rely on anyone but myself."

"Entertain my offer," he pled. "Flying a ship may be more fulfilling than you realize."

Emmeline didn't have the energy to continue this argument. Instead, she peered up at Avery from where she sat huddled in the corner of the basket.

Avery looked over her shoulder, a wide grin on her face.

"Could be fun," she suggested.

"Fine," Emmeline agreed, despite her reservations. She tucked the clay marbles into her pocket with the stone and walked to Avery's side. Her stomach growled and all she could think about was how she needed to keep busy, she needed a complex distraction if she wished to silence the hunger pains. Learning to fly this ship was great while she was here, but soon she would be alone again in her bedroom with only her deteriorating thoughts to keep her company.

"Take note of your surroundings," Avery instructed.

They were a few miles north of Fyree in the upper level of Gaslion and the world below appeared as a churning sea of gears.

Avery explained the first steps of piloting a helium balloon, and though Emmeline listened, her sight kept meandering to the ground. Though Tinkerpunks were invisible from this height, she thought of Gemma—the Tinkie with access to discarded Pyropunk wings.

It was time to cash in on that favor.

Chapter 11

Palms cupping the bottom dish of the heat lamp, Emmeline intensified the flame.

The helium balloon rocketed upward.

"A little less," Avery instructed between inhales and exhales into the copper pipe that zigzagged up into the balloon. Her control of the helium determined their rise and fall. "We need to lower into Fyree."

Emmeline pulled her hands away from the dish.

"Now, crank the silver-knobbed pedal clockwise," Avery said.

Emmeline moved to the wall of the basket covered in levers, pedals, and cranks.

"This one?" Emmeline asked, her hand gripping the lever.

"Yup, that's the one."

There was a strap Avery normally attached to her foot, but Emmeline did not need it. She cranked it clockwise with her hand.

The giant wings on both sides of the basket pumped the air, matching the speed with which Emmeline turned the pedal.

"The bronze lever controls the tilt of the wings," Avery explained. "It has full range of motion. You can use it to alter our course."

"Are we heading the right way?" Emmeline asked.

"We need to aim west."

"How do I do that?"

"Gently shift the bronze lever down and to the left."

Emmeline did as instructed and the wings tilted, turning the balloon's direction.

More exhilarating than anticipated, Emmeline enjoyed the rush of adrenaline.

They worked together like this till they reached the Dawes's golden mansion in Fyree. As they crossed the invisible plane between upper Gaslion and Fyree, the air warmed, their surroundings brightened, and Emmeline was greeted with the familiar feeling of home.

They docked next to the open hangar bay and Avery lassoed two ropes onto golden posts to keep the balloon from floating away.

As Montgomery climbed out of the basket and fussed to correct Avery's hasty ties, the Pilopunk turned to Emmeline.

"Good work, co-pilot," Avery congratulated.

"I'll never be able to fly one of these on my own. Not without helium."

"Let me tell you a secret." Avery leaned in close. "You don't need helium to fly a balloon. Heated oxygen can float, too. Look at your home—that's how it stays levitated."

"Then why do the Pyropunks rely on helium?"

"Burning oxygen is really only good for short-term floats, not for long flights."

"Then how do our homes stay lifted?"

"The golden tethers connect them directly to the source flame—they are fueled by unlimited fire power. Thermapunks, on the other hand, only have so much fire within their hearts. They can only expend so much in any one sitting. That being said, it's still possible to gain lift with fire and air, you just need to be careful you don't run out of fire midflight."

Emmeline absorbed this information, wondering if the challenge was worth the risk.

"Let's get going," Montgomery said, securing the final knot.

"Thanks," Emmeline offered, feeling more hopeful than before. Between her fear of the monsters and her new fear of eating, this was exactly what she needed—a complex task to distract her worried mind. She climbed over the side of the basket and landed on the golden platform.

"Anytime," Avery replied while securing the straps of her copper wings over her shoulders and across her chest. After clicking the gears of each wing into her shoulder gears, she leapt off the side of the basket and took flight. Swooping in circles, she disappeared into the swarm of Aeropunks enjoying their evening floats in Gaslion.

Emmeline glanced over the side of the hangar platform at the world below. Gemma was down there, somewhere, and through her, Emmeline could score a pair of wings.

It was time to pay her a visit.

After stealing a batch of firestones from Helix's room to pay the cable car attendants, Emmeline strapped herself into a harness and rappelled to the ground.

The trip was quicker this time as she felt more comfortable in her descent.

One final release of the rope and her feet landed firmly on the platform. She unlatched her harness, disconnected from the pulley system, and left her equipment on the platform. A quick glance up put her distance from home into perspective. She wasn't sure how she'd get back, but decided that was a puzzle she'd solve later.

Emmeline marched to the edge of the platform and scanned the horizon.

Rows and rows of tall terra gears lined the land. Tall platforms where the Tinkies worked and lived were constructed high above these gears and the Revopunks skated beneath in monotonous cycles. Some platforms were connected and formed bridges over the terra gears, others stood alone like islands. The platform beneath the Dawes family home was isolated—Emmeline either had to climb down and walk to the nearest cable car station, or she could hitch a ride on the passenger conveyer belt in the sky.

She looked up. The complex conveyer belt was designed for Tinkies, not visitors. Strategically so—Terrapunks wanted payment for their services, no outsider was allowed to utilize their part of the world for free.

Deterred by the dangerous nature of the conveyer belt, Emmeline opted for the cable cars.

She climbed down the ladder and walked the long row. Giant gears churned on both sides, creating walls so tall, they dwarfed her. She saw nothing except what lay ahead, behind, and above.

The revolving gears were loud. Greased by the Tinkies, each rotation was smooth, yet the collective sound they made echoed like a distant storm. A slight breeze accompanied the movement, dancing gingerly across Emmeline's soft skin as she charged toward the far-off cable car station.

The gentle atmosphere boomed with noise, startling Emmeline from her mission.

She looked over her shoulder to find two Revopunks racing toward her at full speed. The gears beneath their feet rumbled like thunder.

Though she knew they could not hurt her—they were confined to the tall gear-tops—Emmeline ducked. Body crouched, chin lifted, she watched the Revopunks skate by. Enormous in stature—they had to be in order to move the massive gears of the sun—these two Revopunks held hands as they approached. Unlike the Tinkerpunks, the Revos had patches of moss covering their flesh, and their silver eyes held flecks of dazzling emerald. The woman glanced down at Emmeline, her brief gaze held great contempt. In a flash, she shot a blast of lightning at Emmeline, scorching the gilded, steel-piped ground next to her.

Emmeline gulped—she had been wrong. She was not out of reach of the Revopunk's disdain.

The female Revo returned her sights to the never-ending track before her, still holding the hand of her male counterpart, who never even bothered looking at Emmeline. He simply pretended like she did not exist.

The rumbling of thunder faded as they skated farther away, and Emmeline's terrorized adrenaline settled.

"Are you okay?" a voice called down from above.

Emmeline looked up to find Gemma crossing the sky on the conveyer belt.

"She tried to kill me!"

Gemma shook her head. "If she wanted to kill you, she would have. She was just trying to scare you."

"Why, though?"

Gemma detached herself from her connection to the conveyer belt and plummeted to the ground. Though the fall was chaotic, she landed in a graceful crouch. Gemma stood and lifted the bottom of her dress, revealing a charred lightning bolt scar on her thigh. "That's just what they do."

"Ugh!" Emmeline griped. "They are rotten."

"They are unhappy."

"I get it, but the rest of us didn't make the rules. We didn't assign them to their eternal loops around the sun. They ought to be angry at the gods."

Gemma shrugged. "They can't strike the gods down with lightning. I guess we're the next best option."

"Solédon is cruel."

"He is a god—he has many suns to monitor. So long as our sun functions properly, he doesn't really care *how* we operate." Gemma scanned Emmeline, her silver eyes bright with curiosity. "Why are you here?"

"I was looking for you, actually. I'd like to cash in on that favor."

Gemma limped closer—she hadn't quite mastered walking on her flesh-stripped foot. Though her energy was willing, her eyes narrowed, as if she sensed trouble.

"What will it be, then?"

"Wings. I want a pair of wings."

Gemma's energy relaxed. "Easy. There's a whole pile of them in the scrapyard."

"I need a pair of wings that work."

"I can fix anything," Gemma reminded her.

"Any chance there are discarded tanks of helium there?"

"Tons, but they are empty."

Emmeline crossed her arms and considered Avery's advice. "Maybe I don't need the helium."

"The wings will be useless without it."

"I was told that if I burn oxygen, I can get lift. Like a balloon—do you have any fabric?"

"There are tattered balloons in the scrapyard, too."

"Perfect. Lead the way."

"Can you jump high enough to reach the conveyer?" Gemma asked.

Emmeline looked up and shook her head.

Gemma pulled a clamp gun out of her decorated tool belt, handed it to her, and advised, "Aim it at the top of a vacant metal chair."

The conveyer had an assortment of attachments: rods with metal spheres at the ends that Tinkies clutched with their steel-iron grips, J-shaped bars that travelers looped under their armpits, and metal chairs for newbies like Emmeline.

Gemma explained, "When you shoot, the clamp will latch onto the chair and you'll flip this lever on the side of the gun, which will retract the rope and pull you into the air. From there, you can climb onto the chair."

Emmeline gulped. "I'll try."

Gemma continued, "When the conveyer splits into different directions, you'll use the levers on the chair's armrests. To turn left, lift the left arm rest. To turn right, lift the right arm rest. Follow me."

With a deep squat and a full spring, Gemma launched into the air and snagged the metal sphere of a vacant rod.

"Catch the chair behind me," she shouted down.

Emmeline closed one eye and aimed the clamp gun. The blast knocked her backwards, causing her to stumble as she pulled the trigger, but the clamp still managed to latch onto the chair.

"Flip the lever!" Gemma reminded her.

Disoriented, Emmeline fumbled. The rope pulled tight and dragged her across the copper pipes. Emmeline found and flipped the lever, holding on tight as she rocketed into the sky.

"Don't let go," Gemma advised.

Emmeline kept her eyes closed to help with the vertigo. She came to an abrupt stop as the recoil finished. She peeked through her golden lashes to see that she hung high above the world.

After taking a deep breath to settle her nerves, she pulled her body onto the chair. A clumsy scramble, but successful.

"Good job!" Gemma declared, pointing to her forever-bruised elbow of the arm latched to the metal rod. "I fell on my first try. Had to reconnect my forearm to my bicep. The flesh died before I could stich it up. That's why it's discolored."

"That wasn't easy," Emmeline sympathized with a shudder.

"Left turn coming up!"

Gemma used her body weight to jump the connection and steer herself to the left. Emmeline grabbed the left arm rest, and to her relief, it lifted easily. She followed Gemma onward.

They traveled like this for an hour, Gemma hopping each diversion of the conveyer and Emmeline matching her every turn. She imagined the energy Gemma had to expend to navigate the belt, and though it appeared exhausting, her Tinkie companion showed no signs of fatigue. Every so often, with her free hand, Gemma released a few clay marbles from her belt dispenser and popped them into her mouth.

Emmeline was still running on the few marbles she had eaten earlier that day. They pushed her gears forward slowly, as she attempted to conserve what little energy she had left.

Farther than she had ever traveled in this direction, Emmeline was in awe to find that the Terrapunk structures were far more elaborate and developed on this side of the sun. A mini city built overtop of the terra gears shot into the sky. The conveyer belt zigzagged between the giant towers made of gears.

"I've never been here before," she revealed to Gemma.

"Everything connects to the terra gears. Everything we do enables the kinetic energy of the sun."

Tinkerpunks scaled the towering buildings, greasing the gears and tightening the connector bolts.

"What are these skyscrapers for?"

"Every faction of Solarpunks has leaders. Ours live here."

"What do they do?"

"They monitor the rest of the Terrapunks. They make sure the Revopunks skate at acceptable speeds, and they monitor the Tinkerpunk trade-dealings with outsiders. I probably shouldn't be helping you without written permission, but gifting you a pair of scrap wings is harmless."

"That's all they do?"

"No. They do a lot more. A long time ago, they led the war initiative."

"To steal the source flame?"

"Correct." Gemma spoke as though she held no connection to her own people. "Their greed and hunger for power almost killed us all. We are flammable beings—the fire is not our friend."

"Well, the Thermapunks have no intention of sharing it."

"Good. I've heard rumors in the markets that the Horrigan family plans to try again."

"The Horrigans?"

"The lead family of power among the Terrapunks— similar to your family among the Thermapunks. The alliance between fire and gas put a halt to their plans, as has the increased invasions by the moon monsters, but they still whisper about possessing fire."

"To what end?" Emmeline asked.

"Domination of our sun, I suppose."

"You mean *annihilation* of our sun?"

"Not necessarily. Our world of gears exists within a pocket of oxygen, so as long as the flame does not touch our hearts or veins, we could exist among fire. It's just risky, and certainly ill-advised. I don't support them," she assured.

Emmeline thought this over as they crossed through the mini city. She wondered if her parents knew, and assumed they must—it explained her mother's flagrant dislike of the Terrapunks, but Gemma wasn't like the rest. A theme that kept appearing—not all was as it seemed.

Beyond the Terrapunk city, the ground resumed the appearance Emmeline was accustomed to: rows of visible terra gears and scattered Tinkerpunk platforms.

In the distance, far from the bridged markets on this side of the sun, sat an elevated junkyard piled high with heaps of trash.

"Almost there," Gemma announced.

"How will I get down?"

"Make sure the clamp is locked to the chair. If you can't pry it open with your fingers, you're good. The lever you flipped up to ascend, just flip it down and you'll descend."

The conveyer belt moved at a slow and steady pace, allowing Emmeline time to check the security of the clamp and climb off the chair.

"Time to go," Gemma informed.

"But the scrapyard is still so far away."

"The conveyer belt doesn't run over the yard. We'll walk the rest of the way."

Gemma let go of her attachment and fell to the ground. The drop was erratic, but her landing was agile. She stood, unharmed, and waved for Emmeline to follow.

As instructed, Emmeline flipped the lever down and the rope attached to the clamp unraveled. The descent was gradual and controlled, much to Emmeline's relief. When her feet touched the ground, Gemma snatched the gun from her grip, fiddled with the buttons, and the clamp released and withdrew into the gun. She locked it into the holster of her toolbelt and looked to Emmeline with a smile.

"Great job!" she exclaimed, leading the charge onward toward the scrapyard.

"I feel a bit queasy," Emmeline noted. The vertigo was catching up to her.

"Here," Gemma said, offering a handful of clay marbles.

Emmeline shook her head. "I can't."

"Why not?"

"I already ate."

"A few more won't hurt you."

"It actually will," Emmeline grumbled, thinking of her migraines.

"Appease me, please," Gemma requested. "You look like you might faint."

Emmeline accepted Gemma's offer of marbles and swallowed two of them. They joined the slow-rolling golden marbles, and her energy perked.

"Thank you," she said, fearing a migraine that never arrived.

"Anytime." Gemma's captivating silver eyes showed sympathy. "Why do you want to fly, anyway?"

"I just need a distraction from all the terror that lives inside my head."

"Terror?"

"Just the usual fears that accompany change."

"I understand," Gemma sympathized. "I can't teach you how to fly, but I can give you the tools to teach yourself."

"That's an offer I am happy to accept."

"Anything for a friend," Gemma said as they reached the base of the scrapyard. She walked to the giant pillar situated on the row. A simple tap in the correct location revealed a hidden crank handle. Gemma rotated it, and a ladder descended from the underbelly of the platform.

When the legs hit the steel pipes that ran the length of the row, Gemma began to climb.

Emmeline followed.

As soon as she joined Gemma at the top, Gemma pressed a lever on the side of the ladder and it sprang back to its starting position.

"Let's get to work," she said once the ladder was securely hidden.

Emmeline observed as Gemma tore off into the field of trash, curious why a platform covered with junk had such a complicated access point.

Mounds of scrap metal decorated the field, creating a dynamic landscape. Rolling hills of junk, standing at various heights, stretching as far as the eye could see. Gemma rummaged through fragments of broken contraptions with thorough speed. Quick examinations, before tossing random pieces over her shoulder.

Emmeline watched from where she stood.

"Can I help?"

"You won't know where to look. Stay where you are so you don't get hurt. I've got this."

A steam whistle blew from the opposite side of the scrapyard.

Emmeline turned her attention and saw thick vapor billowing from the top of the tallest junk pile.

"What's that?" she asked Gemma.

"Delivery port to Hydra," she replied without pausing her search. "A giant zinc pipe crosses the plane between Hydra and Terra, and it emerges in the center of this scrapyard."

"Why, though?"

"It's how the Hydropunks build and maintain their ships and Roves—they send us steam, which we harness in jars, and in return, we send them metal materials from this scrapyard. I believe this is how the Thermapunks get water at the Steamery, too."

"There's a different piping system on the other side of Quintessence that sends water vapor to Fyree," Emmeline explained. "I'm not familiar with the mechanics, but I believe the pipes are much smaller. They're so narrow, it's impossible to trade anything other than mist. But here, it looks like you trade an assortment of items."

"Our pipe is big enough to trade an entire terra gear if desired."

Emmeline thought of Louie.

"Can the Nautipunks leave Hydra through the port?"

"Oh gosh, no," Gemma replied. "That's why the guards are there. If you think the idea of us having power is scary, then the Nautipunks with power should terrify you. They have an affinity for cruelty. It's why they're so well-suited to wrangle and detain the monsters."

"I've met them. I have to work alongside them in Hydra."

"Then you know."

"I haven't seen their cruel side yet."

"You're lucky, then. They are vile."

"I am going to go watch the transaction," Emmeline said.

"Be careful. Don't let anyone see you."

"I won't."

Emmeline climbed the nearest mound, then hopped from pile to pile, teetering on the debris of fallen airships as she crossed the yard. On a neighboring mound, close enough to see and hear the exchange between water and minerals, she hid behind a damaged propeller umbrella to observe.

At this distance, she saw the four Terra guards who manned this port.

The steam continued flowing through the cage opening. The Terra guards sequestered as much of the hot, misty air as they could, sealing each of the jars with lids before returning to catch more.

A four-pronged hook launched through the hole and latched to the grate with a loud clang. The sound acted as an alarm, alerting the Terra guards to cease their collection of steam and step back from the port.

Through the steam came a guttural howl.

Emmeline flinched—it sounded like one of the caged moon monsters.

The Terra guards unsheathed spear-tipped javelins from the scabbards on their backs and aimed them at the port.

Another savage howl.

Captivated, Emmeline's attention was glued to the dark space leading to Hydra.

A set of fingers blackened with filth emerged between the bars of the iron grate.

"What do you want?" a Terrapunk guard inquired.

"Come closer," a voice within the darkness hissed.

"We don't take orders from you."

131

"I gave you steam, now, come closer."

"Tell us what you want, or we'll unlatch your hook."

The Terrapunk guard lurched forward, his javelin hovering close to the port.

The dirty hand snatched the javelin and hurled it, sight unseen, into a Terrapunk on the opposite side of the port. The guard fell, injured but alive. He yanked the spear out of his shoulder with an agonizing holler as his comrades swarmed the portal, ready to fight.

"What do you want?" one of the guards demanded.

A pair of icy blue eyes lifted to the edge of the grate. They peered into the world above with illuminated abhorrence.

"Everything you've got."

The force of the ocean blew the grate into the sky and a hundred Nautipunks crawled into the world above.

Chapter 12

Emmeline raced back to Gemma.

"We have a problem!" she shouted, stumbling over staggering piles of junk.

"What's wrong?"

"There's been a breach."

Gemma froze. Attention turned to Emmeline, silver eyes alight with terror.

"What do we do?" Emmeline asked.

"This happens sometimes," Gemma said, her speech racing.

"It does?"

Gemma nodded.

"Are we in danger?"

Gemma gulped. "No one survives."

"How could the guards let this happen?"

"We've reinforced the port countless times. We've made treaties and trade deals with the pirates to persuade them to stop attacking us, but it never fails that they take it upon themselves to pillage us at their pleasure."

"Why not seal the port?"

"We need the steam. It's a valuable commodity in Terra—it's our main source of heat along with the firestones."

The rumbling roar of pirates plundering the scrapyard echoed across the platform.

"They can only take what is on this elevated island of junk," Gemma explained. "That's why this scrapyard is so far away from everything else, and why the conveyer belt does not run overtop of it. It's intentionally marooned, for this reason."

"You could have warned me!"

"They haven't breached in a while." Gemma grabbed the pair of broken wings she had located, along with ripped balloon fabric. The alarm in her eyes intensified. "Fire," she mumbled, as her sights returned to Emmeline. "Did they kidnap the Terrapunk guards?"

"I didn't stick around long enough to see."

"They cannot know that you are here." Her tone was urgent. "Hurry!"

Emmeline raced down the towering heap of scrap metal, tearing wounds into her ankles as she ran. She followed Gemma to the platform's edge.

The raucous jeers of the Nautipunks grew louder, indicating they were closer than before.

"Argh! We got stowaways!" a scratchy voice declared.

Emmeline glanced over her shoulder and saw a gaggle of Nautipunks standing atop the nearest junk pile. The tallest among them caught her eye—he wore a diagonal scar across his face.

"That one ain't a Terrapunk," he noted.

"Look at 'er goldenness," his comrade observed.

"She's a Therma. Seize her!" the largest of the pirates commanded, to which the others darted down the trash heap at terrifying speeds.

Emmeline chased after Gemma, determined to outrun this nightmare.

Gemma reached a box of controls near the platform's edge. The first button she hit sounded the alarms, which blared a screeching echo across the land. She then entered a code, which unlocked a steel-framed box concealing a crank. Gemma quickly turned the handle, lowering a single ladder to the ground below. Inch by inch, the turning gears stretched the coiled spring until the ladder touched the path below.

The Nautipunks were growing near—their ruthless jeers boomed louder with each turn of the crank.

"Hurry! They're getting closer," Emmeline urged.

"I'm going as fast as I can," Gemma promised.

The ladder hit the steel-piped ground below.

"You go first," Gemma instructed, draping the tattered balloon fabric over Emmeline's shoulders.

Emmeline grabbed both sides of the ladder and slid down.

Gemma was right behind, gliding down with the battered golden wings strapped to her back. As soon as her feet touched the ground, she kicked a lever holding the stretched spring, and the ladder recoiled back to where it had been stored beneath the platform. A throng of pirates peered over the platform's edge, shouting obscenities at the girls as they escaped down the long row.

"That was close," Gemma said between strained breaths, her limp more present as she ran.

"It's not easy to kill a Solarpunk of any kind—we are demi-gods. Why do they bother kidnapping the guards?"

"They imprison and farm us for our resources. That's why we couldn't let them capture you—they cannot be trusted with fire."

"I'd die before I let them use me like that."

"They've broken the bravest of Terrapunks. Don't underestimate the persuasiveness of torture."

"Why do they capture and torture Terrapunks?"

"To drain our veins dry and use the petroleum to sail faster. They activate the fuel with steam—the heated ocean water plus petroleum lets them sail at incredible speeds. It takes a while to drain us dry, but once they do, they turn our uranium hearts into cannonballs. I'm surprised you haven't seen the war boats yet."

"We haven't traveled too far from the gates."

"That makes sense then. The main gates to Hydra are a quarter spin from our port. Beneath the port is one of their Roves—the floating city where common Hydropunks live and a spot of solid land for the Nautipunks to rest when they aren't at sea. The Roves are where most of the trouble happens."

"I've seen one of the Roves from a distance," Emmeline said with a gulp. "The pirates I work with in Hydra seem different. I can't imagine any of them, even the most uncivilized among them, kidnaping and harvesting other punks for their natural resources."

"I suppose working with the Dawes family has its perks, and those perks are great enough to persuade the pirates in your charge to behave."

She thought of Louie and wondered if he had it in him to pillage and plunder. If he was no longer paid a handsome fee to protect her, would he leave? Or worse, attempt to steal her fire heart?

Emmeline reached her hand into her pocket, clutching the sea stone. As always, it provided the comfort she sought.

"What's wrong?" Gemma asked. "Why'd you stop?"

Emmeline was so caught up in the comfort of her stone, she had not realized that she stopped running.

"Oh, sorry."

"We can walk if you want. We're far enough away."

Atop the spinning terra gears, darting against the rotation and using long ropes to launch themselves forward, were hundreds of Terrapunks wearing armored vests and stone helmets.

"Who are they?" Emmeline asked.

"A special task force of Terrapunks, hand selected by the Horrigans, to deal with matters such as Nautipunk breaches. Their official group name is the Stone Patrol, because they've been rewired to shoot hardened sediment out of their fingertips, but most of us regular, unchosen Terrapunks call them the Stoneheads. They're awful. They're the ones who report everything we do back to the Horrigans."

"Are the guards at the steam pipe and cable car platforms part of the Stone Patrol?"

"No, they are just regular guards. Not nearly as trained or dangerous. They can be bribed; their loyalty to the Horrigans wavers. The Stoneheads, on the other hand, would die for the Horrigans."

"Is it bad that they can see us now?"

"They can't track you—you don't have the chip."

"The chip?"

"All Terrapunks are injected with a tracker. They monitor everywhere we go. I'm on my second strike, so this will likely land me in the slammer."

Emmeline glanced above at the fast-moving Stoneheads. "They aren't stopping to apprehend you. That's a good sign, right?"

"They have scanners. They'll read the report later and come find me. If those stupid pirates hadn't invaded, I wouldn't have needed to sound the alarm."

"But if you hadn't been there to sound the alarm, no one would have known they invaded."

"I guess you're right. I'll still get in trouble, though."

"I'm sorry," Emmeline offered.

"It's not your fault. Every move I make is a risk—I'm used to the stress. There is no freedom here."

Emmeline's grip on her sea stone was tight, the soothing darkness potent, and she wondered if her stone might offer Gemma some relief.

She pulled it out of her pocket and unfurled her fingers. The shiny silver stone gleamed in her palm.

"What is that?" Gemma asked.

"The simple answer is that it is a sea stone, but I've learned it is much more complex than that. Remember when I had that migraine?"

"Yes."

"This stone helped me heal. It gives me comfort whenever I feel stressed or scared. Maybe it can do the same for you."

Gemma's brow furrowed. "Where did you get it?"

"I found it under the sea."

"Are you sure it's safe?"

"It hasn't caused any harm yet," Emmeline replied.

"Is it made of obsidian?" Gemma asked.

"No."

"Then it does not come from *our* sea."

"But I found it in *our* sea," Emmeline countered, unsure why her offer to help was being scrutinized. "My father said that it was just a common stone."

This forced Gemma to pause. Everyone knew of Montgomery Dawes; his respected reputation reached every facet of Quintessence.

"Has anyone ever taken one of these stones out of Hydra before?" Gemma asked cautiously.

"Forget it. I just was just trying to help."

"Sorry," Gemma offered. "It's in my nature to be inquisitive. I see strange objects regularly in the market. Can I see the stone?"

"Sure."

Emmeline extended it to her, and as the stone transferred into Gemma's possession, the shadows lifted and Emmeline's anxiety returned. Her shoulders tensed as a searing ache shot up her back and into the base of her golden skull. She glanced back at the scrapyard platform, amazed at how calm she had stayed while being chased by murderous pirates. Danger and terror plagued her. No matter where she went, trouble seemed to follow.

Gemma, on the other hand, wore a look of pure respite. The lines of stress etched onto her young face had lessened and her rigid posture had relaxed.

"I don't feel anything," she said, her tone low and smooth.

"Are you sure?" Emmeline asked.

"I feel the same," Gemma said. "Except for the coldness."

"Coldness?"

"Where the stone touches my skin." Gemma shook her head and handed the stone back to Emmeline. "I don't like it."

As Emmeline took the stone, the lines of worry returned between Gemma's silver eyebrows.

"You looked more relaxed while holding it," Emmeline said.

Gemma wiggled her fingers and massaged the center of her palm. "If it works for you, that's all that matters. Thanks for trying."

The steady churn of terra gears grew louder, indicating that a Revopunk was approaching. A solemn note sung in perfect pitch accompanied the thunderous rumble.

"Dahlia," Gemma revealed, her demeanor forlorn.

"Who?"

"My assigned Revopunk. She wails and moans melancholic songs whenever she feels neglected."

Throughout their entire adventure, Gemma showed no signs of exhaustion until now. She unstrapped the golden wings from her back and handed them to Emmeline.

"Time for me to go," Gemma said. "It was nice seeing you again."

"How will I get home?" Emmeline asked aloud. "I guess I can take the cable cars."

"The cable cars are the worst." Gemma handed Emmeline her clamp gun. "Keep it. I can get another."

"I guess I have no need for these, then." Emmeline unlatched the satchel of firestones from her belt. She left one stone in the bag, in case she needed it during her trip home, then handed the rest to Gemma.

Gemma's silver eyes gleamed as Emmeline heated them up and transferred them into her friend's thermapouch.

"I haven't earned this," Gemma remarked.

"You saved my life. I never would have escaped those pirates on my own."

"You also would have never been in that situation if it wasn't for me."

"Don't overthink it."

Gemma's energy lifted. "This is a fortune."

"Will it help you get off the terra tracks?"

"Yes! I can buy a spot at the market in Sector 3 with this."

"Fantastic."

"Now I owe you twice," Gemma said.

"No, you don't, but you can still help me fix these wings."

"Of course. I have free time most evenings. I can help you then."

Despite her excitement, Gemma's attention was frayed, as if her thoughts were far-off in the recesses of her mind. She clenched the hand that had held the sea stone into a tight fist, knuckles protruding violently from the pressure.

"I'll see you soon," Emmeline said as the Revopunk approached.

Gemma glanced over her shoulder and offered a weak smile before launching into the air and latching onto the Revopunk's back.

Gone, as fast as the day had passed.

Sea stone rotating in her grip, Emmeline looked to the sky. She had hoped to give Gemma some relief, but it seemed the stone only worked for her. Like most everything else she'd experienced as of late, the power of the stone was just another figment of her imagination. She tossed the stone into her pocket, strapped the broken wings to her back, and draped the balloon fabric over her shoulders. Clamp gun aimed at a passing chair, she made her shot and securely attached to her ride home. She flipped the lever and ricocheted into the air. Safely situated in the chair, she watched the burning solar shield darken as nighttime approached.

Emmeline needed to get home.

Turn after turn, she found her way back to the platform beneath her house. She dismounted the conveyer with perfect timing, landing safely on the base.

Determined to return to Fyree without being seen by anyone in her family, she recoiled the clamp and prepared to see how far the rope could reach.

First shot, she aimed for the distant hangar bay.

The rope only reached half way, and the metal clamp rocketed back to the ground after failing to make contact.

Emmeline shielded her head with her arms as the heavy clamp fell with speed, landing a few feet to her left.

She recoiled the rope.

Second shot, she aimed at the golden tether attached to the base of her home. The clamp had sharp titanium teeth that dug into the tightly wound golden coils.

Emmeline flipped the lever and was pulled into the air. When she reached the clamp, she wrapped her legs around the thick tether and unlocked the clamp. She was in the lower level of Gaslion. Legs squeezing firmly, she leaned back and shot again, latching the clamp to a higher spot on the tether.

She repeated this until she reached the fire at the base of her home.

From here, she shimmied up the tether, through the fire, and found the latched door. Her brothers had left it unlocked and she was able to crawl through.

Safe at last, she rested her tired body on the floor of the basement, unmoving as her adrenaline settled.

She did it—she had acquired a set of wings. Though they were broken, having them in her possession was a huge hurdle to overcome; an achievement that felt unattainable only a few hours ago. Her heart tugged between the ocean and the sky.

Maybe she could have it all.

Chapter 13

A whirring whoosh tore through her bedroom, whipping Emmeline's sleeping face. Her geared-heart stuttered as she lifted her head from the tattered balloon fabric. Eyes half open, vision fuzzy—how did she get here?

The doors to her bedroom balcony were open, and perched on the railing outside was the winged woman. Massive dragonfly wings spread wide and gently fluttering to keep her in place, she stared at Emmeline with her giant moon-shaped eyes.

Emmeline faltered, unsure if this was real.

She scanned the room, confused—last she remembered she was in the basement.

"Are you a dream?"

"Maybe I am." The woman's voice was so clear, so crisp, it reverberated with a slight echo.

"Do you have a name?" Emmeline asked.

"Luna."

"Why do you come to me in my sleep?"

"To study your undoing."

Emmeline stared at her blankly, hesitant to dissect the meaning of her words.

Luna explained, "It seems I am the only one who cares for your well-being."

"I am fine."

"You are far from fine."

"Why? Because I wish to fly?"

"Your quest to fly is a distraction from a more devious ailment."

Emmeline's heart raced. "You know about my headaches?"

"Starving the pain will not make it go away."

"Then how do I make it stop?"

"I'm trying to figure that out, too." Luna's wide silver eyes blinked with empathy. "The nature of our connection will destroy you, but it's also the only thing that can give you comfort. For now, anyway. I'm working on a solution."

"I don't understand."

"In time, you will. And I will be here to catch you when you fall."

"Why?"

"Because I'm not a monster."

Luna's attention darted toward the sky, seemingly drawn toward a sound only she could hear.

"I must go," she said.

"Wait, I need to know more."

"If you wish to save yourself, stay whole."

Luna chanted a familiar phrase — *Ad lunam* — and as Emmeline tried to decipher the rest of the foreign incantation, her heavy eyelids betrayed her and she succumbed to forced slumber.

"Get up!"

The words startled Emmeline awake.

She was in her bedroom, lying on top of the ratty balloon fabric — she had fallen asleep while sewing. Silver needle under her hand, she pressed herself upright.

She now remembered stumbling from the basement to her bedroom while half asleep.

Vision blurry, she saw the silhouette of a winged creature perched on her balcony railing.

"Luna?" she asked, rubbing her eyes.

"Do I look like a girl to you?" Solís scoffed, jumping off the railing and marching toward her. "Why do you have these?" he asked upon discovering the broken wings near the base of her bed. "I haven't seen a pair of golden wings since we first formed the Pyro-Argo Militia."

"I got them from the scrapyard in Terra."

"How?"

"Gemma helped me."

"Tinkies are no good. You can't trust them."

"I can trust her," Emmeline objected. "She is my friend. She saved my life."

"When?"

"Nautipunks raided the scrapyard and kidnapped the Terra guards. Gemma helped me get away."

"You wouldn't have been there in the first place if it wasn't for her!"

"I asked her to bring me there."

"For these wings? And that tattered balloon?"

Emmeline nodded.

"Why?" he asked.

"You know why."

"I told you I'd teach you. Why can't you be patient?"

"I need a distraction *now*. It's just a hobby."

Solis lifted the mangled metal wings off the floor.

"A dangerous hobby," he scoffed. "We stopped using gold to build our wings because they bend too easily. Plus, they're broken. You can't fly with these."

"Gemma is going to repair them."

Solís tossed the wings to the ground, then knelt beside his sister.

"Why?" he pleaded.

"Why not?" she argued.

"This isn't like you."

"There's nothing wrong with change."

"There sure is if it jeopardizes your life."

145

"Teach me how to fly, then. Show me how, and I won't have to teach myself."

"You need helium, and I only get what the Argopunks give me."

Emmeline's resolve did not falter.

Solís budged a little and added, "I can teach you the basics, though—how to latch the wings to your shoulder gears, the proper arm and shoulder motions, how to turn, raise, and drop."

"Thank you."

"But you won't be able to fly without the helium."

Emmeline smirked. "That's what the balloon is for."

"I don't understand."

"Quintessence is a protected pocket of oxygen within the burning solar shield. Heated air rises—it floats, just like helium."

"I see where you're going with this, and it won't work."

"Why not?"

"Our predecessors already tried this. Thermapunks searched for independence from the Aeropunks for centuries before conceding—it takes too much energy; it requires a level of control that we do not possess. No single Thermapunk has enough fire power to stay aloft for any significant amount of time."

"It's because we are too heavy."

"Maybe so," he agreed. "But there's nothing we can do about that."

"What happened to the Thermapunks who tried to fly?" she asked.

"The attempt drained them dry—their fire hearts were fully extinguished, and they plummeted to their death. After many great losses of noble Thermas, flying via fire was deemed too dangerous."

"It's not fair."

"Just like we don't share our fire, the Aeropunks don't share their helium. It's just the way it goes." He showed great understanding. "I'm sorry."

"I can still tinker with the wings. I can still repair this balloon. Look at how tall my ceiling is—I can still float in this room."

Solís glanced upward at the tall cathedral ceiling, then glanced down at his golden wristwatch. Attention returned to his sister, he offered, "I can take you on a quick ride. I have enough helium to loop around the house a few times before I have to be at training."

Emmeline shook her head. "I've flown with you before—I know what that's like. It's great, but it's not the same as flying alone. I wish you could just spare me a little of your helium."

"You know I can't. If the Aeropunks caught wind of me sharing their helium with an unauthorized Thermapunk, the alliance between gas and fire would be ruined. The fragile fate of our world lies in that treaty. We can't go back to the old ways."

"I get it," Emmeline replied, sulking.

"I don't know what got you on this kick, but don't let it break you. You have a lot to live for."

"My dreams are haunted," she revealed. "I don't know why, but I find myself questioning everything I once believed." Emmeline sighed. "I need a distraction."

"You need to get out of your head. Stop torturing yourself."

"I'm trying. Having a new hobby will help."

"Once you're full-time in Hydra, that'll be distraction enough."

Emmeline thought of Louie—she often forgot about her worries while in his presence.

"You might be right."

"Then your sixteenth soul day can't come soon enough. The sea has a way of setting punks straight. Dad used to bring me there whenever my fits of anger grew too large for Mom to handle. I always felt better afterwards."

"You haven't had an episode in a while."

"I'm a grown-up now," he said, his tone joking. "It was just kid rage."

"Seems I have teenage sorrow."

"We all have something. Just don't let it take over before you get a chance to grow out of it."

He leaned in and hugged her, sharing a brief moment of tenderness, before pressing his lips to her forehead and blowing a raspberry. The tickling, flatulence noise forced Emmeline out of her solemn mood. She pushed her brother away with a laugh.

"You're annoying."

"That's my job."

He stood and walked to the balcony. A glance over his shoulder revealed his concerned golden gaze.

"You've got this," he encouraged.

She nodded. "Thanks."

He jumped off the railing, gracefully twirling in a nosedive before lifting back up into the sky and pounding his wings as he charged toward the Pyro-Argo air base.

Emmeline heard every word Solís had said and knew his advice was wise. Still, seeing him soar away kept the idea of flying alive.

Desperate to think about anything other than her fear of marbles and monsters, she let her depraved thoughts spiral recklessly. She forgot about Louie momentarily and silenced her brother's sound advice—restriction and distractions were the only way to control all that currently unraveled around her.

"Emmeline! Hurry up!" Melora called out to her from downstairs.

Dressed in tight cargo pants with a plethora of pockets, a tight black tank top, and a leather bomber jacket, Emmeline snatched a piece of paper off her dresser and secured the sea stone into her thigh pocket before racing downstairs.

"Nice to *not* see your legs today," Melora remarked, handing Emmeline a bowl of golden marbles. "Though a long skirt would be more ladylike."

Emmeline swiftly handed the bowl back.

"I only eat clay marbles now," she explained.

"Since when?"

"Since I realized they are natural and healthier, not to mention significantly lighter."

"Preposterous. I go to great lengths to feed you and your brothers the best of the best."

"Then stop going to such lengths and just feed us normal marbles. I bet they're cheaper, too."

She handed her mother the paper she grabbed from her room.

"What's this?" her mother asked.

"My guest list for my party."

Melora lowered her reading glasses and read the list out loud.

"Louie, Gemma, Avery—who are these people?"

"My friends."

"From where?"

"Louie lives in Hydra, Gemma lives in Terra, and you know Avery—she's Dad's Pilopunk."

Melora scoffed. "I am only sending invites to Thermapunks."

"Then I'm not going."

"Yes, you are. It's your party."

"I already told you that I don't want a party."

"I told your father that you needed to continue etiquette school! Look at what you're becoming."

"Independent?"

"No. Insolent!"

"Compliance is for the weak, Mother. You asked for a list, and I gave you one. It's not my fault you don't like who I chose."

"Well, it's impossible, anyway. Hydropunks can't leave Hydra, Terrapunks can't leave Terra. I suppose I can see about the Pilopunk." She huffed and left the room, clutching the list so tightly it ripped.

Emmeline took a swig of grease from the communal jug before darting out the door.

The less she ate, the more in control she felt—she was the master of her migraines. The tightening pull of her stomach indicated victory; the slowing churn of her gears meant success. Energy elevated temporarily by her current high, Emmeline raced down the maze of golden staircases attached to the side of the house, which landed her on the hangar bay. She leapt off the final step, landing in a dramatic crouch next to Avery's helium balloon.

"Someone's ready to be a hero today," Avery remarked, a slight grin on her face as she oiled the many levers and checked every bolt and screw.

"I'm just feeling accomplished."

"Oh yeah?"

"I am taking back control. I am starving my fears."

"Good," Avery declared. "Fear is a hinderance. Monsters can smell it, and they'll use it to their advantage."

"I also gave some thought to what you told me."

"And?"

"It might be exactly the information I needed."

Avery stopped tinkering to face Emmeline. Her expression was stern.

"You understand the danger involved, right?"

"Solís reminded me this morning."

"I only told you that nugget of info so you could feel what it's like to levitate, not to inspire a quest to fly."

"But what if I could do both?"

"Years of well-documented failed attempts should be enough to show you that it's not possible."

"You might be right, but I got myself a balloon anyhow. Don't worry, I just want to float."

"Okay, but do it someplace where you won't fall far. No Thermapunk has ever lasted more than ten minutes."

"Ten minutes is plenty."

"Aim for five—the eight-to-ten-minute range was where it always turned lethal. Most fell from the sky, but others overheated and combusted. I saw images. It was gruesome."

Emmeline tightened her lips, expression annoyed. "Solís didn't mention combustion."

"He probably doesn't know. The archives are old and mostly forgotten about—no Thermapunk, except you, has any interest in trying this deadly experiment again."

Emmeline was eager to maintain her high. "Anyway, did they ever catch that hellion?"

"No, and we're no closer to discovering *how* it escaped."

"Maybe it's better that it's gone. It probably went home to its moon," Emmeline replied, shushing the worry that she was somehow to blame for its escape. "If the hunt has been paused, what's on deck for the day?"

"Your father wants to attach a second fire tether to the Pyro-Argo air base. You will get to see more of Hydra today."

Emmeline gulped. "Will we be going to the Rove?"

"Yeah—Smuggler's Rove. That's where we barter and trade with the *other* Nautipunks." Avery shuddered. "They're awful. Nothing like the ones you've met so far."

"I got a little preview yesterday at the scrapyard."

"Why were you there?"

"Hunting for treasure."

Avery clicked her tongue. "You can't trust the Terrapunks."

"So I've been told," Emmeline grumbled.

"Seriously. Their desire for fire is almost as bad as the moon monsters'."

"The Tinkie I know is generous and thoughtful. She has no interest in fire."

"Give it time."

Montgomery came crashing outside, arms filled with scrolled maps and blueprints. He tossed them into Avery's basket.

"I'm riding with you today," he declared, his energy frazzled. "Melora needs Regis to bring her to the market. She's in party planning mode."

"I told her I don't want a party," Emmeline griped.

"Melora's resolve cannot be swayed."

Emmeline turned to Avery. "You're invited."

"I am?"

"Yes, and I hope you can make it."

"I guess it depends if I'm needed in Hydra."

Avery looked to Montgomery, who took a deep breath before expressing remorse.

"Unfortunately," he said, "starting today, we will need to stay full-time in Hydra again. The construction of this fire tether needs to be monitored daily. I'm sorry."

"Sorry," Avery said to Emmeline. "I appreciate you including me."

Emmeline huffed. "Maybe I'll skip the party, too. There won't be anyone there that I want to see."

"All your old classmates will be there," Montgomery said. "And your teachers."

"Great. Ms. Rickard can scold me on how badly my manners have regressed. Sounds like a fantastic way to spend my soul day."

"It's one afternoon. Get through that, and then you'll be with me in Hydra more frequently."

"Do you want to steer us to Hydra?" Avery asked.

"Sure," Emmeline conceded, her mood swaying dramatically between great highs and devastating lows. Energy rapidly waning, she felt the crash coming. She had to regulate herself; she needed to find a steady balance. She took a clay marble out of her pocket and swallowed it, deciding her restriction would be delegated methodically.

The gears in her gut stopped their aching churn and began to move with greater ease. There was a shift, as if her body was starting to recognize this new routine. Her gears reorganized and shrank to accommodate the lack of fuel.

Emmeline doubled over as they rearranged.

"Are you okay?" Avery asked.

Determined to keep her secret, Emmeline stood tall despite the pain and nodded.

"Just a cramp," she answered, before grabbing the steering crank and guiding them to Hydra. Montgomery's ship was hooked to the ceiling, docked out of reach where no Nautipunk could raid the vessel for its cargo. The helium tanks aboard were empty, meaning the boat would not float once detached. Avery docked the balloon onto the special landing pad atop the tallest deck and got to work filling the tanks.

"Will it deplete her?" Emmeline asked her father as she mentally counted the surplus of tanks needing helium.

"No," he answered, "as long as she paces herself. Aeropunks replenish their gas faster than we can replenish our fire."

"I heard the plan is to build a second fire tether to the Pyro-Argo air base?"

"Correct. The moon monsters have been arriving with more frequency, and your brothers informed me that all the Pyropunks need extra help recharging between battles."

Emmeline scanned the watery world of Hydra. As far as she could see, giant tethers made of braided gold extended from the sea and pierced through the ceiling of pipes and gears. They exited Hydra into Terra between rows of terra gears and sourced fire to the Thermapunks in Fyree. Fire from the source flame coursed through the massive cords. One of these tethers attached to her family home, though she had no clue which one.

Montgomery continued, "It will be good for you to help oversee this project, as the tethers are a big part of our responsibility."

"Who builds them?"

"The Nautipunks, in exchange for firestones."

"All done," Avery announced.

"Thank you," Montgomery replied. "Now, rest and recharge. I can steer us to Smuggler's Rove."

Avery happily obliged, retreating into an empty cabin.

"Where is the crew?" Emmeline asked.

"I sent them to investigate a monster sighting south of Smuggler's Rove. They will return tomorrow."

Emmeline walked to the deck railing, leaned into it, and extended her arms. Eyes closed, she let the salty sea air whip through her hair and a calm surge of tranquility coursed through her. Despite all that had transpired here, she felt overwhelming peace. Hydra felt like home.

Maybe this is enough, she thought.

When she opened her eyes, they were hover-sailing at high speeds, farther into Hydra than she had ever traveled before.

Smuggler's Rove came into view.

Stacked huts made of steel planks were precariously perched atop a massive floating raft. The towering columns of homes reached varying heights—there was no uniform construction or order in their design. Ladders and pulley systems decorated the piled huts, and Hydropunks traversed up and down, coming and going with purpose. Between the dilapidated and salt-whipped pillars was a maze of roads lined with vendors selling goods. At the edge of this pirate sanctuary, flanked by the massive village and the various jutted piers, were Hydropunks hawking their merchandise.

At the center of it all was a giant zinc pipe that extended into Terra above. Not only did it serve as a trading port between Hydra and Terra, but it also held the Rove in place, preventing it from floating away.

As Montgomery steered the ship closer, Emmeline noticed that much of the goods being sold along the coast were devious in nature: vials of petroleum, surely farmed from the captured Terrapunks, quartered sheets of dragonfly wing membrane, jewelry made of monster fangs and claws. One booth had a sign that read, *Gaseous Potions.*

"They have access to Aeropunk gas?" Emmeline asked, appalled.

"They're not supposed to," Montgomery replied, his tone irritated. "I'll have to send a team to sweep the market. Another task we're responsible for, I've just been so busy. I let it fall by the wayside."

The Rove at this distance was vibrant with life— Emmeline examined this strange place with wonder. Closer to the piers, they passed countless Nautipunk ships anchored offshore.

Arrival of Montgomery's airship stirred the resting pirates to their feet.

"Ahoy, there, Mr. Flamekeeper," one bellowed from a ship adorned with silver Terrapunk gears. They shimmered in the strobing light source beneath the water.

"Yo ho ho! Fire booty!" shouted another swinging from a mast made of monster skulls.

A pirate on a boat with three giant steam stacks called out to Montgomery, "I got me ship ready! Hire me fer whatever job ye got!"

Emmeline looked to her father. "Who will you hire?"

"There's only one man for this job," he replied, gaze focused on a man-of-war ten clicks to the east. Half of the crew was mopping slick crude oil off the upper deck, while the other half was funneling the thick dark-brown liquid through shafts and into a compartment hidden below deck. Copper pipes snaked around the ship's structure, feeding the engine.

"Monty, boy!" the captain of this gnarly man-of-war greeted.

"Captain Cuda Ray," Montgomery replied, keeping it curt.

The Nautipunk shifted his sights to Emmeline. A long diagonal scar crossed his face and his icy blue stare pierced through her, forcing her to shiver.

As she reached into her pocket, gripping her sea stone for courage, the intimidating man winked in her direction.

Shadows cushioned her view, muffling her fear.

This was the same Nautipunk who had led the raid in Terra.

Chapter 14

"I recognize you," he barked. "I almost had ye as me new fire source."

"What is he talking about?" Montgomery whispered to Emmeline.

"I met him in the Terrapunk scrapyard," she explained.

"What were you doing there?" He was no longer whispering.

"It's a long story."

Cuda Ray went on, "Imagine the possibilities with a Thermapunk as part of me crew."

"You mean, as your prisoner," Emmeline retorted, her courage fierce.

The captain laughed, his deep bellowing guffaws echoed menacingly. They held no joy, no humor.

His crew tensed—Emmeline had struck a nerve.

"You call 'em prisoners, I call 'em friends. Together, we're bridging the gap between our worlds."

"Until you drain them dry."

Cuda Ray did not feign laughter this time. His furious gaze shifted to Montgomery.

"Who is this insolent child?"

"My daughter; your new boss."

Cuda Ray spat. "Not on my watch."

"Then we will find another captain and crew for the tether work."

"Them swabs can't do the job as well as me."

"They'll figure it out." Montgomery turned the wheel of his ship, shifting their direction.

"I'll strike me stanch if ye pay me double," Cuda Ray bellowed.

"I'm not paying you a penny more!"

"Turn around, ye old seadog."

"If you can't respect my daughter, we will take our business elsewhere."

"It was something of a butt," Cuda Ray insisted. "I'll work fer ye and yer daughter!"

Montgomery spoke softly to Emmeline as he turned the wheel. "You cannot trust him. Ever."

"Then why are we turning back?"

"Because he is the best tether weaver in Hydra."

Emmeline glared down at Cuda Ray, who grinned up at her with his gap-toothed smile. In between his few remaining zinc teeth was a combination of black obsidian, seashells, sea glass, and metal scraps drilled into his jaw — a poor attempt to fill the holes.

His long brown hair was knotted into braids and decorated with beads and monster fangs. A deep diagonal scar ran across his face and down his neck, disappearing beneath his monster-hide vest. Eyes a soul-crushing blue, his gaze pierced Emmeline's.

She looked away, afraid that he could see into her soul.

Impossible, she thought. Still, she felt violated.

She scanned the other boats anchored at sea. There was only one she wished to find.

"Where does Red Fang Ralph take his ship when he's not working with us?" Emmeline asked her father.

"He should be down there somewhere."

Emmeline looked again.

"He's not."

"Then they're likely at the Detention Center."

"Will you call on them to help with the tether?"

"Absolutely not. For one, Ralph cannot be trusted with anything technical. His expertise is with the monsters, nothing else. In fact, he has been known to ruin every project he gets involved in that isn't monster-related. Secondly, Nautipunk captains don't take kindly to other Nautipunk captains. Crew members come and go, but there is a volatile rivalry among the captains in Hydra. They don't play nicely together."

"I see."

"It's not worth the headache, or the bloodshed. As an overseer of Hydra, save yourself the drama by picking one captain and crew per project."

"Noted."

Emmeline just wanted to see Louie.

Hand in her pocket, comfort from the sea stone would have to suffice.

"Aye! Emmie!" a voice shouted from below.

No one had ever called her that before.

Emmeline leaned over the rail.

Louie was standing on a ship she did not recognize.

"What are you doing? Where's Red Fang Ralph?"

"He only hires me when he needs divers," Louie replied. "So I freelance in between. Throw me a rope."

Panicked excitement propelled Emmeline to search for a rope ladder. Underneath a pile of old sails, she found a rope wound tightly to a spool. It wasn't a ladder, but it would have to do. She knotted one end to the railing and threw the other overboard.

Louie gave his end a firm tug to check the anchor knot before beginning his climb. As he ascended, his temporary crewmates protested. Their angry grumblings caught the attention of their captain, who jogged with his peg leg to the spot of Louie's escape.

"No prey, no pay!" he shouted up at Louie.

"Fair enough."

"I'll never hire ye again!"

"See ya never, then, Stubbs!"

"That's not me name!"

Louie reached the top rail and launched his body over gracefully, landing on both feet. He pulled the rope back to the deck and never looked back.

"This be why I hate swashbucklers," the captain shouted, then spat.

"Thanks," Louie said to Emmeline. "Captain Allen Peggs is a cheap bastard. Offered me two firestones for a five-day diving expedition. Red Fang Ralph pays me five stones *per dive*."

"Oh. I don't have any firestones to pay you. My dad might, though."

Louie slapped his forehead. "Sorry, that wasn't what I meant. Happy to be here for free."

"Are you sure?"

"Absolutely. So tell me, what's on the agenda?"

"My father just contracted Cuda Ray for a tether job."

Louie's silver-blue eyes widened. "Ol' Captain Croctopus, huh?"

"Who?"

"That's what we call him when he's out of earshot. He's a real devil, that one. He snatches punks from the upper world and farms them for their resources."

"I was almost one of his farm animals."

"What? How?"

"I was in the scrapyard when he did his last raid. I'm not happy that we're working with him now, but my dad insisted. When I'm in charge, Cuda Ray won't be my go-to tether guy."

Louie smirked. "Careful, now. There are reasons to work with the lowliest Nautipunks. Your father tried blackballing Croctopus once, and in response, Croctopus

161

plundered and pillaged every ship your father contracted after. He even set one of the moon monsters free. It was chaos down here till your father created a treaty with him."

"I didn't think it was possible for me to hate him more."

"He's a plague, for sure. His ship is the only one I won't work for."

"Understandably."

"Yes, well, Cuda Ray can't see me when we get to the job site. He has a hit out on me."

"A hit?"

"Yeah. He wants me dead."

"All for saying no to him?"

"That," Louie said, unable to hide his grin, "and because I'm a menace to his farming operation. I've been known to free a punk in my spare time."

"I didn't think it was possible for me to like you more," Emmeline gushed, not realizing what she was admitting till it had already left her lips. She immediately covered her mouth.

Louie's bright eyes shimmered with charm. "Ah, ha! So you do fancy me. I was wondering."

He stepped closer and reached his arm around her shoulder, which Emmeline ducked under.

"Don't get ahead of yourself there, bucko. I'm still the boss around here."

"I wouldn't have it any other way."

Smiling ear to ear, her father's disapproving voice startled her from her revelry.

"What is *he* doing here?" Montgomery barked.

"He's here to help," Emmeline replied.

"No." Montgomery groaned. "No, no, no. He belongs below."

162

"I won't cause you any trouble. I swear."

"You being here is trouble enough. I know about Cuda Ray's hitlist, and I know that you're on it. I don't need that kind of trouble on my ship."

Louie glanced overboard — they were over open seas now. "There's nowhere for me to go."

Montgomery grunted. "Stay out of sight."

"I will."

Montgomery marched away.

Louie raised his brows and made a half-apologetic cringe smile at Emmeline, to which she laughed.

"You're gonna get *me* in trouble," she teased.

"Never! I'll behave. I promise."

The ship flew onward, crossing the vast sea and passing many established tethers along the way. They sizzled loudly, searing the salty air around them.

Louie took Emmeline's hand and pressed it to his heart, then lowered it to the railing, keeping it firmly in his grip. She glanced up at him, a small, curious smile on her face. He looked down at her briefly, his smile matching hers, and then refocused on the horizon. His fingers wrapped between hers, and he held on like he'd never let go.

"Almost there," Montgomery shouted from the helm, which was out of sight from where they stood. He peered around his wheel, frowned upon seeing their intertwined hands, and added, "Don't make me wish I threw you overboard!"

Louie let go of Emmeline's hand.

"He would never," she said.

"I know. Time to hide." He winked, then ducked behind a pile of steel crates. From here, he was out of sight but still within earshot.

Avery emerged from the cabin where she had napped looking refreshed and ready to work.

"Teach Emmeline how to drop an anchor," Montgomery requested of her.

Avery waved Emmeline over to the spooled chain-link rope.

On Montgomery's command, when the ship came to a solid stop next to the existing tether attached to the Pyro-Argo air base, he gave the order.

"Now!"

Avery turned the crank-handle clockwise and the anchor lowered. It fell through the air before submerging into the sea.

"Always drop it at a slow and steady pace," Avery explained.

"Got it," Emmeline replied, taking mental notes of the relatively easy task.

Once the chain showed slack, Avery turned the crank counter-clockwise till it pulled tight.

"We're secured," she announced to Montgomery.

He double-checked his calculations on his map before jumping off the wheelbox, then marched to the starboard and shouted down to the pirate ship below.

"Cuda Ray! The tether will rise into the sky one nautical mile from my starboard." A closer look revealed a wobbling man dressed in diving gear walking the plank of Cuda Ray's ship.

"I haven't given you full instructions yet," Montgomery objected.

"Oh, this here diver ain't fit to work fer ye."

"Why not?"

"He is three sheets to the wind."

"Excuse me?"

"He's loaded to the gunnels. A useless carouser, he is. This is his third strike. He can drown for all I care."

"Do you have another diver on board?"

"I do not," Cuda Ray replied, prodding the drunk diver in the back with a pike.

"You won't get paid till the job is started," Montgomery warned.

"I heard yer crew has a diver." His icy glare was murderous.

"My crew is on the other side of Hydra investigating a monster sighting. They'll return tomorrow."

Cuda Ray clicked his tongue. "Did ye think I'd not notice the boy climbing aboard yer ship? Allen Peggs declared the scoundrel's betrayal loud enough for the gods to hear."

"I did not know he was on my boat until we were out to sea."

"He's known to run a rig, that one. Works out for us both, though. He can do the dive."

"Dad," Emmeline urged. "He will kill Louie."

Montgomery heeded his daughter's warning.

"If you kill him, you will answer to me."

"What're ye gunna do?" Cuda Ray mocked. "You tried ter blackball me once, to no avail."

"This time, I won't play nice. It will be death that you face—a life for a life."

"I'm curious ter know how ye'd pull that off."

"Ever since your last stunt, I started recruiting my own Nautipunk hitmen. They work in disguise—some could be hidden among your crew—there would be no way for you to know till their sword was pressed against your neck."

Cuda Ray spat as he scanned his crew, then smirked, returning his gaze to Montgomery. "Blimey, yer no lily-liver." He spat, a thick loogie landed on the boot of the pirate beside him. "I'll let the lad live this time."

"Louie," Montgomery shouted, to which Louie stood from his hiding place. Montgomery gave him a scowl. "Looks like you'll be working for me after all."

"Sorry," he replied sheepishly.

"It's fine. I suspect you're a far better diver than whoever Cuda Ray had hired."

"I am. Pippin Picklefish, the diver Croctopus—er—Cuda Ray has walking the plank, is the worst. He's always plastered."

A loud splash, followed by a cheer, turned their attention.

Pippin had fallen into the sea. Dressed in his diving suit, he floated away with the tide, too inebriated to swim.

"That's a shame," Montgomery commented.

"Eh, you'll likely see him again. He's been marooned like this before—he always finds his way back to a Rove. It's impressive, really."

"A strange lot, you all are." Montgomery shook his head, yanked a scrolled map from his back pocket, and unfolded it on top of a metal crate. "My only concern is the success of this mission. Have you ever been on a tether job before?"

"Yes, as an apprentice." Though his expression remained stoic, his voice quivered. "I shadowed Sub Anne Marie."

Montgomery raised his brow. "She was the best—the majority of tethers in Hydra were created with her help."

"It's why I refuse to work for Cuda Ray." Louie's eyes welled with angry tears. "He is the reason she is dead."

166

"You operate with honor—I respect that. You're going to have to be alert down there, though. His promises are worth nothing."

"I know. Who will be diving with me?"

"Emmeline and I. She will observe."

Boats anchored, they prepared to spend the night at sea.

The excitement was thrilling—Emmeline had never spent a night in Hydra. It was the perfect distraction from everything that plagued her above ... until they gathered around the gallipot to eat. A plethora of shimmering sea glass marbles awaited consumption, and Emmeline felt a sickening pressure to engage despite every nerve in her body begging her to refuse.

Montgomery held out his hands, and the four punks linked into a circle to share grace.

"Primordial gods," Montgomery began, "we thank you for your many blessings. Marlodon, for safe passage across the sea. Matrigaia, for the gift of life. Incarna, for delivering our souls. And above all, Solédon, our leader. To thee, we are obliged."

"Our gratitude is transferred," Emmeline, Avery, and Louie replied in unison.

"We feast at the mercy of our gods."

"May we feast in their glory."

"Assent."

Montgomery concluded the prayer, "Assent."

Everyone except Emmeline dug into the gallipot of rounded sea glass. Terrified of ruining her night by consuming too many marbles and enabling the migraine to return, Emmeline picked one from the pot and placed it into her mouth. She let it sit there for a minute before allowing it to roll down her throat.

167

The longer she stalled, the more the others gobbled up the remaining marbles. No one was paying much attention to her reluctant consumption.

"Did you have enough?" Louie asked when there were only four marbles left.

"I'll have another," she assuaged him.

"The blue ones are a little sweeter than the rest."

She lifted a blue sea glass marble and placed it onto her tongue. Her eyes widened in delight.

Louie continued, "Not sure why they have a sweet flavor, but they're my favorite."

Emmeline let the sweetness linger before swallowing the marble. The ringing in her head was faint, but present. She closed her eyes, willing the noise away.

Avery cleaned up the pot and Montgomery left the circle to check the ship's anchor.

Louie disappeared into a nearby cabin and returned with pillows and blankets to set up camp beneath the vast sky. The ceiling of Hydra was made of crisscrossing steel pipes, and through them, light from the solar shield above beamed through. As the day faded, the nocturnal shield activated and the light within Hydra faded. Night was much darker here. Twinkling light filtered through the pipes, shimmering like stars. They reflected in Louie's eyes like mirrors.

"It's peaceful down here," Emmeline said.

"Tonight, it is." His voice was calm. "I've never spent a night away from other Nautipunks. Whether it be on a Rove or aboard a ship, my nights are often plagued with snoring, farting, and drunken debauchery." He sighed, taking in the silence. "This is nice."

"You aren't much like the others," Emmeline noted.

He grinned. "I'll take that as a compliment."

168

"You don't speak like them, and you don't seem to think like them."

"I have my mother to thank for that. She wasn't like the others, either."

"Where is she now?"

"She's dead. Cuda Ray killed her."

Emmeline's heart sank as she recalled his conversation with her father.

"Sub Anne Marie?" she asked.

He nodded. "She taught me everything I know."

"I'm thankful for her too, then. I'm glad there is someone down here I can trust."

Louie turned to Emmeline, eyes blazing with enchantment.

Montgomery's booming voice interrupted the moment.

"If you insist on sleeping out here, so will we."

He set up a bed beside Louie, and Avery made herself comfortable on the other side of Emmeline. She glanced over and mouthed the word *sorry*.

Louie reached beneath the blankets and grabbed Emmeline's hand, and like that, they fell asleep.

For the night, with Louie consuming her sleeping thoughts, Emmeline was safe from the monsters that lived in her dreams.

Chapter 15

The sound of quarrelling served as a morning alarm.

Emmeline rubbed her eyes to find herself alone under a pile of blankets.

"What's going on?" she asked between yawns.

Montgomery, Avery, and Louie stood at the edge of the deck, observing the argument happening below.

"Come," Montgomery urged. "This is a great lesson in politics."

The early morning air was cold, so Emmeline wrapped herself in a blanket and waddled over. To her horror, she saw Gemma aboard Cuda Ray's ship.

Descended like puppets on strings, a crew of Terrapunks had entered Hydra from above and were accosting Cuda Ray.

"That's my friend, Gemma," Emmeline whispered to Louie.

"Looks like Gemma got herself into a pickle."

"What's going on?" she asked.

Louie replied, "The leaders of Terra are here to save their people."

Emmeline recognized the Stoneheads, but the other Terrapunks were unfamiliar. They were shorter, stockier, and stern. Their appearance was immaculate—no scars or tattered clothing—and they each wore leather gas masks.

"Are those the Horrigans?" she asked.

"The Terras wearing gas masks? Yes. Torsten Horrigan is the one gripping your friend by the neck. He is the patriarch."

The scene unfolded before them.

"Is this him?" Torsten demanded.

Gemma nodded. "Yes. He's the one that raided the scrapyard."

He let her go, then took a step closer to the menacing pirate. Though he was shorter than Cuda Ray, his confident energy was just as fearsome.

"Return my Terra guards, and we will go."

"I dunno what yer talkin' about," Cuda Ray replied.

"I can smell them," Torsten said with a growl. "Your ship reeks of petroleum."

"The evidence is everywhere," another Horrigan asserted, pointing at the fossil fuel stains all over the ship deck.

"Wish I could help, but ya see, I'm contracted to help that there Therma," he pointed to Montgomery's ship in the sky, "and I got to be gettin' back ter me job."

In unison, the Terrapunks snapped their attention toward Montgomery.

"I have nothing to do with whatever issue you have with him," Montgomery assured them, hands lifted to imply his innocence. "Do with him as you wish."

Torsten stepped forward. "Help us. Give us fire."

"You know I cannot do that."

The Terrapunks retracted upward on their puppet strings, ricocheting onto Montgomery's boat. Gemma was now in the clutches of a Stonehead and avoided making eye contact with Emmeline.

"Monty boy," Cuda Ray shouted from below. "Don't you dare betray me!"

"Use your fire to force his hand," Torsten insisted of Montgomery.

"Cuda Ray is under the protection of my employ ... for now. My detest for him is as potent as yours, but I need him."

"How would you feel if he was kidnapping and farming Thermapunks? You'd do something then!"

"You're going about it all wrong," Louie said, stepping into the conversation.

"Excuse me?" Torsten barked. He ran his geared fingers through his greasy hair and crouched like he was ready to pounce. His brothers and cousins mimicked him. The group of Terrapunks were on the defense.

Montgomery shot a cautionary glare, but Louie continued, "I've saved many of your people over the years. You have to free them from below."

"Lies."

Louie's brow furrowed. "They've never mentioned me? I'm offended."

"It's true," Gemma said, her voice a mere squeak.

"What did you say?" Torsten asked.

"It's true."

"Speak up!"

The Stonehead pushed her forward and she was forced to address the crowd.

"Freed Terras don't often come forward after being rescued … they fear the ridicule. But everyone in the market knows who they are, and they always return with water damage. I've repaired quite a few waterlogged Terra guards myself, and they all told me they were saved by a pirate."

Torsten's furious gaze returned to Louie, who wore a look of smug delight.

"So tell me then, how do I save my people?"

"Can you swim?" he asked.

"No."

"Didn't think so. You should hire me."

Torsten's chrome glare was murderous. "Hire?"

"I mean, I normally do it for free, but since I have the prestigious Horrigan family here, I might as well ask for compensation this time."

Torsten grumbled with fury. "Name your price."

Louie looked at Gemma, who trembled in the clutches of a Stonehead, then over to Emmeline, who hadn't taken her worried eyes off her friend.

"That girl in your charge. When you get back to Terra, set her free."

Gemma looked up at him, eyes bright with greasy black tears.

"She is a prisoner," Torsten objected. "She continually interacts with outsiders without submitting activity reports. This recent indiscretion was her third strike."

"Set her free, and I will free the Terrapunk hostages."

"Who is she to you?" Torsten inquired.

"I have no idea who she is, but I can tell she isn't a menace. Let her live."

"Fine," Torsten agreed, though his conviction wavered. "Free the hostages, then I'll free the girl."

"No. I will free the hostages *after* you free the girl."

Torsten's eyes blazed with rage. He turned to his family members, and in a tight huddle they deliberated the ultimatum. When Torsten turned back around, his demeanor had relaxed.

"Deal." He held out his hand, then added, "The captured guards are worth more to us than her."

Gemma's smile beamed.

Louie stepped forward and shook Torsten's hand.

"Fantastic," Montgomery interjected. "Glad we came to a resolution. Now, you'll need to leave in a furious hurry. Cuda Ray has to believe that we refused to help you."

"Fair enough," Torsten agreed. "Let's go."

With a quick fist to their chests, they leapt off the floating ship and rocketed into the sky. Their angry banter echoed across Hydra as they disappeared into the cracks of light above. Torsten lingered a moment to address Cuda Ray.

"You and your comrades are an enemy to Terra. We will be back with reinforcements."

He then slammed his fist against his plated-chest armor, and the cable within his backpack recoiled. He sprang into the air and disappeared.

"Delightful family," Louie joked.

Montgomery guffawed. "Real charmers. Why didn't you ask for real payment?"

"Seemed more important to help that girl."

Emmeline grabbed Louie's hand and squeezed it.

Before Montgomery noticed, she let go.

Her father nodded, deep in thought, as he leaned over the rail.

"I put my neck on the line for you," he shouted down to Cuda Ray. "You better not have stowaway Terrapunks."

"Are ye really afeared of those wee little punks?"

"Those wee little punks have nuclear hearts. You push them too far and we all go *kaboom*."

"Only if they get their grimy little hands on yer fire," Cuda Ray remarked.

Montgomery stepped away from the railing and spoke to the gods.

"Solédon, I implore You, grant me patience."

Emmeline looked up at the sky and wondered if the gods could hear them; she wondered if they even cared.

The solar flares peeking through the pipes above pulsated—a sign, or a fluke?

Lately, she found more comfort within the sea stone than from the gods.

"Do you pray?" she asked Louie.

"Sometimes. Marlodon, god of the seas, never answers, but He serves me with blessings daily. I thank Him often."

Emmeline nodded. "I used to pray to Solédon a lot."

"Why did you stop?"

"I felt like He wasn't listening."

Louie's expression showed compassion. "Why do I sense you're a different person when you're up there?"

Emmeline's heart contracted—his observation was jarring.

She replied, "Because I am."

"I don't know who you are up there, but I like who you are when you're down here with me."

"I like who I am with you, too," she confessed.

She had completely forgotten about the stone. It sat heavy in her pocket, always there with her, but she had no desire to use it for comfort. She did not need it, not while Louie was nearby.

"Emmeline," her father interrupted her thoughts. "I wanted you to see the start of this project, but you have to head back."

"Why?"

"The situation has become more dangerous than I anticipated."

"So what? I need to learn, don't I?"

"Yes, but not so close to your party. Your mother is already stressed and it would be better if you were home to help her get the house ready."

Louie added, "You also need to make sure they let your friend go. Once I have confirmation from you, I can begin my quest to free the Terrapunks held captive by Captain Croctopus."

Montgomery chuckled. "Croctopus?"

"Oh—er—Cuda Ray."

"No, no. Croctopus is more fitting." Montgomery looked to Emmeline. "He is right. One of your brothers can escort you to Terra where you can check on the girl."

Avery was atop the balloon deck, fussing with the many gears and levers in preparation to take flight.

The dread of returning home was potent—Louie was right; Emmeline wasn't as brave or clearheaded outside of Hydra. She was haunted by visions of monsters, plagued by thoughts of elsewhere, desperate to achieve some sense of control. Above Hydra, everything felt confusing and the dizzying nature of her decaying mind was unmanageable.

"Soon, I will live here full time," she said, mostly to herself, but her father and Louie heard her.

Montgomery's pride swelled. "I eagerly await the day!"

"Me too," Louie whispered as Montgomery marched happily back to the wheel.

"Ready to fly!" Avery announced, standing up from her workspace, covered in black grease.

Emmeline climbed aboard and Avery initiated liftoff.

Louie kept his eyes on Emmeline as she floated away. She tried to smile, but felt the tangible pull of her happiness fading.

She had terrors to face, and she was beginning to realize that the greatest of them all lived inside her mind.

Chapter 16

Everything felt different the moment they crossed through the gates of Hydra.

Montgomery secured the lock behind them, and Emmeline experienced a tidal wave of despair. She was living two lives: one of healthy growth and excitement within Hydra, and another plagued by a crippling obsession with control outside of Hydra. It was the noise in her head, it was the monsters in her dreams—her harrowing desperation to escape these things affected her most when she was alone with her thoughts.

Avery was with her now, but soon, she'd be on her own again.

She reached into her pocket and squeezed the sea stone, hoping to transfer her nervousness, wishing to escape the impending dread. It did not help. Those feelings remained, veiled in a haze of shadows.

"Are you getting out or not?" Avery asked.

Emmeline shook her head, clearing her vision, to find she was home.

"Any chance you can give me a ride to Terra?"

"I need to get back to your father."

"You can just drop me off. I'll find my own way home."

"Fine, but we have to go now."

"Give me three minutes. I need to get something from inside."

Emmeline raced into the house, barging through the kitchen where her mother was sipping grease-tea with Ms. Rickard.

"Emmeline!" her mother shouted. "Where are your manners?"

"There's no time," Emmeline answered between breaths as she darted out of the room and up the stairs. Her gears worked overtime to keep up with her rapidly draining energy. She tossed a clay marble into her mouth, feeding the hungry machine just enough to keep it working. The gears creaked as they shifted in size again, shrinking in order to accommodate the lack of marbles—smaller gears were easier to move with less rolling weight.

Emmeline clutched her belly as the shift occurred.

Every searing twinge reminded her that she was in control.

Progress was painful, but if her stomach was empty, perhaps her tormented mind would mimic the silence.

She raced into Cyrus's room first to snatch a handful of cold firestones from his stash. She tossed them into one of her oversized cargo-pant pockets and sprinted toward her own bedroom. There, she grabbed the broken golden wings off the floor, strapped them to her back, and took an alternate route back to the hangar bay. The golden stairs outside her balcony zigzagged down the side of the house. As she passed the kitchen window, she heard her mother and Ms. Rickard discussing her rude entry.

"She needs to return to class," Ms. Rickard urged.

"I know. I'm trying."

"She's smaller in size, too."

"Is she?"

"Perhaps you see her too often to notice."

Melora did not reply.

Emmeline cringed, aware now that her mother would be on her case after hearing Ms. Rickard say she looked unhealthy.

She kept running down the steps, deciding to deal with this potential conflict later.

"Two minutes and thirty seconds," Avery announced while watching her wristwatch.

"Told you I only needed three," Emmeline declared as she threw her body over the side of the carrier basket. She landed on the wicker floor, out of breath.

"Wings?" Avery asked.

"Yeah. Gemma promised to help me fix them."

"If this quest to fly ends up killing you ..."

"I'm not going to die. It's just something to pass the time till I'm in Hydra more often." Emmeline looked at Avery, expression pleading. "That house is a prison."

Avery groaned. "If I find out you've done anything stupid, I'll take those wings and break them myself."

"Deal."

Avery initiated their trip to Terra. Inhaling helium from the balloon, the basket lowered. Emmeline took charge of the pedal, guiding them forward as she scanned the world of Terra from above.

"Do you know where she'd be?" Avery asked.

"I'm not sure. Every time we've crossed paths it was accidental. She was planning on buying a spot at the market."

"There are countless Tinker markets," Avery griped.

"She wouldn't have gone far. She knew I was coming to see her again. Last time we spoke she mentioned Sector 3."

"Sector 3 is northwest," Avery informed her.

A quick glance at her compass and Emmeline navigated them there; it was the nearest market. As they hovered overhead, hundreds of Tinkies turned their gazes upward to assess their visitor.

"Get out of our skies," one shouted up at them.

"Shoot 'em down," another yelled, though his threat was followed by a chorus of laughter.

179

Avery asked, "Do you see her?"

"Not yet. Will they really try to shoot us out of the sky?"

"No. The peace treaty between gas and minerals forbids it, though I'm sure they'd love to." Avery was agitated. "I told you … Tinkies are rotten scoundrels."

"Gemma really isn't like the rest."

"If you say so."

Emmeline spotted a freshly painted sign wedged between an oil pump and a potion dealer.

It read: *ThingaMaGems*

Inside the booth was Gemma, tinkering fervently on a project.

"I found her!"

Emmeline guided the balloon over her stand and dropped the rope ladder.

"Are you sure you can find your way home?" Avery asked.

"I've done it before, I can do it again."

"Don't try to fly home after she fixes those wings," she warned.

Emmeline laughed. "I wasn't planning on it, but—"

"No! If it comes to that, wait on the platform and I'll give you a ride after my shift in Hydra."

"We'll see," Emmeline teased before jumping over the side of the basket and sliding down the rope. Three prongs from the platform, she latched to one of the footholds and climbed the rest of the way down.

As her foot touched the ground, Avery took off toward Hydra.

Emmeline turned to Gemma, who hadn't noticed her arrival yet.

"Moving up in the world, huh?"

Gemma jumped, concentration startled.

"Emmeline!" she exclaimed, jumping up to greet her friend.

"I'm glad you're okay."

"Yeah, well, the Horrigans gave me a nice lashing before letting me go." She held up her forearm to reveal fresh welts.

"They punished you? You saved those Terra guards! If you hadn't been there, the alarm never would have been pulled and no one would have been able to identify Cuda Ray as the culprit."

Gemma shrugged. "They like to keep us in line and remind us who's in charge. I'm just grateful I got to keep the firestones."

Emmeline stepped back to get a better look at her stand. The sign's lettering was etched into a scrap of tin—Gemma's penmanship was messy, but legible. Smeared into the scratched letters was dirt and moss to add color.

"Looks great! Are you happier now?"

"Very."

"Good! You ought to be proud. Look at what you have achieved."

"Oh right, yeah," Gemma stammered, glancing side to side. "Having this stand is great too. I thought you meant having access to the heat—it has brought me great relief. It's a rush, it's a high. It also gives me a bit of power over the other Tinkies. They don't mess with me anymore."

"That's great. I'll give you some more after you help me fix these wings."

"Really? I wasn't expecting to get paid again."

"It's the least I can do."

Emmeline unstrapped the mangled wings from her back and handed them to Gemma, who already had the necessary tools extracted between her knuckles. Fist clenched, she rotated between screw, hammer, and wrench as she repaired the wings. Swift and precise, using only her right hand, Emmeline watched in awe.

"You're really good."

Gemma replied without looking up. "This is an easy fix."

"You're even doing it one-handed!"

"That's because my left hand is injured."

"From what?"

"Who knows—my body is a battlefield." She held up her rigid left hand. "This hand froze up. It's ice-cold and tender to the touch." She paused, glancing up at Emmeline. "Do you have that stone on you? I've been thinking about it a lot."

"Yeah, I always keep it on me." Emmeline pulled the silver sea stone out of her pocket. "I thought you said it didn't work for you, though?"

"It didn't. I'm just curious if maybe I should try again."

"You can if you want to."

"After I finish," she said, returning her attention to the wings, glancing up every few seconds to look at the stone in Emmeline's palm.

Three solid fist-twists on the final loose screw, and the wings were as good as new.

"All done," Gemma announced, handing them back to her friend.

Emmeline took the wings by the straps and slung them over her shoulders. Buckle yanked tight, she expected the wing gears to attach to her shoulder gears automatically, but they didn't.

"Shouldn't they connect?" she asked.

"There's a technique that flyers use—I'm not sure what it is exactly—an exercise or a stretch that allows the gears to interlock."

"Why can't anything be easy?"

Gemma chuckled. "If it was easy, it would lose its thrill."

"You might be right."

"I am."

"I wonder if I'll be bored with this quest the moment I succeed."

Gemma shrugged. "It's possible."

Her gaze was zeroed in on the stone.

"Oh, right! Here you go," Emmeline said, offering the stone forward.

Using her cold hand, Gemma gently lifted it off of Emmeline's palm. The lines of distress disappeared from her expression as she held the stone.

"Do you feel it this time?"

Gemma shook her head. "No, but it soothes my desire to burn."

"Burn? What do you mean?"

"A coldness has consumed me. I struggle to shake the chill."

"What caused it?"

"I don't know, but my mind has been wandering to dangerous places since it started. I never cared about fire before, but now it consumes my dreams. I can usually silence it during the day when I'm working and surrounded by other Tinkies, but at night, when I'm alone, I find myself tantalized by the urge to burn."

"You would die and kill the rest of us in the process."

"I would never let that happen," Gemma insisted. "I don't want to die; I just want to feel warmth again."

183

"You need to push this desire away."

"Is it really all that different from your quest to fly?"

"It's very different! Me learning to fly won't end with a nuclear explosion."

Gemma sighed, "The firestones help. Whenever I lose control of my thoughts, I just hold onto one of the firestones till the feeling goes away. It's a small burn, a safe burn, and it usually subsides the bigger urge."

"Good thing I brought you more, then." Emmeline retrieved the stones from her pocket, heated them up, and dropped them into an empty thermapouch.

Lines of worry returned between Gemma's brows as she handed back the silver sea stone. Covetous desire illuminated her chromatic gaze.

Emmeline recoiled the thermapouch. "Don't waste them all," she warned. "You need them to maintain your position in the market."

"I know, I know. Just enough to get me through each day."

Emmeline extended the pouch, which Gemma snatched eagerly.

"You're welcome," Emmeline said.

"Thank you—sorry. My head is elsewhere."

"It's okay. Just don't vanish on me."

Gemma's obsessive infatuation with the firestones lifted and her gaze softened. Her chromatic silver eyes shimmered with warmth.

"I won't," she promised. "You're my only friend. Same goes for you, though."

"I'm not going anywhere," Emmeline asserted.

Gemma scanned Emmeline's shrinking body, then pressed her lips into a tight smile and nodded.

"Good. We have to watch out for each other."

"Always," Emmeline agreed, grateful Gemma hadn't further addressed her concerns. "I'll visit again soon."

Emmeline left Gemma's trinket stand and navigated the long row of Tinkerpunk merchants selling gizmos and gadgets. At the edge of the platform, she retrieved the clamp gun Gemma had gifted her on her last visit and used it to make her way home on the conveyer belt.

At the platform base beneath her home, Emmeline took a moment to reflect.

Gemma was coping with the coldness through the firestones, just as Emmeline was coping with the migraines through starvation. Gemma used the bustling market as a distraction from her darkening thoughts, just as Emmeline took on the hobby of flying to distract from her own deteriorating mind. They weren't so different—Gemma had been correct. Her spiral was quite similar to Gemma's—but what was the cause of their afflictions?

Emmeline stewed over this question longer than planned. The bright sky shifted as night approached and the darkening light snapped Emmeline from her thoughts.

She had no answer to her question.

"What are you doing down there?"

Emmeline looked up to see Solís circling above. She clicked her tongue in annoyance and returned her gaze to her interlocked fingers.

"I'm thinking."

"About what?"

"About why you're always lurking and watching over me like I'm a child."

"If I don't look out for you, who will?"

"I can take care of myself."

"How do you plan on getting home? Are you going to try flying?"

"No," Emmeline spat. "I have a clamp gun. I've done it once before, I can do it again."

"Well then, I guess I should rescind the offer I was about to make."

Emmeline groaned. "Yes, I would like a ride home."

Solís smirked. "Thought so."

He swooped down and landed by sliding on his knees. Emmeline stood, energy low, and climbed onto her brother's back.

"Wish I could do this myself," she said.

"I don't mind helping you."

"That's not the point—"

Solís shut her up by launching full speed into the sky. The wind slapped Emmeline's face, forcing her to be quiet and duck behind her brother's neck. When he landed on her bedroom balcony, Emmeline hopped off, grateful that he hadn't delivered her to the main floor where their mother was surely waiting.

"Thanks," she offered.

"Mom made a huge feast if you're hungry. There's even a tray of clay marbles among the spread."

A pang of guilt pinged through Emmeline's heart—her mother had listened, she was trying.

"I'm not hungry," she replied instinctively.

Immediately following, her stomach roared loudly.

Solís crossed his arms over his chest. "You can't lie to me and get away with it."

"I just need a minute."

"Fine, but Mom is trying."

"I see that," she mumbled in reply.

"Don't be so stubborn that you get in your own way," he advised before climbing onto the balcony railing.

"I'm not being stubborn, I'm surviving."

186

Solís glanced over his shoulder, eyes narrowed with curiosity.

"Clay marbles to survive?"

"They hurt less."

"You never had a problem with golden marbles in the past."

"I'm changing. They don't settle right anymore."

"Well, as long as you're eating, it doesn't really matter what kind of marbles you prefer."

"Exactly."

"I won't let you disappear on me," he warned, his tone protective.

"I'm not going anywhere."

"That's right. Now, go eat." He took off into the night, leaving Emmeline alone with his lingering worry.

Refusing to believe there was anything significant to be worried about, she focused all of her attention on the tattered balloon fabric. There were many holes left to stitch.

Each threaded loop that she yanked tight felt like a victory. The methodic motion silenced her mind and distracted her from the ailment growing within.

Like an inescapable obsession, she weaved the thread in and out, never losing focus, never letting her mind wander. It wasn't until she stitched shut the final tear that she noticed her deepening hunger aches.

Recalling now that her mother had taken the time to fix her a special dinner downstairs, she stood, energy weak and limbs fatigued. Everything moved slower: her gears, her body, her mind. The aching lurch of her gears shrinking again forced her to double over in pain. They were adapting to her restrictive consumption; they were making it possible for her to survive this way. Still, it increasingly hurt every time and she was not yet used to the discomfort.

As she hobbled to leave her bedroom, ready to appreciate her mother's efforts to accommodate her changing appetite, the door swung open and Melora stood there, red in the face and fuming.

Instead of addressing the issue at hand, she zeroed in on what Emmeline had chosen to do instead of joining the rest of the family for dinner.

"What are those?" Melora asked, pointing at the recently repaired wings.

Emmeline had wanted to apologize, she had wanted to keep the peace, but her mother's furious energy sent Emmeline into a panic.

"What do they look like?" Emmeline snapped.

"Why do you have a pair of wings?" she inquired, her tone matching Emmeline's anger.

"Who cares?"

"I do!"

"A lot is changing in my life. I'm sorry if you feel left out."

"I am worried!"

"You shouldn't be. I am fine."

"Look at you—I tried to accommodate your request to switch to clay, yet you still won't eat. You're withering away!"

"I was actually making my way downstairs to enjoy the dinner you made before you so rudely barged in and started yelling at me."

"They're cold now."

"I don't mind."

Melora looked down at the wings again.

"You can't fly," she insisted.

"Those wings are for my party," Emmeline lied.

"They're part of an outfit?" she asked, her voice softening. "They're quite intricate for a costume piece."

"You know me—it's all or nothing."

She reluctantly dropped the issue.

"Stop snooping through my stuff," Emmeline added. "It's rude."

"I will do as I please while you live under my roof."

"Then I eagerly await the day I move to Hydra."

Melora huffed, pursing her lips together and storming off. The door slammed close. Though Melora was gone, her agitation lingered and ruined Emmeline's fleeting appetite.

Maybe Solís was right—maybe she was too stubborn for her own good—because now she refused to go downstairs and eat the clay marbles her mother had prepared.

Emmeline silenced the guilt boiling inside of her. Instead, she latched the wings to her back and rotated her shoulders till the gears latched. It took a while to get the motion right, but once she succeeded, she moved her mattress to the floor and climbed on top of her tallest dresser.

Fear, anger, pride, control—she channeled it all into a steady burn. Heart heating to its maximum capacity, her golden-hued skin glowed red and her golden gears became visible beneath her temporarily translucent flesh. She held the balloon fabric tight above her head and jumped.

The wings never moved, the fire never gave her lift, and she landed on the mattress with a hard crash. Injured only in spirit, Emmeline cursed at herself—her fall had bent the left wing.

Emotions stretched too thin, she began to sob. Irrational in theory—this was a silly thing to cry over—but with all that she was carrying, it only took the smallest of inconveniences to break her resolve.

What once felt like strength was now revealing itself to be weakness.

Panicked weeping rendered her useless. Losing breath, losing herself, she fell to the floor and cradled her knees to her chest. She retrieved the stone from her pocket, aware that its comforts were an illusion, but dependent on it anyway.

Fingers latched tightly around the sea stone, she squeezed until her panic lessened and her breathing slowed.

A complete loss of power, a moment of utter unraveling, Emmeline crumbled beneath the realization that she was not in control at all.

Chapter 17

Emmeline awoke with dry, red eyes from crying herself to sleep.

Her dreams were plagued by flying hellions disguised as angels—she could not escape the monsters. She shook off the night terrors with a firm stretch, and her eyes adjusted to the morning light.

It was a new day; a chance to do better.

She rolled out of bed, shuffled to her closet, and chose an outfit. Determined to act more like the version of herself before everything started falling apart, she chose to wear a knee-length leather trench coat over a chenille bodysuit with ruffled bloomers. She wrapped a two-strap holster around each of her bare thighs—one held her pistol, the other held three blades. Emmeline popped the button collar of the coat, pulled on her knee-high combat boots, and threw the silver sea stone into the pocketed waistband she wrapped around the outside of the coat. A quick smear of black grease around her golden eyes and her look was complete. Emmeline took a step back from the mirror to examine herself—she looked fierce, she emulated strength, yet she felt weak. Though the large jacket hid her shrinking body, her golden eyes gave her away. They shimmered with muted sorrow; they revealed a fragile girl hidden under an image of courage.

This was the best she could do.

She threw the damaged wings and a satchel of inactive firestones into a large backpack before marching downstairs.

Melora was in the kitchen brewing a pitcher of grease. She kept her back turned as Emmeline sat down at the table.

"I'm sorry for snapping at you last night," Emmeline offered.

The blunt apology forced Melora to turn with her brow raised. Instead of battling Emmeline, she cautiously accepted the gesture.

"Thank you for saying that."

A long awkward silence revealed that Melora did not plan to return the gesture.

"Nothing?" Emmeline asked.

"What do you mean?"

"Aren't you going to apologize to me, too?"

"What do I have to apologize for? I went out of my way to accommodate your new diet and you thanked me by treating me like trash."

"I was planning on coming downstairs to eat and show my gratitude, but then you barged into my room and screamed at me instead of listening to me."

"It was hours after dinnertime!"

"I needed a minute to myself. Why does everything have to be on your schedule?"

"It's called respect. I thought I taught you better."

Emmeline covered her face with her hands, agitated that her day was starting off as poorly as last night had ended.

"I don't want to fight with you," Emmeline said.

"Then stop!"

Emmeline swallowed her pride and accepted that there was no apology coming her way. She lowered her hands and took a deep breath.

"I'd be grateful to enjoy those clay marbles now."

"I threw them out," Melora replied as she turned back to brewing the pitcher of grease.

"Why would you do that?"

"Why not?"

"They don't spoil … I could've eaten them today."

"I hate the smell of clay. They were stinking up my kitchen."

"Great. Well, I guess I'll be going then."

Emmeline pushed her chair away from the table and the brass legs screeched loudly against the golden floor.

"Excuse you," Melora scolded, turning again to face her daughter. "Don't make a scene."

"I'm not. I'm leaving."

Melora clicked her tongue as Emmeline marched out of the room.

Irritated, Emmeline hardly noticed her angry stomach growls. It wasn't until the elimination of breakfast forced her gears to downsize again that she noticed the pain. She twisted in agony, curling over and resting her hands on her knees as her insides morphed to accommodate her negligence.

She *was* hungry; she *wanted* to eat.

As soon as the pain subsided, she darted to the basement and used her brothers' rope and pulley system to rappel to Terra. Becoming quite skilled at this journey, she navigated the overhead conveyer belt with ease. Clamp gun activated and attached, she was carried to the nearby Tinker Market.

She dropped with perfect timing, landing in a graceful crouch. Before returning to Gemma's booth, she found a merchant selling clay marbles.

"How many marbles are in a pouch?" she asked.

"Thirty," the Tinkerpunk man replied. Though his chrome eyes glimmered in the sunlight, they were otherwise devoid of emotion.

"I'll take three."

"That'll cost you."

"How much?" Emmeline asked.

"How much you got?" he countered.

"I'll give you one firestone per bag."

"Two firestones per bag."

"That's more than the divers get paid in Hydra."

"You're not in Hydra—you're in Terra."

"Fine. I'll buy elsewhere."

As Emmeline turned, the man backpedaled.

"Wait, wait," he urged. "Three for three."

Emmeline slowly turned. "I had a feeling my initial offer was generous."

The man grumbled as he pushed three pouches of clay marbles to her. She retrieved the satchel of firestones from her backpack, took out three, heated them up, and exchanged them for the marbles.

The man put on a thermaglove to lift the red-hot stones and then tossed them into a large thermasafe where he kept his other firestone payments.

Emmeline tossed two of the marble pouches into her backpack with the remaining inactive firestones and knotted the other pouch to her waistband. She tossed two clay marbles into her mouth and took a swig from her flask filled with grease as she marched onward to Gemma's hut.

As the marbles rolled down her throat, a faint hum rang through her head. Small enough to control, she did not eat any more marbles until it ceased. It cleared as she reached ThingaMaGems.

Gemma was nowhere in sight.

Emmeline swallowed two more marbles. This time, the noise was louder and forced her to close her eyes. She rested her forehead against the cool tin table at the front of the stand.

"Not another one," a grouchy Tinkie complained from the stand beside Gemma's.

Emmeline lifted her head, eyes squinted, and tried to locate the source. She landed on a Tinkie woman with a massive hump in her back.

"What do you mean?" Emmeline asked in reply. She reached into her pocket to retrieve the silver sea stone. Pressed against her forehead, the noise began to soften.

"You look just as sick as her."

"Who? Gemma? Do you know where she is?" she asked the woman.

"Gemma? You mean the junkie camping out between the tracks below this platform?"

"Excuse me?"

"I tried talking sense into her, but she wouldn't listen."

"She will listen to me."

"I doubt it."

"How do I get down there?" Emmeline asked.

The old Tinkie grumbled. "You can use the trap door at the back of my shop."

With no assistance from the hunchbacked Tinkie, Emmeline made her way to the back of the shop. Vials of potions in every color and texture imaginable decorated the shelves—some were labeled, others were unmarked. Emmeline wondered if these potions were legal. On the back wall, purple liquid sizzled and smoked. The pungent aroma left her feeling lightheaded.

"Don't touch anything," the old Tinkie bellowed from the front of the shop.

"I'm not," Emmeline answered, then lifted her long jacket to cover her nose. "Where's the door?"

"The only floorboard with a handle."

Emmeline scanned the ground, then noticed a lump near the back left corner of the dirty carpet. She lifted the edge and located the door. It had five locks, all of which were unlatched. Emmeline grabbed the circular hooped handle and yanked upward. It creaked loudly as she used all her might to lift the heavy door.

Darkness awaited below.

"Gemma?" Emmeline shouted.

No reply.

Emmeline climbed down the rickety ladder. She squinted, hoping to adjust to the shadowed surroundings, but it was too dark and she could not see. Emmeline paused to channel her source flame into the palms of her hands and create light.

When she reached the steel-piped ground, she called out for Gemma again.

No reply.

She scoured the area, using the light radiating from her palm to aid her search. On the other side of a pile of discarded glass bottles she found Gemma lying incapacitated with depleted firestones scattered all around her.

"What happened?" Emmeline demanded.

Gemma rustled at the sound of her voice.

"Huh?" she managed to mumble, completely strung out.

"Why are you down here on the tracks instead of working at your stand?"

"I was so cold."

"So you wasted all the firestones I gave you?"

"I gave in," she confessed, eyes barely open. "I wasn't strong enough to resist the temptation. I just wanted warmth."

"You are better than this," Emmeline urged.

Gemma refocused to take a good look at her friend.

"You're just as broken as me," she said.

"No, I am not."

Gemma's lucidity was returning. She sat up, rubbed her eyes, and scanned Emmeline with scrutiny.

"Admit it," Gemma said. "You think you can hide under that trench coat, but I see you."

"You aren't making sense," Emmeline deflected.

"You look starved."

"At least I'm not high."

"They're both slow deaths."

"Get up!" Emmeline demanded.

"What's the point?"

"I set you up for success, and you misused my gift. You will correct this."

"You aren't to blame," she mumbled, slipping back into a stupor.

"It certainly feels like my fault."

"I'm so cold."

Emmeline took the silver sea stone out of her pocket and raced to Gemma's side. She uncurled Gemma's clenched fist and placed the stone into her palm.

Gemma's eyes shot open as the stone filled her body with warmth.

She sat up in awe—instantaneously, her clarity had returned.

"I want to feel this way all the time," she said.

"The stone is just a temporary bandage. We need to determine the cause of your ailment."

"The cause is the stone."

"What? Why would you say that?"

"I've been thinking about it a lot and the unshakable chill began after I held the stone."

"But the stone remedies the pain, it soothes the discomfort."

Silver eyes ablaze with wonder and terror, Gemma stared at the stone.

She insisted, "I think it also *caused* our suffering."

"I am not suffering," Emmeline asserted, snatching the stone from Gemma's palm.

"You can live in denial all you want, but you're just as broken as me. And I blame that stone."

"It's only given me comfort and courage."

"Did you need any of that prior to finding the stone?"

"No, but I also hadn't almost been killed by a hellion prior, so I'd say needing a little comfort and courage after that was warranted."

"Maybe so."

"The stone never made me cold."

Gemma retreated into her forlorn thoughts. "If it's not the stone, then I don't know what's making me feel this way."

"I'm not here to judge you, I'm here to help. You can fix this," Emmeline encouraged.

Gemma's dark silver eyes welled with oily tears. "I want to."

"Good. That's all I needed to hear. I brought you more firestones, but I am going to pay the rent for your booth with them. All you need to do is show up and tinker."

"Thank you," she said. "I will do better. I don't know what came over me."

"We all have moments of weakness."

Emmeline extended her hand and helped Gemma to her feet. Small, wounded, half alive—Gemma shuffled to the ladder, her presence hardly registering; a ghost clinging to life.

Skeletal-geared foot placed on the first rung, Gemma took a dramatic breath, mustering every ounce of energy she had before making the climb.

Emmeline stayed close behind, afraid her friend might lose her balance and fall.

Suffering only a few wobbles and slips, they made it to the top. Heads down, they darted past the crotchety old Tinkerpunk, who shouted insults as they left her potion shop.

"She's a nasty grouch," Gemma said with a shiver once they were back in her hut.

"Pay her no mind. Are you still cold?"

Gemma nodded, chrome teeth clattering.

Emmeline unfastened the belt around the waist of her trench coat and draped the jacket around Gemma like a blanket.

Gemma peered up, still shivering.

Emmeline was exposed. Beneath her chenille unitard, her geared-bones protruded violently.

"You're just as sick as me," Gemma said.

"It's different."

"It's not." Gemma shook her head. "Get rid of that stone."

"I can't. It's the only thing that stops the deafening hum in my head."

"Well, lucky you, then. I've got nothing to help with the cold."

Emmeline perked up. "I can help! I can get you a stone just like this one. It will give you warmth till we figure out a way to stop the cold completely."

"And the noise in your head."

"Yes, that too."

Gemma tightened the trench coat around herself.

Emmeline went on, "Can you fix this before I go?" She pulled her wings out of her large duffel bag and placed them onto the counter. "I dented them last night."

"Sure," Gemma answered, apathetic to the request. Fist clenched, she pressed between her hand bones, massaging the gears, till a small hammer extended between her knuckles. Gaze empty, body trembling, she pounded the dented wing till the layered golden feathers laid flat. After a quick switch of tools—hammer to pliers—she put on a pair of triple-lensed bifocals and began adjusting the edges of each layer with great care. By the time she was done, the wing moved fluidly without any pieces jamming or scraping against each other.

"All done," she said.

"Thank you."

Gemma looked up at her, dark silver eyes desperate. "You are my only friend."

"I will help you. I will get you a stone and you will heal."

"We are in this together, right?"

Emmeline nodded, though she refused to admit she had a problem, too. She was desperate to believe her issues were under control. Determined to solve her problems on her own. Stubborn, sure. Unwise, possibly. But if she hammered these lies into her head long enough, never confessing them aloud, perhaps they'd turn into the truth.

Chapter 18

Home with her repaired wings, Emmeline found herself unable to let go of the doubt Gemma felt toward the sea stone. If she was right and the stone caused their ailments, then why was it the only thing that made her feel better?

It sat on her dresser, silver sheen gleaming in the light of day.

"I need a break from you," she said to the stone. "I need to see what happens if I let you go."

Emmeline changed into her white cotton nightgown. The lace trim around the bodice that used to cling tight to her waist now hung loose. A quick glance in the mirror revealed she was drowning in a gown that once fit her perfectly.

She threw a blanket over the free-standing mirror—if she could not see the truth, it could remain a secret.

Emmeline jumped into bed and let her tired golden bones sink into the comfort of sleep.

The lies she told herself while awake echoed in her dreams.

I'm fine.

I'm surviving.

I'm in control.

Wings of gold sprouted from Emmeline's back as she tore across the fiery sky in confident circles. Destiny realized—she could have it all.

"Be careful, or you might fall," an ethereal voice warned.

Shaken from her delight, Emmeline glanced over her shoulder and through the hazy blur of her golden feathers, she saw Luna.

Fragile, yet fierce, her regal poise shook Emmeline to the core. Luna's iridescent dragonfly wings pounded against the burning sky as she waited for a reply.

"I'm fine," Emmeline said.

Luna's eyes, which were already large, widened in disapproval. The dark spots at the center of her gaze expanded and consumed her shimmering silver irises until all that was left were two orbs of black.

Emmeline cringed and looked away—she was a monster after all.

"Leave me alone!"

"Look at me," Luna demanded, her voice stern.

"No."

"You need to listen."

"I'm fine!"

Luna soared, stopping in front of Emmeline.

Emmeline tried to turn away, but she was caught in the captivating pull of Luna's black-hole eyes.

Her terror turned into a whimper.

"Let me go," she sniveled.

"Open your eyes."

Emmeline shook her head. "I want to stay here."

"This is a dream."

"But I am happy."

"It's an illusion, a dangerous one. Open your eyes."

A tear rolled down Emmeline's cheek.

She did as directed and awoke in her bed. A warm breeze tickled her face. She sat upright, trying to shake herself from the lingering blurriness of sleep, but by the time her vision cleared, it was too late. If Luna had been there, she was already gone.

Emmeline tried to rationalize her hopes—of course Luna was not there; she only arrived inside dreams. But why ruin a pleasant dream? Why not let her enjoy a few moments of imagined bliss?

It was torment. Emmeline couldn't get a break from the stress, not even while she slept.

The dark light of twilight revealed it wasn't yet morning.

Emmeline groaned and fell back onto her pillow. Mind racing, she could not fall back asleep. The only thing louder than her spinning thoughts was her grumbling stomach. She was starving.

Emmeline rolled out of bed and shuffled to the chair her cargo pants were draped over. In one of its many pockets was a small stash of clay marbles.

She swallowed two, an allowance that was manageable in the past, and then waited.

A dull, persistent ache started at the nape of her neck.

Emmeline stood her ground, determined to endure the pain without help from the stone.

The ache crept up her skull and turned into a low, deafening hum.

Stomach still growling, she craved more sustenance, but she couldn't eat more until the pain subsided.

It grew louder.

The rattling drone filled her head and her panicked heart added a desperate rhythm to the noise.

She glanced at the stone, debating her own resolve.

Just one more time, she thought before caving.

Racing toward relief, she lifted the stone and pressed it against her forehead. The cool touch of the smooth stone silenced the noise.

Her surrender felt less like a loss and more like a victory. Though she worried the stone might be the cause of her suffering, it was foolish to forsake the only thing that gave her relief. In fact, she couldn't imagine she'd survive without it. The thought induced a gear-rattling shiver.

She had to retrieve another stone for Gemma—she had to help her friend.

Morning arrived.

The nocturnal light of the sun began to brighten and Emmeline raced to get dressed. She had to get to Regis before her mother; she needed a ride to Hydra.

Emmeline slipped into her swimsuit, preparing to dive for stones. Overtop of her swimming attire, she wore overall shorts with six naval buttons lining the front. Two columns of three, each golden button had her initials etched into anchors. A pair of thigh-high socks kept her legs warm and mostly covered. She laced up her combat boots, threw the stone into a satchel, and climbed over her balcony railing. Four precarious steps and she found her way to the zigzagging stairs that lined the side of the house. A trek she made many times before, Emmeline navigated the narrow escape route with ease and precision.

She snuck out without her mother noticing.

Emmeline reached the platform and hid behind the corner of the house. On the other side, Regis was wide awake and preparing the newly repaired family airship for a day of flying.

"Psst," Emmeline hissed.

Regis's head snapped, looking in all directions.

"Over here," she whispered.

Regis narrowed his gaze to where Emmeline peered around the corner. As he saw who summoned him, his eyes rolled.

"What?" he asked.

Emmeline tiptoed toward him.

"I need a ride to Hydra," she informed him.

"No."

His curt denial confused Emmeline.

"Why not?" she asked.

"I learned a long time ago not to anger Melora."

"This won't make her angry."

Regis chortled. "Of course, it will."

"We can leave before she wakes up, and I'll take the blame once we get back. It's important."

"If it's important, then I'm sure she'll grant you permission to go."

Emmeline groaned.

The sky was lightening; her time was running out.

"Please," Emmeline begged.

Regis shook his head, then glanced at the helium balloon docked beside the airship.

Emmeline's attention turned to the balloon as well.

"Is it gassed up?" she asked.

Regis nodded.

Relief flooded Emmeline, alleviating her panic. She hopped into the basket and recalled everything Avery had taught her. Prepared for flight, she unknotted the rope from the dock.

"No," Regis said, bored. "Don't go."

Emmeline gave him a wink before cranking the foot pedal and taking off. She'd face the wrath of her mother later, but for now, she had a mission to complete.

Not only did she hope to secure a healing sea stone for Gemma, but she also had to let Louie know that Gemma was free so he could save the imprisoned Terrapunks aboard Cuda Ray's ship. As she thought of Louie, a worry she hadn't felt before crept up her spine—she remembered the hit list, she recalled the murderous intent Cuda Ray held for Louie, and now she feared she could be flying into terrible news.

Emmeline added more heat to the lamp and cranked the pedal harder. The wings attached to the side of the basket pumped faster, quickening her trip. When she arrived at Hydra's gates, she hovered the basket as close as she could get and lowered a ladder. Dangling in the sky by a rope, she climbed down till her feet landed on steel rods of the gate. She knotted the rope ladder to a beam of the gate so her balloon did not float away, then assessed her options. She had no key to open the gate, and while her body could fit through the gaps between metal rods, the fall to the ocean below was lethal.

The urge to fly returned—she wished she could solve this problem on her own.

"What are you doing here?" a familiar voice shouted up at her.

Emmeline peered through the gates and saw Avery lifting toward the sky in her own helium balloon.

"I came to report back about Gemma."

"And?"

"She's free."

"Great, I'll let Louie know."

Emmeline frowned. "Let me in so I can tell him."

"You're supposed to be home till after your party."

"Oh, come on. I'm going crazy over there. I just need a morning away."

Avery lifted her brow. "Did my dad escort you here?"

"I came on my own."

Avery shook her head. "You just made your life at home significantly worse."

"I know, I know. My mother is going to be livid. I don't care anymore. I'll be living in Hydra soon."

"I was actually leaving to attend your party."

"Really?"

"Yeah. It's later today, isn't it?"

Emmeline paused. She had lost track of the days. "I think it's tomorrow."

Avery shrugged. "An extra day off, I suppose. Your father has been consumed by the tether build."

"Is Louie okay? Has Cuda Ray tried to hurt him?"

"Louie is fine. The old pirate is behaving himself."

"I still need to get down there," Emmeline revealed.

"Why?"

"I need to dive for sea stones."

"Why?" Avery repeated.

"It's a lot to explain. I just need to."

"Are you sure your party is tomorrow and not today?"

Emmeline counted the days in her head, then confirmed, "Yes."

"It's really easy to lose track of time down here," Avery noted, then assessed Emmeline's predicament. She was stuck above the gates of Hydra. "You didn't think this through, did you?"

"No, not really."

Avery laughed, then advised, "Stand back."

She unraveled a rope with a large hook attached to its end, then swung it in circles over her head. Emmeline crawled along the metal beam, away from where Avery was aiming. With a hearty lob, Avery tossed the hook toward the massive metal gate and latched the hook on the first try. She continued to hold onto the other end, creating a connection for Emmeline to traverse.

"Climb down," she instructed.

Emmeline slithered through the opening of the gate and wrapped the rope firmly around her ankle. With a solid anchor, she inched her way toward Avery's balloon. Surprisingly sturdy, she traversed with little trouble and jumped into the basket with ease.

"You look different," Avery commented.

"I'm the same," Emmeline replied, then quickly changed the subject. "How will you get that rope unhooked?"

"It's staying there—you'll need to climb back up it later."

Emmeline glanced up, unsure if she'd have the energy for such a feat.

"Can't I ride out of the gate with you?"

"Only your father has the key. I dock my balloon near the entrance and fly out," Avery said.

"I see."

"We'll worry about it later," Avery reassured her, then lowered her balloon.

They soared through the salty air, tearing across Hydra as fast as the fire-fueled helium balloon could go. Emmeline fed some flames into the lamp, then leaned against the side of the golden basket to soak in the temporary taste of freedom.

Hydra was healing; something about this place made her forget all her troubles above. And while she wished to hang onto this feeling, she couldn't forsake Gemma. She understood her suffering, she had to help her find reprieve.

Montgomery saw their approach first.

"Why are you back?" he shouted up at Avery.

"Seems the party is tomorrow, not today."

"You haven't even been gone an hour. How do you know the party isn't today?"

"We had a breech at the gate," she said.

"Hey, Dad," Emmeline said, stepping forward with an awkward wave.

"Why are you here?" he demanded.

"I needed a break," she said, her gaze imploring.

"From what?"

"Everything."

Montgomery's golden gaze showed sympathy. He scanned his daughter's appearance. "Your mother said she'd get you clay marbles."

"She did."

"Why do you look so small?"

"Because I am far away," she replied, noting the great distance between them.

"Will you have lunch with me?"

"Yes," she agreed.

"Fine, you can join us for a few hours, then you have to go back."

"Deal."

Avery lowered the balloon to the top deck, where she secured it in place. As she filled the gas lines and secured what remained of the flame, Emmeline hopped over the side of the basket and climbed down to the main deck.

"Couldn't stay away, huh?"

Emmeline turned to find Louie leaning against a mainsail in his diving trunks. Shirtless and smiling, she struggled not to blush.

"I have some matters to attend to," she replied.

"Is seeing me again one of them?" he asked, stepping closer.

Emmeline's fire heart was set ablaze.

She tried to play it cool.

"I did need to see you, actually. Gemma is free, so you can rescue those Terrapunks now."

Louie smirked, ignoring the news. "Well, I missed you, regardless of whether or not you missed me."

Emmeline's thoughts tangled together as her heart melted. "I was worried about you," she finally confessed.

"That's a win in my book," he said.

Emmeline took a deep breath. "And what of the captured Terrapunks?"

"I'll get to them. But first, there's you."

Brow furrowed, Emmeline asked, "Excuse me?"

"I just want to take you in," he explained, a genuine smile of adoration stretched across his face. Though he surely noticed her shrinking size, he did not mention it.

"You're perfect."

"I'm far from perfect."

He leaned in and touched the side of her face. "To me, you are."

The bustling ship around them disappeared and all she saw was Louie's face. She wanted to kiss him, wanted to let her guard down, wanted to let him in. In this moment, nothing else mattered. All her worries, all her pain vanished. Only a budding love remained.

"Excuse me …"

Her father's voice shattered their almost perfect moment.

Louie stepped back and turned to attention. "Ready to dive, sir."

Montgomery zeroed in on Emmeline. He warned, "Whatever is going on here, it needs to stop."

"There's nothing going on. We were just talking about the dive."

Louie glanced at her and winked.

She squeezed her eyes shut, shaking herself free from his captivating allure.

Montgomery remained skeptical, but chose not to press the issue. Instead, he addressed her preparedness. "You haven't dived since that hellion almost killed you. Are you sure you're ready?" he asked.

"I'm ready," she reassured him. "I need to get back in the water."

"Okay, if you're certain. Suit up."

"Is there a new suit for me?"

"In the supply chambers."

"I'll show her," Louie offered.

Montgomery narrowed his gaze. "Be ready to dive in fifteen."

"Yes, sir."

As Montgomery walked away, Emmeline looked to Louie.

"You're trouble," she said.

"I needed a few more minutes alone with you."

Emmeline smirked. "Where's my suit?"

"Follow me, m'lady."

He led her into a small room lined with equipment. Before she could pick a new suit, he had her pinned against the nearest wall.

His forehead pressed into hers, he closed his eyes and breathed deeply. Emmeline's heart raced—everything she felt for him was amplified. And though she wanted to fight the temptation, she found herself giving in. When he opened his eyes, his silver-blue gaze was filled with desire.

"I want to kiss you," he said.

"Then do it," she replied, an uncontrollable grin stretching across her face.

Louie leaned in and pressed his body against hers as their lips touched. Fire and water, an impossible combination, somehow setting their blossoming love ablaze. His passion fanned the flame in her fiery heart, while her blissful surrender set fire to his fluid desire. Guard down, she felt all of him, and for a moment, she felt whole.

He let her go.

"Don't stop," she said, eyes still closed, desperate to hold onto the feeling.

Louie squeezed her tight and gave her a small kiss before stepping away.

"I think I've won your father's favor. I don't want to lose it now."

Emmeline opened her eyes.

Louie observed her with a slaphappy grin.

She gave him a playful frown. "Fine."

"It's going to take him time to accept this."

"Accept what?"

"Us."

"And what exactly is that?" Emmeline asked, her smile widening.

Louie showed a rare display of nervousness. "I mean, I like you. I'd like to be with you."

"I see," she replied, her guard lifting. Though she wanted that too, this was all so new, and saying it aloud felt too real.

"I see?" he repeated. "Is that all? Don't you feel the same?"

"I do."

"Then tell me!"

"You already know."

"No, I don't."

"You're gonna make me say it?"

"Yes!"

Emmeline scrunched her face. "I want to be with you."

"Was that so hard?" he asked.

Emmeline opened one eye, peering through a squint at the boy she adored.

He stood there, sturdy and unwavering, as sure about her as he was the day they first met.

"Saying it makes it real," she said.

"Don't you want it to be real?"

The grin returned. "I do."

Louie leaned in and kissed her forehead. "You don't have to be scared. I'm not going anywhere. Now, pick a suit."

As she selected her diving gear, she recalled the purpose of her trip here.

The stone.

She was here to help Gemma.

Chapter 19

Covered head to toe in her suit, Emmeline stood next to Louie near the edge of the ship, ready to dive.

Cuda Ray had provided a sheath of golden coils that Louie now wore strapped to his back. His ship sailed below, circling the job site like a hungry shark.

"You will be observing," Montgomery said to Emmeline, also dressed in his diving gear.

"Perfect. If I see any monster eggs while I'm down there, should I grab them?"

"You won't. I've already swept the area."

Emmeline cursed inside her head. She needed a reason to dive lower to the obsidian shield and retrieve a sea stone.

"Ready to go?" Louie asked. He glanced sideways over his shoulder, his shimmering protective gaze staring down at her.

"I am."

"Excellent. Follow me." Louie stepped onto the ledge. His bare back expanded as he took a deep breath. The only scar on his body was the one he got while saving her. Though his flesh covered his zinc bones and gears, Emmeline imagined his tank-lungs preparing for submersion. It was an incredible feat only those born to water could achieve. Same with flying, but Emmeline still had hopes she could beat the system on that front.

Louie raised his arms above his head and dove off the side of the ship.

Emmeline glanced over the ledge—he submerged, creating the tiniest splash.

"I need to dive?" she asked her father, voice muffled beneath her giant helmet.

"You can just jump."

"Why can't we be lowered into the water like last time?"

"We could, but it's not standard. I only arranged that because it was your first dive. But if you feel more comfortable being lowered, I can have the crew ready the platform."

"No, no. I will do it the right way."

Montgomery held out his hand.

"We can do it together."

Emmeline took his hand and they stepped onto the ledge.

"Feet first, take a deep breath. On the count of three, jump."

Emmeline nodded.

"One … two … three!"

Still holding hands, Montgomery jumped, pulling Emmeline along with him. The plummet to the ocean was far, and her stomach lurched as she fell. Eyelids squeezed shut, she held her breath, waiting for impact. The ocean hit like a punch. First contact was harsh, but as they broke through the surface, they sank gracefully through the water.

Montgomery began finding buoyancy, and Emmeline copied his every move. A couple clicks of the BC, a few cranks of their motorized fins, and they were floating securely.

He gave her the OK signal, which she returned to indicate all was well.

Serenity washed over her as she floated weightlessly. This was bliss, this was peace. Consumed by the deafening silence, she found her worries were once again put to rest.

The world above was noisy and overwhelming, whereas the world below was calm and comforting. Everything was better here; there were no crushing voids to fill, no chronic pain to battle. There was love and adventure, purpose and peace. She was content and found herself wishing to never go home.

The only noise besides the steady surge of the sea was the slight buzz of the golden tethers. Here, in this part of the ocean, there were many tethers built through the obsidian shield and jutting through the ocean into the world above. A hazy glow illuminated the dark water around each tether, creating an ethereal cloud of energy.

Louie swam ahead to the new tether they were working on. Situated close to an already established tether that connected to the Pyro-Argo air base above, this new build was still in the very early stages.

Montgomery dived lower and Emmeline followed. At a certain depth, Louie lingered, unable to get any closer to the source flame. Her father dove deeper and landed with two feet on the obsidian floor. Emmeline toyed with her BC until she was able to do the same. Heat radiated upward through her suit. Sweltering, but manageable, she prepared for a successful day beneath the sea. After adjusting to the temperature change, she took in her surroundings. Light crept through the cracks in the obsidian shield, casting rays of light through the dark water, and the hazy glow around the countless golden tethers extending into the sky illuminated the darkness above. Then she looked down. All around them, scattered across the ocean floor, were silver sea stones.

While her father communicated with hand signals to Louie above, Emmeline adjusted her fingers within her gloves and grabbed the nearest sea stone. She shoved it into her satchel, then returned her attention to the collaborative construction of the tether.

Louie unsheathed a golden coil from the scabbard strapped to his back. Though it was already very long, he worked the coil, stretching it until its length tripled. He then extended it downward where Montgomery was able to seize the end and braid it into the coils already connected to the source flame. They repeated this process continually, Louie lowering a coil and Montgomery weaving it into the growing tether.

Emmeline checked her oxygen gauge frequently, making sure they were on track and had enough air to return to the surface. She lost track of time as they worked. All that mattered was that she was happy, for the first time in days, and that the happiness came from herself and her surroundings, not from the stone.

Montgomery tapped her on the shoulder and then pointed up.

It was time to go.

Montgomery grabbed Emmeline's hand and they ascended. Legs kicking, ankle and wrist fins fluttering, they made their way back to the surface.

Louie swam above, circling and swimming in loops. Graceful and carefree as he navigated the ocean he called home.

The temperature cooled the higher they rose, and by the time they crested the ocean surface, Emmeline had caught a terrible shiver.

"Are you okay?" Montgomery shouted within his glass helmet.

"I'll be fine. I just need to get out of the water."

A ladder was lowered over the side of the hovering ship, and they climbed it one by one. Emmeline went first and as soon as her feet hit the deck, she stripped off the wet suit. Though she was dry beneath, the suit was cold from the water.

Louie climbed over the ship's ledge next, followed closely by Montgomery.

"Have you shaken the chill?" her father asked.

"Yes, I feel better now."

"Fantastic. Great dive! All around success."

Cuda Ray's scratchy bellow sounded from below.

"Argh! How much longer till the tether breeches the sky? Me crew is getting' restless."

Montgomery replied, "Hard to say. You're getting paid to do a whole lot of nothing though, so stop complaining."

"Ye couldn't build it without me coils of gold."

"That you stole from the Terrapunks' scrapyard."

"I gave 'em steam. Fair trade!"

"I'm sure they'd argue otherwise."

Cuda Ray spat, but quarreled no further.

Montgomery turned to his daughter.

"Time to go."

"I thought we were going to have lunch," she said, desperate to elongate her time in Hydra.

"We will have lunch on the trip home."

"Mother is going to be furious with me. I stole the balloon and left without telling her."

"I'll go back with you to soften the blow."

"Can't I just stay here?"

"No. Though you will spend a lot of time here in the future, your home is above. You have to find balance."

"But I'm happier here."

"You will rust. Though you were trained for Hydra, you weren't built for it—even I need to take breaks from this salty haven."

Emmeline groaned. "Okay, fine."

Avery chimed in, "Plus, your party will be fun."

"Maybe. I'm happy you'll be there." Emmeline glanced over at Louie, who was coordinating the next dive with members of the Thermapunk crew. She looked to her father. "Can Louie come to my party, too?"

"No," Montgomery said. "He needs to stay here."

"Why?"

"There's a lot of work to be done."

"Or is it because Hydropunks aren't allowed above?"

Montgomery sighed. "There's that, too."

"Such stupid rules."

"That's just the way it is," Montgomery said, though his tone held sympathy. He added, "Plus, that would only anger your mother more."

"Another reason why she and I can't see eye to eye."

"She has your best interest at heart."

"She is trying to control me."

"She is trying to love you; she just shows it in strange ways."

"The balloon is ready for liftoff," Avery gently interjected.

"I have to say goodbye to Louie."

Montgomery huffed. "You have five minutes. Meet us at the top deck."

Emmeline raced to Louie, who was wrapping up his conversation.

"I have to go," she said, clearly upset.

Louie looked around for Montgomery's watchful eye before pulling her in close. Bodies connected, a surge of relief coursed through Emmeline. She could stay in his arms forever.

"I will see you in a few days," he said.

"I lose my head when I'm away."

"Think of me when that happens."

Emmeline nodded. She wanted to tell him how she suffered, but didn't want to burden him with her problems. She would solve them on her own.

He kissed her. "I will miss you while you're gone."

Emmeline's eyes glistened. She couldn't say it back, it hurt too much.

She took a deep breath and reassured herself, "It's just for a day or two."

"Exactly. I'll see you again soon."

He gave her another small kiss then let her go. She released a heavy breath before walking away.

It was harder than ever to say goodbye; she was leaving her happiness behind. She climbed the ladder to the top deck without looking back. Doing so would make this departure even more unbearable.

She'd be flying into her mother's fury, soaring back into painful loneliness where her body and mind consistently betrayed her. If she stayed busy, perhaps she could dull the misery, but she'd rather stay where true contentment came easily.

The new sea stone was safely wrapped in her satchel while her original sea stone sat in her overall pocket. She wrapped her fingers around her stone. Its false comfort would have to do.

Montgomery expended five clay marbles from the contraption on his belt. He handed them to Emmeline, then dispensed another five for himself.

"Eat up," he said.

Emmeline took her time, throwing them into her mouth at dramatically spaced intervals. Hand still gripping the stone, the ringing pain in her head never grew louder than a whisper. She was in control.

When they reached their home, Melora was standing on the hangar bay, arms crossed and expression furious.

"Here we go," Emmeline grumbled.

"My dear!" Montgomery shouted in greeting. "How I have missed you."

"You," Melora seethed, staring at Emmeline. "Don't you dare think that having your father escort you home will soften my anger."

"I requested she come," Montgomery interjected. "She was following my request."

"She should have told me."

"It was early," Emmeline said. "I didn't want to wake you. Plus, I told Regis where I was going. It's not like I left without telling anyone."

"Did you tell Regis your father had sent you a summons?"

"No."

"So surely you can understand my misplaced anger."

"I do. I'm sorry."

Montgomery cut in, "Great. That's solved. I need to head back now, but Avery and I will return in time for your party tomorrow."

Emmeline wanted to object but restrained from doing so—it would only upset her mother. She climbed over the basket and landed on the hangar bay. Melora's energy was ice cold.

As Avery redirected the balloon back toward Hydra, Emmeline apologized again.

"I really am sorry."

Melora huffed. "I suppose I need to get used to this— you will be coming and going more often after tomorrow. I just wasn't ready or expecting that this morning."

221

"Is there anything I can help you with for my party?" Emmeline asked.

Melora jolted upright, trying to hide her shock as they walked inside.

"You could polish the great room," she answered. "I haven't gotten to that yet."

"Done," Emmeline said.

They parted ways inside and Emmeline went straight to the great room. She placed her satchel with the new sea stone on the lowest sill of the ceiling-high bookshelf and got to work. Rag, soft-bristled brush, and a spray bottle filled with warm sea water and terrain salts—an expensive concoction to acquire, as both Hydros and Terras were needed to make it—Emmeline began polishing the elaborate room of gold.

Everything was gilded; that which was not solid gold was brushed with pure 24-carat paint. Though the Thermapunks were made of gold, they did not have easy access to the precious metal—it was only found in the terrain—so a mansion made entirely of gold was a luxury few could afford.

To Emmeline, it was excessive, but she had lived her whole life within this golden prison. Polishing the gold was a means to an end; a simple way to mollify her mother's anger.

"Do my eyes deceive me?" Solís entered the great room, expression animated with shock. "Are you *cleaning*?"

"Just trying to keep the peace."

"Cyrus and Helix will never believe it when I tell them."

"Go away."

Solís plopped himself onto the couch.

"Have you ever tried glass marbles?" he asked.

"No," she answered without looking up.

"I have a pocket full. Want some?"

"I'm not hungry."

"You look starved." Solís' tone turned from casual to concerned.

"I just ate lunch with Dad."

"I think you'll like the glass—it's super light."

"Stop," Emmeline shouted. "I don't want any!"

"Geez, no need to pop a coil."

She took a deep breath. "Sorry. Everyone has been on my case."

"Have you looked in a mirror recently?"

"I know ... I'm smaller, but I'm fine."

"Are you still getting those headaches?"

"No, I learned how to control them."

"How?"

Emmeline glared at him. "Take a wild guess."

"You can't starve yourself. Your headaches are probably caused by a loose screw; an easy fix if you'd just see the Thermadoc."

"It's not a loose screw."

"Edwin Doyle works on Dad's ship. He's a great medical mechanic. Has he examined you yet?"

"No."

"Then how do you know it's not a loose screw?"

"I just do."

Aggravated, Solís stood. "You need help."

"Worry about yourself," Emmeline snapped.

Solís dug into his pocket, grabbed a fistful of glass marbles, and slammed them onto the couch.

"You should eat," he advised, then marched out of the room.

Alone again, Emmeline burst into tears.

She didn't want to believe something was wrong with her, yet everyone was acting like there was.

Everyone except Louie. He loved her, flaws and all.

Her soul day could not pass soon enough.

Emmeline took a deep breath and refocused on cleaning. Zeroed in on every nook and cranny, she lost herself in the monotonous task.

Anything to distract her from the constant grumble of her stomach.

A loud crack echoed outside—it startled Emmeline from her task.

The great room was dark, twilight had arrived—she had lost hours consumed by her woeful thoughts.

She raced to the window.

In the darkening sky, Luna soared.

Had she fallen asleep while cleaning?

Emmeline pinched herself.

"Ouch!" she exclaimed as she broke skin. The tiny wound on the back of her hand throbbed as she watched the beautiful monster fly in graceful circles.

Heart pounding, reality sinking in: Luna wasn't a dream, after all.

Chapter 20

"Are you real?" Emmeline asked through the open window.

As the words left her mouth, she realized how loud she was being. She scanned the sky. Mostly empty, besides a few straggling Aeropunks, no one noticed Luna's arrival except Emmeline.

"Why doesn't anyone else see you?" Emmeline asked in a loud whisper.

"Only you hold the key."

"Huh?"

Before Luna could explain, a second crack reverberated through the sky. It shook Emmeline to the bones, rattling her gears as it echoed.

Vision blurred as her nerves settled, the sound of arguing rang like an alarm.

"Why are you here?" Luna demanded.

"I don't know," a different female voice replied. "I should be in the sea."

"Is your shield up?"

Emmeline's vision cleared, revealing a second beautiful hellion pounding the sky with her dragonfly wings. She spun three times in rapid circles, then disappeared.

"Where did she go?" Emmeline asked.

Luna looked to Emmeline, eyes wide with dread, and before she could answer, Emmeline was tackled by an invisible force. A fierce grip grabbed her neck and pinned her to the ground, choking her slowly.

"Let her go!" Luna demanded, flying through the window to help.

"She needs to die!" the second woman replied, though she was still invisible.

"No, she needs to live. She is the key to peace between our people."

"She killed your brother; my husband! How could you protect her?"

"You aren't seeing the bigger picture," Luna rationalized.

The invisible grip let go and Emmeline gagged, desperately refilling her lungs with air. As she sat up, the second woman dropped her shield and reappeared. Her anger was now directed at Luna.

"She is a monster!" she spat, pointing at Emmeline.

"She's actually not as bad as the rest."

"How could you know that?"

"I've been watching her, and I spoke with my father after he returned. She hasn't told anyone about me yet, which was unexpected."

"I thought you were a dream," Emmeline said, massaging her throat.

"I'm not," Luna answered. "Will you run and tell?"

Emmeline paused. "Are you here to hurt me or anyone else?"

"No."

"Speak for yourself," the second woman hissed.

"Ignore Cèla," Luna said. "She is angry."

"No kidding," Emmeline said, rubbing her neck. "Why are you here?"

"I'm here to help you. Her, I'm still not sure why she's here."

"This is where I was brought," Cèla said.

Luna's silver brow furrowed, then her eyes enlarged as she looked at Emmeline. She asked, "Did you take another stone?"

"A sea stone? Yes, for my friend. It soothes our ailments."

"No! It is the *cause* of your ailments," Luna groaned. "Have you touched it?"

Emmeline scoured her memory. "Only with gloves on."

Luna's shoulders relaxed. "Good. You need to throw it back into the sea."

Emmeline's expression dropped with grave realization. She looked to Cèla. "That stone belongs to you?"

"That's none of your concern."

Emmeline reached into her pocket and retrieved her sea stone.

"And this stone belongs to you?" she asked Luna.

Luna wore a grave expression, but did not answer.

Emmeline continued, "Is this the key?"

Luna nodded.

All Emmeline could hear was the swirling flames pounding against the confines of her heart. "They are portals," Emmeline realized, her voice hushed. This revelation was enormous.

"They are also a weapon," Luna informed her. "You are afflicted."

"You've had portals within our ocean all this time?"

"For centuries, and we've never once caused any problems."

Cèla chimed in, "The only conflict we encounter is initiated by your people when they imprison and kill us."

"Why, though? Why do you need portals into Quintessence?" Emmeline asked.

"For the flame, of course," Cèla spat.

"You've captured the flame?" Emmeline's shock was potent.

"Countless times. It protects us from our enemies."

Luna added, "And keeps our mortals alive. Our possession of fire causes no harm. It protects the lives of the mortals our moon serves. The light we emit gives their planet warmth during the cold of night."

It didn't make sense.

"But the holy doctrine," Emmeline stammered. "It specifically states that we cannot share our sun fire with the moons. It depicts chaos and death for all if we were to break this rule."

Cèla laughed, her callous hatred apparent.

Luna showed more empathy. "Solédon and Lunéss have fought for eons. He must have made that part of the rules to mess with Her and Her moon children. It makes our quest to serve our mortals that much harder."

"If what you're telling me is true, then everything we've been taught, everything we believe, is a lie."

Cèla seethed. "You've murdered countless moon beings for a false prophet. Solédon is a pariah among the gods."

"He is not!"

Luna stepped in, "Stop your bickering. What I need to know right now is if our secret is safe."

"If you don't cause any trouble, then yes," Emmeline answered. "It is safe."

"Doesn't matter anyway," Cèla said to Luna. "Your stone has done its job. She'll be dead soon."

"Not if I can heal her."

"Take it back," Emmeline insisted, thrusting the stone toward Luna. "I don't want to die."

"You need to keep it. It's the only thing keeping you alive until I figure out how to leech its toxic magic out of you."

Panicked, Emmeline's thoughts raced. "Gemma—she touched the stone too. She also needs help, that's why I took a second stone. I thought it would help."

Cèla replied, "It won't. My stone is far more lethal. You're lucky you stole Luna's first and not mine."

"You can have it back," Emmeline said to Cèla.

"No, you will drop it back into the sea."

"I cannot help you sneak into Hydra."

"But you will," Cèla threatened. "After all we've suffered because of you, it's the least you can do."

The sound of feet walking around upstairs forced them into silence. They held a collective breath as someone marched above.

"It's probably my brother," Emmeline whispered. "Helix hardly sleeps."

"Will he come down here?" Luna asked.

"Not if we stay quiet."

"I'm not sticking around to find out," Cèla said. She mumbled a few words beneath her breath. "Ad lunam cè. Accipe me!"

Cèla vanished.

Emmeline watched in awe.

"How did she do that?"

"It's better if you don't know," Luna replied, her voice hushed.

Emmeline looked at the stone in her grip. "This is what caused my headaches?"

"The stones affect everyone differently. Impossible to guess how they will afflict someone till the damage is done."

"I can't eat without pain."

"I'm sorry."

Emmeline looked at Luna—she saw her clearly for the first time. She was a Hellion of Obsession; and though she looked similar to those Emmeline had seen in Hydra—dragonfly wings, talon toes, pointed fingernails—there were also differences. Her thick black hair was decorated with stardust, her large eyes were silver instead of black, the cords beneath her flesh weren't knotted, they revolved smoothly. On all accounts, she would be considered a monster by the Solarpunks, but it was clear she was far from monstrous; she held great care for herself and those around her. Her empathetic energy radiated and she showed remorse for the trouble her stone had caused. Instead of letting Emmeline die, or trying to kill her as Cèla had tried to do, she watched over her and monitored her ailment, all while trying to find a cure from afar. How could anyone call her a monster?

"Gemma has an unshakable chill, an unquenchable need for fire. She could kill us all if I don't help her."

Luna's expression was solemn. "If her condition is that dire, more drastic action might be needed."

"What do you mean?"

"Take her out before she takes everyone else out."

"No! Never."

"There is no guarantee that either of you can be saved. I'm trying, but I get no help. My people hold no sympathy toward your people. They don't care if you suffer."

"I suppose we deserve their apathy."

"It's all a misunderstanding," Luna went on. "Solédon altering the doctrine caused a dangerous riff. The flame was meant to be shared."

"I can try to work on things here," Emmeline offered.

"You need to worry about your health."

"I think the war between our people is a tad more important than my health."

"You're the only sun creature who has ever listened. You can't die."

"I won't."

"You don't understand the power of the stone."

"I do. I have lived with it for weeks now. I have it under control."

Luna pursed her plump, pale lips together. "I will keep an eye on you."

The sound of Helix's feet stomping above disappeared.

"I think he went back to sleep," Emmeline said, but as the words left her mouth, the large double doors to the great room swung open.

Luna vanished in a blink.

Helix scanned the room. "Who were you talking to?"

"No one."

"I heard talking," he insisted.

"I was going over all my responsibilities in Hydra. I'll be there more often after my party."

"So you were talking to yourself?"

"Yes."

He shook his head. "I heard a different voice."

"You're tired. Go back to bed."

Helix huffed. "You should go to sleep, too. Mom will be mad if you're anything less than perfect tomorrow."

He was right.

Emmeline put her polishing tools back into the cupboard, grabbed the satchel with Cèla's moon stone, and left the room with Helix. As she followed him into the dark corridor, she glanced over her shoulder.

The great room was empty, Luna was truly gone, but the amazement of all she had discovered lingered.

All she was taught to believe was a lie.

The monsters they fought could be friends if she found a way to share this information with her people.

It would take time; it would take patience.

It was another massive task to distract Emmeline from her withering health.

Another diversion to enable her denial.

Chapter 21

Reality felt like a fever dream.

Emmeline was hopelessly wired, tirelessly awake.

Heart pounding, eyes wide, she lay in bed unable to fall asleep.

How could she be so foolish? So weak? How could she let her courage come from anything other than herself? She had clung to the moon stone like a crutch, allowing it total control of her mental state and relying on it to feel brave. Gemma tried to warn her, and deep down, she had suspected it, too. Still, she chose denial over the truth, and now she paid the price.

The moon stone would kill her. It would kill Gemma, too, and Emmeline had no one to blame but herself.

Anger rising, Emmeline was losing control of her emotions. She got out of bed and paced the room, unaware of her heating heart. The fire grew at a rapid pace, swelling to great temperatures under the camouflage of Emmeline's spiraling thoughts. She did not notice the change until she lifted her hands and saw her golden gears beneath her glowing flesh.

Emmeline growled in frustration, heightening the anger she felt.

She wanted to calm down, but she was consumed by the intensifying fire in her heart.

She needed a distraction, a release. She needed to dispel this growing fury.

The heat simmered, steadily growing and filling every crevice of her being. When it felt like she might set ablaze, she gathered the balloon fabric, closed her eyes, and pressed the opening to her lips. With meticulous breaths, she released the heat from her body into the balloon.

Soothing, liberating, she set herself free with each exhale. The balloon slowly started to rise. As her feet left the cool golden tiles of her bedroom floor, she opened her eyes.

She was air bound.

Hands gripping the balloon above, body dangling awkwardly, she floated. It wasn't graceful, it wasn't skilled, but she had achieved some semblance of flight.

Elated, her anger and exhaustion vanished. She was finally light enough to fly. Though it was unintentional, it seemed that all her suffering had served a greater purpose. With this skill, she could run Hydra like no others had done before. A watchful eye in the sky, unlimited access to and from job sites—productivity would soar, just as she did.

With care, she loosened her grip and let the hot air leak from the balloon, lowering herself to the floor. Her toes touched down softly. She had floated and landed victoriously.

The clicking clock on the wall ticked louder now; her exhaustion was beyond reconcile. She tossed the deflated balloon fabric and collapsed onto her bed. Delirious from the drama and exertion, Emmeline finally fell asleep.

"Happy day of creation!"

The sound of Solís's voice rang through Emmeline's sleeping mind.

"Happy soul day!" Cyrus and Helix added in unison.

Emmeline rustled where she lay, too tired to open her eyes.

Solís plopped himself onto her bed.

"Time to wake up," he said, gently shaking her leg.

Emmeline groaned, then cracked her eyes open ever so slightly. The room was bright, their voices were loud, and the jolted revival of her senses left her jarred.

Had it all been a dream?

She sat up, alarmed by her fuzzy memory. Tired eyes blurry and vision dizzy from exhaustion, she could not trust herself. Her mind had become a haven for delusions.

"I'm so tired. I didn't sleep well," she stated.

"I found her polishing the great room in the wee hours of morning," Helix informed the others.

Emmeline perked. "I didn't dream that?"

"No, you were there. You seemed loopy, though. You might've been sleepwalking."

"More like sleep cleaning," Solís joked.

"Not another insomniac," Cyrus groaned—Helix's insomnia and subsequential sleepwalking had caused many problems over the years.

"We live stressful lives," Helix rationalized. "Sleep is for the undisturbed."

Solís nodded. "We're all a bit disturbed."

Emmeline sighed. This didn't clear up anything.

"I remember everything, but I also can't distinguish what was real and what was just a dream."

"Ah, yes," Helix said. "I know that feeling well. Sleep deprivation makes dreams feel real."

Emmeline fell back onto her bed—she wanted her dreams to be real.

Hopeful, but hesitant, she planned to move forward with caution. All the information she had learned was dangerous if it wasn't truthful.

"Mom made an elaborate clay marble breakfast for you," Cyrus said.

Emmeline's stomach grumbled.

"Sounds like you're hungry," Solís commented. "Come on."

He grabbed Emmeline by the wrist and yanked her upright. She did not resist, nor did she help; her body was deadweight as he pulled her out of bed.

"Perk up," Cyrus advised. "You've got a long day ahead of you."

"I should give her the dust," Helix said.

Cyrus shot him an irritated glare.

"The what?" Emmeline asked.

"Locomo," Helix answered.

"No," Solís chimed in.

"It works for me," Helix said with a shrug.

"Does it, though? You're neurotic half the time after huffing."

"It gets me through the day after a restless night."

"What is it?" Emmeline asked again.

"A narcotic, essentially. Some lowly Tinkie created it using minerals found in the terrain between Terra and Hydra. Originally, it was just a natural remedy to help the Tinkies work with clear heads; prevented a lot of careless injuries. Then the Horrigans caught wind and began experimenting. They bartered with the Holloways, who donated rare gasses to the research, and the dust became potent."

"The Holloways," Emmeline repeated. "A dynasty in the sky. I've yet to meet them."

"They might be at your party today. Mother invited them."

"Why don't you want me to try the dust?" Emmeline asked.

"It's addictive," Solís said.

Helix nodded.

"Plus," Solís added, "you have enough going on with your headaches. Would be stupid to inhale chemicals into your brain."

"She's not going to make it through the day," Helix stated, observing his sister's bone-tired appearance.

"She'll have to find a way." Solís ended the discussion before Emmeline or Helix could press the issue further. "Get dressed."

Cyrus left her room first, followed by Solís. Helix paused before leaving. Once their brothers were out of ear shot, he whispered, "Come see me before you go downstairs. I'll help you out."

He left before she could reply.

Emmeline didn't want to accept his offer. She agreed with Solís—she didn't want to add any remedies with unknown side effects to her already crumbling health—but she also did not know how she'd survive the day without a little help.

Dressed in a tight-laced tank top and suspenders attached to a ruffled skirt with curtained layers of gold, copper, and silver fabric, Emmeline looked in the mirror. Her long bright hair was disheveled, and prominent brown circles sat beneath her pretty gold eyes. She brushed her hair, which sprang into long curls after minimal maintenance, then applied some powder, which only covered a fraction of her fatigue. She'd have to make up for her tired appearance with spirited energy.

She placed her sea stone into a hidden pocket of her skirt, then snuck down the hall into Helix's room.

"Smart," he said as she entered.

"I don't want too much. I don't want to start relying on it to get through the day."

"I'll give you a very small dose. Just enough to make you feel awake."

Helix sat at his desk, which was covered in widgets and contrivances fit for a mad scientist. He lowered a pair of goggles with adjustable magnifying lenses from the top of his head and got to work. With a miniature spoon, he scooped and emptied the tiniest pinch of locomo dust onto a brass scale. The dial on the pressure gauge rocketed back and forth as Helix returned some of the dust to its vial. When the gauge settled on the weight he desired, he took a finger-sized broom and brushed the dust into a tiny bowl. Three droplets of salt water were added, then Helix heated the bowl in the palm of his hand. When the contents began to steam, he waved Emmeline over.

"This is the safest way to consume locomo."

"How?"

"Just breathe in the steam."

Emmeline leaned over the bowl and took a deep breath. The vapor entered her nostrils, coating the inner gears of her skull with a dewy mist, and then seeped into her brain. Immediately, she felt the effects. Like a kick to the head, she was startled to alert attention. Eyes wide, heart pounding, she took a step back.

"Better?" Helix asked.

"I feel like a new person."

Helix laughed. "It's powerful stuff."

As he lessened the heat emanating from his palm, he leaned in to breathe the remaining vapor.

"You do this every day?" she asked.

He nodded, enjoying the hit with his eyes closed before responding. "I'd be useless without it. I don't snort it, though. That's where it becomes a problem. Way more addictive that way."

Emmeline bounced on her heels, unable to control the adrenaline now coursing through her.

"I'm ready to party," she said.

Helix laughed. "Let's go."

They walked downstairs together. Though she felt normal, like she had nothing to hide, Solís knew immediately that she was high. He shot Helix an outraged glare, to which Helix shrugged and smirked.

"You're an idiot," Solís hissed.

"It's her big day. Let her have a little fun."

"I feel normal," Emmeline insisted.

"Don't make this a habit," Solís warned before walking away.

Emmeline scanned the room—her mother had outdone herself. The kitchen was covered in platters of marble-filled delicacies, and billowing streamers of metallic brilliance decorated the hall leading to the great room.

"It's beautiful," she said to her mother, who was pacing around, finishing last-minute details on the food trays. "Thank you."

"Oh, you're welcome," Melora replied dismissively. She looked up briefly, assessed Emmeline's appearance, then asked, "Where are the wings you planned to wear?"

"I decided my outfit looked better without them."

"I agree. Good choice." She returned her attention to the platters. Consumed by perfection—everything needed to be flawless before guests arrived. Without looking up, she added, "Breakfast is on the counter. I made you a plate."

"Thank you. I'm going to take it outside if that's okay."

Melora nodded and waved her hand, too consumed to be bothered with small requests.

Emmeline grabbed her plate and waited a moment, hopeful to receive words of love from her mother on this special day.

Those words never came.

She pocketed her hope and walked to the outside deck connected to the kitchen. Directly below was the hangar bay where the family aircrafts were docked, and above were a few levels of windows and balconies with a golden staircase weaving upward to the roof.

She looked down at her plate. The terrible hunger pains she woke up with had vanished after huffing the locomo dust. She wasn't hungry at all.

Though her restriction was dangerous, she found that her body was adapting in miraculous ways. The marbles already inside of her began recycling themselves. They no longer excreted and instead, churned through the maze of wheels, back to the top to fall again.

Emmeline couldn't believe it. To survive, her body had mutated all on its own.

Countless Thermapunks began showing up to celebrate Emmeline's day of creation. Escorted by Pilopunks, they were dropped off at the hangar bay. Emmeline watched as they filtered into her home—not a single one was her age.

They were all dressed in elaborate fashion, prim and proper, just like her mother.

As Emmeline had anticipated, this party was for Melora, not her.

An hour passed before Montgomery's ship came into view. It grew larger as it neared, and Emmeline exhaled with relief. She licked the maple-slicked marbles clean before dumping them into her pocket with the sea stone. Plate empty, evidence hidden, she stood to greet her father and Avery.

With great skill, Avery swerved the ship next to the kitchen deck.

"Happy soul day!" she greeted.

"Thank you. I'm glad you're here—so far I don't know any of the guests filtering into my party."

Avery grimaced. "I can't stay."

"Why not?"

Montgomery stepped in. "I need eyes in the sky. Cuda Ray tried to pull a fast one after you left yesterday."

Emmeline thought of Louie. "What happened?"

"He tried to sabotage the tether build."

"Why?"

"We think he caught wind of Louie's first attempt to free the captured Terra guards."

"Is Louie okay?"

"Yes. Louie swears no one saw him, but we have no other plausible rationale for Cuda Ray's attempt to destroy the tether."

Avery added, "Louie is pausing the rescue mission till after the tether is finished."

Emmeline nodded, her anxiety lessening.

"I guess it's best that you go back then," she added, bummed that Avery couldn't stay.

"I'm sorry."

"It's okay."

"I'm staying," Montgomery said. "With your brothers and me here, you will have fun."

Montgomery climbed onto the railing of the ship and leapt to the kitchen deck, landing in a graceful crouch. Avery steered the ship back to Hydra and Montgomery pulled Emmeline into a hug. He kissed the top of her head.

"Happy soul day," he said. "I am so glad we built you."

Emmeline smiled. "I'm glad, too."

"Hey, Emmeline!" a familiar voice shouted up.

Emmeline looked over the railing and saw her longtime friend, Clementine Monroe, disembarking her family's airship. Dressed in a stuffy gown covered in ribbons, she looked as stiff and snobbish as the adults in attendance.

"I'll see you inside," Montgomery said, encouraging Emmeline to be with her friend.

Emmeline climbed over the railing and scaled down the nearest pipe. She landed on two feet and before she could turn around, she was buried in a hug.

"I've missed you," Clementine exclaimed, squeezing Emmeline tightly before letting her go.

"I've missed you, too. It's been so long since I've seen you."

"I know! Graduation day at the academy."

Emmeline smirked as she examined Clementine's dress. The fabric hung loosely on her body, not fitting correctly.

"Who dressed you?" Emmeline asked with a snicker.

"Ugh, it's horrible, right? My mother forced me to wear this. It doesn't fit and the fabric itches."

"I'd be wearing something equally as horrible if my mother had her way."

Ms. Rickard arrived at the hangar bay. She rode in a basket attached to the back of a Pilopunk's skycycle. She hopped out, offering no thanks to the Pilopunk.

"Ladies, come inside," she instructed in her sternest tone before marching past them without a second look.

"She's so rude," Emmeline commented under her breath.

Clementine nodded in agreement.

They followed her inside.

The kitchen was bustling with Thermapunks. None of whom greeted Emmeline or acknowledged her presence.

The heat from so many fire-fueled bodies crowded together accumulated, making the air thick and uncomfortable.

"This is horrible," Emmeline commented. "I don't even know these people."

"Where are all of our classmates?" Clementine asked. "No one here is our age."

"This party is more for my mother," Emmeline confessed. "I'm glad she had the decency to invite you at least."

Clementine cringed. "The invite was made out to my parents."

"Figures."

Melora's voice rang from the great room.

"Everyone, please gather!" she shouted.

This coaxed the haughty Thermapunks away from the elaborate feast.

"Do you think we have to go, too?" Emmeline asked, already knowing the answer but wishing to be spared.

"Of course. You're the guest of honor."

Emmeline groaned.

They followed the crowd as they funneled into the great room. As soon as Emmeline crossed the threshold, Melora waved her over.

Emmeline pushed through the group of oblivious Thermapunks, many of whom cursed at her and called her rude as she shoved past. A rather demeaning experience on a day intended to celebrate her.

"My dear daughter, Emmeline, is celebrating a milestone year," Melora began as Emmeline took her place between her mother and father. They stood on an elevated platform near the enormous picture window. Her brothers stood to the side of Montgomery in an orderly row according to their ages: Cyrus, Helix, and Solís.

Melora continued, "On her sixteenth cycle, Emmeline transitions from child to adult. As you all know, my sons were not able to take on the family business due to the continued attacks by the moon monsters. So, Emmeline will carry on the family legacy at Dawes Detention Center for Demons." She paused and smiled. "My courageous boys are needed in the sky."

The crowd cheered, celebrating the Dawes boys, who had built a prestigious reputation for themselves as Pyropunks. Melora let the adoration persist, clearly absorbing their indirect admiration as if it were aimed at her. As the crowd's reverence subsided, she resumed her speech.

"Sixteen years ago, Montgomery and I built ourselves a little girl." She returned her attention to Emmeline. "We toiled over your tiny frame for months, using only the finest gold found in Quintessence, along with bits of ourselves, to craft your body. Countless days accompanied by restless nights, we labored until you were an image of perfection. Golden gears and bones, meticulously placed and bolted to form a daughter we could love. We prayed to Matrigaia, the goddess of life, who blessed us with your functioning body. We then prayed to Incarna, the goddess of souls, and in time She delivered your soul."

Melora and Montgomery turned to face Emmeline and connected their hands above her head. They reenacted the day they delivered Emmeline's soul into her body.

"A golden orb sent from the heavens descended upon us, landing in our loving embrace, and together, we delivered your soul into your body. Birthed by our love and prayers, we were gifted the daughter we always dreamed of." Their hands lowered to Emmeline's shoulders. "Through hard work and devotion, we were given you."

The crowd clapped, less enthusiastically than they had for her brothers. Emmeline grimaced; the whole charade was embarrassing.

Melora looked out at the crowd and continued her speech. "Emmeline's soul lived through five hundred mortal lives before finding its way home. Selected specifically for us, Incarna chose a soul well-traveled." The crowd murmured; impressed or disgusted, Emmeline couldn't tell. "Wise, nurturing, empathetic—Emmeline showcases characteristics far beyond her years. We expect great things from her."

Emmeline wasn't sure if she possessed any of those characteristics, but if it served her mother's farce, she'd play along. Anything to keep Melora content and off her back.

Cyrus retrieved the black-marble cake Melora had made and placed it on a small table near the front of the platform. Slick and piled high, the marbles formed a pyramid bound by hardened sugar. Thick syrup coated the cake and dripped slowly down its many layers.

Everyone in the room joined Melora as she sang the traditional soul day song. Emmeline kept a forced smile on her face despite her desire to disappear. All this attention was uncomfortable.

Gizmos and gadgets,
golden gears and wheels;
built with tinkered love,
we are happy you are here!
Body built by the hands of those who love you most.

Soul nurtured by the mortals till it was fully grown.
Delivered by the deities, who carried your soul home.
Soul to body,
we celebrate the day you became whole.

Emmeline cringed—she hated the next part.

Dear Emmeline,
on this day,
we celebrate your growth.
Happy mind, happy heart, happy soul,
unleash the secrets that you hold.

Common practice, but exceedingly awkward the older she got, Emmeline was expected to release any misgivings that might be holding her back from reaching her fullest potential. Transparency was believed to set the soul free, but really, it was how the Thermapunks monitored their people. In past years, her answers were easy: her struggle to get good grades at the academy, her subtle fear of taking on the responsibilities at the detention center, her desire to make her parents proud.

Now, she could not answer honestly—the truth would not set her free; it would secure her a cage in the detention center. They didn't want to hear that she no longer saw the moon beings as monsters. They didn't want to know that she doubted Solédon. They didn't want to hear that she was in love with a Nautipunk. The slightest mention of any of these truths would turn her into a leper among the Thermas.

"I got injured on my first dive in Hydra," she answered. The room of pompous Thermapunks silently stared at her with critical curiosity. She continued, "I worried I'd be too afraid to try again, but I proved myself wrong. I was able to dive again. I was able to be brave. My secret is that I was afraid, but I will always choose courage over fear."

The crowd responded with polite applause.

Satisfied with her feeble admission, Melora stepped in front of Emmeline.

As she prepared to address the crowd, a giant explosion shook the floating mansion.

Screams of terror echoed through the great room as half the party crouched and searched for cover. The other half, primarily Pyropunks, darted to the windows with eyes scanning at the sky.

"I see nothing," Cyrus said.

"There's no fire in the sky," Helix confirmed from the other side of the room.

Solís opened a window and climbed onto the ledge. Perched, with only his firm grip keeping him in place, he was granted a wider view of Quintessence.

A billowing stream of black smoke rose from below.

"It came from Terra," he announced, to which the entire room gasped.

Their hushed surprise amplified Emmeline's horror.

Gemma, she thought, before racing out of the room unnoticed.

Chapter 22

Emmeline locked herself in her bedroom. As she raced to attach her wings to her shoulder gears, a knock rapped at the door.

"Who is it?"

"Clementine. Are you okay?"

"I'm fine." Emmeline wiggled, struggling with the straps.

"Can I come in? It's chaos down there."

The wings wouldn't lock into place and hung loosely off her shoulders. She needed help.

"You won't like what you see," she warned before opening the door.

Clementine gasped at the sight.

"Are you trying to fly?" she asked in a hushed whisper.

"Hurry, come inside," Emmeline urged, swiftly locking the door after ushering Clementine inside. She looked to her oldest friend with grave severity and asked, "Can I trust you?"

"Yes," she promised.

"Help me latch these wings to my back and I'll explain."

"I've never done this before," Clementine said, her anxiety clear.

"It's impossible to mess up. They're either latched or they aren't."

Emmeline yanked the shoulder straps to hold the weight of the wings while Clementine tried to line up the gears. She fuddled continuously.

"We have to hurry," Emmeline implored.

"Why?"

"I think I know what caused the blast."

Clementine hesitated. "You're going to fly down to investigate?"

"I need to get there before my brothers."

"Your brothers are trained to handle situations like these."

"They won't understand or believe that this was an accident."

"How do you know that it was?"

"I just do."

The gears clicked as they latched, and Emmeline rotated her shoulders to test that the connection was secure. The wings moved fluidly, no glitches or kinks.

"Thank you," she offered.

Clementine crossed her arms over her chest. "Have you done this before?"

"Sort of. I had some accidental success last night."

"You're going to hurt yourself," Clementine groaned. "This feels just like when we were little; you'd do something stupid and I'd get in trouble for being a bystander."

"I have an idea," Emmeline said, adrenaline fueling her excitement. She tied the long rope that was once attached to the balloon fabric to her waist, then handed the loose end to her friend. "You can hold onto this until I get my bearings. If I can't do it, this will at least prevent me from floating away or plummeting to my death."

Clementine squeezed her eyes shut. "I won't be able to talk you out of this, will I?"

"No."

"Fine." She released a heavy huff and grabbed the rope.

Giddy with anticipation, Emmeline grabbed the balloon and exited onto her balcony. Her stomach gears churned, morphing, as they always did, to accommodate her refusal to eat. She ignored the pain. Perhaps an additional downsizing of her gears would assist in this flight.

She climbed onto the railing and channeled the source flame. When her golden body blazed red, she breathed heat into the balloon. It lifted instantaneously, rising into the air. Emmeline clamped the edges of the fabric, sealing the heat inside the balloon, and felt her body lift. She glanced back at Clementine.

"When I give you this signal, it means I'm steady and you can let go of the rope." She showed Clementine the OK signal used beneath the seas of Hydra.

Clementine gulped and nodded.

Elevated onto her toes, Emmeline was ready for takeoff. Still blazing bright with all the heat she could muster, she pounded her wings and launched into the sky.

Five clanging chimes echoed through the upper world of Quintessence, warning those on the other side of the geared orb that danger was afoot. The warning bells were followed by a screeching whistle that filled the skies with eye-scorching steam—the piped ports to Hydra were turned into war sirens, ensuring all trade ceased until this homeland attack was resolved.

Emmeline pulled down her goggles with her free hand.

She scanned the world below and located the spot of detonation. Exactly as she feared—it was the Tinker market in Sector 3.

The rope pulled tight.

Feeling secure, Emmeline gave Clementine the OK signal. Clementine dropped the rope and Emmeline wrapped the excess around her waist, tucking the end to keep it from unraveling before flying onward.

She felt light, she felt free; she was succeeding.

The entire market was catching fire as the Tinkerpunks frantically evacuated. Flames chased them as they ran. Some threw their bodies off the elevated platforms, while others patted down the fire attached to their clothing and descended the ladders.

Emmeline caught sight of the old potion maker whose booth neighbored Gemma's.

"What happened?" she called down. The sound of her voice ringing from above caught the frenzied attention of many Tinkies.

They looked up, pausing their plights in collective awe. Horrified, enamored, bewildered—fire was not meant to fly.

The Tinkies erupted, speaking all at once.

"How?"

"Impossible!"

"You are breaking the rules!"

"Amazing."

"Thermas cannot be allowed to have fire *and* flight!"

"This is preposterous!"

"I'm impressed!"

Emmeline shook her head, shaking off the wildly varied opinions on her ability to fly.

She asked again, "What started the fire?"

"You again," the old potion maker shouted. "It was your junkie buddy."

"Is she okay?"

"She must be. The explosion would've been much worse than this if the fire had detonated her heart."

While the Tinkies continued to shout both angry and awestruck comments at her, Emmeline assessed her next move. She suspected Gemma had found shelter beneath the platform, so she directed her flight to the opposite side of the platform where there was no gathering of evacuated Tinkies.

Between two rows of terra gears, Emmeline slowly released the heated air from her balloon and landed. Far from the astounded jeers of the Tinkerpunks, Emmeline searched for her friend.

She traversed beneath the platform, heating up her hands and using the light in her palms to guide the way. A junkyard of sorts, the Tinkies working above used the space between the terra gears to discard their garbage. Emmeline navigated around piles of tossed trinkets, shouting Gemma's name as she searched.

Atop a pile of depleted firestones, Gemma lay unconscious, body ripped apart. Only her head, torso, and arms were in sight.

Two rows of terra gears were blown off their tracks. It wouldn't be long before the Stone Patrol arrived to investigate and remedy the damage.

Emmeline ran to her.

"Gemma," she said, gently shaking her shoulders.

Gemma groaned.

Relief surged through Emmeline. "Oh, thank Solédon—you're still alive. Where are your legs?"

"What happened?" Gemma grumbled. As she tried to sit up, the reality of her predicament became clear. Her eyes shot open as she began to hyperventilate. "Where are my legs?"

"Do you remember anything?"

Gemma instinctively placed her hands over her chest, relaxing a little upon realizing her heart hadn't exploded.

"I didn't go nuclear," she said, tears of gratitude in the corners of her eyes. "My gears are slowing, though. I need to be reassembled."

Emmeline examined the bottom half of Gemma's torn apart torso and found a rhythmic chute of clay marbles catapulting from the intricate system of gears.

"Where are your legs?" Emmeline asked again. "I can't piece you back together without them."

Oily tears fell from Gemma's silver eyes. "I don't know," she said between sobs. "I'm going to die, aren't I?"

"Not if it's up to me."

Emmeline searched the surrounding area, climbing over the debris from the explosion. On the neighboring track, pinned beneath one of the toppled terra gears, were Gemma's hips and legs.

An alarm sounded—one similar to the blaring siren she heard the day the Nautipunks breached Terra.

The Stoneheads were on their way.

Emmeline tugged Gemma's severed parts from where they were pinned, doing her best to collect all the small screws, bolts, and attachments, before darting back to where the rest of her friend lay.

"We have to go," she urged.

"Where?"

"I'll hide you in my room till I can fix you." Emmeline groaned, thinking of the moon stone. "This is all my fault."

"You live in Fyree. How will we get there?" Gemma asked, her voice a mere whisper now. Her gears were churning to a stop.

"I'll fly us there."

Out of energy, Gemma closed her eyes.

Emmeline was on her own now.

She had no knapsack or device to carry Gemma's broken parts—she only had the balloon fabric.

It would have to do.

Spread across the ground, she dragged her friend onto it, placed the bottom half of her body next to her top half, and pulled the ends together. Though Gemma was light enough, Emmeline wasn't sure if she could fly with their combined weight.

She hauled Gemma out from under the platform. Once again beneath the open sky, a sight of true terror greeted her. Not only could she hear the furious skates of the Stoneheads racing along the terra gears, but littering the sky were livid Pyropunks and Argopunks, darting toward Terra to investigate this breach of the peace treaty.

Emmeline channeled every ounce of heat she could muster from her fire heart and spread her wings wide. She had hardly mastered flying with the balloon, now she needed to succeed without its assistance.

"I am the balloon," she said to herself repeatedly, hoping that mind over matter might elevate her to a level of skill she had yet to achieve. When she felt hot enough to float, she raised onto her tiptoes. Concentration locked, her body lifted.

Delighted shock overtook her senses. She was beating the odds.

As her body achieved levitation, she imagined flying above the seas in Hydra. History in the making—she would carry the Thermapunks' rule to new heights. Her lift came to an abrupt stop as soon as the bundled balloon fabric carrying Gemma pulled tight.

Together, they were too heavy.

Emmeline summoned more of the source flame, heating to temperatures she had never before experienced. Her golden body glowed a furious red as the fire inside of her grew to ill-advised levels.

No matter how hard she tried, they were too heavy together, and their combined weight remained landlocked like an anchor. She pounded the wings attached to her back, desperately trying to fly.

The assault of punks from each faction grew closer, and as she prepared to face the consequences of her friendship with Gemma, a pair of invisible arms scooped her up and carried her away.

Delirious from the heat coursing through her body, Emmeline fell limp in her savior's grip.

"Gemma," she said in an exhausted whisper.

"I've got her, too." The familiar voice rang like a symphony of ethereal bells.

"Luna?" she asked, but received no reply.

Up and away, Emmeline was carried home in Luna's protective shield of invisibility. Luna flew through the open doors of her bedroom balcony and delivered Emmeline to her bed. Eyes fluttering as her spiked adrenaline declined, Emmeline struggled to stay conscious. Luna's soft voice whispered, "Don't let the moon stone win."

"Wait—" she objected, but Luna never showed herself

"*Ad lunam lu. Accipe me,*" Luna whispered before a room-swirling whoosh indicated her departure.

After regaining her whereabouts, Emmeline raced through the open doors of her bedroom balcony and witnessed the chaos she narrowly escaped. Black smoke still billowed from where Gemma had detonated, and Solarpunks from every faction surrounded the scene.

Aeropunks filtered the poisonous smoke, diluting it to prevent it from contaminating their delicate bubble of oxygen. They also helped the Thermapunks contain the fire. Thermapunks absorbed all that they could, while the

Aeropunks smothered small areas with liquid nitrogen. Tinkerpunks repaired the damaged terra gears amidst the chaos. Across the horizon, Montgomery's airship appeared. When it reached the scene, water poured over the gunwales, extinguishing the remaining fire from above. Upon closer examination, Emmeline saw that there were ten Nautipunk watermen on board assisting with this mission.

She scanned each one, hoping to see Louie.

He wasn't there.

Emmeline turned and found Clementine staring at her in shock.

"How long have you been standing there?" Emmeline asked.

"I never left."

"You saw everything?"

Clementine nodded. "You can fly," she said in awe. Her wonder shifted to disgust as she noticed the wiggling, whimpering heap beneath the balloon fabric. "But what is *that*?"

"My friend. I'll explain later. Can you help me fix her?"

Clementine shook her head and backed toward the door. "It's better if I don't."

"Promise you won't tell."

"All I saw was you flying," she reiterated before darting out the door.

"Help," Gemma croaked in a small whisper. "I'm on my last marble."

"Oh, I'm so sorry," Emmeline said as she darted to where Gemma lay bundled in the balloon fabric. She untied the fabric, and before arranging and reassembling Gemma's pieces, she took a few clay marbles out of her pocket and fed them to Gemma. "This should hold you over while I piece you back together."

"Thank you," Gemma said as the marbles reinvigorated her top half.

"What happened?" Emmeline asked.

"I burned too hot."

Luna's parting words replayed inside Emmeline's head. "We can't let the moon stone win."

Chapter 23

"What's a moon stone?" Gemma asked.

"The sea stone—it's really a stone from the Moon of Fixation," Emmeline explained as she tinkered and reconnected Gemma's pieces. "It belongs to a Hellion of Obsession. You and I both have been afflicted by it."

"I knew it. I knew that stone was to blame."

"I'm sorry," Emmeline offered.

"How do we heal?"

"I have a friend working on it. In the meantime, we have to outwit its possession over us."

"Easier said than done," Gemma griped.

"I'm no Tinkerpunk, but I'll do my best to fix you."

"Just get my insides reconnected; I can do the rest." Gemma paused. "Though I'm not sure if there's any point. They'll figure out that it was me, that I caused the explosion. They will execute me the moment they find me."

"We will deal with that later. For now, we need to fix you."

"First, take out my tracker," Gemma advised pointing to the back of her neck.

Emmeline grabbed one of the blades off of her dresser and carefully inserted it where Gemma pointed. The small incision leaked petroleum.

"It shouldn't be too deep," Gemma said.

"I see it," Emmeline said, lowering her blade and pressing against Gemma's flesh with her fingertips till a small metallic ball popped out. "It's out."

"We need to get rid of it."

"What's it made of?" Emmeline asked.

"It's a magnet."

Emmeline closed her fingers around the small magnetic ball and heated her palm. It only took a few seconds before the tracker melted in her grip. When she unfurled her fingers, only a tiny silver puddle remained. She shook her hands, discarding the liquid and returning her attention to Gemma's disassembled parts.

She spent the rest of the night rebuilding her friend. She worked fast, bolting and fastening the various gears, wheels, and chutes within Gemma's torso. She'd never built a punk before, so she did her best to piece the puzzle together in logical order.

Marbles raced down the broken mechanism, shooting out onto the floor where Emmeline hurried to connect the final parts.

Gemma's energy was returning. She tossed a few more clay marbles into her mouth.

"I'm almost done," Emmeline said, brow furrowed as she tightened the final bolt of the intricate digestive system.

She dragged Gemma's flesh-stripped hips and legs closer and connected the bottom of her silver spine to the joist at the base of her hips. Solidifying this link bonded the gears that moved her legs, and with a final twist of the wrench, Gemma was repaired. Her knees could bend, her toes could wiggle, and the marbles in her gut emptied into the proper base pan for excretion.

"I thought I was done for," Gemma said.

"So did I." Emmeline examined her friend. Silver-hued flesh covered only the top half of her body, the bottom half was silver bones and gears. "Your bones are stripped bare."

"I will have to learn to live this way."

Emmeline retrieved a silver frock-dress from her closet and gave it to Gemma, who pulled it over her head. It covered her exposed gut gears, but not her skeletal legs.

The solar shield shifted from dim nocturnal light to blazing morning flares, revealing a new day was upon them.

A knock sounded at the door.

"Hide," Emmeline insisted.

Gemma fell to the floor and crawled beneath the bed, disappearing into the shadows as the door burst open.

"Explain!" Melora shouted, her grip firm on Clementine's bicep as she dragged her into the room.

Emmeline shot a frustrated glare at Clementine, who grimaced in return.

"Explain what?" Emmeline asked.

"You can fly?" Melora demanded.

Sensing that might be all Clementine had revealed, Emmeline relaxed.

"I can," she confirmed.

Melora let go of Clementine's arm.

"Show me," she insisted, her tone harsh.

Emmeline took a step back, spread her golden wings, and closed her eyes. She heated her insides till they raged like a sweltering inferno, and her body lifted ever so gently off the ground. A few inches of levitation was all she needed. She pumped her wings and lifted higher into the air. When she neared the cathedral ceiling, she flew in three circles before lowering and gently landing on her tiptoes. Her wings retracted as she found firm footing.

All of Melora's anger vanished.

"You will be a star," she said, her eyes glazing over with selfish visions of the future.

"I don't want to be anything more than what I am."

"Do not fight destiny. You can do something no one else can. Our name, your name, will be forever remembered."

Emmeline thought of the destruction she had embraced in order to achieve flight. How she got here was not noble, it was not worthy of praise, yet here she was receiving accolades.

"I feel conflicted," she confessed.

"You've finally achieved something worth celebrating." Delivery harsh, the words stung. Melora did not notice her daughter cringe at the insult. She continued, "Do not shrink in the face of greatness. Embrace it, own it, revel in it. This is your moment."

Melora's newest fixation revolved around Emmeline. There was no escaping the path of her conviction.

"Is everyone in Terra okay?" Emmeline asked, shaking Melora from her visions of fame and superiority.

"Oh, yes. As well as they can be after an explosion like that. Your brothers will get to the root of the cause."

"Perhaps it was a faulty diesel shop in the market."

"Do not concern yourself with this. We have greater matters to address, such as your coming out party. We need to reveal to the world what you can do."

"They'll know soon enough."

"What do you mean?" Melora asked.

A strong gust tore through the room, forcing Emmeline, Melora, and Clementine to shield their faces.

"Were you in Terra earlier?" Solís demanded as the wind settled.

He, Cyrus, and Helix stood on her balcony, tall and backlit by the solar flare sky. Though mostly silhouetted by the lighting, Emmeline saw their various expressions. Solís wore a scowl, Cyrus looked concerned, and Helix couldn't hide his fascination.

"I was."

"How? And why?"

"To see if I could help. I realized I couldn't, so I returned home."

"You made quite the scene," Helix noted, a wide grin on his face.

"Of course, she did," Melora chimed in. "Your sister can fly without aid from a helium tank."

"You already know?" Solís asked.

"I know everything. Emmeline will be celebrated, not chastised."

"Don't you want to know how she managed to accomplish such a feat?" Solís asked.

"It really doesn't matter, does it? Look at her; she is alive and well." Everyone looked at Emmeline, and though her mother blindly sang her praises, seemingly forgetting all the turmoil that once existed between them, her brothers weren't as convinced. Solís, in particular. He scanned Emmeline's shrinking body with concern.

"She isn't healthy."

"She's perfectly fine. The clay marble diet helped, right?" Melora asked, but continued speaking before Emmeline could answer. "Perhaps we all should switch to clay marbles. The change has done wonders for Emmeline. Do you think that's part of the mysterious equation? Perhaps that is how you've come to fly. Regardless, what a delight! The Dawes name is already revered—now our infamy will live forever. The Terrapunks will spread the word among themselves. Your father and I will organize a reveal for you in Hydra. We will wait to show the Aeropunks last." Melora's mind was racing faster than she could express her thoughts. A devilish smile stretched across her face. "The Holloways will not be happy to learn of this."

With a skip in her step, Melora left Emmeline's bedroom.

For the first time in her short life, Emmeline wished her mother would have stayed. As a buffer, as a shield, for she knew her brothers would not paint a pretty picture over her recent actions.

"I should go, too," Clementine said in a meek whisper before darting out the door.

"The room is clear. Tell us the truth," Solís barked.

"I told you the truth."

"You flew over the explosion site and then just left?" Solís asked. "Because we have a report from a hunchbacked Tinkie near the explosion site that you touched down in Terra."

"She's probably saying that to distract you. I've been in her shop. She sells illegal potions."

"Did you land in Terra?" Cyrus asked, his tone kinder than Solís's.

"No," she lied, swallowing the guilt she felt. "I flew down, assessed the scene, and flew home. I wasn't sure how long I could stay afloat, and despite what you might think, I'm not that reckless."

Solís snorted. "You're as reckless as it gets."

"You're just jealous that I found a way to fly on my own."

"Jealous? That's a laugh."

"You're mad that I didn't need your help."

"Stop. You sound delusional. And you look terrible. You're going to disappear if you don't get healthy."

"I feel great."

Solís groaned, his frustration apparent.

Helix stepped forward. "Was it the dust? Did the locomo help you fly?"

"I don't think it was that," she answered honestly.

"But it might have helped?"

"I suppose it's possible," Emmeline said, catering to her desperate brother, though she knew it was her lack of weight that allowed her to gain liftoff.

Helix nodded, his hopeful thoughts read plainly across his face. "Whenever you need more, I've got you. And once you get your bearings, maybe you can teach me how to fly."

"Don't encourage her," Solís barked.

Cyrus chimed in. "I am curious to see how her ability is received in Hydra. Ruling without need of a ship gives her access to so much more of that world. The Hydropunks will not be able to pull their usual tricks and debauchery with an overseeing eye that can arrive unannounced."

Emmeline thought of Louie.

"I have to get back there," she said, spreading her mechanical wings.

"You need to wait," Cyrus replied. "Mother wants the Aeropunks to know last."

Emmeline lowered her wings.

Solís added, "You need to rest, anyway. You've already expended a lot of energy. Don't push your limits."

Emmeline nodded. "I don't know my limits yet."

"Exactly. Be careful."

He was right—she was exhausted and attempting to fly to Hydra right now would be foolish. Plus, Gemma was still hiding under her bed. She had to finish taking care of her friend and determine their next move before she departed.

She scanned her three older brothers, who still stood on her balcony, waiting for something unknown.

"Shouldn't you all be in Terra, helping with the clean up?" she asked.

"The Horrigans shooed us away. They said the Terras could handle the mess on their own," Helix answered.

Solís chimed in, "It was clearly an accident of some sort. The Horrigans were just as furious as the rest of us."

"No one was seriously injured, miraculously, and it only affected Terra. None of the other factions were impacted," Cyrus added. "It's likely the whole thing will be dropped and forgotten."

"The Horrigans won't drop it," Helix countered. "They will hunt down the culprit and punish them."

"True, as they should, but that won't involve us."

Emmeline glanced toward her bed, aware that her mission to protect Gemma might last a lifetime.

A horn blared.

Emmeline pushed through her brothers.

Montgomery's ship was lifting from the kitchen deck and leveling up to her bedroom balcony. Red Fang Ralph hung from the main sail, howling between guzzles of his grog.

Avery manned the wheel—one hand on the turnstile, and the other connected to a copper pipe. Through the attachment, she filtered helium into the hull of the ship.

"Lassie!" Red Fang Ralph shouted. "Had to hornswaggle me way out of Hydra, but blimey! The fresh air is a clap o' thunder to the senses."

Avery turned the vessel so the starboard lined up perfectly with Emmeline's balcony.

"Boys," Montgomery said as he charged toward the railing. His long golden-brown hair whipped in the morning wind. "I need you to check on the connection port at the Pyro-Argo air base for the new tether build."

"Is the tether almost complete?" Cyrus asked.

"No, but we are experiencing enough delays on our end. I'd like to ensure there will be none on your end."

"Last I checked, it was nearly complete."

"Triple check the links. We are using seven-millimeter coils, batched together in groups of ten. It needs to be a perfect fit."

"How many connection joints?"

"One hundred. The usual."

"We're on it."

Cyrus and Helix took off. Solís shot Emmeline a brief look of concern before following.

"You," Montgomery continued, turning his attention to Emmeline. "I thought I asked you to drop the quest to fly."

"It just sort of happened."

His expression was exhausted. "Well, I just spoke to your mother and she is elated by the development."

"Are you mad at me?" Emmeline asked.

"Not mad, just concerned."

"I swear, I'm okay."

"I won't lie—what I've heard is impressive."

"Watch," she said, eager to make her father proud. Though she was tired, she mustered the energy to generate heat and after a slow burn, she lifted off the golden tiles of her balcony. A few pumps of her wings, and she lifted higher.

"Enough!" her father bellowed. His booming voice startled Emmeline, causing her to falter and lower erratically. She stumbled to her feet.

"I'm sorry," he said. "I just had a flashback."

"Of what?"

"A long time ago, before the Thermas abandoned their mission to fly, my brother was on the research team. I watched him implode."

"I'm sorry."

"It's not your fault, it's just strange to relive. I never thought I'd see a Therma float on their own again, especially not my own daughter. It's dangerous."

"I haven't once felt close to combustion."

"I want you to soar, I want you to achieve great things, but please do so with care. Too many have fallen while attempting to reach similar heights."

"I will learn my boundaries and will not push past them."

He nodded. "Thank you."

"Darling," Melora called up from the hangar bay attached to the basement. "I'm ready when you are."

Montgomery addressed Emmeline. "You're coming, too. Hop on."

"Give me one second."

Emmeline ran inside, shutting the doors behind her. Lying flat on the ground, she lifted the draped sheets of her bed.

Gemma's glowing silver eyes greeted her.

"You have to stay here. You have to hide," Emmeline advised.

"I can't hide forever."

"At least stay here until I get back."

Gemma closed her eyes and smiled. "I do enjoy the warmth radiating up through the floor."

"I have a jar of clay marbles on my dresser for when you get hungry. Just don't go too close to the windows."

"I'll stay out of sight."

"Good. I will see you soon."

Her short lace skirt was not suitable for a trip to Hydra, so she quickly changed into a pair of skintight black pants. Around her waist she fastened her body straps, which had notches, holsters, pouches, and loops for all her gizmos and defenses. She retrieved a handful of marbles for herself and placed them into a small pouch tied to her waistband. Both moon stones were placed into her pockets—Cèla's remained wrapped in thick cloth to prevent accidental contact. Wings still attached, she darted through her balcony doors.

"Hop on!" Avery shouted upon her reemergence.

No longer afraid of heights, Emmeline climbed onto the railing, spread her wings, and leapt. A little bit of heat gave her enough lift to soar and land gracefully.

"Impressive," Avery said with a grin. "I knew our adventures together were just beginning."

Emmeline peered up from where she had landed in a crouch. "Let's hope the others receive me similarly."

Avery lowered the ship so Melora and Regis could board, then turned the wheel and shot a blast of helium into the hull. Montgomery breathed fire into the engine and the ship rocketed toward Hydra.

Soon she would be with Louie again.

As they approached the gates of Hydra, a cackling screech echoed into the world above.

Disturbed and visceral, Emmeline's nerves stood on edge.

There was a new monster in Hydra.

Chapter 24

"What was that?" Emmeline asked, her horror apparent.

"Ah, yes," Avery replied. "You missed the capture of our newest tenant."

"A new monster?"

She nodded. "A Devil of Delusion from the Moon of Deception."

Montgomery unlocked the gates and the airship lowered. The horrible screeching was gear-rattling.

"This is a great time for you to showcase your new ability," Montgomery advised as they flew closer to the Detention Center. "The Hydropunks are in a state of shock and despair. This monster lived among them on Smuggler's Rove for weeks, maybe months. Many are infected by its delusions."

"How would me flying help them?"

"A watchful eye in the sky might've prevented the elongated nature of this invasion. Seeing you fly might give them hope and reassurance that this won't happen again."

The monster's huge blue eyes were bloodshot and fixated on the ground, leaving the monster unaware of its visitors as it paced in a frenzy.

"It seems a little sad," Emmeline said to her father.

"Not sad—it's calculating its next move. Every few hours, it tries to escape. Then it cries and begs for freedom after being thwarted. It's a wicked and conniving devil. You must be wary of the intelligent monsters; they'll trick you into believing they're good. But you'll see, when they're free, they destroy everything good around them."

Avery chimed in, "This is the first Devil of Delusion we've ever caught. It camouflaged itself to fit in at the

Rove. Remember when you noticed there were some illegal shops? We did a deep investigation there, and this monster had turned decent Hydro merchants into criminals. It targeted the good ones and turned them bad."

"How are you so certain it was the monster who persuaded them to change?"

"Because they all had befriended the monster. In fact, they are the only Hydropunks on Smuggler's Rove who ever even saw the monster. The rest had no idea what we were talking about when we interrogated them."

"I bet it has a story to tell," Emmeline said.

"If it would speak to us, perhaps we could make sense of its existence."

Emmeline examined the wretched creature, who was now cowering in its cage. She knew her father wanted her to express excitement over the capture of another monster, so she faked it, but found herself empathizing more with the monster than her father.

They weren't so different, after all—they both lived in cages to protect their secrets. Emmeline's cage just happened to be her own withering body.

She shook this thought away.

Louie shouted her name, "Emmie!"

From Red Fang Ralph's ship below, he grinned ear to ear.

A beautiful distraction. Everything would be alright.

She tossed him a rope ladder. After he climbed aboard Montgomery's ship, she ran into his open arms and disappeared in his embrace. It was the safest place to hide.

"How was your soul day?" he asked.

"No one told you yet?"

He leaned back. "Told me what?"

"I can fly," she whispered.

270

He let her go. "Impossible."

"I'll show you, just not right now. I'm under strict orders to follow my mother's plans for my debut. But I can show you when we are alone."

Louie did not match her excitement.

"How?" he asked. The distance he had created between them now felt dangerous, like the space was filled with poison she needed to dilute.

"It just sort of happened." She was desperate to keep him close and remedy this new fissure.

"Don't lie to me," he warned.

As much as she wanted to tell him the truth, she wasn't ready. She wasn't ready to admit that she was infected by a moon stone, and even more so, she wasn't ready to admit that she wanted to stay this way. The remedy and the curse were one in the same; her migraines were pacified by starvation, and starvation led to flying. It was a vicious cycle, and the only silver lining was the unexpected gift of flight.

"What do you want to know?" she asked.

"Are you hurting yourself?"

Startled, Emmeline's defenses lifted. "No, of course not."

"I noticed you were smaller last time, but I chose not to mention it. I thought maybe it was the stress. But if you've made yourself smaller in order to fly, you need to stop."

"No, it's not like that. I was sick and stressed, and I became smaller as a result. It wasn't intentional. And flying was an unexpected side effect."

"You were sick? Have you seen a Thermadoc?"

"It was just migraines. I've learned to manage them."

"Well, when you get healthy again, you will have to stop flying. It will be too dangerous."

271

"Why are you so against it?"

"Because you were perfect as you were. You don't need to do or be more."

"You're supposed to support me."

"I do, but not at the expense of your health."

Emmeline groaned. "Please don't do this right now. You are my only reprieve."

Louie sighed and wrapped his arms around her. He kissed the top of her head.

"I will not stand by idly and watch the girl I love wither away. I promised to protect you, and that's the promise I intend to keep."

"Even if it means losing me?" she asked.

"You would choose ruin over love?"

"It's not ruin, it's advancement." Her eyes welled with oily tears. "Plus, I won't have much say in the matter now that everyone knows. My parents expect me to use this gift to help. They expect me to rule with flight."

He held her tight, as if letting her go would be their end.

She added, "I need you now more than ever."

"I made a promise to protect you. Will you make a promise to stop if this becomes too dangerous?" he asked.

Too afraid to lose him, she nodded. "I promise."

She pressed her face against his chest, breathing deeply and taking in all of him: the crisp scent of zinc and salt water, the warm octopus ink coursing through his veins, the way he held her like he never wanted to let go.

The ability to fly, or Louie's love—it was a choice she hoped she'd never have to make. And while she told him an abbreviated version of the truth, she had left out the most damning part. At the root of it all was a Hellion of Obsession. Luna was the only one who could reverse the curse of the moon stone, and Emmeline was no longer sure that she wanted to be healed.

She could have it all, or so she hoped.

"Darling!" Melora shouted over the constant murmuring of the Thermapunk crew.

"I have to go," Emmeline said to Louie, discouraged that their reunion had turned sour.

He let her go without saying a word.

His silver-blue eyes held great love and concern. Her destructive choices would ruin him if she let them spiral out of control.

"You can trust me," she promised before turning away, though she wasn't sure if he could. If she said it enough, to herself and to him, perhaps it would become the truth.

I will have it all, she thought as she marched toward her mother. She reached into her pocket to leech comfort from the moon stone, but instead, accidentally grabbed Cèla's stone wrapped in cloth. Though she was grateful for the barrier, contact with the cloth-covered stone served as a reminder that she had a secret job to do while she was here. Emmeline detoured to an uninhabited part of the ship. After a quick glance over both shoulders, she retrieved Cèla's stone from her pocket and tossed it into the sea. She did not care where it fell, only that it was safely out of her possession. Luna's curse was potent enough, she did not wish to feel the wrath of Cèla ever again.

"What was that?" a raspy feminine voice asked.

Emmeline turned to find Ruthanne the Heartless watching her—she must have followed Louie up the rope ladder. Arms crossed over her chest, red ringlets hanging to her waist, and blue gazed narrowed with suspicion.

"What was what?" Emmeline asked.

"What did you just drop into *my* ocean?" Her tone was menacing.

"A sea stone," she answered. "I found it on a dive and decided to return it to the sea."

"One of those silver ones?"

"Yes. I thought they were interesting souvenirs, but then realized they are kind of boring."

"And heavy. Too many of those would be a load to carry."

"Exactly. I have one I'm keeping from my first dive. Just a little token to remember the day."

Ruthanne examined Emmeline, seemingly detecting for lies. After a thorough assessment of her energy, her defenses lowered and she changed the subject.

"Louie is like a little brother to me," she said. "Don't hurt him."

"I won't."

Her gaze returned to the sea. "It was just a sea stone?" she asked again.

"I swear. You can dive down and see for yourself. You won't find anything but stones in the water below this ship."

Though Ruthanne dropped her line of questioning, her expression revealed a lingering misgiving. Emmeline hoped Ruthanne would forget about the stone after seeing her fly.

"Emmeline!" Melora shouted again.

"Duty calls," Emmeline said to Ruthanne, her energy deflated.

"You better hurry," Ruthanne said. "She sounds angry."

Emmeline raced to where her parents stood near the bow of the ship.

Melora had gathered the Thermapunk crew and arranged the crowd into a semi-circle. She and Montgomery stood in the open space, waving Emmeline toward them.

As Emmeline took her place beside them, Melora spoke.

"If word has not already reached you, we have revolutionary news—our dear Emmeline has mastered the art of flying."

The crew let out a collective murmur of disbelief, followed by hushed mumblings.

Melora continued, "For those of you wondering—yes, she flies without aid from the Aeropunks. She takes flight by fire alone."

The murmurings grew louder, the excited energy electric.

"This discovery is groundbreaking," Melora said.

"How does she stay aloft?" one brave Thermapunk inquired.

"We are still determining the logistics. For now, embrace this news with jubilation, for it indicates hope that all Thermapunks might fly someday."

The crew cheered. Having fire and flight would give them all an unattainable edge above the other Solarpunks of Quintessence.

"Can we see?" one of the welders asked.

"Of course!" Melora pressed her hand into the middle of Emmeline's back and pushed her forward.

Emmeline took a single clay marble out of her pocket and popped it into her mouth. As is rolled down her throat-chute, she scanned the crowd. Their golden eyes were filled with hope; they gleamed with anticipation. Louie hung from the foremast. He and Ruthanne were the only Nautipunks aboard the ship.

She locked gazes with him—hers was filled with worry, his showed concerned encouragement. He gave her a small smile, which eased her apprehension.

No migraine, no deafening hum; the marble settled, locking into the top gear of her inner workings. Its weight pushed the gear forward, faster than it was turning prior, and the whole mechanism accelerated. Energy boosted, Emmeline channeled the source flame and filled her body with heat.

Her golden-hued flesh glowed with ruby brilliance as her temperature increased. Golden gears visible through her burning skin, she embraced the heat. The sight before her faded as the fire took over—her parents, the Thermapunk crew, and Louie were cloaked in a fiery haze. Concentration locked and heat amplified, Emmeline did not notice her feet leaving the ship deck until the crew gasped in unison. She was levitating; she was aloft. Without breaking focus, she rotated her shoulder gears, churning her golden wings into action.

In a grand swoop, she took flight. Golden wings pounding the salty sky, she soared in circles around the ship. The higher she flew, the smaller those below her became.

"She soars with grace!" one of the Thermapunks exclaimed.

"Like a golden orb of fire!" said another.

When the Nautipunks stationed in their sea-bound ships caught sight, their cackling guffaws and crude bellows of disbelief echoed throughout Hydra. They shouted in amazement—some cheering praise, some yelling profanities—and their raucous response caught the attention of nearby ships. Countless vessels sailed over the horizon toward Dawes Detention Center for Demons to investigate the commotion. One by one, they joined Red Fang Ralph and crew in their guarded astonishment.

Emmeline glanced down. Her mother dramatically waved her onward, encouraging her to further display her talents. Emmeline felt strong enough to showcase her ability, her energy had not yet begun to wane, so she left the aerial perimeter of her father's airship and flew laps around the caged monsters.

Sight of her triggered their anger, and they lashed out in unique ways.

The Beast of Panic continued flying in monotonous circles, but had flipped its body and now flew upside down so it could observe Emmeline. It hissed, spitting acidic poison, which sizzled small dents into the titanium bars.

A low and menacing rumble came from the Behemoth of Fatigue, who pressed its giant face into the top bars of its cage. It released a solemn exhalation. Lethargic and soul-draining, its potent moan echoed upward, consuming all sparks of energy. Emmeline flew higher to avoid its reach.

The most furious among them was the Ogre of Irritability. This rageful monster scratched itself in fury, tearing open the many blistered sores across its face. Oozing pus and blood, the monster howled at Emmeline, too confused by its own anger to see the hurt it inflicted upon itself.

Determined not to be outdone, the Demon of Destruction matched and then surpassed the caged energy of its fellow prisoners. Repeated slams of its rock-hard head into the bars of its cage shook the entire foundation upon which it was perched. The freshly welded fissures began to crack open again. Thermapunk welders lassoed their hooks and swung to the scene, swiftly repairing the titanium and preventing a catastrophic escape.

The only monster who watched Emmeline quietly was the Devil of Delusion. Its bright blue eyes bore into Emmeline through the long, stringy red hair hanging in front of its face. Toxic energy radiated in her direction. Invisible and soundless, Emmeline did not notice the change until she flew into a pungent patch of odor. The stench forced her to halt and backtrack. Body rotated and wings pounding forward, Emmeline pushed against the toxins and flew backwards. The Devil of Delusion followed her with its eyes, breathing dark magic her way. Aware this little jaunt needed to end, Emmeline redirected her flight and lowered herself back onto the ship deck next to her parents.

Though she was rattled by the monster's ability to reach her in the sky, she had no time to relay her concerns, as the entire Thermapunk crew swarmed her with cheers and adoration.

Louie snuck through the crowd and wrapped his arms around her from behind. He whispered into her ear, "That was really impressive."

Emmeline's adrenaline shifted from panic to delight as he kissed her cheek.

Melora's furious golden gaze captured the sweet moment. Her disgust read plainly across her face.

"Absolutely not," she barked, grabbing Emmeline by the arm and dragging her out of the jubilant crowd.

Louie stood in place, his expression forlorn as they were separated.

"Does your father know about this?" Melora demanded as soon as they were out of earshot from the others.

"About what?"

"Whatever *that* was."

"The fact that I have a friend in Hydra? Yes, he knows."

"He kissed you!"

"So what?"

"You cannot intermingle with the Nautipunks. Not like *that*. Not only is it beneath you, but it is forbidden. Solarpunks of different factions cannot mate."

Emmeline cringed. "You're so embarrassing."

"You're an adult now. These are real issues you'll be facing. You have to think of your future."

"Even if we were to mate, we could build a child to our liking. We don't need to mix our elemental traits."

"Did you learn nothing in school? You cannot pick and choose pieces from a scrapyard—that is not how building a child works."

"Then tell me how?"

Melora shifted uncomfortably. "Ms. Rickard was supposed to teach you this in the academy."

"Well, she didn't."

Melora huffed. After straightening the collar of her lace blouse and crossing her arms tightly over her chest, she spoke. "It requires intimacy. It requires love. Punks must meld themselves together time and time again to create the parts needed to build a child."

"What do you mean by *meld*?"

"Blend, comingle, coalesce!"

"How, though?"

Melora inhaled and closed her eyes. Her words came out rapidly. "Melding is intercourse. Each species of punk does this differently. For Thermapunks, it takes shared heat. We join gears at the hips and the male Therma secretes fertile flares into the female's reproductive pan.

Her body then forges bones, gears, springs, screws, and bolts—various parts to build the baby."

"Each meld results in one part?"

"Yes. It's a long process. Both punks must be fully committed to succeed."

"How do other punks meld?" Emmeline asked cautiously.

"You have no need for that information."

"Well," Emmeline said, deciding not to push the matter further. "I have no intention of making babies anytime soon."

"Don't waste your love on someone you cannot build a future with," her mother warned.

"I prefer our relationship when you focus on my flying. Can we stick to that for now?" Emmeline asked.

"Fine," Melora conceded. "That really is our greatest challenge—securing your place in the sky."

"Exactly. Can we rejoin the others now? You wanted me to embrace this gift, you wanted Solarpunks of all factions to accept my ability to fly, yet you're making me miss my own celebration."

"You're right," Melora agreed. "I'm sorry. I was just caught off guard when I saw you with that Nautipunk."

"His name is Louie."

"His name doesn't matter," she snapped. "Go join the others."

Emmeline wanted to battle her further, wanted to demand that she respect Louie, but determined that was a fight for another day.

Melora departed and Emmeline enjoyed a moment alone for the first time since landing. The pungent smell the Devil of Delusion excreted clung to the rims of her nostrils. She rubbed her nose, trying to wipe it away, but it lingered.

The moon stone grew heavier.

Emmeline reached into her pocket and wrapped her fingers around the stone. Her other senses engaged. Shadowed vision and soft voices chanting now accompanied the smell. Her mouth became so dry, her breath tasted stale, and the stone grew cold to her touch.

"The reek of sulfur and corpse lily—our shared enemy is nearby."

"Luna?" Emmeline asked, startled by the voice. "Is that you?"

"Fire is the figment's only foe."

Chapter 25

Emmeline disconnected from the stone, terrified by the voices that now spoke to her. She did not like this development. She preferred the incoherent hums.

"How much trouble are you in?"

Emmeline turned to find Louie approaching.

"She'll get over it. We won't have to deal with her much in Hydra."

"Did she disapprove of me?" he asked.

"Yes, but it doesn't matter. She doesn't like anyone who isn't a high-born Thermapunk."

"I understand that your future would be better served if you spent it with a fellow Thermapunk," he said, gaze lowered and shoulders slouched.

"Being unhappy is better?" she retorted. "I highly doubt that."

Louie grinned. "You make me happy, too."

"You weren't too happy with me earlier."

"I just don't want to lose you. Flying is dangerous for Thermapunks. But after seeing you do it and witnessing your control, maybe I was wrong to assume the worst."

"I have it under control. I promise. And if I ever feel myself losing control, I will stop."

Louie pulled her in close. "I trust you. And I'm here to help however I can."

He kissed the top of her head.

She wanted to tell him everything, but worried the whole truth might be too much. He promised forever, no matter the conditions; still, she struggled to believe him. Her peculiar connection to the hellions would send most punks running.

"Hope has been restored," Montgomery announced as he marched toward them, no longer bothered by the affection she and Louie shared. "Timing could not have been more perfect. If we had shown them your ability a few days ago, they might have perceived it as a threat. But in the wake of the Devil of Delusion's terror, they see your gift as a blessing for all. An added security."

"I'm glad it was received well," Emmeline replied. "Though you ought to add some sort of shield around the devil. It excretes its toxins through the bars of its cage. I felt it, well—*smelled* it, in the sky."

"Fantastic intel," Montgomery gushed. "Your gift is already proving to be quite helpful."

He rushed away to consult his crew on how best to better contain the devil.

Louie placed his hands on Emmeline's cheeks, his blue gaze bright with concern.

"Did it hurt you?" he asked.

"No, I'm fine. I left the moment I realized what it was doing."

"It doesn't take much poison to be afflicted."

"I don't feel any different," she said, though that was a lie. The confidence she felt now was greater than how she felt a few hours ago.

"Well, if you start having illusions of grandeur or brushes with invincibility, be sure to tell me or your father. All the infected Hydropunks tiptoed a fine line between reality and fantasy."

"Understood. I'll be aware."

She lifted to her toes, closed her eyes, and puckered her lips. A moment lingered as she waited for her kiss. Louie leaned in, obliging her silent request. As their lips touched,

Emmeline pulled Louie closer and smiled, then proceeded to dispense countless tiny kisses.

Louie accepted them, also grinning throughout their delivery.

When she finally let him go, Louie stumbled backward, feigning dizziness from the onslaught of affection.

"Time to leave!" Melora shouted from the deck Louie and Emmeline stood beneath. She could not see them, but her call rang loud and clear.

Emmeline sighed. "That's my ride."

"You'll be back soon," he replied.

"Everything is so different above Hydra. I prefer being here."

"When things get tough up there, just remember that this is your home now, too."

"And that you're here, waiting for me," she added.

Louie grinned. "Yes. That, too."

He leaned in to deliver a farewell kiss.

She wished this could be her permanent reality, but the repeated shouts of her mother were a harsh reminder that her reality must exist both above and below.

"Ruthanne climbed aboard, too," she said, remembering that Louie wasn't the only Nautipunk on the ship.

"I haven't seen her," he said, brow furrowed. "But I'll make sure she leaves with me before you depart."

They walked to the side of the boat where the rope ladder still hung. A quick glance over the edge revealed Ruthanne dueling the largest of her Nautipunk crewmates.

"I guess she found her way back to Ralph's ship," Louie said with a laugh as he straddled the gunwale and found his footing on the ladder.

"It appears so," Emmeline noted.

Louie gave her one last kiss before lowering.

Emmeline walked across the large ship to join her family on the top deck. The ladder to get there was tall, but she made the climb. Joints creaking, gears weak, she felt the fatigue of her imbalanced energy consumption and expulsion. What she put out was more than what she took in—she needed grease and marbles to refuel.

Regis and Avery stood behind the wheel of the airship, and Melora paced near the ladder. When Emmeline's head appeared over the ledge, Melora extended her hand and helped Emmeline climb onboard.

"I have a platter of clay marbles prepared if you're hungry."

"Oh, I am! Thank you," Emmeline replied before carefully consuming a few marbles. She spaced their intake, careful not to overload her gears and give herself a migraine. Skilled at recognizing her limits, she managed to reenergize without suffering the consequences.

Regis flew the airship out of Hydra, silent, as usual. Quiet, just as Melora preferred.

After a small but filling meal, Emmeline turned her attention to the world below. Gemma's explosion in Terra was still being remedied, though great progress had been made. The Revopunks had resumed their progression across the terra gears, and the Tinkerpunks had rebuilt half of the market in Sector 3.

Emmeline thought of Gemma and how she'd have to fight hard to protect her from the wrath of the Horrigans.

Regis delivered them home, and Emmeline raced up to her room.

Solís stood in front of the door, arms crossed and golden gaze furious.

"Did you think you were slick? That we wouldn't find out?" he asked.

Emmeline gulped. "Find out what?"

"It should be obvious," he stated, "unless you're keeping many secrets."

"Move out of my way," Emmeline demanded, pushing her brother aside to enter her room, but he pressed the door wide open and followed her inside.

"Stop!" she shouted, but her defiance lessened as she witnessed the chaos before her.

Her room was littered with clothes and jewelry. Armoires emptied, dresser drawers stripped, everything she owned was scattered across the floor.

Gemma stood in the middle of the mess, staring at herself and striking odd poses in the mirror. She was dressed in a mismatched assortment of Emmeline's clothes: a cropped jacket with decorated shoulder pads overtop of an oversized nightgown that hung to her shins, combat boots that were too big for her feet, and a patchwork bowler hat that was put on backwards.

"What are you doing?" Emmeline asked.

Gemma turned, startled—she hadn't heard them open the door.

"Oh, gosh," she said, falling to the floor and pulling a large trench coat over her body.

"He's already seen you," Emmeline stated, trying not to laugh. "You don't need to hide."

"I'm sorry," she said, her apology muffled beneath the heavy coat.

Emmeline glanced over her shoulder at Solís, who wore a perplexed expression.

"She's not a threat," Emmeline assured him.

"Did she cause the explosion in Terra?"

"No," Emmeline said. "I did."

Solís scoffed. "You were in the great hall, celebrating your soul day. I was there with you."

"It's my fault that she is sick. I am to blame for her current state."

Solís glared at his sister, then at Gemma, whose head now peeked out from under the trench coat.

"I told you that befriending a Tinkie was trouble," he said.

"I caused her more trouble than she has caused me," Emmeline rebutted.

"Well, you can't keep her here."

"I can do whatever I want."

"I won't allow it," Solís persisted.

"Are you going to tell Mom?"

"If I have to."

"I never took you for a snitch," Emmeline spat.

Solís's expression tightened. "Are you trying to self-destruct?"

"Of course not."

"It sure seems like you are. First the shrinking, then the flying, now the harboring of explosive fugitives. You're playing a dangerous game."

"This is not a game. This is my life."

"Then you ought to treat it with a little more care. You aren't invincible."

Emmeline groaned. "I'm doing the best I can."

Solís sensed her aggravation and lessened his aggression. "How can I help?" he asked.

"By leaving me alone," Emmeline said, unwilling to accept his sudden, more docile demeanor.

"You are your own worst enemy," he spat.

"Maybe, but I am also the only one who can save me from myself."

"Well, try not to get in your own way."

Solís stormed out of her room.

Emmeline turned to Gemma. "I'm glad to see you're feeling better …"

"Yes! I ate some more marbles and all my gears are churning normally again."

"Gemma," Emmeline said, her tone stern. "You were supposed to hide."

"I thought I was! I never left your room."

"The window drapes are wide open!"

"Yes, to let the light in," Gemma said.

Emmeline shook her head. "Anyone can see inside. My brothers fly to and from this house daily."

"Oh, I see. I'm sorry."

"It's okay. I'm sure Solís made sure no Aeropunks flew too close to watch your fashion show through the windows."

"You have so many beautiful clothes. I've only ever owned one garment at a time, and I usually keep it till it's so tattered that I have to replace it."

"Take whatever outfit you like. I have too many."

Gemma's silver eyes lit up as she scanned the mess strewn across the floor.

"I should probably pick an outfit that covers my exposed bones," she noted while lifting a pair of full-length overalls off the floor. "Plenty of pockets, and straps to keep them on. I tried a pair of regular pants before—not even a belt could keep them on. My hip bones are too bare."

"Looks like it's overalls or dresses for you."

"Seems so. I like these."

"Great. You can have them."

While Gemma changed outfits, Emmeline closed the window drapes. She thought of Luna as she blocked the outside world from her bedroom. There was no telling if there'd ever be a cure for this curse.

"The good news is that without my tracker, the Horrigans can't find me," Gemma offered. "They'll assume I died in the explosion. I'm free."

"Still, I am relocating you to Hydra," Emmeline said. "I can keep you safe there."

"How will you manage that? Tinkies aren't allowed in Hydra. Plus, I'll be in constant danger from the Nautipunks trying to harvest my petroleum. Or worse— my uranium heart."

"I am in charge down there. My commands are law. You will be my new assistant, there to help me upkeep my wings. Salt water will wear them down quicker."

"Yes, true," Gemma said. "The gold will warp and rust in that potent salt air without maintenance."

"The perfect alibi."

"And if I keep my legs covered, maybe no one will ever realize that I am to blame for that explosion."

"We can hope."

"Thank you for helping me," Gemma said gratefully.

"I truly believe what I said before—this is my fault. You were fine before you met me, fine before you touched the moon stone."

Gemma did not argue. "Do you think we will find a way to heal?"

"I have a friend who is working on it. Hopefully she returns soon."

Melora's voice echoed through the house. "Emmeline! It is time to showcase your abilities to the rest of Quintessence."

"Keep the drapes shut this time," Emmeline advised her friend.

"Yes, I will. Sorry again."

"I'll be back soon."

Emmeline grabbed a handful of clay marbles from the jar on her dresser and ate two before racing downstairs. The moon stone, which once felt light, hung heavy in her pocket—it was quickly becoming the heaviest part of her.

She threw a third marble down the chute, preparing for another energy-expending flight, and as it rolled into the holding pan, the voice in her head returned.

"You are doing too much." The ethereal warning was accompanied by a low hum. It started at the nape of Emmeline's neck and slowly pulsated upward.

"I'm fine," she replied, clutching the moon stone to stop the migraine from fully forming.

"Do not embrace the delusion."

Silence resumed as her migraine dissipated.

Emmeline reached the kitchen. Melora was waiting there for her, armed with her posse of high-ranking Thermapunks. They stared at Emmeline, their intrigue covetous—a strange contrast from their utter disregard only a few days prior at her soul day celebration.

"Are you ready to fly?" Melora asked her daughter.

"Always."

Chapter 26

Emmeline stood at the edge of the airship as Regis flew them to the Pyro-Argo air base. Melora had made a few calls and orchestrated a large gathering to witness Emmeline in fight.

When they arrived, the crowds were already there. Thermapunks congregated on the open hangar bay, while Aeropunks filled the sky on their various hovering contraptions.

Melora and Montgomery stood at the ship's bow, preparing to address the crowd. Avery stood beside Emmeline's brothers—everyone showed concern, except for Emmeline.

"Aren't you nervous?" Helix asked.

"Not at all," Emmeline answered honestly.

"You ought to be," Solís retorted. "Blind confidence will be the reason you fall one day."

"He's right," Cyrus added. "All it'll take is one slip or error to end in catastrophe."

"It's not blind confidence … I know the risks," Emmeline snapped.

"I told you guys we should've argued harder to get her a helium tank," Helix griped. "That would've prevented all of this."

Solís silently scrutinized his sister's shrinking body, then said, "I don't think it would have."

"He's right," Emmeline said. "While that would've been nice, the outcome would have been the same. I don't need helium to fly."

"What she needs is support," Avery chimed in, appalled by their insensitive barrage. "You are her brothers. There is no stopping her momentum now, and whether it turns out great or it ends poorly, just be there for her."

This silenced Cyrus and Helix, but Solís was not so easily assuaged.

"Personally, I'd prefer to prevent the tragedy *before* it happens."

"Stop trying to save me," Emmeline complained, exasperated by Solís's smothering show of concern. "I'm fine."

Solís threw his hands into the air and walked away.

"I really am fine," Emmeline repeated to Cyrus, Helix, and Avery.

"You seem fine to me," Avery encouraged.

"Yeah … you're a little smaller, but you still look healthy," Helix noted, trying to make sense of it all.

Cyrus agreed, and added, "Just stay how you are now."

"I will," Emmeline promised.

Cyrus and Helix opened their arms and buried her in a group hug. Delighted to have their support, her sullen spirits lifted.

"I know you've known each other all your lives," Avery stated as the group hug ceased, "but I've only gotten to know Emmeline recently. I have seen a side of her that none of you have witnessed. She is brave, she is fearless, and she is selfless. Her heart is good, and if the gift of flight is her blessing, then in my eyes, she is more than worthy."

Cyrus nodded. "I haven't seen you in Hydra, but I know you are all of those things. Through the good and bad, I am here for you."

"Me, too," Helix agreed.

"Thank you," Emmeline said, her eyes wide with oily tears. "I've felt so alone up here, above Hydra, so it's a relief to know you'll be there for me regardless."

292

"We love you," Helix said. "So does Solís. He will come around."

"I know he will. He's just a stubborn pain."

"I think it's time," Avery said, her voice hushed.

Melora and Montgomery had finished their address to the crowd and were waving her to join them.

Instead of walking, Emmeline channeled the flame in her heart and levitated, floating ever so slightly above the ship deck and using her wings to gently propel her forward. Sunlight beaming behind her created a radiant silhouette. Heart ablaze, she fluttered toward them like an angel of fire sent by Solédon.

The crowd gasped—a mixture of awe and horror. The Thermapunks in attendance saw Emmeline as a vision of hope; perhaps they, too, could learn how to fly. The Aeropunks saw her arrival as a threat; the upper hand they once had would vanish if other Thermapunks followed her lead.

Emmeline floated past her parents and left the safety of the ship. Hovering at lethal heights, she stayed there for all to witness her fiery glory.

"Preposterous!" Deandra Holloway shouted from the cushy throne atop her regal dirigible. She was the matriarch of the Holloway family—the most prestigious Aeropunk family. They lived in faraway castles, existing in the highest and farthest level of Gaslion. Residing so close to the solar shield, only their assigned Pilopunks and the Pryopunks and Argopunks guarding against moon monster invasions ever saw them. Though they oversaw all Aeropunks, they worked as gas spinners. Maintaining the gaseous balance of the solar shield and conserving the delicate atmospheric balance was a noble job, one that ostracized them from the rest of the punks. Deandra's social status was similar to Melora's, and her irritated outburst filled Melora with delight.

"Do not fight the changing tides," Melora shouted to her foe.

Deandra's Pilopunks pedaled the Holloways closer. Heads down and geared knees creaking, they steered their leaders to the edge of the Dawes's family airship. Emmeline hovered between the two opposing forces, caught in the middle of an ancient rivalry that had been pacified until this day—until she revealed her cursed gift.

"Do not challenge the balance of nature," Deandra spat in reply. "This is unnatural! Your daughter is a monster!"

"How dare you," Melora seethed.

"Ladies, ladies," Montgomery interceded. "Our families must work together."

"You must admit, this is abnormal," Reuben said from his throne next to Deandra. Patriarch of the Holloway family, he ruled over the Aeropunks with staunch rigidity.

"Don't be bitter."

"Bitter? I just wish to protect what is rightfully ours," Reuben said. "Thermapunks are the only beings in Quintessence with access to the source flame. Isn't that enough? Can't we have one thing to claim as our own?"

"You will always rule the sky."

"Why must you have flight, too?"

"Her ability came as a surprise to us all," Montgomery said as gently as possible. "If you were more in touch with the rest of us, perhaps this news wouldn't feel so shocking. Thermapunks work in brilliant unison with the Pilopunks and Argopunks, while you hide away near the solar shield, disengaged from the happenings below. Only you and your fellow conservationists hold tight to this desire to feel superior to us through flight."

"If that were true, then why don't you share the source flame with us?"

Montgomery smirked. "It is a vicious circle we spin in. If flight for the Thermapunks is what the gods decree, then so it will be."

"I will be the judge of this so-called gift. Surely you will agree to an Aeropunk chaperone for your daughter's safety."

"Excuse me?" Melora snapped.

"My children, Raven and Remington—they will serve as guides for young Emmeline. They will make sure her techniques are safe, and most importantly, natural."

"You have no expertise with fire. How dare you act like you have some superior knowledge as to how Thermapunks achieve flight."

"If you want our acceptance of this jarring, and frankly, freakish development, you will need to appease my requests."

Fatigue was beginning to take hold of Emmeline. She held her position in the sky, determined not to let anyone see her wavering strength.

"They will not chaperone, but they are welcome to join us for dinner whenever they please," Montgomery replied, his voice calm and stern. "They can learn about us and Emmeline, and ask her questions. But there will be no formal watch or guardianship. They will not monitor her every move."

"Do you want a war between our people?"

"Do you?" Montgomery retorted, his golden skin glowing brighter as his anger intensified. "My offer is plenty generous."

The threat of the source flame was enough to remind Reuben of his place in this hierarchy.

Reuben's expression tightened as he conceded.

"Raven! Remington!" he shouted into the nothingness above. Despite the open sky, his voice carried like an echo in a valley, dancing along with the wind until it reached the outer edges of Quintessence.

In mere seconds, two rushing streams of air blasted onto the scene, circling Emmeline with such speed, the forms of those within could not be seen.

After a thorough and invasive sweep of the airship, Raven and Remington ceased their assault and occupied the empty seats beside their parents.

Unlike the other Aeropunks, their methods for flying were sleek and sophisticated. Simplistic in design, they had small steel propellers attached to the ankles, knees, hips, and shoulders of their flesh-hugging body suits. Webbed gloves helped them steer through the air at dizzying speeds.

Raven had hair as dark as night, which matched the sullen energy emanating from her pinkish-orange eyes. Remington had the same dark hair, but his gaze held mischief. Sorrow and trouble—a devious pairing.

"What is this freak show you've summoned us to?" Raven asked, glaring at Emmeline.

"The Thermapunks seem to have discovered flight. I called you here to investigate."

"She feels weak," Raven stated to her parents, bored.

"I don't think her ability to fly will last long," Remington agreed.

Emmeline could no longer feign strength. She lowered to the ship's deck before anyone suspected their accusations were correct.

Avery stood beside Emmeline, her presence comforting during the Holloways' pretentious display of power.

"Don't listen to them," she whispered into Emmeline's ear. "They are obnoxious and poorly socialized."

Emmeline took a deep breath and stepped to the edge of the ship.

She spoke directly to the Holloway family.

"My strength far surpasses yours, as I am one with water, terrain, gas, and fire. If you cannot accept me as I am, you will be left behind in the days of glory yet to come."

Her threatening promise rang with such confidence, everyone in earshot was stunned into silence. A roaring cheer from the Thermapunks watching from the hangar bay below broke the quiet tension, further confirming that Emmeline was a force for all to fear. Join, or get left behind. Her poise in the face of adversity was admirable, and she had solidified the support of her own people.

The Pilopunks and Argopunks in attendance looked less convinced.

Emmeline looked to Avery, who offered an encouraging smile, then she thought of Louie and Gemma—her greatest friends.

For the first time, she realized what she truly wanted. Like a bolt of clarity, she understood the true potential of her cursed gift.

"My ability to fly is no threat to any of you. I only wish to help. My desire is to form a coalition that unites all the Solarpunks of Quintessence. Instead of working separately, we ought to combine forces. Together, we are stronger. We are neighbors, not enemies. Our only foes exist beyond the reaches of the sun."

Another promise Emmeline was unsure if she could keep, though it seemed to sway the reluctant Aeropunks. Mumbling among them grew as they considered this idea.

For the first time in history, they were being presented with the proposition to unite rather than remain divided.

Avery stepped forward and added, "If it counts for anything, I've worked alongside Emmeline for months now, and while I cannot guarantee that her grand visions will prevail, I can promise that her intentions are truthful. Do not fear the unknown, embrace it."

Regis hitched a lock in the wheel and hobbled to stand beside his daughter. He took a deep breath before adding, "Many of you know me, and you know how I feel about the Thermapunks." He grumbled and side-eyed Emmeline. "Well, she is different than the rest. Her heart is open. The Nautipunks are already on board … I say we give this a chance, too."

Regis and Avery had sway over the common folk Aeropunks. Both were beloved figures in the Pilopunk and Argopunk community.

Reassurance from both Regis and Avery was enough to tip the balance in Emmeline's favor. There was no cheering, only a tiny, hopeful applause. Reserved, yet optimistic, they were willing to try something new.

This did not please the Holloway family. Deandra scoffed in disgust, while Raven and Remington observed the shift with utter confusion.

"Their willingness to trust you does not squash the deal we made," Reuben said to Montgomery.

"The invitation for your family to join us in unity stands. You'd be wise to accept."

"We will be monitoring this development. My people may be open, but I will maintain a steady guard in case their trust has been misplaced."

"Whatever makes you feel better. We do not wish to fight."

Aggravated by Montgomery's docile nature, Reuben shouted orders for their Pilopunks to return them home. This was not the end of their dissonance, and they'd likely return with reinforcements next time, as their fellow conservationists would have similar reservations.

As the cheering and applause continued, Melora and Montgomery turned to Emmeline.

"You did it!" Melora exclaimed. "I'm not too certain about your promises of unity, but it seemed to work."

"That's how I truly feel," Emmeline countered.

"Well, that will be a battle for another day." Melora did not wish to argue; she wanted to enjoy this glorious moment—another notch of greatness for the Dawes family.

Montgomery pulled Emmeline into a hug.

"I support your desires for unity," he said.

"Thank you."

"It will be hard, but far from impossible."

"I know. I will do my best."

Unable to remedy the destructive magic of the moon stone, Emmeline was determined to turn her curse into a blessing.

Chapter 27

Gemma sat on the mauve velvet chaise lounge in the corner of Emmeline's room, spinning an active firestone between her fingers. Body stripped of flesh and rebuilt in a manner that allowed more ventilation for her petroleum veins, Gemma could now withstand more heat than any other Terrapunk. Her heart was still explosive, but there was little left of her to detonate.

"They'll be back soon," she assured Emmeline, who stood on her balcony, waiting for her father to return home from Hydra.

A week had passed since her big reveal, and Melora had Emmeline on a strict schedule of flights. She flew every morning, afternoon, and evening to showcase her ability, reminding all of Quintessence of her power. The longer she was forced to obey her mother's regimented schedule, the more she desired to escape into Hydra.

Montgomery had agreed, though—Emmeline needed to solidify her new standing in the upper world of Quintessence before returning to Hydra—which was why he left without her.

Emmeline obeyed, hoping her compliance might lead to a quicker return to the only place she really wanted to be.

As she stared out the window waiting for her father's dragon-winged airship to return, she thought of Louie. Everything was changing too quickly, and she feared not being by his side as these changes occurred. Would it cause a rift in their bond? Would they grow apart? She needed to be with him so they could navigate these changes together.

Thoughts of all the time she was missing with him stirred the fire in her heart. Emmeline stepped away from the window and began to pace.

"You're stressing me out," Gemma stated, her confidence growing by the day.

"Sorry. We just need to get out of here. I want to be in Hydra."

"Try to enjoy the spotlight a little. Everyone idolizes you."

"That's because they don't know the truth. I am sick, you are sick. Our abilities stem from destruction."

"You sound like me a few weeks ago," Gemma said with a laugh. "I was so worried, but maybe it takes a breakdown to be built back better."

Emmeline groaned. "Despite my better judgment, I've been thinking the same thing. My friend is working on a cure, but I don't think I want it anymore."

"I think we are managing just fine."

"Yeah," Emmeline agreed. "Somehow, we both found ways to cope. We took the curse and turned it into a blessing. Look at us! We are beating all the odds."

"Exactly."

"Still, I'd rather be in Hydra."

"We will be there soon."

A small knock rapped against her bedroom door.

Gemma stopped talking and Emmeline tiptoed to the door, pressing her ear against the thin golden frame.

The person on the other side sensed her presence and asked, "How do you do it?"

Soft, sweet, and demure—Emmeline recognized the voice.

"Clementine?" she asked, cracking the door open.

Clementine stood on the other side, her expression desperate.

"I need to get out of my responsibilities at the Steamery," Clementine stated.

"Your parents need you there."

"My younger siblings can take on the responsibility. Please teach me. Let me join you," Clementine pled.

Behind Emmeline, Gemma sat quietly.

Emmeline warned, "I'm not sure if you're ready to know the truth."

"Please let me in."

"Okay, but everything you see and hear is sworn to secrecy."

"I swear," Clementine promised.

Emmeline opened the door and Clementine gasped at the sight of Gemma.

"Is that a Tinkerpunk?" she asked as Gemma's silver gaze met her golden concern.

"Yes. That is my friend, Gemma."

"Is that who you flew down to see in Terra? Is she the one who caused the explosion?"

Gemma bent her knees and yanked up her pants, exposing the silver bones and gears beneath.

Clementine's question was answered.

Emmeline sensed her confusion.

"My ability to fly began as a curse. Gemma was cursed as well, it just materialized differently. We've done all we can to turn these lethal afflictions into miracles. We survived, despite the odds."

"So to fly, I'd need to suffer and defeat a curse?"

Emmeline nodded. "And there's no telling how the curse would afflict you. It's not worth the risk."

"I should be the one to determine that," Clementine replied.

"Except you're not. I hold the key. I won't subject you or anyone else to it."

"Have you looked outside recently? Thermas are maiming themselves in an attempt to emulate you. They deserve to know the truth."

"You promised secrecy."

"And I plan to keep that promise, just let me in on the magic. I need to break away from my monotonous routine at the Steamery. It's soul crushing."

"I imagine that seeing me fly stirs envy in others, but I swear, it comes with a cost—an irreversible cost. One that comes with great sacrifice."

"Just name me as a member of your team. Please, I beg you. I'll be an extra heart of fire down in Hydra. Surely that could be useful."

Emmeline considered this. It would be worthwhile to have another source flame around at all times.

"If I agree, you will not badger me about flying again."

"Deal."

Emmeline now had two friends in her crew, and soon, Avery would join them. Unifying the factions—she would succeed in this mission.

"We are leaving for Hydra as soon as my father returns. You ought to settle up any matters you have up here before we leave."

"Yes, I need to let my boss at the Steamery know that I quit." Clementine bounced with excitement. "Oh, I can't wait!"

"Hurry back. There's no telling when we will leave."

Clementine nodded before darting out the door.

"You ought to let her touch the moon stone," Gemma said.

"Are you crazy?"

"Do you really think your father will let her join us if all she can offer is a normal dose of fire? He has a whole crew of Thermapunks for that. You're already pushing your luck trying to bring me. You have more pull now, but your father is still in charge."

Emmeline halted — Gemma was right.

"She can't quit, not yet."

Emmeline raced out of her bedroom and caught Clementine before she reached the first flight of stairs.

"Wait!" she shouted.

Helix left his bedroom at the same time, high on a recent hit of locomo.

"Like old times," he said, a nostalgic grin on his face. "What game are you two playing? Tag? Dolls?"

"No games ... we are adults now. Move along," Emmeline said, shooing Helix away.

He snickered before charging down the steps. Once out of earshot, Emmeline spoke to Clementine.

"Don't quit yet."

"Why not?"

"I need to present my case to my father. I am building my own crew, he knows that, but I need to ensure that he approves your admittance into Hydra first. It would be foolish for you to quit before guaranteeing you have something to replace it with."

"Why isn't your word enough?"

"Because my dad is still in charge down there. He has the final say."

Clementine's shoulders slouched, her enthusiasm dissipating.

Emmeline added, "Don't be discouraged. I suspect he will say yes. I'd just rather play it safe."

"If you let me in on the magic, I could pave my own way, just like you did."

"Shh," Emmeline insisted. "Just be patient."

Clementine grumbled as she marched down the stairs.

"Magic, huh?" Solís said, leaning against his bedroom door frame.

Emmeline squeezed her eyes shut, annoyed that he was hovering yet again.

"It's a lie," she said.

"Are you sure?"

She turned to face him. "Very sure. There is no such thing as magic."

"There are tales of dark magic in the holy doctrine. Spells, potions, curses."

"Fables of fantasy, just like all the other stories in that book."

"You doubt Solédon?"

"He's a liar."

Her adamant blasphemy caught Solís by surprise.

"I hope you aren't desecrating His holiness in public."

"Of course not. I'm just sick of the lies."

"Why do you think it's all lies?"

Emmeline groaned. "You wouldn't believe me if I told you."

"Try me."

"No. I have more important things to do."

She marched back to her room, leaving Solís baffled where he stood.

He was onto her and she did not appreciate it.

"My brother is a nuisance," she complained to Gemma as she reentered her room.

"Which one?"

"Which one do you think?" Emmeline snapped. "Solís, of course. If he had his way, he'd dissect every last secret from my brain and heal me against my will."

"Sounds like he worries about you."

"He does. I know he cares and that it comes from a place of love, but he's too invested, too controlling. He cares too much! I just want him to leave me alone."

"We will be in Hydra soon enough. He won't bother you there, right?"

"As long as he doesn't get into my father's ear, I should be free of him there."

Emmeline executed the nighttime flight her mother insisted she perform. She paid little attention to the gawking crowds of Thermas and Aeros enamored by her blazing theatrics. Instead, she eagerly imagined the day she'd have more control over her schedule. She thought her soul day would be a marker of freedom, but with this new ability, her mother's grip had tightened, and a strange peace had formed between them. Melora was so elated to have a renowned and revered child, she no longer harped on Emmeline for little stuff, and Emmeline was not yet ready to test the boundaries of her mother's flimsy appeasement. One wrong move, and their war would resume.

For now, it was better to keep the peace.

After landing on the basement hangar bay, Emmeline tore past her brothers without saying a word, grabbed a large bowl of clay marbles her mother had set out in the kitchen, and retreated to her bedroom. Only her brothers knew about Gemma, and she intended to keep it that way until her father returned.

She and Gemma ate dinner together with the balcony doors open. They watched the daytime solar flares shift from orange and red to pink and purple. Gemma had no food restrictions, whereas Emmeline had to be careful with each marble consumed.

"How many can you eat before the migraine starts?" Gemma asked.

"If I pace myself, five. If I eat too fast, or if I'm stressed, it can happen after one or two."

"Five is the max? No wonder you're shrinking!"

"I think I've found a sustainable routine. Where I'm at is small, but manageable. If I plan it right, I should stay this size."

"Sounds miserable."

"Not as miserable as the migraines."

"I suppose your migraines are a lot like the agonizing chill and restlessness I feel when I desire fire. I want to crawl out of my skin, and only heat soothes the discomfort."

"Well," Emmeline said with a smirk, "now you have half the amount of skin to crawl out of."

Her dark joke landed, and Gemma laughed so hard, the marble in her mouth shot across the room.

"You're rotten," Gemma said through the laughter.

"At least we can joke about it."

"Yeah, I'd rather laugh than cry."

The mood turned solemn again. Despite their ability to turn their ailments into something positive, they both knew that their gifts stemmed from the decimation of their health and that time might not be on their sides. Surviving like this was a gamble, and it was yet to be determined if it was sustainable.

"I'm full," Gemma announced, the tinkering of her inner gears audible from beneath her overalls. "Time to sleep."

She curled up on the chaise lounge and pulled a wool blanket over her body, covering everything from her skeletal toes to her silver-haired head.

Emmeline was still working on her second marble. Though she had learned to silence the hunger pains, it didn't stop her gears from creaking forward devastatingly slow. She felt every bolt and nut scrape against her golden hinges, poorly greased and rusting. Emmeline took a swig of oil, as if one sip would remedy a full day's worth of neglect.

A gentle breeze blew Emmeline's golden hair off her shoulders.

"You need to take better care of yourself."

It was Luna, but she was nowhere to be seen.

"Where are you?" Emmeline asked.

"Meet me on the rooftop. Bring the stone."

The breeze circled overhead once before departing through the open balcony doors.

Emmeline took another swig of oil, cupped four marbles in her grip, and tiptoed out of her room. She closed the door gently, so as not to disturb Gemma's slumber, then crept through the hallway past her brothers' rooms, dodging the creaky golden floorboards. Five skips and a jump, she hopped down the corridor toward the attic staircase.

The doorknob was made of bronze and had ornate floral patterns etched into the metal. Ancient, just like all the artifacts stored behind this door.

As a child, Emmeline enjoyed getting lost in the attic for hours, rediscovering the past through antiquated paintings, journals, and relics. She hadn't been up there in years, and the dust from inactivity made her cough.

She shooed away the plume of dust as she walked through a long row of golden chests. They varied in shapes and sizes, but all were sealed with ruby-coated padlocks. Mannequins dressed in her great grandparents' finest gowns and suits lined the walls, along with an array of broken clocks all stuck at different times.

There were six windows in the attic, but only one provided access to the roof. The cosmic pink and purple light from outside lit up the scattered dust with interstellar brilliance, creating the illusion of space. Emmeline sifted through, imagining she was floating far beyond the confines of Quintessence as she made her way to the window.

It hadn't been opened in years.

Emmeline used all her strength to pry open the rusted lock. After a minute of struggle, it cracked and twisted. She lifted the heavy frame, cringing as the corroded seams screeched in protest. Moving slowly did not lessen the noise. It was so loud, she decided it was best to push the window up with force to get it over with. After one giant heave and one earsplitting scrape, she was granted access to the rooftop.

She ate another marble, allowing a slow roll down her throat chute, then placed the rest in her pocket and climbed over the window ledge.

It was an easy scale over two small peaks to get to the place where Luna waited. Dragonfly wings wide and glowing in the beautiful light of night, her silver-disced eyes were filled with concern.

"Are you visible to anyone who flies by?"

"No, just you. While you have the stone, I can allow you to see me through my invisibility shield. I can speak telepathically to you through the stone also."

"That explains a lot," Emmeline said. "I was hearing voices and thought I might be going crazy."

"It's just me," Luna assured her, then changed the topic. "I haven't been able to find a cure yet," she said, her remorse apparent.

"It's okay. A lot has changed here. I have found a way to turn this curse into a blessing."

"Excuse me?"

"My sickness graced me with the ability to fly, and I am learning how to manage the migraines in a way that keeps me this exact size."

"You cannot control the curse. You might think you have it subdued, but it feeds off the challenge. It will adapt and attack more fiercely. Do not let this moment of calm fool you."

"There's nothing calm about this moment—I am in a constant battle—but I feel confident that I am managing. This curse could unite the people of my world, and one day, after they see the good I have contributed to our society, I will tell them it was a gift from you and we can end the war between the sun and your moon."

"It is not a gift," Luna reminded her.

"It is a blessing in disguise."

"You can call it whatever you want—a gift, a blessing, a miracle—but it will always be a curse. If you lose sight of that fact, you will not live to see the other side of your affliction."

Emmeline huffed, annoyed that Luna was not listening to her.

"Can't you see that I'm just trying to make the best of this terrible situation?"

"You are going about it wrong. You are trying to live with it, thrive with it, instead of healing from it. It is delusional." Luna's eyes widened. "The devil," she said in a whisper. "It got to you."

"The Devil of Delusion?" Emmeline asked, recalling her brief brush with the monster in Hydra. "No, I never got close enough."

"You don't have to get close for it to infect you. Its noxious fragrance can reach victims from great distances."

"I did smell something foul."

"It's poison. It's gaseous delusion."

"I don't feel any different," Emmeline insisted.

"Delusion is sneaky—it often goes undetected until it emerges in a person's impulsive actions."

"I am not impulsive, nor have I acted in any rash manner. I'm just trying to adapt as best I can."

"Delusion also shows itself in a victim's thoughts and decision making. I'd say it has affected your thoughts."

"I do not agree."

"Just the other day you tried giving back the moon stone," Luna argued. "Now, you want to keep it and benefit from its dark powers. You must see the shift—it is so clear."

"You are looking at this from the outside, whereas I am actively living in this nightmare. I cannot defeat the curse—you said yourself that you haven't found a cure yet—so what other option do I have than to learn to live with it? My choice is to be miserable, or to make the best of it. I choose the latter."

"I get it, but be careful. This isn't a game. And if the Devil of Delusion has hold of you too, then your battle has become much harder. We fight them often," Luna said. "They are a huge nuisance on our moon."

"If you fight them, tell me how to defeat them."

"Fire is your best bet. It's one of many reasons we need access to the source flame. They'd have overtaken our moon by now if we didn't have fire as a defense."

"Well, I am made of fire. The devil has no chance against me."

"But the moon stone does—it will kill you if you let it take too much of you."

"I am aware. It almost killed Gemma."

"What happened?" Luna asked.

"The curse made her so cold, she held too many active firestones at once and exploded. It didn't reach her heart, thankfully, but her whole lower half had to be rebuilt. She's doing better now. In fact, she's thriving. When she rebuilt herself, she wrapped thermacloth around her petroleum veins and can now withstand more heat than before."

"She sounds delusional, too. You two are bad influences on each other."

"It wasn't my idea," Emmeline objected.

"I'll keep working on a solution. There's a lot of turmoil back home—my people are divided about my mission to save you."

"You don't need to save me. I am saving myself."

"Except you aren't."

Emmeline groaned. "Don't get yourself into trouble on my behalf. I have this handled."

Luna ignored her deranged declaration. "The king and queen support my mission. They see it as a possible avenue to a truce between our people. With their support, I will continue my quest to help you."

"Fine. If you insist. I just can't make any promises that I'll be able to accept your help. Things have changed here—I want a truce between this sun and your moon, but I also want to unify the Solarpunks of Quintessence. And to do that, I need to be able to fly."

Luna frowned. "Be careful not to get in your own way."

"You sound like my brother," Emmeline griped.

Luna's eyes widened and she vanished.

Emmeline's brow furrowed in confusion.

"Who, me?" Solís asked, his tone serious.

Emmeline turned and found her older brother standing atop the nearest roof peak with his arms crossed over his chest.

She gulped, terrified to learn how long he had been standing there.

Chapter 28

"Why can't you leave me alone?" Emmeline demanded.

"Why are you on the roof in the wee hours of morning?" he countered. "It's a bit odd, don't you think? And who were you talking to?"

Emmeline exhaled, trying to hide her relief—she momentarily forgot that he couldn't see Luna.

"I was talking to myself," she replied.

"No, you weren't. I heard a woman's voice. Where is she? Was it an Aeropunk?"

"You're hearing things. You must be tired."

"Of course, I'm tired! I'm in a panic, chasing my baby sister onto the roof at god-awful hours, praying to Solédon that she isn't planning to jump."

"You really thought I was going to jump off the roof?"

"I can't guess with you anymore! You worry me."

"I don't have a death wish," she assured him.

He didn't look convinced. "I wish you'd clue me in on what's going on. I would be a great ally."

"I want to believe that," she countered, "but I don't think you're ready to hear or accept the truth."

"Please, try. I will do my best to listen without reacting."

"It would be too devastating to my mission if you took the truth and used it against me."

"I would never. I only want to help."

"I know, that's the problem. You'll see the truth as dangerous, as something that it isn't. You will try to take matters into your own hands instead of following my plan."

"You don't give me enough credit," he said while walking to the edge of the roof, searching for the mysterious person Emmeline had been talking to.

Emmeline glanced upward, wondering if Luna had left, or if she was hovering within an extra layer of invisibility that blocked Emmeline, too. If Solís saw her, he'd only see her as a monster. He wasn't ready to see the moon beings as anything other than enemies. Or so Emmeline believed.

It wasn't worth the risk.

He sniffed the air. "It smells like burned moon lilies."

"I've never smelled a moon lily," Emmeline countered, although she suspected that was the distinct aroma of Luna that she hadn't been able to place previously.

"They are lovely, normally—honied magnolia, crisp cosmic zephyr, untouched stardust." He closed his eyes and smiled. "Soft, sweet, and youthful, with a hint of rock musk." He opened his eyes and shook his head. "This one is tainted with the scent of char and ash, though."

"Where do moon lilies grow?"

"On moons, obviously."

"All of them?"

"Only the moons with warm-blooded beings."

This forced Emmeline to pause. "Beings?"

"Monsters," Solís said, correcting himself. "The flowers need warmth to grow."

"Don't you think the same could be said about the beings there, too? That they need warmth to survive?"

"No. The lilies are 'watered' with monster blood. That's how they are given life. It needs to be warm blood to work. In return, the flowers provide countless magical properties for the monsters to utilize—healing ointments, aromatic mind control, paralytic balms, confounding pollen. The list goes on and on."

"How do you know all of this? And when did you ever get close enough to a moon to know the scent so well?"

"They've used the flowers against us in battle. After breaching our solar flare shield, they've used the poisonous powers of the moon lilies to try to defeat us." He paused in consideration. "It's usually the Hellions of Obsession who use the flower as a weapon. I got to see the flower in its beautiful, docile state after one of our first battles as Pyropunks. It was seized as evidence after we won the fight."

"Where is it now?"

"Oh, it was destroyed during a thorough dissection."

An audible huff came from above.

Emmeline's eyes widened, hoping Solís hadn't heard Luna's horror, but he had.

"What was that?" he asked.

"It was me."

"No, it wasn't. It came from above."

"You're wrong," she insisted.

"What is going on?" he demanded, his patience waning.

"I'm going back to bed," Emmeline said, marching past her brother and scaling the peaked roof. After crossing over to the other side, she realized that Solís was not following her.

Worried what he might be doing, she peeked over the top of the roof and found her brother in the same spot, staring at the empty night sky. Swirling pink and purple solar flares illuminated his irate golden gaze. He reached into a satchel attached to his toolbelt and threw white powder into the sky.

Emmeline held her breath, afraid it might reveal Luna's form within her invisibility shield, but the powder fell without any realizations.

Solís growled under his breath before reaching for a second handful of powder to throw in a different direction.

Confident that Luna had vacated the area, Emmeline slid down the opposite side of the roof and crawled through the open attic window.

She pushed through the cosmic dust and raced down the attic stairs, eager to retreat into her bedroom before Solís decided to follow and reinitiate his interrogation.

She locked the door behind her and slid to sit on the floor. Gemma slept soundly on the chaise lounge, giving Emmeline a moment to collect her thoughts without interruption.

Luna was still an ally, though she did not support Emmeline's intentions to wrangle the curse. She did not think it was possible to control the affliction and live with it successfully. Emmeline still believed she could prove her wrong.

Solís was also an ally, but his suffocating attempts to help her often made him feel more like a foe. He was too irrational, too impulsive, and though she loved him, she did not trust that he was levelheaded enough to accept the truth.

She needed to return to Hydra where everything made more sense.

After a restless sleep, Emmeline awoke the following morning to the sound of a foghorn trumpeting. She rubbed her eyes as she sat up in bed.

Gemma was no longer on the chaise lounge.

Emmeline snapped her attention to the other side of the room and found Gemma, Clementine, and Avery huddled around the moon stone Emmeline had left on the dresser near her bedroom door.

"What are you all doing?" she demanded.

Gemma looked up, her silver eyes wide with guilt. "I was just showing them the stone."

Terrified, Emmeline sprang out of bed, nearly tripping on the mess of clothes still littered all over the floor as she charged toward them. She reached between Avery and Clementine and seized the stone. Grip firm around its smooth surface, Emmeline's panic was temporarily subdued by the shadows.

She promptly shoved the moon stone underneath her pillow.

"Did either of you touch it?" she asked as her heightened dread returned.

"No," Avery and Clementine responded in unison.

"What did you tell them?" she asked Gemma. Her heart pounding with such fury, the flame turned her cheeks red.

"Calm down," Gemma said. "You have nothing to worry about. I only told them that it came from a distant moon."

"Why would you tell them that?"

Avery stepped in. "Because the stone was convulsing violently on the counter, making a racket and acting unlike any normal rock found on Quintessence. Why do you have a moon stone? And how did you get it?" she asked.

"I found it in the ocean," Emmeline answered honestly.

"It stopped shaking the moment you spoke," Clementine added. "Does it have magical properties?"

"No. You can find better, more interesting extraterrestrial artifacts in the underground Tinker markets. This one is just a stone."

"Then why did you get so worked up when you saw us looking at it?" Clementine asked.

"Because what if I'm wrong and it's capable of more than I realize? I don't want either of you getting hurt because of me."

"You found it in the ocean?" Avery asked.

"Yes," Emmeline answered, exasperated by this conversation and wishing to divert the topic.

"I wonder what it was doing there."

"It doesn't really matter. It is benevolent."

"You should tell your father. He would want to investigate it thoroughly to make sure."

"He already knows that I have it."

"He does?" Avery asked, shocked.

"Yes, he is fine with it. It's a souvenir from my first underwater hunt."

Avery's orangey-pink eyebrows furrowed, expressing a mixture of disbelief and submission.

Emmeline hoped sharing small bits of the truth was enough to prevent this information from spreading. She reassessed the scene she woke up to.

"Why are you two in my room?" she asked Avery and Clementine.

"I came here to wake you up," Avery answered. "You slept through the first thirty minutes of your father's airship horn. Imagine my surprise to find a fugitive Tinkerpunk hiding out in your room."

"I'm not *technically* a fugitive if no one knows I survived," Gemma countered.

"They'll know soon enough. I imagine you plan on bringing her with us to Hydra?" Avery asked Emmeline.

"Yes. Clementine, too. I'm building a crew."

"That's why I'm here," Clementine said excitedly. "To let you know that I settled all matters here and can leave with you."

"You didn't quit your job at the Steamery yet, did you?"

"They fired me," she admitted, her smile shifting into a cringe. "It was an accident. I only intended to warn them that I had a new opportunity on the table, and they let me go."

Emmeline groaned. "I can't promise that you'll be allowed to join me yet. I still have to talk to my father."

"I have no other options now. It has to work out."

Avery scoffed. "Quite the predicament you two have conjured."

"Do you think my dad will agree?" Emmeline asked.

"All depends on how you present your case."

Emmeline's shoulders slouched. "I'll think of something good."

The foghorn sounded again.

"We better get going," Avery said.

Emmeline grabbed a fresh outfit—black suede pants with golden buttons lining the outer hem and two large pockets. She tucked a white collared blouse with trumpet sleeves into the wide waistband, secured the buckles of her holster belt, and laced her black combat boots. She tugged her goggle-adorned captain's cap over her braided hair and took a deep breath. She was ready for whatever adventure awaited her in Hydra.

She opened the doors to her balcony and found Montgomery's airship docked directly beside her bedroom.

"Father!" she shouted, to which Montgomery peeked his head out of the small circular window of his captain's chamber.

"Finally awake, I see!" He dipped back inside, then emerged through the rounded door. "Welcome to the world, dear child. It's almost midday!"

"I had a long night," she tried to explain. "I've been thinking about what I told the Holloways; how I want to unify the groups of Quintessence."

"Yes?"

"I want to build a crew."

"Like the Pyropunks?" he asked.

"Not that big. Something smaller, and more focused on overseeing the community. A crew to be my support system as I navigate my new role as a flying Thermapunk."

"You want to build your own personal team?"

"Yes. I could use the assistance."

Montgomery's expression tightened as he considered this. "I don't see the harm in that."

Emmeline jumped with delight. "Oh, thank you!"

"I assume Avery will be part of the crew."

"Of course."

"Louie, too?"

"Yes, if he agrees to it."

"I have no doubt that he will," Montgomery replied. His tone half annoyed, half amused. "Who else?"

Emmeline turned and waved Gemma and Clementine forward.

At the sight of them, Montgomery's energy changed from lighthearted to grave.

"Emmeline …" he began.

"Hear me out," she pled. "I will need constant maintenance on my wings, and Gemma can help with that."

"Okay …"

"And I will burn dry often, with no fire left to spare for Avery. Clementine can provide fire for our airship when I'm depleted from flying all day."

"First of all, Tinkies aren't welcome in Hydra. It's not my rule, it's a Hydropunk rule, and I really don't wish to push my luck any further with them."

"She will never leave my side."

"Secondly," Montgomery went on, "you have my entire Thermapunk crew at your disposal for fire when you've used all of yours to fly."

"But I'm not friends with any of them like I am with Clementine. I'm trying to build something special, a loyal crew I can always count on."

"This is a lot to digest. Let's take it one step at a time. I suspect it's most urgent to get the Tinkie out of our home before Melora finds out she is here … or does she already know?"

"No, she doesn't know."

"As I thought." He looked to Clementine. "You would be welcome in Hydra, the issue is your parents. They are aristocrats, like my dear wife, and they won't like you working alongside Nautipunks."

"I'd be working alongside Emmeline," Clementine argued.

"Still, that work would bring you into Hydra. I will need to consult your parents on this matter."

"I turned sixteen a few months ago! I'm an adult now—I don't need their approval."

"Sadly, due to the rigid dynamic of our people, I need their blessing, and you cannot enter Hydra without my approval."

Clementine's excitement deflated.

He added, "Be patient. Perhaps they will be okay with it. When I speak to them, I'll present this role as a wonderful opportunity."

"I guess we'll see," she said, her tone defeated, then whispered to Emmeline, "They'll never allow it."

"Everyone else, hop aboard! We are behind schedule," Montgomery said before turning to address his Thermapunk crew on the day's itinerary.

"I'm sorry," Emmeline said to Clementine. "Just hang tight. We will find a way to make it work."

"We have to—I have no other options. My parents don't know about me losing my job yet ... I didn't want to tell them till I had some good news to cushion it with."

"Be patient. Don't panic."

Clementine's eyes glimmered with teary oil.

Emmeline understood the pressure she was under—it was only a few weeks ago that her own mother had saddled her with a similar type of burden. She gave her friend a hug.

Clementine's tense shoulders relaxed for a moment in Emmeline's embrace.

"I'll be back soon," Emmeline promised before letting go.

"Hurry along," Montgomery urged as the Thermapunk crew heated the balloon lamps. Avery took the wheel, ready to depart at Montgomery's command.

Emmeline raced to the balcony, climbed the rope ladder, and launched herself onto the ship's deck.

Clementine waved as they departed, holding back tears of dread as she wished them farewell.

The burning gazes of the Thermapunk crew were locked on Gemma, who stood uncomfortably behind Avery.

Avery wore an expression of impatience as Emmeline approached.

"She won't be welcome here *or* in Hydra," Avery griped. "Everyone is too stuck in their judgments."

"All the more reason to bring her. Squashing this unfounded hate is long overdue."

Emmeline closed her eyes, carefully timed the consumption of three clay marbles, and her fire heart was activated. She was getting good at this, and the time it took for her to heat to a level worthy of flight was decreasing. In seconds, she was levitating, rising above the crowd and diverting their repulsed gazes to her. Their hate rapidly shifted to admiration as they watched Emmeline in the sky.

"Do you support me?" she asked, her voice a menacing bellow.

"Of course!"

"Yes!"

"Always!"

The Thermapunk crew cheered.

Emmeline continued, "Then you must also support my decisions. The Tinkerpunk onboard is part of my personal crew. She is my friend. Her name is Gemma and she is in charge of the maintenance of my golden wings. They will need constant upkeep to preserve their functionality, so she is an essential key to my success. Pestering her will result in as grave a punishment as if you had disrespected me. Do you understand?"

The crowd mumbled as their golden heads nodded.

There was no dissention, no pushback, and Emmeline released the breath she unknowingly held. They respected her authority and trusted her choices.

"Fantastic, thank you," Emmeline said, gracing them with appreciation—a rare gift from an elite Thermapunk. "Avery! Take us to Hydra!"

Montgomery had climbed the main mast and hung from the rope with his free arm extended wide. Golden-brown hair whipping in the wind, he was so engulfed in appreciating the little moments, he paid no mind to the bustling of his crew below. Grateful, content, free—the way he prized even the smallest adventure was admirable, and Emmeline intended to mimick his spirit as she became a leader.

She wanted her followers to be inspired daily; she wanted them to view each new day as a glorious adventure. Together, they would unify the masses, connecting the different factions through friendship and teamwork. It would take time, but they would rebuild the trust that had been tarnished over the centuries.

This was her hope.

This was her mission.

If Luna was right and the moon stone's curse was destined to be Emmeline's end, she would leave a blazing trail of prosperity in her wake.

Chapter 29

Montgomery swung down the rope, ricocheting off the mast till he reached the deck. He tied the line to his waist then dove over the gunwale. It only took a moment for him to unlock the gate to Hydra, and as the intricate gears turned, the Thermapunk crew heaved Montgomery's rope, pulling him back onto the ship.

Avery lowered the airship just enough for Montgomery to climb the mast and lock the gate from below. He moved about as if he had minimal years collected in his aging golden joists. With youthful energy, he darted from the gunwales up the mast to finish sealing Hydra from the world above.

Emmeline thought to offer her service of flight to assist in locking the gate, but held back—her father's joy while performing this duty was infectious; he would not relinquish this responsibility until it was officially time to pass the torch. That day was still far off, and with Emmeline's unexpected journey down a new path, it was possible that day might never come.

She glanced over the edge of the ship, searching for her greatest source of comfort within Hydra: Louie.

Red Fang Ralph's pirate ship was nowhere in sight.

Dormant fears of abandonment crept to the surface. She reached into her pocket instinctively to find comfort in the moon stone, but her pocket was empty.

Emmeline gasped—she had left it under her pillow. This was the first time she had entered Hydra without it since finding it. A true test—without Louie or the stone, she'd need to be brave on her own.

She had done it once before. On her first trip to Hydra, she had neither of those crutches. She could do it again.

"Will Red Fang Ralph and his crew be joining us?" she asked her father as he climbed down the main mast.

"I'm not sure when you will see Louie," he replied. "He had to relinquish his role as diver on the tether job due to a crisis aboard Ralph's ship."

"What kind of crisis?"

"I don't have all the details. Something to do with Ruthanne. I believe she caught a terrible illness."

Emmeline halted. "What kind of illness?"

"I really don't have the details. What you need to be focused on is taking over Louie's role as lead diver. The tether has almost breached the surface of the sea, and once it does, the job will be halfway done." Montgomery leaned in close and lowered his voice. "Louie discovered a secret hatch near the base of Cuda Ray's ship that leads to the Terrapunk prisoners. Cuda Ray is bleeding them dry. The sooner we finish the job, the sooner Louie can free them."

"I understand," Emmeline said. "We will make great progress today. And with my ability to fly, perhaps I can speed along the tether build in the sky."

"Fantastic idea!" Montgomery exclaimed. "What a day we will have," he added, scanning his daughter, silently assessing her health. "Have you eaten yet today?"

"I had a few marbles earlier."

"You ought to eat some more. You have a long day ahead of you." He squeezed Emmeline's skinny shoulder in excitement before walking toward Avery to give her navigational commands.

The airship redirected toward the tether build, soaring in the opposite direction of Smuggler's Rove, where Louie most likely was.

She tried not to think about him, or how much she missed him.

She had a job to do.

Gemma sat beside Avery, her posture rigid and uncomfortable. Though the Thermapunks left her alone, their skeptical gazes landed on her frequently.

"I am not wanted here," she said as Emmeline approached.

"Yes, you are," Avery countered. "Both Emmeline and I are happy to have you here."

Emmeline added, "And once they see how helpful you are, they'll be more welcoming."

"What's on the agenda today?" Gemma asked, hoping to change the subject.

"Continuation of the tether build," Emmeline answered. "We should breach the ocean surface today, then we just need to build it up."

"I can help with that."

Emmeline's golden brow furrowed. "You can?"

Gemma extended her hands and began raking the tips of her fingers against her fleshy palms. Shimmering particles materialized within the friction.

"What do you need?" she asked. "I can produce any mineral—natural or compound."

"That's incredible," Emmeline said. "I forgot Tinkerpunks could do that. Can all Terrapunks produce minerals on command?"

"Yes, all Terrapunks have two functions, two purposes: how we fuel the sun and our natural state of being—fossil fuels and minerals. The Horrigans made our entire existence revolve around fuel. So much so, our gift of mineral creation is often overlooked." Gemma sighed. "But it's integral to everything we do. I've created all sorts of minerals to aid and ease my builds."

"If you can make adhesive minerals, like glue or cement, it would strengthen the tether."

"I can do that," Gemma said.

"Excellent! I better get to work on bringing the tether air-side then," Emmeline said, leaving Gemma and Avery to change into her dive suit.

A quick switch of outfits and Emmeline was geared up to dive. Montgomery led her onto the extended platform, and together they dove into the sea.

Cuda Ray's ship circled above, oil leaking through the metal planks nailed to its hull. Such a fine substance, it was able to escape despite the watertight construction of the boat, revealing the nefarious secret Cuda Ray kept locked away in the bilge of his boat.

Emmeline worked fast, eager to finish this build so Louie could free the captured Terrapunks. Within the hour, she and Montgomery had weaved enough golden cords together to break through the ocean's surface.

They returned to Montgomery's ship to dry off while Cuda Ray's crew installed the floating base with anchors to the weaved stub of cords now protruding from the sea.

Emmeline changed into her button-seamed pants and collared blouse before tossing a few clay marbles into her mouth.

Careless, because she was in a rush, six marbles rolled down her throat with speed, landing in the pan with rapid succession.

The migraine started immediately.

Emmeline reached into her pocket, desperate for relief, only to remember that the sea stone wasn't there.

She cursed at herself beneath her breath—she would have to work through the discomfort.

Emmeline had her hands pressed against the side of her head when a knock sounded on the cabin door.

"Give me a minute," she said, clenching her teeth through the piercing pain.

"I swam all the way here and you're going to make me wait to see you?"

It was Louie.

Emmeline raced to unlock the door. As it opened, she fell into his arms. Forehead pressed against his chest, she attempted to soothe the pain through his embrace.

It wasn't enough.

"I missed you, too," he said with a laugh.

"I was upset when I got here and was told I wouldn't see you."

"Something is wrong with Ruthanne. I stayed behind to help her."

"I heard. Has a medic examined her yet? Will she be okay?"

"When I left, she had stopped shaking. We recruited a Hydrodoc from the Rove, so she's in good hands now. I waited till they got there to leave."

"I'm happy you're here now."

"Are *you* okay?"

Emmeline shook her head. "I have a migraine, but it'll go away if I keep my eyes closed."

Louie held her close, letting her bury her face in his chest to simulate darkness. After a moment, her quickened breathing began to slow to a more normal pace.

"Feeling better?" he asked.

She slowly opened her eyes and then looked up at him. Her migraine was not gone, but she did not want him to worry. "I think so." She paused, then asked, "Did you really swim here?"

"Yes," he replied. "A bit foolish, perhaps, but I had no other way to get to you. Ralph's boat is docked for the week."

Emmeline grinned. "I'd have flown to you after the day's work."

"I couldn't wait that long." He kissed her forehead. "Let's get going. Everyone is waiting for you outside."

Emmeline fastened her wings to her shoulder gears and tightened the harness around her chest. Louie took her hand and led her onto the main deck where the entire Thermapunk crew eagerly awaited her debut of pairing her ability to fly with the tether work.

If she focused on the task at hand, perhaps she could temporarily silence the headache. She closed her eyes and initiated the burn. Temperature rising, skin glowing red, the sizzle of her heart overpowered the agonizing hum in her head.

Desperate to hang onto this fleeting relief, she lifted into the sky and got to work.

As suspected, having the gift of flight dramatically accelerated the process. Instead of being bound to contraptions built and towed by Aeropunks, Emmeline was able to braid and secure the tethers at her own pace, without needing to collaborate or coordinate with a Pilopunk.

Everyone watched in awe as it took her half the time to get the tether to the height of Montgomery's flying airship.

At this level, as they had preplanned, Avery and Gemma joined her in the build. Gemma was light enough to ride Avery's back, and like this, they followed Emmeline, enhancing and strengthening the spots she constructed. Avery got as close as she could to the tether, and Gemma smeared the adhesive minerals into the cracks and crannies.

Gemma's ability to get close to the fire was invaluable and aided her capacity to assist. The heat from the tether warmed the coldness that still lingered within her daily. Healing and helpful, Gemma performed her role with precision, proving just how useful her presence here would be.

The trio demonstrated how productive Solarpunks could be if they worked together. It was a silent, but powerful lesson as the Thermas and Nautis observed their teamwork.

They made it halfway to the ceiling of Hydra; halfway to where the Tinkerpunks would help drill a hole through the base of Terra so the tether could extend to the Pyro-Argo air base floating high above. At a high cost, of course—a delivery of real fire to the Horrigan skyscraper. Just enough for them to maintain ultimate power over the Terrapunks, but not enough to take over Quintessence. It was one of the rare times they were paid with real flames.

Drilling through Terra was the trickiest part of the tether job. They had to make sure the terra pipes and gears were not altered too much while making space for the tether to fit through.

Emmeline led her small crew back to the airship, and they were greeted with cheers upon their return.

Louie wore an impressed smirk.

"That's quite the girl gang you're assembling," he noted.

"Well, I was actually hoping to recruit you, too," Emmeline replied.

"I don't have any special skills outside the water, and I can't leave Hydra."

"But you could help us when we're down here."

Louie smiled and pulled her close. "I can and will do that."

"Maybe I'll figure out a way for you to leave Hydra, too."

"I'm not allowed up there," he said.

"If I gain enough power, perhaps I can change that."

"It goes beyond that, though. We struggle to breathe outside of Hydra. The air is slightly different down here."

"How can I breathe down here then?" she asked.

"The air is less dense down here. Saltier, sure, but less gas and humidity. You are used to the thick air above, so breathing lighter air is an easy transition. But going from light air to heavy air is much more difficult."

"Ralph said it was a delight to breathe the air above."

"Ralph is a freak," Louie said with a laugh.

"I see." She paused. "Would the air above kill you?"

"No, but it would weaken me significantly. I could never live a full and healthy life above Hydra," he said. "I was built for the sea."

"Can't you train for the sky like I trained for the sea?"

"I suppose I could, but it would take years."

"Luckily, our lives are eternal if we're careful," Emmeline said.

Louie's grip of her loosened. "I like it down here."

Worried she might be pressing an irrelevant issue, Emmeline caved.

"Good thing I can be with you down here, then," she offered, to which his tense energy softened. Though the topic was dropped for now, Emmeline sensed that this discussion would arise again.

Montgomery shouted new orders to the crew.

"Shift the sails eastward and prepare for the Detention Center," he ordered. "Welders and wranglers, fuel up."

"Wranglers?" Emmeline asked, looking to Louie. "Why are they needed?"

"Ah, you missed the commotion this morning. Ruthanne swore she saw a Hellion of Obsession. It's hard to tell if she's hallucinating, due to her fever, but it's best to be prepared in case."

"What exactly is wrong with her?"

"Fever, tremors, paranoid outbursts. She can't go in the water anymore—the seawater burns her skin. It's awful, and we have no idea what's causing it."

"That sounds terrible!"

"I'm hoping the Hydrodoc has discovered a better ointment for her burns—everything we've tried only caused her more pain."

"I'm so sorry."

"She's a fighter," Louie said, holding back his fear. "She will get through this."

Emmeline nodded as she took his hand and held it tight. They stood together in supportive silence as Avery steered the airship toward the Detention Center.

She did not have her moonstone, and now that she was simmering back to a normal temperature, the migraine returned. It was dull, but present, and for the first time in a long time, she was looking forward to leaving Hydra in order to obtain relief.

The Demon of Destruction roared as the airship approached, alerting the other caged monsters of their arrival.

"Happy to see us, ay?" Montgomery guffawed from the crow's nest where he observed the monsters through binoculars. He shifted the lenses rapidly, switching between various magnifications and tinted colors. Night vision, thermal tracking, coolant detector, and infrared radiation tracker—Montgomery was equipped to monitor all the monsters. He turned his focus away from the caged monsters to scan the surrounding area. Flipping between lenses, he searched for the mysterious hellion Ruthanne swore she saw.

The Ogre of Irritability howled within its cage, scratching the pus-filled boils on its arms till they burst.

The Behemoth of Fatigue was quiet, rubbing its clay-covered eyelids and ignoring the arrival of the Thermapunks, while the Beast of Panic flew in its usual monotonous circles, side-eyeing the punks as they approached.

Sulfur and corpse lily—the familiar scent assaulted Emmeline's nose.

"Can you smell that?" she asked Louie.

Gemma approached them from behind.

"It reeks," she said.

"I don't smell anything," Louie noted while sniffing the air aggressively.

"Strange," Emmeline said. "Why can we smell it, but you can't?"

"No idea. What is it that you are smelling?"

"Hmm." Emmeline pondered how to describe the smell. "Rotten monster eggs and fermented flowers."

"Gross."

She nodded. "Yes, it is quite disgusting."

"Where is it coming from?" he asked.

"The Devil of Delusion."

"How do you know?"

"It's the same poisonous odor I smelled last time."

Louie's posture became rigid with alarm. "We have to kill it."

"Why? It's contained in its cage."

"It is reaching you from its cage. Clearly, no one is safe while it lives."

"Actually," Emmeline said, recalling her conversation with Luna, "I know how to subdue it."

"How?"

"Fire is the figment's foe."

"Fire is the foe of every monster," Louie countered.

This forced Emmeline to pause in consideration, which led her to an idea.

"I think I know how to stop the devil from breathing poison. I'll need to fly again, though." She turned to Gemma, who stood quietly beside them. "I'll need your help."

"That's what I'm here for."

Emmeline led Gemma to Avery, and together they came up with a plan.

"Gemma will ride on your back and coat the bars of the cage with petroleum. I will then light it on fire. How long do you think the burn will last?"

"A few months," Gemma answered.

"Great! We can reapply and reignite the prison bars once the petroleum starts to wear off."

The trio prepared for their mission—Avery refueled with glass marbles, Gemma slit a small incision in her wrist where her petroleum veins were largest, and Emmeline primed her heart for another burn. A quick swig of oil and her gears were greased and ready to fly.

The Devil of Delusion spewed copious amounts of poison their way as they worked together to better contain the monster. While hanging onto Avery's back, Gemma lathered the bars with her highly flammable blood. She excreted a surplus of petroleum onto the cage; the excess fell through the bars and into the devil's hair. Its long, red locks became drenched in petroleum. Emmeline stayed a few paces behind, waiting till they had moved far enough away to ignite the cage. Her source flame heart increased in temperature as she prepared to strike. The magma in her veins gurgled, and with the heat, she created a single fireball. With a simple toss, the nearest side of the devil's prison went up in flames.

As the wall caught fire, the devil screeched in horror, backing its frail body into the neighboring wall, covering its head and cowering. Gemma finished applying the fuel and Emmeline set the opposite side ablaze.

Raw fury emitted from the devil—a scream so scratched and splintered, it sounded like it traveled through razor blades.

The third wall lit up with flames, quickly followed by the fourth wall and then the ceiling.

The poisonous odor was gone and the devil was subdued beneath five walls of fire. The only part of the cage left untouched was the floor where the devil cowered at the center. Engulfed by flames, this monster would not be causing problems for a while.

Again, the Thermapunks and Nautipunks watched in awe. Though it was similar to how they interrogated the hellion that had escaped, the mixture of fossil fuel and fire was everlasting—a superior combination no one thought to try before.

Emmeline was revolutionizing operations within Hydra, and if she stayed this course, it was plausible that punks from all factions would eventually look to her for leadership.

A tickle crossed the inside of her nostrils, causing her to wiggle and scrunch her nose to get the itch.

The scent of the sulfur and corpse lily returned.

"Do you smell that?" she asked Avery and Gemma, who hovered between the airship and the tether, awaiting further instructions.

"Smell what?" Avery asked.

"I only smell the smoke from the burning cage," Gemma added.

Emmeline hesitated, not wanting to reveal that she still smelled the devil's poison.

"Yeah," she finally replied. "That must be what I smell, too."

Chapter 30

Red Fang Ralph sailed below.

The vicious winds of Hydra spun the gears of the skeletons fastened to all sides of the hull, animating their limbs and giving the illusion of life among the dead. The giant mirror-eyed monster skull speared to the bow caught the pulsating light from the source flame below. Blinding refractions, Emmeline averted her gaze.

"Let's get back to the airship," she said to her friends, then led the way.

"Great work!" Montgomery exclaimed as the trio landed safely on the main deck.

"Hopefully it keeps the monster bound for a few months," Emmeline replied.

"It should," Gemma chimed in, her confidence within Hydra growing. "Unattended petroleum burns last a while."

"Fantastic. Amazing teamwork," Montgomery gushed, then proclaimed, "Who knew!"

Louie joined the small group, silver-blue eyes wide with worry.

"I have to go see Ruthanne," he said, mostly to Emmeline.

"Can I join you?" she asked.

"Sure, but it's hard to see her so fragile."

Montgomery chimed in, "I will join you as well. I need to hear how the Hydrodoc has diagnosed her."

Louie did not argue.

Avery and Gemma followed, and though there were two within the small group that could fly, they took the traditional way down—a long rope ladder hanging over the starboard gunwale of the airship.

When they reached the main deck made of stained zinc planks, Montgomery joined Ralph and the Hydrodoc near the captain's cabin while Louie led Emmeline, Avery, and Gemma to the bunk where Ruthanne was resting.

He turned the doorknob softly, pushing the door open quietly. As he entered, Ruthanne stirred from her slumber.

Her heavy eyelids cracked open and the shimmering blue gaze within beamed at the sight of him. A tired smile stretched across her face as he walked toward her bedside.

Then she caught sight of the girls standing in the doorway.

Ruthanne's happiness transformed into annoyance.

"Why are they here?" she asked, her voice a whisper.

"They wanted to wish you well."

"Well wishes won't help me," she barked, though it came out with a hoarse cough.

"It's the thought that counts," he gently argued.

Ruthanne's angry gaze shifted to Emmeline. "This is her doing."

"Excuse me?" Emmeline said, stepping forward.

"I got sick after diving to investigate that *thing* you threw overboard."

Emmeline's eyes widened.

Louie looked to her. "What is she talking about?"

"Oh no," Gemma said from the doorway.

Emmeline took a deep breath, then answered. "It was a stone."

"A cursed stone," Ruthanne spat. "What did you do to it? It was riddled with dark magic."

"I did nothing to it," Emmeline swore. "I returned it as I found it."

340

"You carry a stone with you," Louie said, deep in thought.

"They aren't the same. Not exactly," Emmeline stammered.

"Is that how you can fly?" he asked, putting the pieces of the puzzle together.

"No," she answered. Emmeline turned and motioned for Gemma to close the door.

Gemma and Avery stepped farther into the room before shutting themselves inside.

Avery looked to Emmeline and commented, "I'd like to hear the full truth as well."

"I'm afraid you won't like it."

"An ugly truth is better than a pretty lie," Louie said, his tone stern.

Emmeline covered her face with her hands and spoke.

"Those silver rocks aren't sea stones—they're moon stones."

"I already know that," Avery said.

"You did?" Louie asked, offended.

"Give me a second to explain!" Emmeline pled, gathering her thoughts and deciding how much of the truth was safe to reveal. "You know the migraines I get?" she asked Louie.

"Yes."

"Well, the stone I carry caused them."

"Then why haven't you gotten rid of the stone?"

"Because it is also the only thing that soothes them."

Louie considered this as he looked back to Ruthanne. "So you're saying the remedy to Ruthanne's sickness is the moon stone that infected her? We need to dive down and get it."

341

"I don't think that's wise," Emmeline said, thinking of Cèla—the malicious hellion who was out for punk blood.

"Why not?" he demanded.

Emmeline did not want to reveal that these moon stones belonged to hellions.

"I threw that one back into the sea because its magic was far more dangerous than the one I had originally found."

"How do you know? What aren't you telling us?"

Emmeline cringed as Louie assaulted her with questions.

"Give Ruthanne your stone," he said. "Maybe it will heal her."

"Only the stone you touch can offer reprieve. If she touches my stone, she'll suffer a second curse." Emmeline grimaced, her migraine worsening. "Plus, I accidentally left my stone at home. I forgot to bring it with me and I've been suffering through a migraine since I got here."

Louie stood and paced the room, his rampaging thoughts of confusion reading plainly on his face. He asked, "How do we heal her then?"

Emmeline looked to Ruthanne, who shivered under the covers. Her face was covered in salt burns.

"We need to find a salve for her burns." She thought of how restricting her marble intake remedied the migraines. "There must be something to soothe her pain."

"A salve is not a cure," Louie argued.

"You're right, but it's a good place to start."

Gemma stepped forward. "I think I can help."

She raked her fingertips against the palms of her hands, producing a thick clay-like substance. With permission from Ruthanne, she began smearing the cool clay on the burns. Ruthanne exhaled with relief as the putty soothed her wounds.

A few moments after the application, Ruthanne inhaled deeply and exhaled like she had been holding her breath for days.

"It's working," Louie said in disbelief.

She sat up for the first time since falling ill. Color returned to her bluish cheeks and her weary eyes reanimated with energy.

"I feel so much better," she expressed with relief.

"I'm so glad," Gemma said.

"It won't solve your sudden allergy to the ocean, though," Louie added.

Ruthanne's gaze was spellbound as she stared at Gemma. She was silent for a moment, but once she spoke, her confidence was unwavering.

"I am no longer built for the sea."

"We will find a solution," Louie said.

"No—I belong above. Whatever cursed me has made me crave terrain minerals."

"You only think that because Gemma soothed your pain. Your lungs, gears, and veins are still built the same. Your heart belongs to the sea."

Ruthanne shook her head. "I'm not so sure anymore."

"You can dive in our suits," Emmeline suggested. "That will keep the salt water off your skin while you dive."

"I want to mine the soil above. I want to be free."

Avery gasped. "She sounds like my uncle before he jumped into the ocean. He kept saying he wanted to be free."

"I heard about him," Louie said. "Wasn't he infected by a hellion? His death is the reason we learned their powers and developed the hellion salve."

Avery nodded.

They both looked to Emmeline, a thousand questions reading silently in their horrified expressions.

"I can explain," she said.

"Those stones are from the Moon of Fixation?" Avery asked.

"They are—"

"They're all over the ocean floor!" Louie exclaimed.

"They are—"

"Why didn't you tell us sooner?" he demanded.

"Because I knew it would cause panic!" Emmeline said, finally finishing a full thought. "I never thought Ruthanne would go and touch one. I never thought anyone would after my father insisted they were plain sea stones."

"But they infected you," Louie said,

"And me," Gemma chimed in.

"And now Ruthanne," he continued. "How many more people needed to get hurt by these stones before you told someone?"

"I didn't want to start a war," Emmeline tried to explain.

"We are already in a war!" he shouted, his anger growing. "We fight it every day."

"Yes, I know, but it would become so much worse if this information reached my father and the sky fighters. The stones have been there for centuries and they've never caused problems before," Emmeline tried to rationalize. "Why make the war worse over something that is mostly benign."

"Perhaps they were benign before, but they aren't anymore."

"Well, we have to tell Montgomery," Avery said.

"What will you say?" Emmeline asked, holding tight to the few remaining secrets she had left.

"The truth! That the stones belong to the hellions," she replied.

Emmeline couldn't let that happen.

"If you tell him, he will remove every moon stone from the sea and catapult them past the solar shield and into space."

"As he should."

"He'd take my stone, too."

Avery paused, slowly realizing Emmeline's point.

"You need that to survive?" she asked.

Emmeline nodded. "Yes, it cursed me, but it's also the only thing keeping me alive. I can only eat with assistance from the stone. Without it, the migraines are crippling."

"I see," Avery said, her mind racing. "There must be another way."

"You need to trust me. I'm working on a way to fix me and everyone else who has been infected, but I need the stone to do that." She needed Luna's help, but she couldn't tell them that.

"Fine. I won't say anything. I just hope you find a cure before it kills you."

"Me too," Emmeline said. Everyone except Gemma was mad at her, which was ironic considering Gemma had the most reason to be angry with her. Avery wore a frightening scowl and Louie wouldn't look at her.

"I need to go home," Emmeline said, defeated. She did not wish to fight with her friends. "My head hurts."

She needed space to think.

She needed to speak with Luna.

Louie's anger softened. "I know you thought you were doing the right thing by keeping this a secret from us, but the truth will set us all free. The more of us who know, the more we can help each other." He opened his arms to hug her, but she leaned away.

"I need a minute," she said, leaving the room without a goodbye.

Overwhelmed, attacked, disappointed—that was not how she wanted her friends, especially Louie, to learn about the moon stones. She wondered if she should have told them the full truth, but in that moment, their energy was too tense and aggressive. It did not feel right.

She knew in her heart that Luna was good. She also believed that the hellions were misunderstood. If they were out to destroy Quintessence, or planned to use the source flame for evil, they would have done so long ago. The war against them was misguided, and she wished to protect them from further suffering at the hands of her people.

"Father," she called out as she marched toward him. "Would you mind escorting me home?"

"We still have work to do," he protested.

"I'll come back tomorrow to help finish the tether. I have a migraine and don't think I can sleep here tonight."

Montgomery's expression tightened with concern. "I thought you liked it down here."

"I do. I love it. I just need a minute away."

"But we just got here," he contested.

Emmeline sighed, then confessed, "I left the sea stone in my room. Like I told you before, having it with me is a reminder that I'm brave enough for this world. It gives me confidence, and I'd like to retrieve it."

"Alright, well, I suppose we can make the trip back and have dinner with your mother and brothers. I suggest that Gemma comes with us—I'm not sure if I trust the crew to treat her kindly in our absence. Her position here is too new."

"She will come, too."

Avery flew them back on the winged hot air balloon. She fed helium into the balloon while pedaling and steering the giant wings attached to the basket. Montgomery occasionally fed the fire pan, stoking the flame whenever it got too low.

Emmeline said nothing on the trip home. Avery side-eyed her every so often, her expression a mix of disappointment and concern.

Avery docked the balloon at the Dawes's hangar bay, then used her harnessed wings to fly home to Gaslion. Gemma climbed up the side of the house, aware that Melora could not see her. Agile and quick, she scaled the golden ladders, climbed over Emmeline's balcony, and disappeared into her room.

"Back so soon?" Cyrus said to Emmeline and Montgomery as he entered the basement.

"Emmeline forgot something, so we decided to come back and have dinner with the family."

"Ah, well, Helix is in a locomo stupor and Solís has been acting like a raving madman all day."

"Helix promised me he'd stop taking the dust," Montgomery growled.

"It's addictive," Cyrus replied.

Montgomery grumbled, then asked, "And what is Solís raging on about?"

Cyrus looked at Emmeline. "You."

"Me?" she asked.

"Yeah. He says you're in trouble."

"I'm not."

"He swears you are. Says he caught you talking to yourself on the roof the other night."

"He needs to relax and mind his own business."

Montgomery gave Emmeline a concerned glance. "Have all my children lost their minds?"

"I might be the only one who hasn't lost it yet," Cyrus commented.

"I'm fine!" Emmeline insisted.

"With all this chaos, Melora must be in a tizzy," Montgomery added. "I should check on her."

Montgomery departed in a hurry.

Cyrus looked to Emmeline. "What is going on?"

"Nothing out of the usual. Solís is making something out of nothing."

"Is he, though? His instincts are usually spot on."

Emmeline groaned. "He is so overbearing. Please don't do that to me, too."

"He cares about you, and so do I. If something is wrong, you should tell us. We can help you."

"Everyone keeps saying that, but I don't need help. I have everything under control."

"Psst," a hiss came from the open hangar bay.

Emmeline and Cyrus redirected their attention to the sound, and found Gemma hanging upside down, head peeping over the ledge and long silver hair blowing in the warm wind.

"Ah, the Tinkerpunk fugitive is back," Cyrus commented, then looked back at his sister. "And you wonder why we're concerned about you?"

"What are you doing?" Emmeline hissed at Gemma.

"We have a problem," she replied.

Cyrus shook his head. "You two are trouble."

"What kind of problem?" Emmeline asked.

"You should see it for yourself," Gemma replied.

"I'll see you later," Emmeline said to Cyrus, leaving him no opportunity to join. She climbed up the side of the house, following Gemma into her bedroom.

The moment they crossed through the billowing curtains of her balcony door, they were greeted by Clementine performing reconstructive surgery on herself.

Chest cut open, gears and bolts strewn all over— Clementine worked in such a concentrated fervor, she did not notice Emmeline's arrival.

"What are you doing?" Emmeline demanded.

Her voice shook Clementine from her fixated focus.

"You're back!" she greeted, then resumed her work as she spoke. "I figured out what I needed."

"What do you mean?"

"To have purpose," Clementine stated. "To feel free."

Emmeline's attention turned to her bed, which was ransacked—blankets in a heap on the floor and pillows overturned.

The stone was missing.

"Where is it?" Emmeline questioned.

Clementine glanced up from her work briefly, then returned to tightening a screw near her heart. "I need it," she answered.

"It's mine!"

"It has shown me the way."

"Where is it?" Emmeline repeated, her voice shaking.

"You can be mad if you want, or you can let me be part of your crew. Soon, I will be one with the water. I will be able to possess fire and manipulate water simultaneously."

"It always comes at a cost. What is your curse?"

Clementine faltered, golden eyes showing fear for the first time. "I start to suffocate, like I was drowning, but the stone returns my breath. That's why I need it."

Emmeline groaned.

Clementine continued, "But I'm fixing myself so I don't need to rely on the stone so much. I'm building an air tank around my lungs and heart that will help me breathe underwater and protect my source flame from getting extinguished by the sea." She smiled. "I'll be a really great addition to your team."

"You could've been part of my team as a healthy Thermapunk."

"I'll be more useful this way."

"Put yourself back together before one of my brothers barges into my room and sees you like this."

Gemma noted, "They do often show up unexpectedly."

With a wrench and screwdriver, Clementine began reassembling herself. She found new homes within her chest for the displaced gears and reinserted them in a way that built a shield around her fire heart. Her original lungs were still there, breathing in the oxygen of this bubble in Quintessence. Next to them was the half-constructed air tank made of gold.

"Where did you get the material to build the tank?" Emmeline asked.

Clementine kept her gaze low. "I melted down some of my excess gears."

"You will kill yourself if you aren't careful," Emmeline scolded.

To which Clementine laughed. "You're one to talk. Look at you! You're a skeleton. I'm surprised you haven't floated away yet."

Her tone was snarky; it was cruel.

Emmeline looked to Gemma, who's skeletal bottom half was covered by her overalls, then back to Clementine, who was removing and melting her gears.

All of Emmeline's friendships now revolved around destruction, and the root of the problem was her. She kept the stone around, and now everyone she cared about was suffering, too.

Her migraine swelled.

"Give me the stone," she demanded through gritted teeth.

Clementine handed it over.

The moment its smooth, cool surface touched Emmeline's palm, the deafening hum of her headache ceased and Luna's voice emerged.

"Where have you been?"

Emmeline pressed the stone to her forehead and walked out onto her balcony, closing the doors behind her. She whispered, "I'm here now."

"We have a problem. Someone touched Cèla's stone."

"I am aware. I saw Ruthanne in the aftermath. She was really ill until we found a salve for her burns. How do you know?"

"Cèla was there. She teleported to ensure you followed through on your promise. As she was about to exit through her stone's portal, the Nautipunk dove down and caught it before it hit the ocean floor."

"She saw me toss the stone overboard. I never thought she would dive down to investigate," Emmeline whispered.

"Watch over her. Cèla's curse is far stronger than mine."

Emmeline nodded then removed the stone from her forehead.

The migraine was gone.

She placed the stone in her pocket where it would be safe from hurting anyone else.

"You'll need to stay close," she said to Clementine. "If the feeling of suffocation returns, I'll let you borrow the stone for relief."

Clementine nodded in understanding.

Though it was not her intention to recruit through forced necessity, the universe was unravelling her noble intentions in this manner.

She was losing her grip.

She was losing control.

One by one, bound by the stone's curse, Emmeline's crew was growing.

Chapter 31

Desperate to make something beautiful out of the nightmare she was nurturing, Emmeline clung to the tiny scraps of control she still possessed.

The secret of her friendship with Luna remained, as did the true purpose of the stones. War was not necessary, and she intended to keep it this way.

Though everyone around her swore she was shrinking, she felt like she was managing her marble consumption well.

Her friends were loyal, even if their loyalty stemmed from necessity.

Emmeline could manage this spiral—she was determined to succeed in unifying the Solarpunks and creating a truce between Quintessence and the Moon of Fixation.

While Clementine and Gemma continued to sleep, Emmeline went to her balcony for fresh air and space to think.

The solar sky was shifting from night to morning. Purple and pink flares swirled overhead, dancing with the red and orange rays of daylight. A beautiful sight to observe; captivating and calming, Emmeline exhaled deeply as she enjoyed this brief moment of serenity.

Dueling bursts of wind ripped her from her tranquility.

Circling above were Raven and Remington Holloway. They hovered where the upper level of Gaslion met Fyree.

"What do you want?" Emmeline called to them.

"Join us," Raven responded, her silky voice weaving between the wind currents.

"I just woke up. I need to collect my energy."

"We've been watching you," Remington said. "We know your secrets."

"Excuse me?"

In unison, the Holloway siblings twirled and disappeared, shifting their forms in a way that blended with the dancing solar flares above.

Emmeline gasped—they were gas spinners; they had mastered invisibility. How long had they been spying on her? And what did they see?

"Where did you go?" she asked, hoping to play it cool.

"We are evolved Aeropunks. We can manipulate our gaseous hearts to mask our solid forms and blend in with the sky."

"I see. Have you been watching me in that state?" she asked.

"We have," Raven said, spinning back into sight. "We know you have magic."

"I don't have magic."

"No need to be defensive," Remington stated, his raspy voice too calm, too calculated. "We want to be friends."

Emmeline's guard was up. "How much have you reported back to your parents?"

"Nothing at all," Raven swore. "We are the next generation of leaders. You for the Thermas, us for the Aeros. We ought to work together. We don't need our parents meddling."

With this, Emmeline agreed.

"Alright, well, let's start off slow. Show me that you wish to build a genuine friendship, and I'll let you into my world as we build trust."

Remington's expression tightened—he wasn't as good at hiding his thoughts as Raven.

"A slow build of trust," Raven said. "That's fair."

"Great."

"Go eat something," Remington said. "Restore your energy and come fly with us."

Emmeline had no solid excuse to decline the invitation, but something about their offer of friendship felt wrong—something devious lingered beneath the surface.

It was better if she played along.

She grabbed five clay marbles, tossing them into her mouth with rhythmic care. By the fourth, the soft hum of a migraine formed, so she clutched the stone until it went away. Still holding the stone, she ate her fifth marble, ensuring she had enough energy to keep up with the Holloways. She put on her wings, and after a quick heat-up, Emmeline was air bound. Glowing red beneath her golden-flecked flesh, she was a vision of regality. She soared alongside Raven and Remington in the upper level of Gaslion, letting them lead the way while monitoring the strength of her flame. Unlike them, her ability to fly had limitations, and she needed to remain aware of them.

The Holloway siblings seemed to understand her limits and did not fly too far or too fast. They monitored and matched her pace—a sign of respect and comradery.

They lowered into Fyree and stopped at the Pyro-Argo air base where Pyropunks fueled their source flame hearts and Argopunks patrolled the nearby sky.

Emmeline's brothers were on the hangar bay consulting with the Argopunk commanders. Helix noticed her first.

"Emmeline!" he shouted, alerting Cyrus and Solís to her presence. "What are you up to?"

"Just a casual flight with the Holloways. This is good practice for my endurance."

Solís's gaze was locked on Raven and Remington.

Helix shouted in reply, "Be careful!"

"I will!"

The Holloways turned their flight upward, back into Gaslion.

"I'm getting tired," Emmeline called out to them as she began to lag behind.

"We wanted to show you where the noble Aeropunks reside."

"I don't think I'll make it."

Remington circled back. The pinkish-orange gleam of his copper gaze narrowed flirtatiously.

"I'll catch you if you fall," he said.

Emmeline scowled. "I'd rather not fall at all. I'm heading back." Before redirecting her flight, she added, "If you want to earn my trust and friendship, stop spying on me."

Remington smirked. "But you're so much fun to watch."

"Well, stop."

"Beauty and bravery," he commented, eyes sparkling with desire.

Emmeline ignored his flirtation and flew home while the Holloway siblings continued soaring toward the solar shield.

She missed Louie, and she regretted leaving him on such a sour note.

Halfway home, she passed Cecelia and Ambrose Monroe—Clementine's parents—being taxied by a Pilopunk. They rode in a cart attached to an airscrew unicycle and glared at Emmeline as they passed.

Waiting on the hangar bay were Melora and Montgomery, accompanied by Clementine, who was the only one smiling.

"I received my parents' blessing!" she exclaimed once Emmeline was in earshot.

"It was less of a blessing, and more of a surrender," Melora noted.

"Either way," Clementine said, "I can join you in Hydra."

Montgomery chimed in, "Another set of hands for your growing crew."

"Wait till you see what I can do," Clementine said, unable to hide her glee.

Emmeline shook her head at Clementine, but her parents were already intrigued.

"And what is that?" Melora asked.

Aware she had said too much, Clementine backpedaled. "Well, I can't do it yet, but I have plans to mix fire and water. I plan to master the sea."

Vague, but also crazy enough for Melora to accept her answer.

"Good luck with that," she said, disinterested with the wild fantasies of a child who was not her own—she had enough chaos to navigate among her own kids. She retreated indoors.

"Can we return to Hydra soon?" Emmeline asked her father.

"I planned to leave this morning, but you were nowhere to be found."

"Sorry, I was appeasing the Holloways. They wanted me to join them in flight."

Montgomery sighed. "Good choice to participate. We need to maintain that alliance."

"They've been spying on me," she revealed.

"I'm not surprised. The noble Aeropunks are sneaky. Exercise caution around them; don't tell them too much."

Emmeline sighed—she wished she could tell her father the truth.

She reached into her pocket and wrapped her fingers around the moon stone. As she gripped it for comfort, a gush of wind smacked them both in the face.

"Sorry about that," Avery said as she slid to a wobbly halt beside them, copper wings wide to slow her momentum. She tossed the key to Hydra to Montgomery. "You need to see what's happening in Hydra. Now."

"Is everything okay?"

"Ruthanne has transformed."

"What do you mean?" Emmeline asked, letting the stone go.

"You have to see it for yourself."

"We're leaving!" Emmeline shouted upward, hoping Gemma would hear her.

Montgomery hopped into the hot air balloon basket and tooted the foghorn.

"Ayo, let's go!"

Gemma peeked her head out of the balcony doors, then climbed down. Clementine joined them in the basket and once everyone was safely aboard, Avery guided the balloon toward Hydra.

Emmeline refueled slowly, spacing out each clay marble with care. As time went on, her tolerance worsened. The migraine now began after two marbles instead of five. She relied on the moon stone to lessen the pain while she did her best to stay nourished.

As they reached Hydra, her thoughts of hunger were replaced by stunned amazement.

Atop the gates stood Ruthanne—tall and proud with her frenzied silver-blue eyes scanning the geared landscape. Shoulders tense and hunched, she appeared ready to take on the world.

"Ahoy there," Montgomery called down to her, cautiously toeing the line of comradery and authoritarian. "How'd you manage to get all the way up here?"

His question diverted Ruthanne's manic gaze upward, and she answered his question with action.

Arm raised above her head, concentration locked on the steel reinforcements along the basket walls of the hot air balloon, Ruthanne launched herself into the sky.

Hand to steel, she gracefully leapt into the basket, a huge grin on her face.

"I am something else now," she revealed.

"You are magnetized," Gemma said with a gasp.

Chapter 32

"You should join my crew," Emmeline said, hoping to direct Ruthanne toward a noble cause rather than leaving her to her own devices.

"I haven't decided what I want ta do with me power yet," she replied, staring at her hands as she spoke.

Afraid to say too much in front of her father, Emmeline decided to investigate how Cèla's moonstone had transformed Ruthanne so dramatically later. For now, she needed to encourage Ruthanne to behave.

"Join us for the day. See if you like working with us. We could really use someone like you on our team," Emmeline said.

"Will I be yer captain?"

Emmeline pursed her lips. "We work together."

"I've been a slave to Nautipunk captains all me life. I don't want another captain."

"It won't be like that, I promise. Just give it a try."

"Fine. I'll give yer team a shot."

Still in shock, Montgomery stepped into the conversation with caution. "How does your breathing feel?"

"The air is thick up here, but I'll survive," Ruthanne barked in reply. "Me body will adapt."

"Seems like your body is in the middle of a serious transition. Don't overdo it," he warned.

Ruthanne spat on the ground, her salty saliva bubbled like sea foam. "I ain't afeard."

"We have to finish the tether job in Hydra," Emmeline informed her.

Ruthanne laughed. "You'll need ta find a new Nautipunk crew."

"Why?" Montgomery asked.

"I tore Cuda Ray's ship apart, plank by plank. All that be left are metal scraps littering the ocean floor."

"Why did you do that?" Montgomery asked, slow to judge but also unable to hide his grave concern.

"Croctopus deserves a worse fate than that fer what he did ta Sub Anne Marie."

Emmeline thought of Louie and wondered if he felt like justice was served.

Gemma asked, "What happened to the imprisoned Terrapunks aboard his ship?"

"Louie saved 'em. We worked together. They're safe on Red Fang Ralph's ship. Figured you could deliver 'em home."

"We will," Montgomery said, his energy tense—he had a lot of damage control to enact with Cuda Ray. "The Horrigans will be pleased."

"I didn't do it for them," Ruthanne snapped.

"Understood. For now, let's just finish the tether job. The Pyropunks need this additional access to the source flame."

Montgomery unlocked the gates of Hydra and Avery steered the balloon through.

Ruthanne clenched the metal rims of the basket, excited to revisit the scene of her wreckage.

Emmeline looked to Gemma, who wore a similar expression of concern—they both realized that Ruthanne's curse was far worse than theirs. What started as a debilitating allergy to her home habitat had morphed into incredible strength—and she hadn't even been infected for a full week yet.

Emmeline feared this would not end well.

When they reached the jobsite, Cuda Ray and his entire crew were floundering in the water, swimming toward Smuggler's Rove, while scraps of his ship floated all around them. The air reeked of metallic destruction.

Ruthanne wore a delighted expression.

"Argh!" Red Fang Ralph shouted from below. "Look at them bilge rats swimming like shore hogs." He cackled at Cuda Ray and his crew. "Slathered in stolen oil and pockets full o' firestones. Careful, or you'll drown!"

"I'll regroup and kill yer whole crew when I do!" Cuda Ray shouted, coughing out water as he swam.

"Ahoy, maties!" Ruthanne shouted down to Ralph and crew.

"The lady o' the hour! Back so soon? I thought you'd be up there paving paths for the rest of us scallywags to follow."

"One day soon. Fer now, I'm trying out a gig with Miss Flying Firepunk."

"Aye, that's where ye belong," Ralph said with a nod. "You're a Superpunk, just like her."

"Is that what we are?" she asked, endeared by the title.

"It's what me crew be calling her and her friends, and you too after yer little show this morning."

"Superpunks," Ruthanne repeated to herself. "I like it."

She tossed a rope ladder overboard and descended toward Ralph's ship.

Halfway down, her elbow jammed, freezing in a bent position. She paused to work it out, grimacing through the pain as she slowly straightened her arm. Gears back in motion, she finished the climb and immediately greased her elbow joint.

"What happened?" Louie asked Ruthanne as he approached.

"Me joints have been sticking. Amidst all these changes me body is going through, I need to stay well-oiled 'n' greased."

"Please take care of yourself," Louie requested. "I already thought I lost you once."

"I ain't goin' nowhere," she said, wrapping her freshly greased elbow around his neck and pulling him in close. With her free hand, she ruffled his shaggy hair.

"Good," he said, allowing her to roughhouse him with sisterly affection. "I don't want to lose anyone else I care about."

Ruthanne sighed. "I miss yer mom, too. She was me mentor, me friend. I considered her family. I will watch over you. I promised her I would."

"I can watch over myself; I just want you to be healthy."

"I'll get better at greasing me gears on the regular."

"You better," Louie chastised, his tone teasing, before pushing Ruthanne off of him.

Overhead, Emmeline soared around the golden tether, braiding the golden cords while Avery flew beneath with Gemma on her back. Gemma reinforced each braid with coagulated minerals that strengthened the tether.

It only took a few hours for them to reach the underside of Terra. Their job within Hydra was done. A team of Tinkerpunks would drill through the terrain pipes to make room for the tether to ascend through, and a team of Pyropunks would take over the tether build above Hydra.

Emmeline shouted down to her father, "We are ready for the Tinkies to start digging!"

Before he could answer, Ruthanne raised her arm and rocketed into the sky via magnetized flight. Her fist collided with a steel pipe, stopping her upward progression.

She hung there securely, palm to steel.

"You don't need help from the Tinkies," she said. "I can move 'n' relocate all this metal."

"You have to be careful, though," Gemma warned from Avery's back. "These pipes are strategically placed. Some aid the sedimentary flow, others filter heat into the universe beyond—they need to be rerouted into matching neighboring pipes."

"We really should let the Horrigans handle this," Avery advised.

"She's right," Emmeline added, "they know the piping system better than anyone else and they look forward to their infrequent payment of fire—they'll be furious if you steal it from them by doing the work yourself."

"Who cares what they think?" Ruthanne spat. "We are Superpunks—we are in charge now."

"Superpunks?" Emmeline asked.

"That's what everyone is calling us." Ruthanne's confidence was infectious. "If ya want to be a leader, ya better start leading."

She was right—Emmeline needed to seize this moment and make it her own.

"Fine. You can do this job, but you must heed Gemma's guidance. She knows more about these pipes than the rest of us."

"Aye, aye," Ruthanne agreed, visibly excited to use the magnetized minerals in her flesh to tear the pipes apart.

"This is a bad idea," Avery grumbled, but her concerns were ignored. She was outnumbered and overpowered by the cursed punks around her. All she could do was monitor their delusions and attempt to prevent them from making a huge mess. Right now, she needed to keep Gemma in the sky to prevent Ruthanne from irreversibly wrecking the intricate piping system of Terra.

Emmeline observed as Gemma gave Ruthanne specific instructions on how to carefully reroute the contents of the pipes. All was going well until her flame began to falter. She fell a few feet before catching herself with a giant flap of her golden wings.

"I'm running out of energy," Emmeline told her friends. "I need to return to the ship to refuel."

"Tell your father what's going on up here," Avery said. "He will need to prepare for the Horrigan's wrath once they find out."

Emmeline nodded before departing.

She flew in spirals back to the airship, using gravity and her wings to guide her descent while giving her fire heart a break.

As she landed, she scanned the ship for her father, but found Louie first. He wore a small smile as they made eye contact.

"Am I allowed to hug you today?" he asked.

Emmeline nodded and opened her arms wide. Louie scooped her up and held her close. He kissed the side of her neck as he spun in a circle. Then he sighed.

"Will you have lunch with me?" he asked.

"Yes," she replied. "I need to refuel."

Her willingness soothed his tense energy.

He grabbed two gallipots of sea glass marbles from the galley and they ate on the back deck.

"Have you heard what they're calling us?" she asked, a small smirk on her face as she ate her first marble.

"Superpunks!" he replied with a laugh, then a proud smile stretched across his face. "I'm dating a Superpunk."

Emmeline chuckled. The marble hit the waiting pan and immediately entered her shrunken system of gears.

Without delay, a migraine appeared at the base of her skull. She reached into her pocket to grip the moon stone.

Louie noticed.

"Migraine?" he asked.

She nodded.

"You're getting too small," he said, his voice low.

"I know. It's not intentional."

"I get the draw to having super abilities, but it's not worth the cost of your health."

"I'm working on it," she insisted.

"How? Let me help."

"It's complicated." The moon stone finally soothed her budding migraine. She tossed a second marble into her mouth with her free hand, still gripping the moon stone with the other.

"I wish you'd trust me a little more."

"I trust you with my whole heart," she countered.

"But you don't trust me with the truth."

"It's not that simple."

Louie sighed. "I don't want to argue with you. Just know that I will listen with an open mind if you ever want to talk."

Emmeline's shoulders relaxed as he dropped the issue. "Thank you."

Louie's eyes held a deep sympathy—he knew she suffered, and though she attempted to keep her woes silent, they read loudly in her every move and facial expression. His love for her was patient, and for that, Emmeline was truly grateful.

"Everyone will be okay," he said, more so to himself.

"We will be. I will find a way."

She leaned in and gave him a soft kiss. Her forehead pressed against his.

Like this, she could linger awhile.

"Emmeline!" Montgomery shouted.

She pulled away from Louie and found her father scouring the main deck for her.

"Up here! Having lunch with Louie."

"You're eating. Excellent." He hurried toward them. "What is going on up there?"

Montgomery pointed at the faraway scene where Ruthanne, Avery, and Gemma hovered around the top of the finished tether. Loud booms echoed through the sky like thunder.

"Sorry," Emmeline replied. "I was supposed to return and find you, but I was so depleted, I needed to refuel."

"It's fine. Tell me now."

"Avery and I tried to talk Ruthanne out of it, but she was insistent." Emmeline paused. "She's mining a hole for the tether."

"No!" Montgomery objected.

"I know. The Horrigans will be furious."

"They will be livid—this is the only job where we pay them with direct flames. This will tarnish our alliance with them."

"I tried to tell her that."

"Go back up there and make her stop."

Louie stepped in. "You're better off coming up with a plan to mollify the Horrigans; once Ruthanne is set to do something, there is no stopping her."

"These are evolved times," Emmeline gently reminded her father. "My crew and I are able to assist all factions of punks in many capacities."

"Still, we can't ruin alliances in the process. At the least, I should have given them a warning before stripping them of this job."

"Perhaps we can soften the blow by delivering this news at the same time we deliver their freed Terrapunks," Louie offered.

"That's a brilliant idea," Emmeline said in support.

Montgomery nodded slowly. "Yes, maybe that would be wise."

Lost in his racing thoughts, Montgomery stared off into the distance.

"Should we prepare to meet with the Terrapunks?" Emmeline asked. "I don't suspect it will take long for Ruthanne to break through into Terra."

"Yes, good thinking. Have Avery return and she will take us up to the new hole in the sky in the thermal balloon."

Light was beginning to peek through the cracks Ruthanne was making.

Emmeline ate one more marble before giving Louie a kiss and taking off. She flew halfway to her friends before calling out.

"Avery, we need you."

"Gemma is still giving Ruthanne valuable directions," Avery shouted down.

"My father wants to intercept the Horrigans. They are inevitably waiting on the other side of those pipes."

"I can magnetize my palms," Gemma said. "Give me a minute."

She rubbed her hands together, creating friction, then lifted them above her head. The metal pipes snatched her magnetism and yanked her off Avery's back. She flew toward the ceiling, making secure contact—her palms firmly connected to the pipes.

"You can go," she told Avery. "The magnetic pull should last until you return."

"Okay, we will hurry," Avery promised.

Together, Avery and Emmeline flew back to Montgomery's airship where the freed Terrapunks were being escorted into the thermal balloon basket.

"Today is the day you get to go home," Louie said as he ushered them onboard.

"Finally," one of them said.

"Don't forget who saved you," Louie added.

As soon as Emmeline and Avery joined them in the basket, Avery shifted her attention to flying the balloon. Five deep helium breaths into the tube that ran up into the balloon, accompanied by Montgomery adding a burst of flames to the fire pan, and they took off.

Avery steered them to Gemma. Her little body hung from the ceiling; only one of her hands was still attached to the steel pipe. Relief flooded her expression as Avery maneuvered the balloon toward her.

Emmeline took over the steering gears while Avery retrieved Gemma.

"I don't know how Ruthanne holds onto such solid magnetism," Gemma said once she was safely returned to the basket. "I've never seen anything like it."

Montgomery replied, "And I've never seen a Tinkerpunk withstand direct contact with a heated golden tether, but here you are."

"Fair point," Gemma said, side-eyeing Emmeline.

Neither revealed their secret.

"Aye, Ruthanne! How are you doing?" Louie shouted while leaning over the side of the basket.

"All sediments are rerouted. No sand, gravel, or silt has spilled. Same with the heat. The pipes above are quartered 'n' emptied. Now I just need ter remove this top section 'n' break through into Terra."

"Hang on!" Gemma shouted. "You need to perforate the edges so you don't tear apart the pipe that you just sectioned.

"How?" she asked.

"I have the tools. Fire would work, too. You just need to weaken the edges."

"I'll help her," Emmeline said before heating up and launching into the sky. Golden wings spread wide, she joined Ruthanne. "Show me where you want it to break."

Palm to metal, Ruthanne walked the perimeter of the section she wished to remove. After completing a full circle, she moved aside so Emmeline could burn deep ruts into the defined section. It took a lot of energy, and by the time she finished searing a circle into the steel, she felt drained—but the job was done.

She lowered herself into the balloon basket to refuel while Ruthanne prepared to complete her task.

Riding on an adrenaline high, Ruthanne's focus was intense. She swung from a nearby pipe—one hand attached to the steel, the other aimed at the section she wished to remove. With a mighty growl, she channeled her magnetic powers and tore the circular section of steel from the sky single-handedly.

She flung the heavy slab of metal into the sea, releasing it before its weight dragged her down with it. A giant splash accompanied its entrance into the ocean, followed by a giant wave that rocked Ralph's boat.

"Extend the plank," Montgomery instructed Avery, who turned a wheel that protracted a platform from the base of the basket. Once secure, Montgomery and Emmeline climbed over the basket wall and took their place on the extended platform—from here, the giant balloon did not block their view and they could see into Terra through the freshly made hole.

Waiting on the other side were angry Terrapunks. Tinkies, guards, Digipunk miners, and nobles lined the opening, expressions a mix of outrage and shock.

Torsten Horrigan pushed through the crowd and reached the edge where he could locate the perpetrator below.

A low growl emanated from his gut when Montgomery greeted him with a smile.

Chapter 33

"What is the meaning of this?" Torsten bellowed, waving his arms at the new hole in his territory.

"It's for the Pyropunk tether," Montgomery answered.

"I'm not an idiot, I gathered that much, but who made it? It wasn't my team of Digipunk miners."

"Right, you see," Montgomery began, "it was done unbeknownst to me, initially, but now I am well aware. Things have changed."

Torsten's fury boiled. With a flick of his chrome coiled wrist, he flung a neodymium magnet onto the metal edge of the hole and ricocheted into Hydra on a silver cord that extended from his belt buckle. Once he was eye level with Montgomery, he slapped the buckle and came to a stop.

"This is *our* job," Torsten barked. "We rely on your payment of fire."

"Yes, I know, and this time, I will pay despite the job being done without you. I should have ended our contract prior to reassigning the job. It all happened so fast, I had no time to communicate properly, and for that, I apologize."

Torsten crossed his arms over his chest. "And we will be hired for future tether jobs?"

"That, I cannot promise."

"Who mined the hole?" he demanded.

"Ruthanne the Heartless," Montgomery answered, extending an arm to Ruthanne, who still hung from the pipe above.

Torsten's gaze lifted—he hadn't seen her there before.

Ruthanne gave him a little wave with her free hand.

"A Nautipunk?" he asked, outraged.

"She is indeed a Nautipunk," Montgomery answered.

"How? Why?" Torsten demanded.

"We aren't sure how she gained magnetic powers, but she has them, and she has graciously offered to join my daughter's crew."

Torsten fumed. "How did she know how to mine the pipes without devastating the entire system?"

"So," Montgomery began, fully aware this next bit of info would further infuriate Torsten. "My daughter has a Tinkerpunk in her crew as well."

Torsten finally turned his attention to Emmeline. "You are messing with the balance."

"I am fixing the balance," she corrected him. "The factions ought to work together."

"Which of my Tinkies is the traitor?" He looked to the balloon for the first time and saw Gemma standing there. He spat. "You? I should've known."

"I am doing good work," she insisted, and though she tried to sound confident, her meek voice betrayed her.

"I thought you were dead," he retorted. "I'll be sending the Stone Patrol to seize you."

"You will not," Emmeline interjected.

"She detonated an entire Tinker market. She is a threat to everyone's safety."

"She is under my protection and you have no authority outside of Terra."

Torsten growled. "Then she better never step foot in Terra again. If she does, I will find out, and she will be detained."

"On a brighter note," Louie shouted from the balloon basket while pushing the freed Terrapunks forward, "we were able to follow through on our promise. Your Terrapunk guards are safe and ready to return home."

Torsten grumbled, eyes locked on Gemma. "Good news tarnished by treachery."

He waved the guards toward him, hardly pleased by their survival. The guards, who also wore special tool belts, each latched a carabiner to Torsten's belt.

Before departing, Torsten spoke to Emmeline.

"You might have built some kind of super crew, but if you neglect the factions of power that have existed for centuries and fail to honor them in your pursuit of greatness, you will never prevail."

Torsten slapped his belt buckle and the silver cord retracted, carrying himself and the guards back to Terra.

"He's right, you know," Montgomery said.

"I know. We tried to tell Ruthanne to stop, but there was no convincing her."

"If you're the leader of this group, you'll need to find a way. You cannot disrespect the established order and expect no pushback. Don't make this harder for yourself."

Emmeline nodded. "I'll talk to her."

Except there was no talking to Ruthanne. She listened to no one. Emmeline tried, but time and time again, Ruthanne insisted she knew better.

While they cleaned up Smuggler's Rove of lingering remnants from the Marzan's time there, Emmeline told her crew that fire would cleanse the devil's poison from the air, yet Ruthanne proceeded to seize every bit of metal from the nooks and crannies of every home.

"The metallic alloys affect rational thought processes," she explained.

"I promise you—the cause of the delusional outbreak was the devil's toxic breath. Fire is the cure."

"You do it yer way, then. But I'm still freeing me people from the metal."

Emmeline flew overhead, heating the sky above the Rove enough to singe any lingering poison. Avery rode a pilobike, towing Clementine and Gemma through the sky. They kept an eye on Ruthanne, who prowled the crowded streets with magnets activated and stripping every Hydropunk of their metal possessions. Many lost valuable artifacts during the cleanup, which caused outrage among them. When the job was done, Emmeline went to Louie with a plea.

"Distract her," Emmeline begged of him. "Please."

"What's wrong?"

"She won't listen to me. She's sabotaging our missions."

"I'll talk to her."

While he kept Ruthanne busy aboard Ralph's ship, Emmeline returned the stolen artifacts to the Hydropunks. Though this gained her favor among them, it also wasted valuable time and doubled her work.

Their next task was to aid the reconstruction of damaged terra gears. Gemma told the crew it would take patience and manual labor to hammer out the dents in each wheel, yet Ruthanne ignored this advice and began popping each indent back into place with her magnetic palm. Three giant gears later, she looked up at Gemma with a pompous smirk.

"I told you it would work," she barked. As the words left her mouth, she pulled too hard and tilted the gear on its axis, which created an even larger problem to fix.

"The gear is misaligned!" Gemma shouted in horror from above. She rode with Clementine in the cart attached to Avery's pilobike, afraid to get too close to Terra and be captured by the Stoneheads.

375

"I'll fix it," Ruthanne stammered, fussing with her hand placement on the giant tilted gear. It spun, scraping the terrain with earsplitting scratches.

"The whole system will fail if you don't get it back in place immediately," Gemma warned.

Ruthanne closed her eyes and pushed, reversing the magnetic pull to shove the enormous gear back into place. Emmeline flew lower and placed her hands on the gear, manually pushing to help speed up the process.

Dahlia, the sullen Terrapunk Gemma used to serve, skated with fury toward the scene, attached to the neighboring track.

"Superpunks, huh?" she shouted as she approached. "Appears you're hurting more than helping."

"I will fix it," Ruthanne growled. A furious surge of power knocked the gear back into place and the loud abrasive gears scraping against the terrain ceased.

Dahlia shook her head as she tore past them.

"She will tell everyone about this," Gemma said. "No one will trust us with important missions if we don't learn to work as a team."

"If you had let me focus, that wouldn't have happened," Ruthanne argued.

"Or you could have listened to me from the start! Every Terrapunk has the ability to manipulate metal through magnets—don't you think we've tried repairs this way before? It's too risky, for the exact reason you just displayed."

Ruthanne's hands were still attached to the moving gear.

"Let go," Gemma warned, "or you'll be severed by the turning gears."

Ruthanne's eyes filled with fear.

"I can't," she said. "I can't move my fingers!"

"Why not?" Emmeline asked.

"They're stuck."

Emmeline looked to Gemma. "How do we help her?"

Gemma scanned the area, panic in her gaze, then whispered to Avery, "Lower me to her."

Avery did as requested and Gemma hopped off her back.

"I'll keep an eye out for Stoneheads," Emmeline offered.

Gemma raced to Ruthanne, placing both of her hands over Ruthanne's right hand first. With deep concentration, she channeled her own magnetic powers and with extreme force, yanked Ruthanne's hand off the gear.

Ruthanne howled in pain.

Gemma moved to her left hand, repeated the process and removed her hand just in time. A second later, and Ruthanne's arm would have been amputated.

"You really need to start listening to us," Gemma said as she fell to the ground in exhaustion.

"I don't know why I froze like that."

"Your body is still navigating the moon stone curse," Emmeline said from above.

Ruthanne shook her head. "I'm fine."

"If you don't start working with us instead of against us, you're out of the crew," Emmeline warned.

"I don't want a captain."

"Stop thinking of it like that. We are a team. If we don't work together, we won't succeed."

Ruthanne groaned. Her lack of fight was a sign of progress.

"We need a break," Avery decided for the group, swooping low to retrieve Gemma.

The terra gears they were working on weren't far from the gates to Hydra.

After regaining full mobility, Ruthanne lifted her arms and attached to the metal conveyor belt above. She swung, working her way hand by hand along the conveyor cord, over the terra gears, and back to Hydra. Emmeline followed her in flight. At the gates, Emmeline put two fingers into her mouth and whistled, to which Montgomery flew his airship beneath the gate. Close enough for Ruthanne to jump, she leapt and reentered Hydra.

"How'd it go?" Montgomery called up to his daughter.

"Could've gone better, but we got it done. We have some teamwork issues."

"I'll try ter listen better, aright?" Ruthanne shouted.

"The fact that the Horrigans allowed your crew to work on the gears after the debacle with the tether is amazing," Montgomery said to Emmeline. "You don't want to mess that up."

"To be honest with you, I really don't care to work with them. I don't want to serve the old heads of power—I want to create new leaders, new rules, new alliances."

"You won't get far if you don't appease those in charge. You will be stopped before you gain any influence. You need to play the game."

"I hope to win the game sooner rather than later."

"Luckily, you have the element of awe on your side— everyone is still enamored by the fact that four of your crew members can channel elements they were not born with."

"Hopefully their admiration lasts long enough for us to do some real good, otherwise they'll start to see us as a giant disappointment."

"Your time will come," he assured her. "I believe in you and your mission. Have patience."

"Thanks, Dad," Emmeline stated, genuinely grateful for his encouragement, then thought of needing to return home. "I wish I had someplace to call home that was my own."

"Talk to your brothers," Montgomery suggested. "With the expansion of the Pyro-Argo air base, I bet there's room for you and your crew to make that your new home base."

"Really?" she asked. "I hadn't considered that."

"It's worth a shot. Just don't tell your mother I suggested it—she likes having all her children at home with her."

"I won't tell her it was your idea," Emmeline promised. "Thanks!"

She took off and rejoined Avery, Gemma, and Clementine above.

"They are a load," Avery griped, side-eyeing her cart. Gemma rocked back and forth, fidgeting in place, while Clementine sat very still with her eyes closed, her breathing slow and methodical.

"You can park the pilobike at the Pyro-Argo air base," Emmeline told Avery.

"Why are we going there?" she asked.

"I'm hoping to secure us space for a new home base."

Avery considered this. "It would put us in the heart of the action, too. We'd get real-time updates about each faction."

"You're right. This could be our ticket to gaining better insight into where we are most needed in Quintessence."

"Actually, if you really want to help, you should sit in on one of the Aeropunk rallies."

"Rallies? About what?"

Avery lowered her voice. "About ditching the Holloways and taking back control. For whatever reason, we are required to report back to the nobles, even though the nobles are totally out of touch with the happenings beneath their solar shield thrones. We also have to obey every order they send down to us. It's infuriating. We want freedom. We want to govern ourselves."

"I support this, but how can I help?"

"You are an elite; you are a Thermapunk noble. I suspect your mere presence would empower the people."

"Why, though?"

"If the next generation of leaders supports the movement, it means there is hope for change."

Emmeline nodded. "We could empower the people, with the condition that change comes under the pursuit of unity."

"I think they would receive that arrangement well."

"I'd be happy to help, but first, we need to secure ourselves a home base."

Emmeline led the way. It was a short flight, as the Pyro-Argo air base wasn't far from Hydra's gates.

Their arrival was a spectacle: Emmeline blazed like a star tearing through the cosmos, Gemma's restless fidgeting created sparkling flecks of bornite that rained glittering bronze and turquoise over the world below, and Clementine hummed a whimsical tune to control her breathing and prevent the surging suffocation that threatened to take hold. Avery wore an expression of fatigue as she flew within this comet of unintentional pageantry.

"Look who it is," Helix said in greeting from the Pyro-Argo hangar bay. "Supercrew to the rescue!" He faked a kick and a punch before posing on one knee with his fist raised.

"I believe they're calling us Superpunks," Emmeline corrected him, her tone teasing. "Thank you very much."

"What has you gracing us with your presence?" he asked.

"I was hoping to secure some space in the new build."

"Good luck with that." Helix stood. "Solís is in charge of that project and he's not particularly pleased with you right now."

"What did I do now to upset him?"

"You'll have to ask him. He's a moody nightmare these days."

"Where is he?"

"Somewhere inside." Helix waved his hand flippantly.

"Real helpful, thanks." She looked to her friends. "Wait for me here. I might need to fight it out with my brother."

"Aye, aye, Captain," Gemma said from the cart.

Emmeline laughed. "Don't call me that in front of Ruthanne."

"Right-o," Gemma said, rubbing her eyes then pointing at the sky. "Noted!"

Emmeline took a deep breath to steady her nerves, then entered the basement filled with Pyropunks. Trained to fight, hardened by wars and tragedy, these Thermapunks were nothing like the aristocrats Melora brought around. Gritty, tough, and resilient—Emmeline preferred their company.

"Little Dawes," a Pyropunk who she did not recognize greeted. "I'm Kiran."

"Nice to meet you," she offered, though she wasn't interested in making new friends right now.

"Surprised it took you so long to visit the base," Kiran said.

"My mother kept me away."

"But now you can fly anywhere you want."

"Indeed." She scanned the room—spacious and comfortable with plenty of seating for everyone. Simple in design; no gaudy decorations. Built for function, not fashion. "I like it here. Hoping to create a home base for my crew in the addition."

"Ah, so you're looking for Solís?" he asked. Emmeline nodded. Kiran answered, "You'll find him through the door at the end of that hallway."

"Thanks," she offered before charging down the long metal-plated hallway.

As she lifted her fist to knock, she heard multiple voices behind the door. She lowered her hand and pressed her ear to the gold-tinted door.

"She's been talking to someone in the sky," Solís said, his voice urgent.

"We're still waiting to witness this for ourselves," another familiar voice said—Emmeline could not identify who it was.

"I think you ought to back off," Cyrus stated. "Clearly, she's ill, but her intentions are good. She's not causing problems and it appears she is trying to heal."

"I want to know who hurt her so I can return the favor," Solís spat. "She's our sister. If we don't protect her, who will?"

"If she wanted us to know, she'd have told us." Cyrus sighed. "There's clearly more to this than what she's telling us, and I suspect she has her reasons for keeping certain secrets."

"I could help her if she'd just tell me the whole truth."

"You're too intense. I wouldn't trust you with a delicate secret either," Cyrus commented.

"Leave it to us," the strange yet familiar voice interrupted. "We have already befriended her. In time, we will learn all her secrets."

Having heard enough, Emmeline skipped the courtesy of knocking and barged through the unlocked door.

Standing next to her brothers were Raven and Remington Holloway.

Their supposed friendship was a lie.

Chapter 34

"Spies? Really?" Emmeline shouted at Solís.

"You wouldn't talk to me."

"For good reason—you're crazy!"

"Am I though?"

"Yes!"

"I disagree. I know you're fighting some massive battle alone, and I just want to help. If you die and I didn't try, I'd never forgive myself."

Emmeline groaned. "Why do you make everything about yourself?"

"It's not about me, it's about you."

Emmeline slammed her hands on his desk and leaned in. Her voice was soft, but furious. "If you don't stop meddling, you will make an enormous problem much, much worse."

Solís heeded this warning, though the determination in his golden gaze was not quite resolved.

"And you two," Emmeline said, turning to Raven and Remington. "You are terribly shortsighted. No wonder your people hate you."

"Excuse me?" Raven said, offended.

"You run around spying on me, when you should be focusing on remedying the tension among the Aeropunks."

"What tension? Our family runs smooth operations. Never a glitch, never a hitch; all gas and air functions are seamless."

"Perhaps you ought to pay better attention."

Remington stepped forward. "Perhaps you ought to stop meddling in matters that don't concern you."

"How ironic! I'd like to offer you that same advice."

Remington laughed. "I like you; you're quick."

"And you're dimwitted. At the risk of stating the obvious, our budding friendship has withered and died. If I catch you spying on me again, I will greet you with blasts of fire."

Raven raised her copper eyebrows in shock, while Remington responded to her threat with a flirtatious smirk.

"Do not test me," Emmeline added, looking directly at Remington.

"What if it sounds like a good time?"

"It won't be."

Remington shrugged. "I like a challenge."

"Enough," Solís cut in. "Your services are no longer needed. If I catch you near my sister, I'll singe every last strand of hair on your head."

"Such a sudden change of heart," Remington spat at Solís. "Moments ago, you'd have let us do whatever was necessary to discover your sister's secrets. Now, you're casting us away."

"I can admit when I am wrong. In this case, I let my fear get the best of me."

"We are nobles. We are elite Aeropunks, just as you are elite Thermapunks. We do not take orders, we give them."

"You were happy to take orders from me up until now," Solís seethed.

"I viewed it as teamwork. Clearly, I was mistaken."

"Listen," Cyrus interjected, "there's no need for new tension. We are all friends here. Let's just go back to how things were before."

"It's too late for that," Remington said. "You want her secrets. I want her magic."

"It's not magic," Emmeline quarreled, utterly frustrated by everyone in the room. "I already told you that."

"Well, I don't believe you, and I want in."

"Leave me alone, or I'll incinerate you to your flimsy copper bones." Emmeline then shifted her furious gaze to Solís. "You will add a section in the new addition for me and my crew. Five rooms joined by a common area."

"The blueprints are already finalized—"

"Change them. After all of this nonsense and undue stress, it's the only form of apology I'll accept."

Emmeline marched out of the room and down the long corridor.

"How'd it go?" Helix asked as she reentered the common area.

"Did you know they were using the Holloway siblings to spy on me?"

"I had no idea." His shock was genuine, as was his confusion within the high of his recent hit of locomo. "They treat me like a kid."

"Maybe that's because you act like one," she said as gently as possible.

"It's easier to deal with the world when I'm not really in it," he said, eyes half open.

In his own way, and by his own doing, his suffering was similar to hers.

"I'm trying to make the world better," Emmeline promised him.

"I hope you succeed." He grabbed her shoulder, squeezing it slightly, then walked away to join Kiran and his other buddies on the other side of the basement.

Unwilling to help, but offering his support—Emmeline supposed this was the best she could expect from him while he was in a constant state of intoxication.

386

She enabled him, he enabled her; perhaps they needed someone like Solís to offer tough love. The idea made her groan, and the sight of her friends shook the notion from her mind.

"How'd it go?" Avery asked.

"He had the Holloways spying on me," she blurted out.

"They are the worst," Avery commiserated.

"But in regard to securing a home base here, I think I've got that covered. Solís owes me big time."

"Be careful. Raven and Remington are skilled gas spinners—they could be hovering above us right now and we'd never know."

Emmeline lifted her eyes to the sky. The swirling red and orange flares of the solar shield reflected in her golden gaze as she contemplated this dilemma. Now that they were onto her, it was not safe for Luna to appear here.

"Can they spin gas indoors, too?"

"That's a lot harder. There's less gas to manipulate inside, so their ability to stay invisible wouldn't last long."

"Good to know."

"While this Superpunk stuff has great potential, I think it would be better if we figured out how to help you heal," Avery suggested.

Emmeline stepped in closer and lowered her voice. "I'm afraid we can't."

"Why not?"

"It's complicated. Just trust that I am trying."

"So are Louie and I."

"How?"

Avery tilted her head upward and breathed mint-tinted vapor into the sky. It swirled and dissipated without revealing any hidden figures. Raven and Remington were not hovering overhead.

"Well," Avery began, "we know the curse comes from the stones, and those stones are from the Moon of Fixation. Louie has access to the ointment used on wounds caused by hellions, and he's talking to potion dealers at the Rove to learn about curses. I'm collecting the gases he needs to brew curative tonics. If you can't find an antidote, we will."

"I really didn't want to burden anyone else with all of this."

"Too late for that. We are invested."

Emmeline sighed. "Fine. I just worry you are wasting your time."

"It's not a waste of time when it's an effort to help our friends."

Behind her sat Gemma and Clementine, neither of whom were handling their curses as gracefully as Emmeline. Gemma's fidgety nature and Clementine's newfound fear of breathing were grave reminders that none of this was sustainable. Everything Emmeline had achieved was an illusion that had tricked others into thinking she was some kind of superhero to be envied, when really, she was the sickest of them all.

She wanted to believe that she could beat this curse, that she could turn its misfortune into something positive, but the more she tried, the more people she inadvertently hurt along the way. And now the Holloway siblings were after her secrets. If they discovered the stones, they'd exploit the dark magic, potentially harming more Solarpunks.

Emmeline was determined to keep her secrets and use them to help however she could. "Where do the Aeropunks meet for their rallies?"

"It's top secret. If I show you, you're with us. There's no going back."

"I'm with you, unwaveringly," Emmeline promised. She passed her moon stone to Gemma and Clementine, who took turns absorbing its healing powers.

Avery nodded. "You're in luck—there's a meeting tonight. Follow me."

They dropped Gemma and Clementine off at the Dawes home, leaving the moon stone with them, and then flew north into the upper level of Gaslion—a direction Emmeline had not yet traveled. Still new to this life of freedom, she had much of Quintessence left to discover. She followed Avery, and when they reached a copperplated home suspended by four giant netted helium balloons, they came to a stop.

"This is it," Avery said.

"What is this place?" Emmeline asked.

"My home."

"I thought Aeropunks roamed free, with no set roots or ties to keep them bound."

"Some Aeropunks are vagabonds, but not all. I grew up here with my entire extended family. They're all scattered now, though. That's how I am able to use this space for secret rallies."

"It's beautiful," Emmeline said, studying the floating home from afar. Four roof peaks covered in copper shingles stood at varying heights, but the two tallest stood apart from the rest. They had steeples adorned with bronze emblems of the gods: Solédon's hands gripping a sun, and Lunéss's hand cradling a moon.

"Did you know that my family used to be nobles?" Avery asked.

"Really?"

Avery nodded. "A long, long time ago. That's the only reason we have a home like this; it's been passed down through the generations."

"What happened? Why isn't your family still ranked among the nobles?"

"We were in charge of the Pilopunks, while the Holloways were in charge of the solar shield. It was an even distribution of power until the Holloways decided they no longer wanted to share. My great grandfather was defeated in a duel against the lead Holloway at the time. We've been considered 'peasants' ever since."

"Wow, I'm sorry. Makes sense why you'd let the rallies happen in your home."

Avery nodded, and before she could say more, Aeropunks began arriving.

Pilopunks on helium-powered aircrafts and Argopunks with titanium-feathered wings arrived in droves. When they saw Emmeline standing beside Avery, many gave worried glances.

"It's okay. She stands with us," Avery assured multiple times to the many uncertain Aeropunks filtering into the floating home. Similar to Avery, these Pilopunks were dressed in bomber jackets with fleece collars, aviator goggles attached to leather caps, and bulky buckled combat boots. The Argopunks wore aerodynamic bodysuits made of thick elastic material. Copper stripes defined their toned slenderness and wings of polished titanium rested in a retracted state against their backs.

Their uniform was similar to the Pyropunks', the only difference was that the suits of the Pyropunks had gold stripes outlined in red and the fabric was fireproof.

After the last Pilopunk parked his unicopter cycle, Emmeline turned to Avery.

"This is a large gathering," she noted.

Avery nodded. "We have the numbers, we're just missing the influence. We don't want to fight; we just want what's fair."

"That is understandable." Emmeline thought of the congregation that had filtered into the home, and how each Aeropunk looked to Avery for assurance before entering. "It seems they trust you."

"I would hope so." Avery grinned. "I am the leader of this revolution."

Chapter 35

"Why didn't you tell me this sooner?" Emmeline asked.

"I had to make sure I could trust you."

"How long has this group been meeting?"

"A little over a year. We are growing stronger, and our time to make a move is fast approaching. I'm hoping you might be the missing piece we've been waiting for. You have the influence we need."

"I don't have any influence," Emmeline countered.

"Of course, you do! Not only are you the leader of the Superpunks, but you're also an elite Thermapunk and a governor of Hydra. You hold great influence."

Emmeline had not considered the privileged role she held within Quintessence. She could inspire great change if she channeled her efforts toward noble causes.

"I will help you however I can."

"Great, let's go inside."

Avery led her through the front door and into a great room. The entire house was hollowed out—no rooms, no stories, attic, or basement; just one giant room with nooks, ledges, and crannies for the Aeropunks to perch, burrow, and hang. Hundreds of them lined the various niches, and many hung from crisscrossing cords bolted to the walls.

Their polished copper eyes gleamed with pinkish-orange curiosity as they studied Emmeline's cautious entrance into their den.

"She is with us," Avery promised. "In fact, she may be the missing link to our success."

The flock of Aeropunks shared energetic whispers at this announcement. Avery let them digest this news for a moment before continuing.

"As you know, she is an elite Thermapunk, scheduled to not only take over leadership of the Thermapunks, but also governorship of Hydra. With her on our side, supporting our cause, we can reestablish autonomy from the Holloways."

"She will lead them to us," an Argopunk argued from atop the highest windowsill. "They watch her, they follow her—I've seen them spying on her. If she hasn't already done so today, she will inadvertently lead Raven and Remington to one of our meetings and our mission will end before it has truly begun."

"I recently learned of their task to spy on me," Emmeline explained. "It's a long story, but those orders have been redacted. If they continue, they'd be breaching the Therma-Aero alliance. Please inform me if you see them following me."

"All it would take is one misstep to ruin everything," a Pilopunk wearing a crown of tin feathers said. She was perched on a rafter, balancing on her fingers and toes.

"Which is why we need to move soon," Avery said. "No more hiding in the shadows, no more secret meetings. We need to make our voices heard. Once our intention is publicized, there will be no stopping the movement."

The Aeropunks whispered among themselves once more.

Emmeline was impressed by Avery's democratic approach to leadership. Everyone's voice mattered, and Avery listened to their concerns. It was drastically different from the authoritarian rule Emmeline was used to seeing among the Thermapunks, Terrapunks, and Aeropunks. She appreciated this approach and was excited to replicate her own version of this type of leadership.

"What's our first move?" an Argopunk hanging upside down from one of the cables asked.

Before Avery could answer, Emmeline stepped in. "Reinstating Avery and her family as nobles. The Morrells will rule the Aeropunks alongside the Holloways."

"While I appreciate that sentiment, it isn't possible," Avery objected. "The Holloways would never agree."

"I know what they want," she said, thinking of the moon stone. "I can give it to them in exchange for your reinstatement."

The Aeropunks cheered.

Avery gave Emmeline a cautionary glare, unable to ask what this arrangement would cost in front of the crowd.

She changed the topic. "Emmeline and I will discuss the possibility of this matter in private. In the meantime, continue on as we were. Practice patience. Change is coming."

The Aeropunks departed with hopeful spirits— Emmeline's presence offered new possibilities for their prosperity. She could initiate the change they so desperately wanted. The Argopunks flew out of the many windows lining the walls, while the Pilopunks retrieved their flying apparatuses docked outside the house.

Once the giant room was cleared, Avery questioned Emmeline.

"What will you trade?" she asked.

"They want magic … I'll give it to them."

"We don't want to give them more power," Avery argued.

"The moon stone magic is a curse, first and foremost. It's only powerful if you discover your specific remedy. Otherwise, it's debilitating."

"We aren't trying to maim or kill them."

Avery placed the back of her hand to Emmeline forehead, checking her temperature and insinuating that she was talking crazy.

"Are you feeling okay?" she asked.

Emmeline shrugged and took a step back. "Perhaps I'm still angry. There's so much happening all at once, and right now, I'm still reeling from the fact that Raven and Remington have been spying on me by order of Solís. I feel violated."

"I get it. Take a breath," Avery said. "We can't act recklessly."

"You're right. I don't want to make things worse. It would be a good bargaining chip, though."

"First, we need to figure out how to heal you, Gemma, Clementine, and Ruthanne. Let's not add more patients to the roster."

Emmeline sighed. She'd let Luna, Louie, and Avery try, but if she was being honest with herself, she wasn't ready to let go of control.

Avery continued, "Speaking of our friends, we ought to check on them."

They flew south, back to Fyree.

Gemma and Clementine were safely waiting in her bedroom, but to Emmeline's dismay, her mother was waiting there with them.

"It's amazing," Melora said in greeting; everyone appeared in good spirits. "A Terrapunk with a tolerance for fire, and a Thermapunk able to breathe underwater. Only a few weeks ago I'd have called this an abomination, but with a Dawes at the helm of this peculiar turn of events, I'd call this a glorious win."

"A true miracle," Emmeline said, hardly hiding her sarcasm. "Did you know the Holloway siblings have been spying on me?"

"No!" Melora insisted. "That is a breach of our alliance."

"Solís gave them permission. He has since retracted it, but you ought to check in with Reuben and Deandra to ensure it ends."

"I will, although I think you ought to attend. You are revered as a leader among the nobles now. You ought to make your authority known."

"You're right. I will go with you."

"Perfect. We will go in the morning. I will also have a word with Solís—he has been acting strange lately."

"Thank you," Emmeline said, her gratitude genuine. Though it was strange for her mother take her side, she was happy to accept the gesture.

Melora left the room, closing the door behind her, and Clementine handed the moon stone back to Emmeline.

"I was able to finish the construction of my tank lungs," she revealed. "I shouldn't need help from the stone as often anymore."

Avery cut in, "And once we find the remedy, all of your ailments will go away for good."

"In the meantime," Emmeline said, "let's keep using our abilities to help. Now that you can spend extended time underwater, I ought to teach you how to dive."

Clementine perked up, golden eyes glowing with excitement. Without saying a word, Emmeline knew that Clementine did not wish to heal either. Like her, she had developed an unhealthy dependency on her sickness.

"When can we return to Hydra?" Clementine asked.

Emmeline glanced out the window—night was approaching.

"Tomorrow, after my meeting with the Holloways" she answered. "For now, we rest."

Avery departed, returning home for the night, while Gemma and Clementine made themselves comfortable in different corners of Emmeline's bedroom. Everyone was eager for the day they'd have more comfortable living arrangements at the Pyro-Argo air base.

Emmeline fell onto her bed and laid there with her eyes open. Mind racing and unable to sleep, she remained restless for hours. She wasn't sure how much time had passed, but once Gemma's gentle rattling snore and Clementine's wheezing breaths began to harmonize like a song, she realized sleep was not in the cards for her just yet.

She twirled the moon stone in her hands, wondering what Luna was doing and when she'd see her again.

As the thought crossed her mind, Luna's voice appeared in her head.

"Meet me outside."

Emmeline jumped out of bed and then tiptoed in a hurry to her balcony door.

"Stay beneath your shield," Emmeline said in a whisper as soon as she got outside. "There's a chance I am being watched."

"We need to talk," Luna said, continuing to speak telepathically for fear of being heard.

Emmeline nodded, eyes scanning the sky for signs of Raven or Remington hiding within a whirlwind of gas.

"I was able to recruit a few scientists who also want the war between the sun and our moon to end. They say they can help, but you'd need to travel with me through the portal. They can only help you in person."

"I can't," Emmeline said in a whisper.

"It's the only way. You might feel strong now, but I promise—in time, the curse will kill you."

"It's too risky," she said, trying to keep her responses short in case they had eavesdroppers in their midst.

"You don't trust me?"

"I do."

"Then what's the problem?"

"My trust ends with you."

Luna pieced together her vague answer. "You don't trust my people."

Emmeline nodded, then asked, "Can I?"

"You can. I promise. Ending this war means everything to me—I will protect you with my life."

"I believe you," she said, then contemplated her choice of words before saying more. "I have a lot of people counting on me here."

"You're willing to die for them?"

"I feel stronger than ever."

"It won't last. Soon, my warnings will mean nothing because it will be too late to reverse the damage."

"What I'm feeling doesn't match what you're saying."

"You need to heed my warning."

"I'm not ready."

"You will die and all of this will have been for nothing. The war between our people will wage on, and our friendship will be wasted."

Emmeline clenched her fists, torn between two noble missions. Assist in the Aeropunk revolution, or end the war between Quintessence and the Moon of Fixation—both tasks were enormous and neither guaranteed certain victory.

"I need to think."

"You've had weeks to think," Luna argued. "Each time I see you you're drastically smaller. You're withering away and the only one who seems to notice, or care, is your brother Solís."

"How do you know about him?"

"I don't reveal myself to you every time I visit. I see him on the rooftop, searching for answers to your illness."

"He is crazy."

"He is the only person in your circle of friends who seems to fully grasp the dire nature of your situation. Which is impressive, considering he knows the least out of the bunch. I'm often tempted to show myself and recruit his help."

"Don't! I promise, it will not go well."

"Then you need to shake the delusions still lingering in your head and take care of yourself. Remember, it's not only you that you need to save. The mortals living on the planet we serve would be better taken care of if the sun coexisted in peace with us."

"I understand."

"Help me."

"I want to, you just need to give me a little more time."

"Fine, but your time is running out," Luna warned before mumbling the incantation and disappearing through the portal with a whoosh.

Emmeline did not feel delusional, nor did she feel like she needed to be fixed. She was the leader of the Superpunks and was idolized by all—the nobles wanted her in their presence, her crew of cursed friends needed her guidance, and the Aeropunks needed her influence. Luna and Solís were separately trying to save her, but she just wanted to exist blissfully without reminders of how sick she was.

She'd find a way to accomplish it all.

If she was to go down with this ship, she'd do so with a blazing, irreversible sweep of change.

Chapter 36

Regis escorted Emmeline and Melora to the Holloway home near the outer edges of the solar shield. Another part of Quintessence Emmeline was unfamiliar with, she examined this level of their world in awe as they approached. Warm, spacious, and remote, she now understood why the Holloways were so out of touch—they were secluded here. The only contact they had outside their elite group were the Argopunks stationed to protect the shield, the Pilopunks assigned to keep their machinery afloat, and occasional visits from the noble Thermapunks.

"Oh, Reuben!" Melora shouted, feigning friendliness. "We have matters to discuss."

Her voice echoed across the expansive atmosphere. Regis steered their airship beneath the gigantic conservation machinery built to assist the Aeropunks in replenishing the gaseous shield. These contraptions stayed aloft by a rotating shift of Pilopunks who breathed helium into the tanks and spun the pedals that turned the turbines. Made of copper pipes and tubes attached to a mixing station for gaseous vapors, these machines were heavy and it took great energy to keep them aloft at such great heights.

Reuben flew out of his massive floating home, navigating the winds with a copper pair of wings. His mansion looked a lot like Avery's, minus the years of neglect. Two rotors on opposite sides of the house, four stories tall with peaked steeples adorned with divine emblems. Three netted helium balloons with copper piping rising into their base kept the home in the sky.

"Why are you here?" he barked.

Melora pushed Emmeline forward.

Emmeline cleared her throat. "Your children were spying on me, which is a breach of the Therma-Aero treaty. If they are caught doing this again, our alliance will be broken and we will look elsewhere for Aeropunk leadership."

"You don't get to decide who is in charge of each faction," Reuben spat.

"No, but we get to choose who we work with, and it won't be your family anymore."

Melora smiled with delight as Emmeline served pure, authoritative confidence to Reuben Holloway.

"I was told they were given permission by your brother, who holds as much authority as you."

"They were, which is why this is a warning and not an official end to our treaty. Solís has since retracted that temporary permission, and if they are caught spinning gas to spy again, friendly ties between the Dawes family and Holloway family will be severed."

Reuben grumbled. "I hear you. It won't happen again."

He turned and flew away, mumbling curses at his children beneath his breath.

Melora squealed with delight. "You are a force to be seen! I wish your father had witnessed that display of power. What a flower you have blossomed into," she gushed.

As Melora went on and on, shifting her compliments of Emmeline into compliments toward herself for raising Emmeline, Regis glanced over his shoulder and gave Emmeline a wink. He then nodded upward.

Emmeline shifted her gaze and saw that countless Argos and Pilos had witnessed her moment with Reuben Holloway. She stood her ground and got her way, which further strengthened their trust in her. From above, they offered small gestures of allegiance—wide smiles with solid, yet subtle fist shakes.

Their faith in her strengthened her desire to reinstate the Morrells as nobles. With Avery in charge, the Aeropunk revolution would be quick and clean—no fighting, no bloodshed, no turmoil.

"Time to head back," Emmeline advised Regis. "I have work to do in Hydra."

"Aye, aye, Captain," he replied—a shock to both Emmeline and Melora; Regis hardly ever spoke.

They dropped Melora off at home and scooped up Gemma and Clementine, then flew toward the gates of Hydra. Avery met them halfway, softly landing on the main deck and retracting her copper wings.

Emmeline immediately pulled her aside.

"We can get you back into power without the moon stones and without a civil war."

"How?"

"I think that Raven and Remington are still spying on me, despite orders to stand down. If we can catch them, I can sever ties with the Holloways and the Dawes will recognize you as the Aeropunk family to conduct business with."

"Wait, what did I miss?"

"The meeting with Reuben Holloway went more perfectly than I had planned. He knows what's on the line; he knows what he risks losing if his children misbehave. And I know they still hover around, especially at night."

"Why at night?"

"Because they are trying to learn my secrets," Emmeline revealed. "If you want an easy resolution to the Aeropunk revolution, set up spies of your own. Catch them gas spinning around me. The moment we do, the treaty between our families will be broken and I can name who I'd prefer to conduct an Aeropunk alliance with."

"If Reuben is aware of this, he will see to it that his kids behave."

"He will try, but I know how badly Remington wants my magic. They won't listen to their father."

Avery sighed. "It's worth a try. I know a few Argopunks who are adequate gas spinners. I'll assign them to the perimeter of your home during the night. If this works, it'll be a miraculous win."

Emmeline smiled. "It will work. I am certain of it."

Regis began lowering the airship as they reached the gates to Hydra. He pulled the golden cord of the foghorn to alert Montgomery of their arrival. A few minutes later, Montgomery arrived to unlock the gates from below.

He did not greet them or say hello.

As the gates opened, Emmeline heated her heart and extended her wings, then flew over the side of the ship to join her father below. Avery followed, towing Gemma and Clementine in a pilobike cart.

"What's wrong?"

"How do you feel?" Montgomery asked.

"I feel fine."

Emmeline landed on the ship deck, her blazing smolder softly fading as she cooled her heart.

"Is the sickness you have similar to what Ruthanne is suffering from?"

Emmeline furrowed her brow. "No," she lied.

"It seems awfully similar."

"I'm not sick."

Montgomery's expression became visibly agitated.

"You do realize I'm not stupid, right? I see your deterioration, and I've been patient because you seem to have some sort of control over it, but now I'm watching Ruthanne lose control and I can't help but imagine the same thing happening to you."

"What do you mean? How is she losing control?"

"She's a destructive mess! Too powerful—she can move ships across the sea like they are toys. And every time she displays her magnetic capacity, it is followed immediately by crippling immobility. She's going to kill herself. Whenever Louie, Ralph, or I try to warn her to slow down, she throws a fit and inevitably destroys something in her path. She dismantled the main mast on Red Fang Ralph's ship yesterday after crashing Allen Peggs's ship into Smuggler's Rove."

Emmeline groaned—Ruthanne was a reckless liability to her mission, and proof that not all Solarpunks could be trusted with the cursed magic of the moon stones.

"Take me to her," she requested.

Avery topped off the helium tanks, then steered the airship to the Rove where Red Fang Ralph had his boat docked.

Emmeline gripped the moon stone in her pocket while consuming three clay marbles, siphoning the stone's magic to ease the migraines the marbles caused. Once she was certain the migraines would not take root, she let go of the stone and flew down to Ralph's ship.

Louie stood in the crow's nest, his handsome face lined with exhaustion. When he saw Emmeline's radiant approach, a smile stretched across his tired face.

"I've missed you," he called out.

"I'm sorry I was away for so long. I missed you, too."

Emmeline landed in the crow's nest next to him and he wrapped her in his arms, withstanding the painful heat from her activated heart. She did her best to cool down quickly.

"What's going on with Ruthanne?" she asked from the safety of his hug.

"She is not well. I think the curse has infected her brain, too. She's acting delusional."

A loud growl echoed from below. They looked over the side of the basket and saw Ruthanne accosting the blacksmith who was repairing the mast she wrecked.

Emmeline could not make out what she said, but the sound of her anger resonated into the sky. As Ruthanne finished her verbal assault on the terrified blacksmith, she turned to leave, limping as she walked away.

"Why is she limping?" Emmeline asked Louie.

"Her left ankle has hardened. The gears are crusted over with calcified minerals and she's lost all mobility in that ankle. I told her to rest, but she won't listen to anyone's warnings. I applied the salve we use on hellion wounds to her ankle gears, but it didn't help. I've spent days adjusting the chemical makeup of the salve, hoping to find a combination that works for this hellion curse, but I haven't discovered the correct formula yet."

"It's an extraterrestrial curse. I struggle to believe we will have the tools or resources to combat it here."

"But the salve works on direct wounds caused by the hellions," Louie argued.

"Those are surface wounds. What we are dealing with runs much deeper."

"Then tell me how I can help. I don't want this happening to you, too."

"I just need you to be here for me."

He pulled her tighter.

"Always."

Seeing Ruthanne's deterioration worried Emmeline. Prior to today, she had not fully understood the gravity of Luna's warnings—but now, it was crystal clear. She did not want herself, Gemma, or Clementine to deteriorate like Ruthanne. Luna's stone was not as potent as Cèla's—she still had time to fix this before it affected them, too.

She had to focus. She had a lot left to accomplish; countless punks to make proud.

"Do you know what's on the agenda today?" she asked him.

"A cage repair for the Ogre of Irritability. It will require divers, flyers, and welders."

"I suppose I can mash two tasks into one. I need to teach Clementine how to dive," she informed Louie.

"Why?"

"The curse materialized as suffocation for her, so she built a waterproof tank around her heart and lungs, and now, with enough octopus ink applied to her golden gears, we think she might be able to dive without a suit."

"Well, that's something," Louie said, both impressed and disappointed—it was hard to appreciate the evolution when it stemmed from destruction. "Good luck with that."

He pulled her in, gave her a sweet kiss, and then let her go. Emmeline took off and joined Avery, Gemma, Clementine, and Montgomery below. Louie slid down the main mast with speed.

"While you're down there," Montgomery instructed Clementine, "bring me one of those silver sea stones."

Clementine side-eyed Emmeline as she landed.

"Why?" Emmeline asked her father, afraid he might be discovering the truth before she got the chance to tell him herself.

"I think we need to study them. Ruthanne made an incoherent mention of them during one of her fits, and I know you keep one close. I just want to make sure they are safe."

"Okay, we will try to find one while we are down there," Emmeline said, prepared to think of a reason that explained why she returned with no moon stones.

"You'll be in the sky," Montgomery corrected her. "Avery can't do it alone. We need two sets of eyes up there."

"I need to teach Clementine how to dive."

"Louie can teach her."

Emmeline wished to argue, but her father was still in charge. This wasn't her mission, it was his. Montgomery returned his attention to Clementine, who was being taught how to grease her gears with octopus ink by two codgers from Red Fang Ralph's crew. A tiny slit to the back of their wrists and they shared some of their octopus ink with her. She applied the slick, viscous liquid to her gear joints of her shoulders, elbows, wrists, hips, knees, and ankles. Once applied, Montgomery gave her a pair of finned wrist and ankle cuffs. With a few twists of their cranks, they'd help her swim.

Emmeline turned to Louie and whispered, "Don't bring back any stones."

"We won't," he assured her.

She trusted Louie to fulfill this promise. As he began giving Clementine basic tips on how to swim and dive, Emmeline joined Avery near the edge of the group. Ruthanne stood beside her, fidgeting with discomfort.

"Are you okay?" Emmeline asked Ruthanne.

Ruthanne grumbled before responding. "The stiffness in me ankle has snuck up me leg."

"Why is that happening?"

"Dunno. I ain't afeard, though."

"I think it's the curse. The stone you touched is far more potent than the one the rest of us touched. You need to rest to prevent further acceleration of your injury."

"If I rest, I stiffen up. If I move, I stiffen up. It doesn't matter either way." Ruthanne spat a whopping clunk of seafoam saliva onto the deck. "I'd rather go out swinging."

"I understand," Emmeline said, very aware she was currently doing the same. The only difference was that they were at different stages of deterioration. She remembered that the remedy to all their woes existed on the other side of the moon stone portal, and for the first time, Emmeline felt the pressure of time. Not for herself, but for Ruthanne. If she could attain the cure, perhaps she could save Ruthanne from further decline.

Emmeline added, "Just try to hang in there. Go easy today. I might know a way to help you heal."

"Go easy?" Ruthanne said with a laugh. "It's all or nuthin' with me."

A loud crack echoed from the Detention Center; the ogre had cracked another bar of its cage.

"Is everyone ready to go?" Montgomery asked the group, his voice booming.

The relatively large task force mumbled and nodded, then took action.

Avery and Emmeline took to the skies, monitoring the project from above.

The Nautipunk divers dove; Clementine shadowed Louie on her first water mission. The Thermapunk welders swung their hooked ropes, latching onto the ogre's cage and catapulting themselves into action. Ruthanne summoned all her strength, then flung through the sky by magnetic force and attached to the side of the steel cage. Her left leg hung stiff and immobile, while the rest of her body moved with focused intention.

While the welders reattached the bases of each bar with fire, Ruthanne worked on the top joists, securing them with concrete. Able to excrete the minerals that were overloading her water-based flesh, she patted a mixture of cement, sand, and water into every crack, which dried into concrete. Catching onto her methods, Emmeline dipped lower so that her high-temperature body heat helped dry the mixture faster.

Unconventional, but successful, the ogre's cage was being rebuilt with speed.

Beneath the sea's surface, the divers monitored the base post that the cage sat upon, making sure the foundation remained solid.

Delighted that her crew was able to help so thoroughly, Emmeline did not notice Ruthanne's struggle until she howled in pain.

"What's wrong?" Emmeline asked.

"Me whole left side be stiff."

"Can you get back to the airship?"

Ruthanne clung to the cage through the magnetic power in her right hand.

"If I let go," she said, "I will fall."

"Avery!" Emmeline shouted.

Avery was on the opposite side of the cage, supervising the welders there, but Emmeline's call diverted her attention.

"What?" she replied.

"You need to get the Pilobike cart. Ruthanne is stiffening and can't get herself back to the airship."

Avery nodded and took off, darting off in a blur of copper.

Time was of the essence.

"Did I do a good job?" Ruthanne asked, gritting through the pain.

"Yes," Emmeline said. "There's a lot more for you to do, too. Don't give up. We will figure this out."

Ruthanne shook her head. "Look at me left arm."

What had hardened on the inside was now visible on the outside—coarse and jagged concrete had taken over the left side of Ruthanne's body. And upon closer inspection, Emmeline noticed that the slow takeover was crawling over Ruthanne's torso and up her neck. The moment it fossilized her organs and brain, there'd be no way to save her.

Emmeline looked over her shoulder, hopeful that Avery was on her way, but there was no sight of her.

"Don't let go," Emmeline pled, the dire gravity of the situation painfully apparent. She was going to lose a friend, and worse, Louie would be forced to grieve another devastating loss. Ruthanne was like a sister to him.

"Argh," Ruthanne howled. She threw her head back in pain as the calcification attacked her vital organs and geared gut. The agony was so immense, her magnetic pull ceased and her right fingers began to loosen around the bar.

Emmeline grabbed Ruthanne's right wrist, hoping to hold her in place as they waited for Avery to return.

"Tell Louie I love him," she said, her voice meek as she struggled to breathe.

"You tell him yourself," Emmeline countered, determined to save Ruthanne.

"Take care of him." She coughed, spitting out ashy soot from her lungs.

Delusions dissipated, the full reality of their similar ailments struck a nerve in Emmeline's heart: this would be her fate, too. She looked down at her skeletal arms and realized it already was. Frail and fragile, she survived by accommodating the migraines, disregarding the new sickness she had caused. The marbles in her gut churned her gears slowly, and it would not be long before they stopped rolling completely.

Ruthanne clung to the cage by two fingers.

Emmeline was not big enough, or strong enough, to hold them both in the sky.

The ocean below beckoned, calling Ruthanne home.

"Louie needs you," Ruthanne said, gasping for air. "Don't let this curse take you away from him." These were her final words before the concrete took over her right hand and she was forced to let go.

Emmeline was only able to hold her full bodyweight for a moment before it became too much and Ruthanne plummeted toward the sea.

As she fell, the concrete crept up her neck and took over her face, fossilizing her panicked expression. Body turned to stone, Ruthanne disappeared beneath waves.

Chapter 37

Emmeline thought of Louie.

Golden wings pinched together, she held her breath and dove into the sea. Her blazing body extinguished as she hit the water, but as long as she kept her mouth closed, her fiery insides would remain dry.

She didn't have much time.

Vision blurry as the salt water stung her eyes, Emmeline found Louie floating nearby, his body slouched with defeat as Ruthanne's stone form sank before him. He began to sink, too, as the trauma of what he was witnessing kicked in.

Emmeline swam to him, wrapped her arms around him, and tugged him to the surface. Weak, but determined, she would not let him face this loss alone.

As they breached the waves, Emmeline gasped for air. Clementine, accompanied by the other divers, surfaced nearby. While they swam back to Ralph's boat, Louie and Emmeline waded in place.

"What happened?" Louie asked, distraught.

"It happened so quick," Emmeline said, holding back her tears. "The minerals took over her body. She turned to stone."

"I have to go get her," Louie said. "She can't be left alone down there."

"In that state, she is too heavy for you to carry on your own. We will get a team that can help you retrieve her."

Louie's composure vanished and he began to sob. This was the first time Emmeline had seen him cry, and seeing his strength vanish caused her eyes to well with tears.

They processed their sorrow away from watching eyes. Tears rolled down Louie's cheeks as he unleashed his grief.

The waves came and went, splashing their faces and wiping the tears from his face, proving to offer more comfort than Emmeline could—she inadvertently caused this tragedy and risked adding more to it if she didn't heed Luna's warnings.

"We need to get back to the ship," Emmeline said, her voice gentle.

Louie nodded, suppressing his lingering emotions and donning a brave face. They swam back to Red Fang Ralph's boat, where the crew had a rope ladder waiting for them. A quick climb and they were safely out of the water.

Louie tried to appear strong, but his vacant eyes and sullen expression gave him away. He looked lost, chest rising and falling slowly—his breathing the only thing he could control in this moment.

"Get him outta here," Ralph grumbled in a whisper to Emmeline.

She glanced up—her father's airship was out of reach and there were no ladders lowered to climb. She could not carry Louie in flight, so she took his hand and led him into a vacant cabin.

After closing the door behind her, Emmeline placed her hands on both sides of Louie's face. She stared into his mournful blue gaze, sharing in his sadness.

"I'm so sorry," she offered.

"How did it happen?" he asked as he sliced the back of his wrist and gave Emmeline copious amount of octopus ink to coat her golden gears that were touched by the corrosive ocean salt water.

"She turned to stone," Emmeline answered.

"But *how*?"

"The curse … it seems the combination of minerals coursing through her and mixing with her water-based flesh turned her into concrete."

He shook his head. "It happened so fast."

"I know. I'm sorry."

His expression shifted from grief to fear. "It will happen to you, too."

"We touched different stones; our curses are different," she tried to assure him. "My deterioration is happening slower."

"I can't lose you, too," he said.

"You won't."

"You promise?" he asked.

Emmeline hesitated—she could not make this guarantee. Still torn between accepting Luna's offer to help and revolutionizing Quintessence, Emmeline struggled to choose between herself and everyone else.

"I am making things better here," Emmeline said. "Everyone is counting on me to succeed."

"At what cost?" he asked.

His question halted her delusional excuses to avoid healing.

Her selfish refusal to admit that she could not craft beauty out of this nightmare was hurting everyone around her. Not only had she fooled the masses into adoring her, but she also accidentally helped birth obsessive monsters in the minds of her friends and broke the hearts of those she was closest to. Louie was losing everyone he loved, Solís had gone mad in an attempt to save her, her father toiled over discovering the cause of her ailment, and Avery futilely helped Louie concoct remedies that would never work.

A waste of their time, energy, and love, when all Emmeline had to do to stop this nightmare was accept Luna's help.

"I know what I have to do, but it will require me leaving for a while."

"Why? Where will you go?"

"It's better if you don't know."

Louie's expression constricted. "Why don't you trust me?"

"I do trust you. There's just a lot riding on this, and if it doesn't work, I don't want you or anyone else taking it out on the person who is trying to help me."

"I would never."

Emmeline thought of Luna and how everyone she loved hated the hellions.

She replied, "You might."

"You are infuriating."

"I need *you* to trust *me*. I have every intention of coming back healed."

"If you take too long, I will try to find you."

Emmeline considered the enormous risk she was taking by attempting to heal in enemy territory and decided this was a reasonable trade-off.

"Fair enough," she replied.

Louie pulled her in close, choosing to end this argument and trust her instead.

"I am just grateful you are finally choosing to heal."

Emmeline said nothing; she was not yet sure if Luna could truly help her or not.

"Can you promise to look after Gemma and Clementine while I'm gone?"

"I will do my best."

"And the moon stone," she added. "Do not touch it with your bare hands, but please keep it safe."

"Why?"

"It's my one sure way back to you."

"Then I will protect it with my life."

Too distraught to put together the pieces of information she just shared, Louie kissed the top of her head, refusing to let her go. Emmeline savored every second. After a long moment, he spoke again.

"I suppose you need to say your goodbyes."

"It's better if I don't."

Louie pulled back, shocked. "Why?"

"My family will ask questions I cannot answer yet."

"I see."

"Plus, this goodbye is hard enough."

"This is not a goodbye," he argued. "You'll be coming back."

She nodded. "Thank you for loving me enough to let me go."

Louie responded with a curt nod, displaying clear uncertainty about this decision.

Emmeline raised to her tiptoes, gave him a sincere kiss, then stepped back. She pulled the moon stone out of her pocket and cradled it in both of her hands. It grew heavy in her grip, shadowing her peripherals as its magic consumed her.

"I do this for you, for my family, and for our people. To prevent heartbreak and war." She glanced down at her skinny arms, for the first time truly seeing her own self-destruction. "But most of all, I do it for me. I will no longer choose ruin over love."

She lifted the moon stone to her lips and whispered, "I'm ready."

417

It took a moment before she received a reply.

"Repeat after me," Luna said telepathically.

Emmeline listened, then echoed the incantation.

"Ad lunam lu. Accipe me."

The stone fell to the floor.

Emmeline vanished.

Louie stood there in shock—his greatest fear realized: another love gone.

His heart ached with ferocity.

"To love is to let go," he reassured himself. "She will come back to me whole."

He picked up the moon stone with a handkerchief and dropped it into a leather pouch. He would ensure the curse infected no one else.

Aware now that the stone was a portal—to where, he was unsure—Louie pulled the drawstrings tight and held the pouch close to his heart, prepared to protect it with his life.

This was how they'd meet again.

Thank you for reading *Gears of the Sun*—I hope you enjoyed the story! If you have a moment, please consider rating and reviewing it on Amazon and sharing your thoughts via social media. All feedback is greatly appreciated!

Amazon Author Account:
www.amazon.com/author/nicolineevans

Instagram:
www.instagram.com/nicolinenovels

Facebook:
www.facebook.com/nicolinenovels

Twitter:
www.twitter.com/nicolinenovels

To learn more about my other novels, please visit my official author website:

www.nicolineevans.com

Made in the USA
Middletown, DE
03 December 2022

16707553R00239